PLAYING ARMY

A NOVEL

NANCY STROER

VIRGINIA BEACH
CAPE CHARLES

PRAISE FOR
PLAYING ARMY

"A deeply affecting, nuanced portrait of one woman's struggle to find herself while serving in the US Army of 1995. Stroer deftly turns the Army's aspirational 'be all you can be' tagline on its head with a feisty protagonist who sometimes awkwardly and often courageously confronts issues of sexism, racism, and leadership shortcomings as well as the painful legacy of Vietnam. *Playing Army* is a captivating read that serves as a reminder of what has changed and what hasn't for women in the military."

—**Daria Sommers**, writer/filmmaker, *Lioness*

"*Playing Army* is a page-turner that kept me hooked from the beginning, while doing a phenomenal job of putting the reader into the story so that they can experience what it is like to be a woman in the military—the pride, and the never ending, ever-present challenges. It's not easy to describe the world of the military while also making it accessible to those who have not served. Nancy has done a phenomenal job here. Understanding my service and everything it meant to be a woman in uniform is something I am still working on, and *Playing Army* helped me find an extra piece of the puzzle. As someone who's written a military memoir, I can say that this book has an immediate place in the canon of works by military women."

—**Daniella Mestyanek Young**, author, *Uncultured*

"Battling self-doubt, self-sabotage, prickly soldiers and staff officers, and a minefield of battalion politics, US Army Lieutenant Minerva Mills takes command of an "ash-and-trash" headquarters company preparing for a possible deployment to 1990s Southeastern Europe. Whether readers are officers, enlisted, or civilians, this is a nuanced, realistic narrative guaranteed to generate leadership insights, ethics discussions, and professional empathy. Promote this book ahead of more-familiar peers, such as Anton Myrer's *Once an Eagle* and James McDonough's *Platoon Leader!*"

—**Randy Brown**, author, *Twelve O'clock Haiku: Leadership Lessons from Old War Movies & New Poems*

"In *Playing Army*, Nancy Stroer has given us a new kind of heroine in Lieutenant Min Mills. At once both awkward and strong, Min fights for her place among her peers in the US Army and becomes the leader her ragtag bunch of soldiers need. While privately battling unresolved grief, maternal neglect, and a past that won't seem to rest, Min still finds a way to shine. A powerful and moving story."

—**Carrie Talick**, author, *Beware the Mermaids*

"There are moments of exquisite prose, punchy one-liners, and a real sense that Lt. Minerva Mills is on an emotional rollercoaster that doesn't have any brakes. The complex negotiations of adult female friendships are played out against a complicated childhood and the tensions of life as a woman in a man's army. This is juxtaposed with the heart-stopping moments of being a soldier in a world always at war. Every soldier has a part to play, and lives on the edge of tragedy no matter how ordinary their job may seem. Stroer captures this beautifully, leaving us in no doubt the price soldiers pay for our freedom."

—**Bev Morris**, military history researcher and author, *An Average Pilot*

Playing Army

by Nancy Stroer

Published by

 köehlerbooks™

3705 Shore Drive
Virginia Beach, VA 23455
800-435-4811
www.koehlerbooks.com

PLAYING ARMY

For Clan Strovis

And in memory of Captain Martin Hans Cesana, who was the best of us

FAKE IT TILL YOU MAKE IT

I stood in the Headquarters Company day room, fists balled on my hips, feet planted wide. The surface of a Claymore antipersonnel mine is smooth, curved plastic. It gives no indication of its destructive potential except the reminder in raised letters to place "front toward enemy." Soldiers in Vietnam, having grown accustomed to the landmines they carried like so many school books in so many rucksacks, stripped Claymores to use the C4 to heat their rations, unconcerned that the benign-looking tablets might blow up in their faces. And on that nondescript day in late June of 1995, none of the soldiers swirling around me realized they might be on the business end of a Claymore in the form of their new commander.

Me.

Inert, but dangerous.

But also uncomfortably aware of the tightness of my waistband. My guts roiled and the armpits of my olive-drab green T-shirt were damp in the muggy, crowded room. My fingernails dug into my palms as I watched my mother direct soldiers to unpack coolers and unfold tables. They scurried to her bidding although she was in a pastel pink skirt and creamy silk blouse, cool as a reverse strawberry ice cream cone, and I was the one in uniform.

"Honey, let me smooth that tablecloth before you put the tray down," she said to Private Washburn, whose face contrasted pink against white-blond hair. He stepped aside with a smile and wiped the sheen from his forehead. Young guys like Washburn probably missed their bossy mothers, and they loved it when their leaders pitched in. When they walked the talk, so to speak. But Washburn was completely unaware that my mother and I were faking our way through the next few hours.

I resisted the urge to sweep my arm down the carefully laid table, bunching the pink cloth around serving bowls and stacks of paper plates as I pushed—plastic cutlery rattling and spilling onto the buffed linoleum floor as everyone's boots danced to avoid crunching the fork tines. In my mind's eye I pivoted on my immaculately polished heel and stalked out. I drove across Fort Stewart, through the main gate, and straight to the Atlanta airport without stopping. If I hurried, I could have made my cross-country flight to LAX with enough time for the connection to Seoul. That'd show the Old Man. That would show all these knuckleheads.

Keep your head down, I told myself. *Pay attention.* I'd been ambushed by the Old Man, but in the Army as in life it was the best course of action to camouflage. It took strength to remain still, and my plan was to get the job done and then scuttle backward out of there, leaving no trace. I didn't want to cause a stir if I could avoid it.

"Hand me the pink frosting out of that cooler, will you, Minerva?" At home in Athens my mother's accent was like mine: straight pine trees and chickens. Here, forty miles southwest of Savannah, it swooped and curled like Spanish moss dangling from a live oak. My mother was a chameleon, adept at merging with her surroundings. She'd glided into that day's role as smoothly as she inhaled the secondhand smoke wafting from the handful of soldiers by a far window.

I pinched at the beginning of a headache on the bridge of my nose then bent to root through the nearest cooler. "The Army eyeball does not recognize the color pink, Mom." My head went fuzzy as I straightened. A Diet Coke lunch will do that to a person. "You have no idea how much shit I'm going to take for this."

"Language, Minerva." Rather than take the tube of frosting, my mother pulled me into an embrace. Sometimes, when I was little, my mother would stop fussing about whatever I was doing and grab me into a hug. "I'm sorry," she'd whisper, clinging to me like I was the only solid object in a world rattling apart. "I love you." At four, five, six years old, I learned to stand as still as a tree, so unshakable that I neither cried nor returned my mother's words. In her arms I felt rough-skinned and unmoving, my own love running too invisibly deep to tap. Now, as then, I allowed her hug but didn't return it.

My mother pushed back to search my face. The outer rings of her blue eyes matched the deep half moons under them, and a pulse blinked under her right eye like a distress signal. "Some of us are happy you're staying in-country for a while longer."

"Thanks, Ma." I smiled and handed her the frosting but turned away to avoid her optic interrogation. Down the length of one table, pink divinity candy preened on doily-covered plates. Fruit balls filled a scallop-edged watermelon and slices of grapefruit and maraschino cherries floated on top of pink lemonade in a cut-glass punch bowl. Rolls of honey-baked ham and rare roast beef covered a rectangular tray and a platter of red velvet cupcakes waited to be fluted with frosting. My mouth watered, not that I intended to eat in public. I tugged at my sweaty waistband. The soldiers would've been happy with a burger burn, cans of Budweiser, and an early escape on a Friday afternoon, but instead we were having a traditional Pink Tea. At certain points in my life I'd have found my mother's flair for the absurd amusing—a Pink Tea! For soldiers!—but these soldiers were thoroughly sick of officers. Fancy pink food would remind them of why we were there and this, too, I needed to play down. If my mother insisted on performing for a bunch of demoralized grunts I'd let her. Someone had to host the party an incoming commander was expected to throw for her soldiers. But I didn't have the juice for it. I could barely keep up my own act.

But I could do a little damage control. I picked up the bowl of cherry Jell-O and cottage cheese Watergate salad, whipped into a lumpy pink mound. It had been a fixture at every POW/MIA potluck my mother and I ever attended, like a pimply teenager sitting alone at the end of the picnic table. Despite Watergate salad's appearance it tasted okay, and soldiers would eat it. Lord knows, soldiers would eat raw sewage if you sprinkled powdered sugar on it and left it next to the coffee pot. But this glop, more than anything else on the table, would draw unnecessary attention.

"Put it down, Minerva."

I put it down. I was going to have to defend the Watergate salad at some point, or join the others making fun of it and risk hurting my mother's feelings. It was a no-win situation.

"We could have done this at the officers' club, you know," my mother chirped. "Your father and I used to love to go to the O Club on a Friday afternoon."

My jaw went slack and my eyebrows raised, my face in a tug of war with itself. It was rare to hear the past tense in reference to my father. He'd been MIA my whole life, his body never recovered from Vietnam, but every time I looked in the mirror, there was his wavy blond hair. There were his same light brown eyes, permanently crinkled in the corners. My mother winced sometimes when she turned too quickly and found me standing there instead of him, even after twenty-six years.

But I was built strong like my father, too, and dragged the conversation to safer ground. "The enlisted guys wouldn't be comfortable in a building full of drunk officers," I said. "And I don't want them to think I'm some kind of princess. I need them to know I'm on their side."

My mother smiled as she piped frosting onto the cupcakes. "Well, then, you get what you get. So don't have a fit." *Get* and *fit* rhymed today.

I studied the silver hair invading my mother's otherwise blond part line. She never missed the weekly wash and set that had anchored her hair in 1969, but she'd probably skipped professional coloring this time to pay for all the food. Those visible roots made me want to hover over her like she was a cupcake, to slip a little something into her pocketbook. But the last time she caught me sneaking her money she said, "Don't be boring, Minerva." Nothing made her happier than pretending everything was all right.

I glanced at my watch. Soldiers from my old job next door at Battalion Headquarters, and from my new job here at Headquarters Company, had started to fill the day room. The Old Man would be turning up any minute and I needed to get my head on straight for the assumption of command ceremony that started at 1300 sharp. I should have been checking my bags right about then. I should have been drinking a celebratory beer as I waited to board the flight that would take me to Korea.

"I need to pee." I'd have plunged straight into a rice paddy to flee the crowded room but if I couldn't escape, I could at least take a minute to regroup. When the Old Man arrived all eyes would be on him—on me!—and I didn't want even a flicker of resentment to cross my face. I would not give him that power.

"Why don't you give your mouth a little scrub while you're in the restroom," my mother suggested to the cupcakes.

It wasn't a restroom, it was a latrine—retrofitted to accommodate females, although the old urinals remained bolted to the wall as a reminder of whose building this had been first. From inside a stall I studied a message scratched into the paint, flat yellow peeking from under the current chipped government green: "Shumacher sucks Washburn's dick." A response was scrawled nearby: "Shumacher sucks her OWN dick!" My heart hurt for Shumacher, perpetually at odds with everyone. Too much woman for the men in the motor pool, and not woman enough for the other female soldiers in the barracks. It was an impossible space to occupy.

I sucked in my gut and forced the top button of my BDU trousers through the hole. Pounds never melted off me like they did in the diet pill commercials. As I wrestled with my body's ill-fitting container the latrine door opened and two pairs of boots tromped in. Specialist Pettit's voice floated over the sound of running water. "Not to be mean or anything, but female commanders are the worst. And Lieutenant

Mills is the *absolute* worst. I worked for her for two years in personnel and she ragged on me the whole time."

Whoa, shit. Enemy inside the wire. I stopped breathing altogether and leaned so close to the stall door my eyes crossed.

"Hey, now." That was Lieutenant Logan, my replacement at my old job. Female soldiers carved their hierarchies along different lines—never straight down the military ranks—and new alliances were being tested. Would Logan stick up for me, officer to officer? "It's a short-term thing. She won't be here long." Instead of reproach, Logan's voice was edged with mirth. "The colonel needs a body in that chair until a real commander comes in, and now that I'm here, Lieutenant Mills is over strength. She's the body."

My face grew hot. *Real commander? Body?* I clamped my lips shut against the urge to burst out of the stall roaring. I imagined inhaling the entire room then blowing them away with the release of my torso, all tightly packed plastic explosives and buckshot. These two, Logan especially, had no freaking clue. My predecessor had lost his job because he was inept and First Sergeant had caught him at it, plain and simple. The inspector general had paid an unannounced visit to Headquarters Company and in the space of a week Captain Williams was gone.

Then the Old Man had slithered to me, amended orders in hand. "I know you were promised Korea, but we need you to stay long enough to get Headquarters Company through annual training." He was trying to make it sound like I had a choice. "It's only two months, Lieutenant."

Stunned, I didn't respond. We both knew two months was bullshit.

"Three months tops." He tilted his head and smiled, a used-car salesman attempting to foist a lemon on an unsuspecting customer. "Any good officer would jump at the chance to command soldiers, especially a personnel officer."

Any other officer, maybe. Captain Williams had certainly loved the limelight. The Old Man was not at all averse to presiding over a conference table. But I'd only ever wanted jobs that kept me out of the line of fire while I worked my way toward Asia. Headquarters

Company was a complete mess—on paper and in real, complicated life. And I was on the literal doorstep of getting where I'd waited my whole life to go. I'd earned this tour to Korea.

As though he sensed my reasons for hesitating, the Old Man threw the trump card. "I got the results of your out-processing physical, Lieutenant. What are we going to do about these extra pounds?"

Shock stopped and fury took over. He was honestly going to hold me back for eight lousy pounds? I'd passed the measuring tape test. I was within regs.

"Officers have to set the standards." The Old Man tried to sound tough, but his jawline remained soft. "The Army is getting lean in every way these days. The North Korean guards on the DMZ? Gargantuan. Solid wall of muscle. We can't have people representing the U-S-of-A who don't look the part." He patted his own comfortable waistline, hiding behind the so-called needs of the mission but within his rights to pull my tour to Korea. It was infuriating. "Think of this summer as a chance to prove yourself as a leader," he'd said. "Square Headquarters Company away for me and square your weight away as an example to the rest of us. Then we'll talk about Korea."

So there I stood—feet wedged into the Georgia red clay until Headquarters Company passed the training evaluation at the end of September and I lost the weight, whichever came second. And in that moment, stuck in the latrine stall listening to Logan and Pettit's shit-talk, I was getting my first taste of what the next three months held in store. Sweat surfaced on the bridge of my nose and panic gripped my heart. I wanted to chew my arm off like an animal in a trap.

"I guess you're right, ma'am," Pettit said to Logan. "She's just a short-term pain in the ass." They giggled and I pictured the two of them angled over the sinks, touching up their mascara and lip gloss with the tubes they carried in their cargo pockets.

Breathe, girl. I closed my eyes and inhaled slowly through my nose. Relationships with other female soldiers were tricky to navigate. There was an unspoken interview process, a sizing-up period when we encountered each other for the first time. Logan had gone to Cornell. She was probably the competitive type. In the Army there can only be one top girl, so best to step aside and let the alpha female be the popular one. But Logan had a Vietnamese first name and Vietnam was my private obsession, so I'd tried to be extra nice as I showed her the ropes around personnel. Fat lot of good that had done.

I braced my hands on either side of the stall door and exhaled slowly, expelling what remained of my tattered confidence. Paper towels shunted from the dispenser and the latrine door squeaked then shuddered on its pneumatic elbow as Logan and Pettit shuffled out. In the wake of their leaving, the room settled into quiet. I sank down on the toilet seat lid and buried my burning face in my hands.

The Army rewarded soldiers who looked a certain way and said the right things. Appearance, and the script, were sometimes more important than performance, but it wasn't like I was incapable of playing the game. I rendered crisp salutes and responded in lockstep to commands too. But going through the motions was its own kind of deception. There was power in keeping one's true self on the down low. If you struck the right balance, no one looked at you too hard and that was the way I liked it. Why, then, did it hurt so much when others undervalued me?

There were a lot of women in Headquarters Company. They'd sense how tenuous my balance was and go straight for the jugular because a shaky woman was fun to topple. But I couldn't let anger or insecurity stop my momentum. Just getting through the next few hours, let alone the next three months, would take all my focus. Sniffling, I pulled a wad of toilet paper from the roll and blew my nose. I unrolled another handful of toilet paper and wiped under my eyes and across the sweaty bridge of my nose. *Get it together, Minerva*, I thought. *Maybe this time you'll surprise everyone, even yourself.*

I pushed up from the toilet seat and squared my shoulders. It was time to swear in.

THE MANAGEMENT OF VIOLENCE

The Headquarters Company First Sergeant entered the day room from the front of the building, followed by the Old Man. Like me, First Sergeant St. John was a Georgia girl. Unlike me, she was as dark as the silty loam where coastal rice flourished. Her starched uniform hung perfectly on her trim frame. I reached under my BDU blouse and adjusted my waistband again. My mother was holding court with the group of soldiers by the window, a red and gold pack of Dunhills in her nonsmoking hand.

"Attention to orders!" First Sergeant announced. One raised eyebrow in the direction of the smokers made it clear she'd be cracking down on them as soon as the guests left. Two presidents had tried to ban smoking in government buildings and word was she was picking up that unsuccessful flag and leading her own charge. I should have said something to my mother about that.

Conversation ceased. The soldiers stubbed their cigarettes out and, shoulders hunched, slipped lighters into pockets and cast embarrassed smiles at my mother. We were all going to have to prove ourselves in the coming days. This was the first sergeant who'd taken Captain Williams down and she could do the same to any of us if we got on her bad side.

The lone holdout was Staff Sergeant Davis, the motor sergeant, who took a deep drag on his cigarette, exhaled from the corner of his mouth while looking straight at First Sergeant, then ground his butt into the lid of a Coke can. My hackles raised but neither she nor I were going to jack him up just then. It was go time.

I walked to the front of the room, stomach sizzling with nerves. As I passed Logan and Pettit I felt my neck grow splotchy like it always did when I was in the spotlight. It was hard to take a full breath, and not just because of my tight trousers.

"Mom," I said in a stage whisper, and beckoned for her to come and stand next to me. When she reached my side, I locked my posture and faced the two flags in the corner of the room. Mere mortals took command of military units every day. They faced down gossipy soldiers too. All I had to do was project a confidence I didn't feel until I convinced them I was more than a body in a billet.

"The transfer of the company guidon is significant in many ways," Logan read from a script tucked into a green plastic folder. "The history, traditions, and accomplishments of a unit are embodied within it . . ."

My mother's posture straightened, too, ever-responsive to the needs of the situation, but she shifted slightly to keep the door of the day room in her line of sight. This many years into the habit she probably didn't realize she was doing it, but she was always oriented to the door, always looking for my father. For me, my father resided in the abstract in my head, but to my mother, any of the assembled soldiers could step forward from the crowd, their smile settling into familiar, beloved lines. This could be the day he returned.

I wanted this for my mother with my whole heart. Hell, *I* longed to be folded into those arms I'd never felt. *Just look at you*, my father would say. *Look how pretty my baby turned out.*

Which was utter nonsense, of course. My father wasn't going to materialize out of thin air. Furthermore, he hadn't wanted any babies at all. I carried a worn and creased letter in my left breast pocket, under the embroidered US ARMY tape and over my heart, in which he'd written those very words.

First Sergeant St. John handed me the company guidon, a pennant with a few limp streamers, and I placed it back into the flag stand next to the Stars and Bars. I shook the Old Man's hand, soft and halfhearted in my firm grip. There should have been more pomp and circumstance. We should have been on the parade field with a band playing ruffles and flourishes. A chaplain should have opened with a semimeaningful request for blessings on me and Headquarters Company, and my mother should have sat in a folding chair with a lap full of flowers, beaming with pride. But Captain Williams's rapid departure and my three-month stop gap command didn't warrant all the bells and whistles. And while I was sure my mother was proud, and happy I was staying stateside for a few more months, I knew it was strange for her to be here, surrounded by soldiers. The decorum she projected was a thin veneer for the perpetual rage at the Army flowing through her veins.

Keep it simple, I prayed as the Old Man put the soldiers at ease then produced a soggy index card and cleared his throat. He ran a finger over his sweaty upper lip—the feeble window air conditioning units being no match for a room full of uniformed soldiers during a coastal Georgia summer—then consulted his index card. "Now, I know . . . Lieutenant Mills is already a familiar face to most of y'all, since it's the first one you see when you report to Battalion."

Had he just checked his notes to make sure he got my name right? Had he never taken any real notice of me until he had an emergency billet to fill? I didn't need to be loved, I reminded myself for the millionth time. Or admired or respected or even recognized. It didn't matter if no one wanted me here. I had a job to do and then I was beating feet to Korea. But I had a name for crying out loud.

"It's a sad day for the battalion staff that we're losing Lieutenant Mills, but she's only moving one door over. And her replacement is already here, which is outstanding." The Old Man bestowed an indulgent smile on Lieutenant Logan, but she'd turned her face away and was studying something in the top corner of the room. Maybe Logan didn't like being singled out either. She certainly seemed comfortable sniping at people from the sidelines, though. "So let's give a big Headquarters Company welcome to your new commander!"

It was the faintest praise any officer had ever been damned with, and the applause scattered like a short burst of blank ammunition. I dipped my head to avoid it. Lieutenants didn't get companies to command unless they were shit-hot, or in this case, because battalion commanders were desperate. Pettit and Logan were right—I was just a body. And a not right-sized one at that.

"Thanks, sir." I paused and scanned thirty-something faces, each projecting a mixture of curiosity and defensiveness. Did everyone know the Old Man was dangling the assignment to Korea in front of me like a carrot? I hoped not. "And thank you all for coming. I imagine we'll all get to know each other fast in a company as tight as this one. We have a lot of work to do in a short period of time, so I'll be asking a lot of you." The hollow officer-speak grossed me out but it was what I was supposed to say.

Storey, the new supply sergeant, winked and gave me a thumbs-up, and I allowed my face to soften at him. He was another recent arrival to Headquarters Company and so far, unfazed by the inventory wreckage Captain Williams had left in his wake. Storey was an oasis of enthusiasm in a desert of apathy, but the rest of the soldiers squinted at my words and a few mumbled among themselves. They knew they were being blamed for the poor performance on the inspector general's visit and would assume I was a mouthpiece for the Old Man. One more wind-up junior officer. That, and the fact I'd only be there for the summer—not even long enough to evaluate any of the sergeants— would make me easy to blow off. Judging from the sullen atmosphere, all the soldiers were aware of the situation. I tried to ignore the lack of reaction. I'd trudged through life without many alliances, and I could get through this more or less alone too.

"Rest assured, I'll be working hardest of anyone," I continued. *Hard enough to keep the Old Man off my back, anyway.* "But for now, please come up and say hello. Enjoy the food. We'll get down to business next week." There was no point saying more.

Everyone hung back at first, Pink Tea jokes flickering around the corners of a few lips, but after the initial hesitation the soldiers tucked in. It was free food after all. My mother beamed.

In contrast, Sergeant Cigarette—Davis—examined the red velvet cupcake in his grease-stained hand before sidling over to Storey, mouth curled like a waxed mustache. "Forget the Jim Beam and the stripper! Female commanders get their mommies to throw a tea party!" He didn't bother lowering his voice.

Storey shook his head. "It's a kinder, gentler Army, Sar'n Davis." My estimation of Storey ratcheted down. These guys better keep their witticisms to themselves, or I was going to have something to say about it. But now was not the time.

The party spilled onto the sidewalk when First Sergeant threw the smokers outside. The late afternoon seethed with a prelude to the sweltering summer ahead and Lieutenant Logan put a cup of punch in the hand I wasn't using to accept salutes. "Congratulations, Lieutenant Mills." Nothing but innocence shone in Logan's dark eyes, but they might have been a little too shining, a little too innocent. I gulped the cold drink and sugar raced through my bloodstream at double time, leaving an aftertaste of gin. Had my mother spiked the pink lemonade? Shit. I needed to make sure she didn't get drunk and make a fool of herself in front of everyone.

"Thanks." I took another swig and returned Logan's gaze. Prolonged eye contact felt like arm-wrestling, and I worried Logan would see something I didn't want to share. There was toughness in Logan's eyes, diluted with a drop of something I couldn't diagnose. Was she feeling guilty about being bitchy in the latrine? Would she apologize if I confronted her?

My head buzzed like a bush full of cicadas. How had Logan done it? She'd walked into my old job two weeks ago and already wielded more clout than I ever had. Worse, the Old Man seemed to like her and since I needed to stay on the Old Man's good side, I had to butter her up too. I gripped the plastic cup tightly. Power gradients among women were a drain. "You can call me Min, you know," I said. "It's short for Minerva. And how do you pronounce your name? Is it *Le Anh*?"

"Most people call me Leann," she said, elongating the *e* and shortening the *a*. She tilted her head and squinted, as if to get a better angle on me. "It's easier."

In the sunlight, Logan's hair glinted with gold strands, too fine to have come from a hairdresser. Her skin was almost as fair as mine but that didn't mean anything—Asian people came in a whole range of shades. Reyes was from the Philippines and her skin was the exact Coppertone tan I'd coveted in high school. But Logan wasn't married, so where had her last name come from? Where had that blond come from? These weren't questions you could ask, at least not in the world of polite constraint where I'd grown up. I regretted not taking a closer look at Logan's 201 file when I'd had it in my hands.

"Anyway. Good luck." Logan tilted her head again to exit and walked over to the cluster of staff officers. Left alone, I tapped tumblers with Pettit as she skulked toward the barracks, one arm wrapped around her midsection like she was holding in her guts. "Good job on the inspection, Pettit," I said. I could play at being friendly too. Toast my hurt pride with this tasty pink punch.

"Back at you, ma'am," Pettit said, eyes lit with the same false innocence as Logan's. She waved her punch cup at her abdomen. "Cramps." Pettit developed cramps whenever the situation required her to do something beneath her. "We're going to miss you in personnel."

"I'm sure you'll be just fine with Lieutenant Logan." Alcohol seeped into my observation. "You two seem to be getting along real well." No more squandering emotional energy on these people. I needed to knock this joint into shape and get to Korea, ASAP. In the meantime, I had some drinking to do.

I lost track of time as the plastic tumblers replaced themselves whenever I held out my hand. I justified the calories because it was hot—you had to keep hydrated, right?—and because I hadn't eaten yet. Surely some of the sweat soaking my T-shirt was fat melting away.

My head hummed and my face grew as red as my blotchy neck. I could barely listen as Storey held forth on the merits of air assault operations. He'd just come from Fort Campbell, the home of the knuckleheads whose job it was to rappel into combat from helicopters. "We should do some rappelling, LT," he was saying. Storey had tawny, freckled skin, reddish-brown hair and reddish-brown eyes to match, a combination I liked in spite of myself. "I can set up some training for us."

My heart raced, not in a good way, as a helicopter thudded overhead toward Hunter Army Airfield twenty miles away. Had my father died in a helicopter assault? The notification only said he'd gone missing in a firefight, but he'd been assigned to the air cavalry. He hadn't been a movie star like Robert Duvall in *Apocalypse Now,* though—just another Air Cav soldier who disappeared in the Mekong Delta in April of 1969. I imagined myself crouched backward over the skids of a Huey. Terrified, with the sound of AK-47s firing below and nothing to connect me to safety but a nylon rope. Nothing but the empty black maw of my ignorance waiting to swallow me whole. You would think, if my father had been liked and respected, the soldiers from his platoon would have responded to the letters I'd written, but no one ever had, leaving me only questions so corrosive my insides burned.

It was strange how the absence of a person could occupy so much mental real estate, but the Army—all of America, really—was obsessed with the bodies of the soldiers left behind. The dead were probably at peace—I had to believe that—but those who remained were not. For me, nothing but boots on the ground in Vietnam would satisfy my relentless drive to understand, and Korea was the closest place to Vietnam the Army would send me. Storey's offer to teach rappelling was well-meant, but neither I nor Headquarters Company could afford any distractions. I babbled something noncommittal and went to make sure my mother wasn't embarrassing herself with the punch.

Back in the day room Davis, the motor sergeant, looked at the ring on my mother's left hand. "You want me to get some soldiers to take things out to your car, Miz Mills?" The soldiers with families wanted to get home and the single soldiers were sneaking toward the barracks like I'd caught Pettit doing. It was the beginning of the long Fourth of July weekend, and everyone needed to gird themselves for the work ahead.

With a quickness that set the room spinning, bowls were covered, coolers packed, and tables folded. First Sergeant roped Private Washburn, perpetually on extra duty, into mopping the floor. All the other soldiers faded away except Shumacher, who flipped through a six-month-old copy of *Popular Mechanics* on the sofa. Because of one thing or another I hadn't spoken to Shumacher all afternoon, but she'd been in my peripheral vision as she attempted to insinuate herself into the group of motor pool soldiers. It reminded me of my own struggle to fit a slightly-too-wide body among the ranks of the slim, but Shumacher was the kind of person who took up space without apology. Through the fog of my buzz I remembered that she and Washburn had a thing going on. Probably she was waiting for him.

I reached for the garbage bag in Washburn's hand. "I'll take that out." Let the lovebirds have their Friday afternoon.

"No, ma'am—let me do it." Rather than relinquishing the bag, Washburn tightened his grip, blue eyes intense under cottony-white eyebrows.

"Company commanders aren't too good to take out the trash, Private." My words slurred as I tugged at the neck of the bag, mouth loose from the gin-laced punch.

"Lieutenant Mills is trying to lead by example, son." The Old Man's voice rang artificially bright. Had he been hitting the punch too? But he always waxed bombastic when he had an audience of junior soldiers. "Do you know what the definition of military leadership is, Private?"

"The management of violence." Shumacher licked her index finger and flipped a page of the magazine. She didn't raise her eyes to collect the impressed look on the Old Man's face, or the fleeting disappointment that his question had been answered so quickly. I gave a boozy snort, then suppressed it with a cough.

The Old Man waited several seconds for Shumacher to say

something else, like she was some kind of motor pool oracle, but when neither she nor Washburn spoke, he turned back to First Sergeant, Storey, and my mother. First Sergeant shifted her weight onto her left leg, an inch closer to the door. As she leaned, my inner ear recalibrated, and a wave of alcohol lapped at my balance.

Washburn pulled the garbage bag toward himself. "It's a bit late in the day to be making a statement, ma'am," he said.

"I'm not making a statement," I insisted. Maybe I'd sought out quiet administrative jobs when I joined the Army but now I had to prove to the Old Man—and everyone—that I was a leader of soldiers.

Washburn let go. "Suit yourself. I'm trying to keep you from going outside is all."

I took the trash bag to the dumpster behind the building and my emotions detangled in the sandy heat of the afternoon. Soon I'd be able to go home and sleep off the punch and maybe I'd wake up transformed. Together the soldiers and I would pull Headquarters Company out of the mess it was in and afterward, they'd look back on our time together with fondness and pride. "Good old Lieutenant Mills," they'd say. "Wasn't she the shit?"

I shook my head to clear it. I could be totally forgettable as long as I got the job done and got out of there. The booze was diluting my focus.

A puff of breeze cleared away the secondhand smoke that had settled in my hair and uniform. I slung the plastic bag into the top of the dumpster, holding my breath against the lazy sweet smell and fat flies. I exhaled as I turned around and felt ten pounds lighter.

Then something soft and pink swished through the air. I heard it right before it splatted on the side of my head. I yelped and ducked as Davis appeared from behind a parked car with the still-full bowl of Watergate salad tucked in the crook of his elbow, whooping and lobbing spoonfuls as he ran. I swiped at the glop plastered to my ear as I turned, still in a crouch, in time to see Pettit dashing across the parking lot. She fished a large plastic baggie of Vienna sausages from under her BDU blouse and began to hurl them like grenades.

In seconds I was surrounded. I cowered by the dumpster and tried to keep my mouth shut, because every time I opened it someone shoved red velvet cake or a ham roll in. I panicked, feeling suffocated and claustrophobic. The hazing that accompanied promotions, hails, and farewells was usually good-natured but these soldiers were enjoying themselves a little too much and my first instinct was to fight. Hands held my arms and I struggled against them, breath coming fast. My top trouser button, strained to its breaking point already, popped off. *For the love of god*, I prayed. *Let the rest of the buttons stay where they are.*

Ammunition spent, the soldiers let go, laughing. Okay, then. You had to treat it like a joke. Still in my protective crouch, I wiped my eyes clear of Watergate salad and looked around the asphalt, littered now with candied almonds and Sister Shubert yeast rolls. Logan was a few feet away, bent double, also laughing.

This was funny? I'd show her funny. In one fluid movement, I grabbed a cupcake off the ground and drove it upward into her smug, gossiping face. I hoped it smeared her makeup. I hoped it made her fat. "Welcome to the battalion," I said, dusting crumbs off my trousers. Logan's mouth, half-obscured with pink frosting, was a perfect, surprised circle.

I extricated myself from the cluster of soldiers, who clapped me on the back with more handfuls of Watergate salad, saying, "No offense, ma'am."

"Congratulations, ma'am."

"Good to have you aboard."

"Okay, okay, okay, you clowns." I dug a limp, broken chunk of Vienna sausage out of my ear and chuckled, more at the look on Logan's face than anything else. Revenge was a dish best served pink. "You win."

Still swiping muck off my uniform, I returned to the day room. My mother whirled away from the conversation. "Good Lord, Minerva— what happened to you?"

"The violence of management." I laughed at how the saying worked in both directions. Reeling with sudden vertigo, I sank onto the edge of the vinyl sofa to stop the movement of the room. The afternoon heat and adrenaline rush had worsened my nausea instead of dissipating it. Shumacher scooted to the other end of the sofa, nostrils flared. I looked up into the shocked faces of my mother, First Sergeant, and the Old Man. Storey looked amused, but also worried. Even Washburn, who played his whole life for jokes, pulled those white eyebrows into a line of concern.

My feeling of momentary triumph faded. The soldiers outside had taken their frustrations out on me, and this fact bobbed on the surface of my understanding like apples in a barrel of water. No, that was too friendly and fun. This awareness bobbed like a body in a river. Like a body in the Mekong River being nibbled by fish, coming apart slowly in the water.

Tears pricked my eyes. There was something seriously wrong with the way my mind worked and a gullet full of spiked punch was not helping matters.

Shumacher leaned over and whispered, "I've been waiting to talk to you all afternoon, ma'am."

I grimaced at Shumacher to shut her up and swiped a finger along my hairline. It came away full of Watergate salad, curdled after a day of riding in a car and sitting out in a hot room. The lumps of cottage cheese were separating from the crushed pineapple and my skin oil was breaking down the unnatural chemical colors and artificial sweeteners. It was not a pleasant smell, but when people showed you they didn't want you around, you couldn't act like you cared. "We've got all the time in the world, Shumacher," I said. "Three. Whole. Months." I licked the salad off my finger.

My mother's chest went concave as she backed away in disgust. No more hugs from her today. Frosting slid down my neck into the gap between my collar and my OD green T-shirt, still sweaty from all those hours in the sun. Breadcrumbs studded my face, stuck on with ham grease and sugar. First Sergeant cleared her throat and Storey laughed. You could always count on at least one masochist in every Army crowd.

Under the cover of everyone's reactions Shumacher murmured, "I just need, like, five minutes."

I nodded but said, "Not now, Shumacher." My saliva thinned and it was all I could do to hold my gorge.

The Old Man took a stack of green paper towels from First Sergeant's hand and walked over. "Looks like they got you good, Lieutenant." Even in my addled state I could hear the lack of approval in his voice. My stomach heaved against a wave of lemonade and rancid salad. I tried everything to stop myself but could not. As the bugle over the loudspeaker on the parade field signaled the end of the official workday, I grabbed the paper towels and ran to the latrine to unload the pink contents of my stomach. Shocked silence, broken by Storey's laughter, chased me down the hall.

POPPING POSITIVE

I n the late afternoon light, the ten-year-old Camry gleamed like it had been touched by the hand of Midas. My mother turned the key in the ignition and it coughed, something stuck deep in its throat. I wrenched open the passenger door, praying we could make our getaway before any of the battalion mechanics overheard and came to investigate the noise. I'd had quite enough of them for one afternoon.

I plopped into the car and my mother looked at me, unimpressed. "Put a towel down, Minerva. You're getting that mess all over the seat." All the curlicues from her speech shriveled in the baking-hot interior of the car.

"Well, I tried to tell you about the Jell-O." I felt like I might throw up again. I wanted to go home, peel off my food-smeared uniform, and take a shower, but I lumbered back out in search of the emergency blanket in the trunk.

"Ma'am?" Shumacher came jogging over the asphalt. Great—a mechanic on the scene.

"I know, I know—the muffler needs to be replaced." I shoved bags and boxes around, my synapses dissolved by gin, arms and brain disconnected. No blanket. "Damn." The pink tablecloth would have to do.

Shumacher drew to a halt, puzzlement descending over her features.

"What is it, Shumacher?" I couldn't keep the irritation out of my voice. Shumacher and Washburn had stayed out of the food fight, but I was lumping all of Headquarters Company together in my mind. They didn't want me there. Check. Well, I didn't want to be there either, so the feelings were mutual.

Shumacher pulled something from a trouser pocket and held it out. It was a white stick, narrowed to a metallic point at one end.

"What's this—oh, shit, Shumacher!" It was a home pregnancy test with two pink lines glowing in the rectangular window—the twin tally marks of doom.

"I was trying to tell you." Shumacher looked uncharacteristically sheepish. She stuffed the pregnancy test back in her pocket. Washburn was nowhere to be seen.

I heaved a sigh. The whole afternoon pivoted on this little stick and Shumacher knew it. Every female soldier knew this. Where to begin? With the first question to ask a pregnant woman, always. "Do you want this baby? Are you happy about it?" A pregnant soldier was not a cosmetic issue that could be buffed away with Turtle Wax. While everyone thumped Washburn on the back Shumacher was going to take a lot of shit for getting knocked up. She'd need a solid core of wanting this baby to weather the criticism heading her way.

Shumacher shrugged and her eyes filled with tears. My pickled brain wandered, as it so often did, to the letter from my father inside my pocket—the pocket now adorned with frosting melting in the late June heat. *We shouldn't bring children into this world.* I knew a thing or two about unwanted babies but had no idea what to say.

I rested a hand on the trunk of my mother's car then jerked it away. It was like a stove burner. The engine was still running, the muffler still grumbling like an ogre in need of a nap. The timing could not have been worse. The female commander of Headquarters Company, with her female first sergeant, was having, on her very first afternoon of command, a female soldier pop positive for pregnancy on top of everything else that needed fixing. A child was a good thing, I was adamant about that. But a pregnancy, a baby, a single mother in the

Army, were impossible things, and I wasn't cut out to handle them just then. Or ever.

"Listen," I said. "Accidents happen. Let's send you on sick call after the long weekend. Get this thing confirmed. We'll deal with it after—" I waved my red hand in a frustrated circle, to encompass the entire past week, my throbbing head, my uniform encrusted with a table-load of party food.

"Get this thing confirmed," Shumacher repeated softly. Her head dropped and her hand moved toward her pocket, then stopped.

I liked Shumacher. I'd helped her get promoted to specialist not long ago. When I was sobered up and fresh after the long weekend, maybe I could show Logan and Pettit what it looked like when women supported each other. "Let's keep this between us, okay? Go to sick call on Monday. Shit—Tuesday. *Wednesday.*" How long *was* this long weekend? Sweat trickled into my eyes from under my BDU cap and I longed for the air conditioning inside my mother's car. The car that was still running, still waiting for me, still too loud and too likely to attract unwanted attention. "Get it confirmed, and we'll square you away first thing after the holiday."

Shumacher shook her head slowly at the pavement. From that angle it looked like she was grinding her teeth. "Yes, ma'am," she said, not looking up.

BE ALL YOU CAN BE!

The next morning my mother dropped me back at Headquarters Company, exhaust system roaring as she drove home to Athens. A silver BMW was parked in the spot designated for the company first sergeant, next to my ratty Honda. "Shit," I sighed. So much for sneaking in for a little quiet time in the new office.

I eased through the front door of the clapboard building, hoping to go undetected as long as possible. I respected the strength First Sergeant St. John must have needed to systematically observe, document, and take down a well-liked officer like Captain Williams, but her actions had shaken Headquarters to its rickety foundations. I didn't know where her loyalties lay as we all emerged from the rubble. In my old job at battalion personnel, the two sergeants I worked with were a strange combination of obsequiousness and hubris. When I was new they met me at the door every morning and pressed cups of coffee into my hand while waving papers under my nose in hopes I wouldn't read them too carefully. You couldn't pencil-whip much when it came to personnel issues, though—either the soldier was there, occupying a billet and doing a job, or they weren't. But those guys sure did try to fudge everything else. I never understood the inclination to cheat except that it made an otherwise tedious job more entertaining. After a couple of months of taking the papers from them and reading them in my own sweet time, asking questions and consulting regulations, Obsequious and Hubris gave up trying to blow smoke. But my sense was that working with First Sergeant St. John would be a whole different ball game.

I turned the overhead lights on in my office and the cheap cylindrical bulbs hummed like malevolent bees. I turned them off. The sunlight was already baking the cramped room and the smell did a number on my stomach, still weak from yesterday's gin punch. I swallowed hard and got to work. I wiped the desktop and the center drawer clean of lint balls and broken rubber bands and folded paper footballs and dozens of individual staples and a whole load of unrecognizable dreck. The file drawers remained locked, and the key was nowhere to be found. I filled a garbage bag with outdated Army manuals and the Victoria's Secret catalogs tucked between them on the shelves. "For crying out loud, lady," I said to the chick in the see-through catsuit on the cover of one of them. "I know I'm a fish on a bicycle, but you *really* don't belong here."

Compartmentalizing the hypermasculine excesses of the Army was the only way to survive them. Stuff 'em in a bag, as it were. I first learned this in Basic Camp the summer after my sophomore year at the University of Georgia. It was a six-week program to catch late starters up with our peers back on campus, the kids with scholarships who'd been in ROTC from the beginning. "You think we're being tough on you, Cadet?" My primary drill instructor was a lizard-faced Vietnam vet named Gallagher. There must have been a story behind why he was still a staff sergeant after twenty years in the Army, something to explain why he was riding out his career harassing college kids. "We got to break you down before we build you back up."

We did Hello Dollies in the beating sun, lying on our backs in the grass while the drill sergeants patrolled the ranks. "Open 'em! Close 'em!" Sergeant Gallagher laughed and leered, and I opened and closed my raised legs for inspection. I was already broken down. I'd been broken down before I was born, and I'd known it for sure when I found that box of letters in the trunk of my father's old car, way before I joined ROTC. My father was so broken he hadn't wanted me to be born. So broken he'd gotten himself killed. Broken people did not always make the best soldiers, but sometimes, in spite of it all, we soldiered on.

Take the current operation: I scrubbed at the spit stains from around the sofa. "On my literal hands and knees," I grumbled, "Cleaning up their mess." Oh, how the sergeants must have loved gathering here for meetings with Captain Williams at the bookends of the days! Victoria's Secret catalogs and Copenhagen! But the grunt work didn't matter as long as it got me to Korea in the end.

"You okay, ma'am?" Outside, the sun went behind a cloud and First Sergeant appeared in the doorway. "Thought I heard you talking to somebody in here."

"Hey, First Sergeant." I wiped sweat from the back of my splotchy neck. I'd louvered the blinds against the sun but it was too hot in there, and no matter how much industrial pine cleaner I doused it with I couldn't banish Captain Williams's bad vibes, which smelled like old socks. The air freshener I'd stuck to the inside of the trash can layered floral artifice over everything but improved nothing. "What brings you here this fine Saturday?"

She scanned the stuffy, darkened room. "It's cooler in here without them fluorescent lights on but we should find you a fan." Was she fighting a smile? The last time she'd seen me I was running for the latrine. "And I'm just getting myself organized then I'm out to my mother's for the weekend. You want some coffee? You look a little raggedy."

I unfolded myself from the linoleum floor and closed my eyes against a wave of nausea brought on by crouching for too long. My mouth was tacky from dehydration. I wanted to leave the mop bucket next to the pile of catalogs of half-naked women and drive home. I wanted a Styrofoam cup of coffee put in my hand and for my ego to be stroked, just for a minute before First Sergeant and I got down to the nitty-gritty of how to get Headquarters back on track. I might end up missing the slightly suspect congeniality of my old sergeants—the balm that soothed my ferocious internal critic—because my overriding suspicion was that First Sergeant St. John was a high-efficiency machine and that no officer in the world possessed the skills to handle such a competent NCO. She didn't need anyone, least of all me. But maybe she was not as big a hardass as everyone said. Had she hinted she had a mother within commuting distance? Maybe she and I would be okay. "Coffee would be great, thanks."

First Sergeant returned with two steaming cups and I barricaded myself behind the sturdy governmental vastness of my desk as she took a seat on the sofa in front of me. "I hope we can be honest with each other," I said, acutely aware of our differences—in rank, in age, in skin color, in body size. I diagnosed my jumbled feelings as a byproduct of hangover and embarrassment about the day before and folded my hands. That looked like I was praying, and also too fake and commandery. I detangled my fingers and laid them on the blotter where they left faint handprints.

In contrast, First Sergeant looked perfectly at ease, her green mug shouting *Be All You Can Be!* "That would be good, ma'am. The colonel asked me to put this company right six months ago and we don't have a lot of time left. I could use your help."

I startled at the word choice. Who was helping whom, here? I was the company commander. A first sergeant, working under me, carried out my orders. But First Sergeant St. John had seventeen years in the Army to my not-quite four. "When you say we don't have time, are you talking about the summer field exercise?" I asked.

"Yes, but also Yugoslavia. There are rumors floating around that we'll have to go." First Sergeant paused, weighing her words like any senior sergeant would with a new commander, or like any female soldier engaged in the eternal dance of keeping her shiny boot toes unstepped upon by another one. "We can make the company look good on paper, ma'am. That's easy enough to do. But we might have more at stake than just a passing grade on the training evaluation."

A passing grade on the field exercise was all that was important to me, but I couldn't admit that out loud. Of course I wouldn't want the company to deploy unprepared to a war zone, but Yugoslavia felt like a distant threat. Like somebody else's problem. Before I could respond First Sergeant drew a breath. "Since you want straight talk, there's something you should know."

I leaned forward in my seat, thinking she might be about to share a confidence. To seek me out, like Shumacher had, even though I didn't dare think the word *friend*. "What's that, First Sergeant?"

"The IG visit confirmed there were irregularities with training since that last failure on the field exercise. And big problems with the accounting. You know this."

I did know this and deflated like a tired party balloon. First Sergeant was neither seeking my counsel nor pulling me close. She was just talking shop. "I know about as much as anyone on the periphery although the colonel didn't go into specifics," I said. "You don't have to gossip about Captain Williams, but I guess I need to hear what happened, because I sure don't intend to make the same mistakes."

She turned toward the sunlight that striped her face from between the blinds. "Progress has been slow since the company failed annual training, maybe even nonexistent in some cases. I'm not trying to make excuses, but things have most definitely *not* been on the up and up. Captain Williams covered for equipment losses, I'm sure of that." She looked at me out of the corner of her eye. "And I'm pretty sure he was pilfering some of it himself."

"Whoa." Stealing equipment—to do what with?—could get an officer thrown into Leavenworth. "I mean, if you say so, I believe you. But this—whoa. This is big." Was Captain Williams that dumb? Arrogant for sure—I'd seen him out socially. The guy did not lack for confidence. But stealing? If this was true, he was an idiot.

"Well, at first I just came up on some whispered conversations between him and the old supply sergeant, Sergeant Lutes, before Lutes left. I didn't think much of it until I saw Captain Williams loading cases of MREs into his personal vehicle. Then another time it was wet-weather gear and field jackets, but he told me he was taking them out to the training area."

"Maybe he was just making sure his soldiers had what they needed?"

A cloud scudded across First Sergeant's face. "It was a sunny day, ma'am."

My neck flushed at the naivete of my question.

She went on. "We should have done a proper inventory before Lutes left but Captain Williams signed off on Lutes's clearing paperwork himself. When Sergeant Storey took over supply, it was about five minutes before he was in my office saying the inventory sheets didn't match what was on the shelves. I told him to leave it all where it was. That's when I went to the colonel and, well—you know the rest."

I did. The Old Man hadn't wanted to hear about a unit supply room's inability to do simple math. He was preoccupied with keeping the other Fort Stewart colonels off his back—the commanders of the mechanized infantry units whose hundreds of tanks and other tracked vehicles our battalion repaired. The ones who were the Old Man's neighbors in the housing area, who lorded it over him because they were combat soldiers, and he was a lowly maintenance guy. The Old Man used words like *picayune* and *minuscule* in his response to the concerns First Sergeant raised, so she left his office and got the inspector general on the horn. Most soldiers would have low-crawled back to their desks out of self-preservation. That's probably what I would have done. It wasn't her confidence but her follow-through that made her an anomaly.

"If you don't have documentation, it's your word against his," I said. The closer I got to the door the braver I might get, too, but at the moment I didn't have that luxury. We needed to keep our heads down. I had to fix the big problems and leave.

"We need to finish the job," First Sergeant said as if she were arguing with my thoughts. "If some of these NCOs don't see some consequences—real, hard consequences—they'll keep pushing their luck."

The Army was rife with petty thievery. It was like playing Whack-A-Mole, trying to fix all the corner-cutting. "I'll keep my eyes open for proof as I'm doing inventories, First Sergeant. For sure. But don't you think we should leave well enough alone? You were heroic to do what you did, but let's move forward. Focus on improvements."

"Of course, ma'am." First Sergeant's eyelids came down. They were shiny, as if coated with Vaseline. The flatness of her delivery, the way she dropped eye contact, made me start to pay attention to when she used the word *we* and when she switched to *you*. I wasn't telling her why I didn't want to investigate Captain Williams's possible life of crime. I didn't need to divulge why I didn't have time to sleuth and crucify. I was also—I'd forgotten until just that minute, as my hungover brain started to clear—not telling her about Shumacher's pregnancy test. Because when those shiny eyelids of hers lowered my own walls came up. Everything worked better when officers and enlisted trusted each other, but trust took time to earn. It took honesty and compromise and shared success to develop, and First Sergeant and I had none of those things under our belts. I watched myself shift into officer mode with equal measures of wonderment and annoyance. She didn't need to get all pissed off and resentful during our very first conversation. It was possible for a senior NCO to be wrong.

"I mean it," I insisted. "I'll document everything while we're doing inventories."

First Sergeant opened her eyes. "Improprieties aside, you do need to get going on equipment layouts and inventories." I squirmed, ever so slightly, at the word *you*. "You should also spend some time in the different work sections. Get to know your people. Headquarters isn't a big company, but it's responsible for a lot. It may seem like the best opening move to beat everyone over the head with inspection reports, but share a little bit of yourself with them, ma'am. Be authentic. Soldiers don't know who to trust right now."

I picked beads of Styrofoam from my coffee cup and forced myself to breathe. She wanted me to walk around glad-handing like a politician. She knew the Old Man had pulled my orders to Korea, but she didn't know why—or how desperately—I wanted to go there. She didn't know the Old Man was holding my orders ransom for a few measly pounds, and because of that I had no intention of holding myself up for close inspection. "Winning hearts and minds? Sounds good, First Sergeant." The best defense is a good offense, right? I narrowed my eyes and smiled. It had to come off as gentle ribbing. "Is that how you've gotten everyone on your side?"

First Sergeant laughed at my dig. "No, ma'am. I wouldn't say I've gotten everyone on my side. I'm not sure that's even the goal."

"I agree with you there." I spoke quickly, trying to strike a balance between having the upper hand and not being too heavy-handed. "I mean, I agree that we have to keep some distance from the soldiers. And I agree on the need for inventories ASAP. But don't you think some of these NCOs slacked off under Captain Williams? Aren't they at all responsible for their poor performance?"

"Some of them are wrong and they know it." First Sergeant's dark eyes flashed in the shaded light of the room, tipping her cards just far enough that I could see the anger she'd been holding close for the last six months. "But that is NCO business, and you can leave the NCOs to me. I've got my own reasons and ways to make things right. You're only here for a few months but I mean to see this one through."

What were her reasons for wanting to make things right and why wasn't she sharing them? Apparently we both had things to hide. "Headquarters' performance is my responsibility now," I said. This was not completely true. Headquarters' performance was the responsibility of a lot of people, but the Old Man would be evaluating me.

"I guess the question I'm really asking is, do you want things done or do you want them done right?" First Sergeant's arm rested like a tension wire across the top of the sofa. It was the ultimate getting-to-know-you question between NCOs and officers.

I couldn't make myself simply hand over the reins. I'd worked with too many smooth-talking NCOs before. I could compromise, but my life's ambition was riding on the outcome. "I want things done correctly. And immediately. I think we can agree on that."

First Sergeant nodded.

"I also want things to work between us, so by all means, handle the NCOs how you see fit. I'll try to cool my jets long enough to earn people's trust."

She nodded again and pushed up from the sofa. "I'll set you up a schedule to start on the inventories. These NCOs know what they should be doing. It won't take them long to square their sections away now that Captain Williams is gone. But if you push them too soon, they're going to dig in and slow down like the bunch of balky mules they are."

My mind flashed to the Charge of the Pink Brigade the afternoon before. "Davis?" I asked. The mouthy motor sergeant was probably the lead mule.

First Sergeant took a final swig of coffee, the watchful expression on her face confirming my suspicion. "I'll have the inventory schedule on your desk first thing next week." She left without volunteering any more information, and I tapped my Styrofoam cup with a dirty fingernail, still completely in the dark about what made this woman tick. One thing was for sure—I needed to watch my six. Her eyes were open, but her mouth was clamped shut.

201 FILE

I drummed my fingers on the desktop my first real morning at work. I'd kept my hands to myself on Saturday while First Sergeant was around. I read training files and charted their information, curiosity nagging the edges of my conscience. What was her story? I couldn't very well ask. But now everyone was back to work and too shy or too busy or too disinterested to talk to me, and a desire to get the inside scoop burned its way past my better judgment. Pushing back from my desk, I strode out of my office and into the Orderly Room.

Reyes, the clerk on loan from the post office, squinted at her computer monitor as she typed with two fingers. Red blotches heating up my neck, I nodded a greeting as I approached the cabinet containing the personnel files like I didn't have a care in the world. I jiggled the top drawer, but it was locked, as was the key control box hanging on the wall next to it.

"*Now* the key control box is locked?" It had all been open all weekend, a big no-go. I'd meant to address it with First Sergeant but that had seemed minor compared to everything else.

"Can I help you, ma'am?"

"I need a few files." I put some oomph in the statement in case Reyes questioned my reasons, but Reyes didn't even blink. She opened her middle desk drawer and handed me a key. "We've got to start keeping stuff secured," I said.

"Sorry, ma'am." Reyes rooted through the tray in her drawer and pulled out another key. "The keys kept going missing, so I've been stashing them here."

"Seems like a lot of things have been going missing." I retrieved the file I wanted, watching Reyes for a reaction but got nothing. "How about we start putting things back where they belong when we're done with them?"

"Yes, ma'am." Reyes returned to hunting and pecking, unperturbed. A commander could look at whatever she wanted. I didn't have to explain anything to anyone—as long as First Sergeant didn't catch me at it.

Back at my desk I smoothed my hand over the light brown cover, suddenly reluctant. If I'd been looking for something work-related that would be one thing, but trawling for insight was perilously close to snooping. People were protective of their stories. But if First Sergeant's file was in the common drawer it was fair game. I took a breath and opened the cover.

A full-length photo was tucked inside, perhaps left from a promotion packet or in preparation for one. My own packet for promotion was making its way through channels. I studied the details of the photograph, impressed at the way a slender person could make even an unflattering polyester skirt and plastic Corfam shoes look good. An expert marksmanship badge was pinned next to her Airborne wings, two symbols of an irrefutable badass, and she held her shoulders level with the rows of ribbons. She didn't glower, the usual facial expression on official military portraits, but her faint smile hinted at levels of competence I could only dream of. That smile was just as dangerous, though. A warning against trespass. I slapped the cover shut.

201 FILE, Part II

thumped my fist against the closed cover. Dammit, the Old Man stomped around the battalion offices demanding information on a whim, interrupting the work flow, rearranging people's schedules, sucking up all the oxygen and spewing it back as though it was his government-issued right. Why was I hesitating over one soldier's file?

I opened the cover then closed it again at the sight of that Mona Lisa smile. Because it was intrusive, that's why. What was I even hoping to learn?

I needed insight, I told myself. I needed to know what First Sergeant meant when she'd said she wanted to handle "NCO business" on her own. I needed to keep interpersonal drama from slowing the company's progress.

If I was being scrupulously honest, I just wanted to know more about the woman. I wanted to understand her. That wasn't a crime, was it? In his letters, my father had agonized over his relationships with his NCOs. Maybe the best way to avoid that kind of pain, that kind of misunderstanding, was to head it off at the pass.

I opened the file and set the photo aside, face down on the desk, and began to flip through the layers of paperwork. Her most recent evaluations were more than fine—lots of above-and-beyonds; oak leaf clusters to add to previous awards. Very few leave slips. Home of record: Sunbury, Georgia—not far from post if you took the back gate out of Fort Stewart. I'd never been out there but I'd seen the signs. The recipient of her life insurance policy was a Martha St. John, born in 1930. Nothing to indicate that First Sergeant was married or had kids.

I paused, ashamed. I didn't need to infiltrate her private life to work better with her. But, sick with self-loathing, I flipped another page and kept reading. It was the same compulsion that drove me to overeat, the feeling that I needed something I couldn't name, and wouldn't know until the revulsion was so bad it overrode the automatic movements of my hands and jaws. I never hit that point with food until I was coming out of a trance to find myself scraping the plate, and in this case, not until I got to the bottom of First Sergeant's evaluation from her assignment in Karlsruhe, Germany in February of 1990. "An unusual lapse in judgment," the statement read. "Inappropriate relationship with a local national. Recommend for positions with close supervision."

Whoa. I lifted the evaluation but there was no letter of counseling underneath to explain the incident. Counseling statements weren't permanent. First Sergeant, a personnelist herself, could have made a letter disappear when she left Germany. There was no evidence she'd been formally punished for whatever the lapse of judgment was, but those bullets were killers. They'd have shot her upward career trajectory straight out of the sky.

I closed the cover of the file again, wishing I could turn the hands of the loudly ticking government clock back five minutes, to the point where I'd looked at the photo then stopped myself. I wished I'd returned the file to the drawer without reading it. Some things, even if you didn't know what they were, you didn't need to know.

INDIGO ST. JOHN

Hunched into her old suede jacket against the cold November night, Indigo walked down the wet street wishing she'd put something nicer on. Wearing a uniform took the stress out of getting dressed in the morning but left her perplexed by clothes and fretting that she didn't understand how to pull an outfit together like European women. Maybe if she took more trouble with the externals she'd have a group of friends to walk into town with, but she wasn't in Germany to keep up appearances. And anyway, she had plenty of friends back home.

Indigo found herself moving in the direction of the palace, the hub from which the spokes of Karlsruhe's streets radiated. Originally the Schloss served as a pleasure dome for a former Grand Duke and his mistresses. These days, in 1989, it contained a somewhat dull museum for the history of the area, minus any reminders of the 1930s and 40s. Outside the Schloss, the gardens were a popular meeting place. A place for concerts, picnics, naps, or public displays of affection when the weather was nice.

As Indigo approached the Waldpark she was joined by more people on the sidewalks and paths. Some wore party hats and carried bottles of Sekt, German sparkling wine. Everyone talked animatedly, and although her skin color usually provoked double takes, for once everyone was too distracted by the goings-on in Berlin to remark on one dark face. The dark faces were almost always Americans anyway, and Americans were everywhere in this Southwest corner of Germany. Indigo crouched to tighten a shoelace on her running shoe, wishing again that she'd put more thought into her wardrobe. Choice of footwear was another obvious marker of an American and it was never smart to make yourself a target in Cold War Germany. But she'd wanted to see what was going on for herself. She didn't want to miss a thing.

As she rounded the corner, the Schloss curved into view and Indigo caught her breath. Klieg lights illuminated the baroque buttercream exterior. The hubbub in the air became a roar of noise. Despite the cold and damp, tens of thousands of people had gravitated to the park. Bottle rockets fired randomly from all corners. A string of firecrackers skittered, cackling with glee, across the path in front of her.

She stepped away from the pyrotechnics and toward the relative quiet of the avenue of classical statues that flanked the fountain, sitting on an empty bench overlooked by the goddess Diana. She ran her shoes back and forth across the gravel, fading into the shadows to enjoy the pure happiness that surrounded her. Ordinarily Germans didn't allow themselves to express strong emotions. She herself could only take them in small doses. But she couldn't have stayed away. The Schloss was the perfect stage to witness the most earth-shattering event in the second half of the twentieth century.

A man in full scuba gear stood in the fountain pouring beer over his head, first from a bottle in one hand and then from a bottle in the other. On the next bench over, a young couple shared a cigarette and kissed passionately between puffs. Then Indigo saw Top about a hundred meters away, surrounded by the other platoon sergeants. They stuck to the path like good soldiers rather than cutting across the grass. McDonnell was noticeably absent from the group.

The company had hailed McDonnell's arrival four months ago like he was R. Lee Ermey in the flesh. Top let fly a litany of happy curses and the young soldiers buzzed with excitement at having a drill sergeant for their new training NCO. Indigo hated how easy it was for McDonnell to walk down the stairs his first day, razzle springing from his lips and dazzle bouncing from the toes of his jump boots, casting a spell over everyone except her. Well, almost everyone—Knight knew him from basic training. He'd been her drill sergeant and Indigo gathered there was some unfinished business between the two of them. But all summer, as the borders to Eastern Bloc countries loosened and faltered, McDonnell made inroads into the soldiers' hearts and minds. As the protests of those same countries became louder, month after month, Indigo's dislike of McDonnell solidified. He was just another soldier who hid behind a spit shine, all bluster and no follow-through. She didn't understand how others could miss this and was annoyed with herself at how much she allowed him into her thoughts. His absence that night was a reprieve, but there she was, thinking about him again.

The more Top drank the louder he got, and he was bellowing at the top of his lungs as the group walked in the opposite direction from Indigo. So much for keeping a low profile to minimize security threats. But the atmosphere was so jubilant that Indigo understood how people might get carried away that night, even the ones who'd just lectured their soldiers about staying out of trouble. The other NCOs didn't appear to see her, and she was glad. Even on the sidelines a wallflower was still at the dance. She was still a company leader even if she hadn't been invited to run after Top like the other strap-hangers. She was the one filtering this moment through all her courses in European history. The one experiencing it without an American buffer.

"It is too magical an evening for a beautiful woman to sit alone." Indigo looked up at a long pair of legs encased in brown leather trousers, laced and fringed along the sides with suede. The legs led to an olive green coat, wrapped around a tall White man with shaggy brown hair, and up to a smile that revealed the uneven, yellowed teeth of a European—probably a smoker. He looked a little like Ted. "May I sit down?" he asked.

OPPOSING FORCES (OPFOR)

It was Thursday, training day, the most hated day of the week. Across the Army soldiers came to work in helmets and web belts, signed weapons out of arms rooms and sat in bored half circles as NCOs read from rote scripts about how to call in mortar fire or respond to nuclear, biological, and chemical weapons strikes. Cooks and postal clerks practiced how to set up land mines and throw hand grenades. Every soldier was a rifleman and blah blah blah, but all the support soldiers bitched about it. *We've got actual work to do and instead we're playing Army.*

I hovered at the door to First Sergeant's office. Outside, a rainstorm hammered down so hard it raised a mist over the parking lot but instead of cooling things off it just made the air thicker. It scrubbed the windows of dust and pollen but refused to wash away the itchy guilt I was feeling, and the paranoia that she would figure out I'd snooped in her file just by the way I shifted my weight in my boots as I stood there. "Do you want to come with me to the motor pool?" I asked.

In penance for my sins against First Sergeant, I'd visited every work section to say hello. Every section except the motor pool, since I dreaded having to make nice around Sergeant Davis. If I didn't show my face Davis would think I was avoiding him or, god forbid, afraid of him. But I wanted reinforcements.

First Sergeant demurred. "I've got a task to go over with the orderly room, ma'am." I didn't fault her for dodging the drama. Motor pool had been hit hardest during the IG inspection and Davis blamed her for bringing down the heat.

Shouldering responsibility like a heavy Alice pack, I went to Storey, who'd volunteered to take on training duties as well as supply. "I need you to go with me to the motor pool," I sighed.

The rain shower had passed, and the sun was peeking out from behind the clouds, growing brighter and hotter by the time Storey and I got to the motor pool. Davis had pulled the M88 Armored Recovery Vehicle, a huge, tracked rhinoceros with a boom arm and winch, from its spot at the back of the motor park. An M88 was strong enough to haul an Abrams main battle tank out of the swampy quarter million acres of Fort Stewart's training area and the mechanics didn't get to play with it very often. So unlike the rest of Headquarters Company, they were excited about Thursday training. I didn't know how to feel about the fact that Davis had gotten something right.

"I got a cold Co-Cola for the first shithead that finds the switch for the smoke generator!" Davis stood to the side of the M88 while the mechanics clambered in and around the fifty-ton vehicle. He rattled the ice cubes in a tumbler of soda, emblazoned with the logo of a restaurant chain called the Dixie Chicken. I squinted in the stark sunlight, intensified by the concrete of the motor park. Rainbows popped from the mist evaporating off the pavement, and the soldiers wiped the sweat that dripped from under their Kevlar helmets. I would have loved a cold Coke myself—diet, of course.

Shumacher poked her head out of the driver's hatch. "Got it, Sar'n Davis," she said. Davis walked over and peered down into the vehicle. Satisfied, he handed her the tumbler. Had Shumacher gone on sick call yet? I made a mental note to take her aside. If Shumacher was pregnant she needed to start telling people what was going on. We'd need to find her a less noxious place to work than the motor pool.

"Fire in the hole!" Davis bellowed, like he was coordinating an artillery barrage instead of a mechanic firing up the smoke generator on a glorified tow truck. He swaggered, probably imagining that he, himself, might someday open a can of whoop-ass instead of being the grease monkey who bolted whooped-up-on stuff back together.

Shumacher's head ducked down. The engine revved into gear and thick white smoke rolled from the rear of the vehicle, enveloping me and Storey. We waved our hands in front of our faces and moved out of the way of the diesel exhaust.

"The M88's smoke generator can be used to conceal its location from opposing forces!" Davis called over the noise. The mechanics cackled, casting glances over their shoulders at me. It was the kind of thing you had to be a good sport about, like getting food smashed into your ear canals after an assumption of command ceremony, but Davis was inching his boot over the line again. I remained stone-faced but my neck heated up, the dumpy lieutenant in the bulky web belt and baggy BDU trousers. I stood up straighter.

Storey harrumphed. "We'll see who's laughing after the motor pool inventory."

Davis's smile faded and the red of his face deepened. "What'd you say, Storey?"

I adjusted my web belt to allow some of the sweat pooling at my waist to drain. I didn't want Storey to rescue me, I just needed him to stand there like a North Korean guard and keep his mouth shut. "We're doing hundred-percent inventories in every section, Sergeant Davis, not only the motor pool," I said.

"Females." Davis disappeared around the side of the M88. He didn't mutter; he wanted to make sure I heard him over the idling engine. "Can't handle their liquor. Got to hide behind a stack of paperwork."

At the word "female," a noun that made me feel like a breeding animal instead of a human, my vision went starry. I might not have looked like much, but I wasn't the one sneaking behind fifty-ton vehicles to take potshots. "Your inventory starts tomorrow, Sergeant Davis," I called to him.

"We'll be ready to start Monday," Davis said.

"Tomorrow," I repeated, sounding tougher than I felt. "I don't want to throw off First Sergeant's schedule."

Davis's head appeared from behind the M88, a sly twist to his lips. "Oh, let's not make Mommy mad." This time when the mechanics snickered they were joined by Washburn. Apparently he wasn't on Team Lieutenant Mills anymore.

Heat radiated off the concrete, up through the soles of my boots, through my damp T-shirt, to my cheeks. I narrowed my eyes. "It's not about whether First Sergeant gets mad, Sergeant Davis. We've all got a job to do." A sharp edge cut through my words, but the M88's engine chose that moment to gun.

"Sorry, ma'am!" Shumacher's head emerged, eyes wide. "My foot slipped!"

My synapses zapped like lightening. Adrenaline surged and threatened to shut me down. From a spot above the motor park I watched myself impale Davis, twist, then pull out the bayonet. Next to me, a soldier in a plain green pickle suit and steel pot materialized. My father. I paused midair, regarding Shumacher, not wanting to bash a pregnant soldier with even an imaginary butt stock and my father nodded grimly. The management of violence, indeed. "First Sergeant already told you that you're scheduled to go first," I said to Davis. "I'm sure she'd be happy to tell you again during motor stables this afternoon. But you need to plan to start inventories tomorrow."

"Roger that, LT." Davis fiddled with a bolt on the side of the M88. My rage battled with the inclination to back down. I might turn up to the motor pool with a clipboard the next morning and have nothing to count but the mechanics' smirking, unprepared faces. What would I do then, besides disappoint my father?

I made a note in the green training ledger I carried, hand shaking on the pen. "Stay or go?" I held it so Storey could see. He shook his head and remained where he was, off to the side of the dissipating smoke, arms crossed. I wanted to believe his anger at Davis was genuine and not just because he was sucking up to me. I was lightheaded with stress and mistrusted everyone's motivations at that point.

We stayed for another forty-five minutes while my blood pressure returned to something closer to normal. My insecurities regained a solid foothold, too, but there would be plenty of Thursdays to check up on the cooks and the postal clerks and the orderly room, and only this moment to show Davis that I could stand and watch him as long as I jolly well wanted to. I scribbled nonsense into my green notebook to steady my trembling hands, and eventually the discussion—self-conscious after our face-off—devolved into the silliness that meant everyone had had enough, and Storey left to open the arms room so the soldiers could turn in their weapons.

Back in the headquarters building I peeked in at the orderly room as First Sergeant wrapped up a lesson on firing a light antitank weapon. With their murmurs in the background, I flicked on the fan in my office and pulled a package of granola bars from the rucksack I'd carried in that morning, taking one bar from the box and putting the rest in the shallow center drawer of my desk. I had to smash the box to get it to fit, but I hadn't found the key that opened the larger bottom drawers yet.

Listening for First Sergeant's boot steps padding down the hallway, I removed a folded metal photo frame from my ruck. My cat Rambo glared from one side of the frame and on the other side my parents smiled and leaned against my father's 1968 Mustang. I didn't want anyone, least of all myself, to think I was getting comfortable at Headquarters Company. I wasn't putting up an "I Love Me" wall of diplomas and training certificates; I would not be decorating with inspirational posters, throw rugs, or potted plants. I didn't even want anyone to see these pictures. Their only purpose was to remind me to get the job done and get out. This morning at the motor pool had emphasized the importance of that.

"Moving in?" First Sergeant drawled like a sleepy honey bee in search of a flower to curl up in.

I slapped the frame shut. "You're so quiet coming down the hall, First Sergeant."

"I don't mean to sneak up." Her eyes sparked in the light filtering through the half-closed blinds. "It just happens."

"Probably comes in handy on patrol," I said, cringing at how awkward I was. She didn't know about my guilty conscience. I cleared my throat. "Anyway. Most of my stuff got shipped to Korea before the colonel canceled my orders. But I brought a few things from home." I opened the photo frame and held it out. It was the least I could offer after gobbling that generous helping of her work history.

"I've met your mother." First Sergeant examined the photos. "Is that your father?"

"Yes." My voice sounded too clipped, even to me. "Not long before he shipped out to Vietnam."

"Ah." A light dawned across her face, but she had the good manners not to remark. My father hadn't been at my assumption of command ceremony—given this factor First Sergeant could at least partially solve the equation. "You favor him."

"That's what they say." I waited for her to reciprocate with some nugget about her own family, but she divulged nothing. Most soldiers spewed their backstory without being prompted, but the ones with skeletons in the closet possessed stronger filters.

Instead she said, "I've got a friend who's a Vietnam vet."

"Oh?" A friend-friend? A boyfriend? A woman friend? I wasn't allowed to ask, nor could anyone tell, about the personal life of an unmarried first sergeant. My thoughts careened toward the "inappropriate relationship" in her evaluation from Germany, but another wave of guilt swept them away. None of it was my business, and Davis had sapped my strength. I rested my hand on the granola bar.

"I know him through a cousin," she continued. "He owns a taxi company."

My heart ached with yearning to understand, to delve into information more important than training requirements and the bluster of obstreperous sergeants. Getting stuck at Fort Stewart wouldn't be a total waste of time if I could get to know a Vietnam vet, the kind who talked. I'd met a few over the years, but they paid out details of their time in-country like misers pinching pennies. I drew a breath. Asking for things was almost as difficult as self-disclosure. "Could you put me in touch? I'd love to talk to him, if you think he wouldn't mind."

"I'm sure he wouldn't mind a bit." First Sergeant gave the photo frame a little pat and handed it back to me. I moved it out of sight behind the computer monitor. "Remind me to give you his card. You going to motor stables after lunch?"

"*Oh*, yes," I said, relieved at the change of topic, and at the sudden lightness in First Sergeant's tone. "I need to watch these soldiers doing preventive maintenance on their vehicles. And it wouldn't hurt me to learn how to take care of my own Humvee, either." I paused, deciding how much to push the conversation. What the hell—there was no time to tap-dance. "And Sergeant Davis is whining about the inventory schedule. Says he won't be ready to start tomorrow."

"Is that right?" She didn't sound surprised. "What'd you tell him?"

"That he should be ready to start tomorrow," I said stoutly, leaving out the part where I told Davis to check his facts with her, because it made me sound feeble. "Although I'm worried he's only going to half-ass it if we do. Is there any flexibility in the schedule?" Maybe First Sergeant would offer to move the dates around. This would be a great time for her to handle NCO business herself.

"Sergeant Davis." She sighed and hooked her thumbs around her web belt suspenders.

"Is there some kind of bad blood?" I tried not to sound too eager, but this was how it should be—two people on the same page, thumbs looped like cowgirls at the rodeo, elbows jostling like pardners.

Her face changed from frustrated to firm. "There is," she said. "And the bad blood is between me and him. But we're working it out."

At least she wasn't lying and saying everything was peachy. First Sergeant was a woman, and a Black one. Davis was the kind of guy who drank from tumblers decorated with dancing Confederate chickens. The probabilities were clear. "Do I need to know what it's about?" I asked.

"No, ma'am. If Davis keeps stirring the pot I'm going to have more to say about it, but I'm dealing with it." Her hands gripped the harness of her web belt and her words landed hard, like punches. Secrets held power and sometimes the only control you had was over your own mouth. She was holding on to what was hers.

"Okay," I said. "I'm not fishing for gossip, unless whatever it is starts to interfere with the mission." My fingers drifted to the ear plug case on my own web harness, over the pocket where my father's letter lived. He'd written about personality conflicts among his NCOs, and conflicts between his NCOs and himself. These were some of the few facts I had about him as a soldier, proof that the Army was and always had been a mess of human fallibility.

"It won't interfere with the mission." First Sergeant unhooked her thumbs and flexed her fingers. Back to business.

"Okay," I said again, watching her face for any sort of clue to what was going on behind it. "How strict do you want me to be about the inventory schedule?" It would be sort of fun to piss Davis off, to insist on starting the motor pool count the next day—but in reality he might make a fool out of me in front of everyone if I showed up to inventory and he hadn't laid out a single piece of equipment.

"Your decision, ma'am," she said, obviously wanting me to go with the original schedule. "The rest of us will follow."

MOTOR STABLES

My visit to the motor pool ripped off the bandage and dumped salt on the wound of my working relationship with Davis. "A dozen vehicles are on open work orders, and that's not counting the trucks that wouldn't start during the IG inspection," he said when I cornered him about the inventory later that day. "A full equipment layout takes weeks to get ready, and I don't got a body to spare." Davis did not remove his boots from the top of his desk. He turned a Styrofoam cup over onto the end of a broken antenna and flipped it across the office into the trash can, baptizing his calendar with coffee droplets. Music blared from behind a Plexiglass window that looked onto the maintenance bays but the jovial banter between mechanics ceased. Davis and I were gunslingers at opposite ends of a dusty street, the townsfolk on the sidelines afraid to make a move.

"None of this is happening the way it should, Sergeant Davis." I shifted my web belt to tug on the sodden waistband of my BDU trousers. I'd only had that granola bar and a diet Coke from the vending machine. Surely I was losing weight.

The air in the motor pool was heavy with diesel fumes and barely restrained fury. Davis glowered, shining with self-righteous sweat, pores visible on his red nose. I wanted to turn on my heel and stalk out, which was probably part of his calculus—to be such a heart attack on the hoof that the womenfolk scurried off—but I was the commander.

My father had dealt with sergeants like this and hated it. I was just one of a long line of officers who would have loved to grab a motor sergeant by his slippery beak and fling him into the Plexiglass window, but instead I scraped together my few remaining shreds of bluster. "We'll start your inventories tomorrow," I said.

BY THE NUMBERS

S o, the next morning I straightened my uniform blouse, pulled a Skilcraft pen from my breast pocket and held out a hand. Storey put a clipboard in it, loaded with inventory sheets. We were joined at the gate to the motor pool by Master Sergeant Jones, a tall, heavily muscled Black soldier, the NCO in charge of logistics for the whole battalion. He and I had crossed paths a lot when I worked on staff. He was a former motor sergeant and his word carried a lot of weight, and my hope was that Davis would shut up and color if Master Sergeant Jones was the one handing him the crayons. "You ready, ma'am?" Jones asked. The sun baked our shoulders and the tops of our cloth BDU caps.

"Ready as I'll ever be." Storey and I had spent a big chunk of time in the supply room counting every last sticky note. He'd taught me the correct procedures to follow and how to document missing items. He brought microwave pizzas and cans of soda—not knowing, of course, that I was not supposed to be eating stuff like that, and he'd offered to help with the motor pool count. Storey was working some kind of angle, but I was low on allies. I had to trust other people. The kind of loyalty that assumed I had the right to eat pizza and was teaching me how to stay out of financial trouble with the US government would have to do.

"We looking at everything?"

"Down to the last rivet." Commanders could be made to pay for equipment losses, but no one should have to pay for Captain Williams's inability to keep track of his property except him. "I'm not going to be financially liable for this guy's mistakes. I'm cleaning up enough after him as it is."

Jones nodded. "Roger that. Be glad it's not a command inventory of one of the maintenance companies. They have a shit-ton of widgets to account for."

Trouble began with a temperamental two-and-a-half ton cargo truck assigned to Shumacher. A deuce and a half was a work horse, and we'd struggle to transport soldiers and equipment to the field exercise at the end of the summer unless this one stayed operational. But when I glanced through the inventory sheets and then at the accessories laid out higgledy-piggledy on tarps in front of the truck, I could see that several of the basic items were missing. Little but important things like the fire extinguisher. Big, very important things like the jack. My radar pinged, going immediately to First Sergeant's accusation that Captain Williams had been pilfering goods. I didn't know whether to be angry or impressed at Davis's attempts to creatively display the items to make it look like everything was there.

"Where's Specialist Shumacher?" I asked. It was customary for a vehicle's operator to be standing by during an inventory, but only Davis was there, looking beyond my left shoulder instead of making eye contact.

"I got her working on the M88." Davis made no reference to my rank or name, which bothered me more than I cared to admit. "I told the soldiers I'd handle this round of inspectors."

"It ain't an inspection." Master Sergeant Jones clicked his pen and made a note on his clipboard. He cleared his throat and attempted to put a positive spin on a potentially disastrous situation. "But let's just see how the inventories go before we make any snap decisions. Worst case scenario, we set up a repayment plan for missing items. That's usually pretty painless."

"I'll be got-damned if me or the soldiers pay back anything!" Davis exploded. "Maybe an E-8 or an unmarried officer wouldn't notice a chunk out of their checks, but I got a wife and kid. We need every cent of my pay." Davis's voice cracked and sweat trickled down his face like frustrated tears. I got the sense he was trotting his family out for sympathy points, and I couldn't muster even a molecule of pity for him. Maybe for the wife and kid. But maybe he should have thought about them before now.

"If things have been going missing, why the hell haven't you documented it?" Storey asked, reading my mind. "You should've known better." Maybe Davis assumed I wouldn't look all that carefully at the tally. But just like Obsequious and Hubris had, this guy would learn I was always going to read the fine print.

"You don't think I could've made things look better than I did? And I'm the one getting fucked over?"

"Pardon your French," Storey said, freckled face going redder after a quick glance at me.

I didn't need Storey to protect my delicate sensibilities. To me, cussing felt like flinging a handful of golden coins into the sun. But Davis's disrespectful tone was getting harder to ignore. He was everything wrong with the Army and I was going to squash his insubordination. "You've tried to cover up the missing items, Sergeant Davis, hoping we wouldn't notice. Are the taxpayers supposed to cover for you?" This statement bounced around between the vehicles in the motor park, along with the question of whether it balanced the equation in some way to make an example of one motor pool's worth of underpaid soldiers. The taxpayers weren't aware of how routinely they underwrote mistakes in military spending.

On either side of me, Storey and Master Sergeant Jones shifted with discomfort as tension thickened the air. Soldiers got put in awful binds—open your mouth and incur the wrath of your boss. Keep your mouth shut and pay for it later.

"Hoo-ah," Storey said, but he sounded sad.

Master Sergeant Jones clicked his pen and made another note. "Like I said, we don't have to make any decisions this minute. All we gotta do is count." None of us were decision-makers in the current situation. The count would be reported up through Battalion to Brigade. Instructions would come back down the chain, and I'd have to detangle the knot of Army regulations one at a time—just like I had in personnel, just like I did with everything—in service of getting Headquarters Company out of the red.

Davis didn't even try to speak. He stalked across the motor park and slammed into his office.

I pictured my mother, running a finger down the check register before making a purchase. She wasn't mentally subtracting money when she did that; she didn't know what her real balance was when she wrote another check. Either she loved the thrill of financial roulette, or she was too terrified to face reality, or somehow didn't think the rules applied to her. As a kid I'd been the one on the front lines, facing down the random nature of money, ashamed that the contents of my school lunch box—a perfectly acceptable peanut butter and jelly sandwich and thermos of milk—were a lie. There wasn't any other normal food in the house, just random boxes of stale saltines and half jars of applesauce. People with responsibilities—children to support, or nations to defend—should do better.

"So I guess this is as good a time as any to take a break." I fought to keep the shake out of my voice as I consulted my watch. In the battle between winning soldiers' hearts and minds and pleasing my boss so I could get the hell out of Fort Stewart, I was coming down on the side of the Old Man and I hated myself for it. I fantasized about one of Storey's frozen pizzas and a can of cold Coke, then I imagined that the sweat soaking the neoprene bike shorts under my BDU trousers was making me swell instead of shrink. Everything backfired.

"I'll get my clerk to update these inventory sheets as we go," Jones said as we went our separate ways. "We've got a bunch of discrepancies already, but the S-3 is rumbling about a possible humanitarian aid mission to Yugoslavia for the whole division. If that happens, the colonel will want all this squared away and that training exercise aced even faster than he already does."

My heart stopped. Fort Stewart, and more specifically, the 24th Infantry Division, was a tactical unit, tapped for involvement on the world stage at a moment's notice. Since the Persian Gulf War, the 24th ID had been asked to make good on that mandate with increasing regularity. If the battalion staff officer responsible for training and readiness was starting to talk about a big troop movement to the former Yugoslavia, we were probably going. And a humanitarian aid mission posed a very real threat to my plans to be heading in the opposite direction by the end of the summer.

"I need to talk to the colonel ASAP," I said as I rifled through the inventory paperwork. There were no answers in the pile, I just needed something to do with my hands to cover for the sudden rapidity of my breathing. My answers were in the Old Man's office. If he confirmed the rumors, I'd have to remind him that after I squared Headquarters Company away I was leaving—for Korea, not war-torn Eastern Europe.

"Let's just finish the count first, okay, ma'am?" Master Sergeant Jones must have thought I was talking about the irregularities with the motor pool numbers but there was no time to set him straight—not that my reasons for meeting with the Old Man were any of his business. "Let me and Storey talk to Davis, and we'll all meet back in half an hour."

"Okay," I said. "But this is not a good situation." As long as everything led pretty directly to a conversation about Yugoslavia with the Old Man, I'd do whatever Jones thought best.

Storey and Jones went after Davis in his office, and I slunk, alone, back to the Headquarters Company building to think without the sun giving me a migraine. I fetched a cup of bad coffee and went to my desk to muster the energy required to finesse Davis, and to strategize how I might finesse the Old Man. I fished a granola bar from the crushed box in my middle desk drawer and entertained a fleeting, exhausted thought that I still needed to find the key to the bottom file drawer.

The silhouette of First Sergeant paused, backlit in the doorway. "Things got ugly down in the motor pool?" At first I thought she must have been sneaking around in her soft-soled boots and seen Davis pitching his fit, then I realized Storey had probably just called to let her know.

"Davis thought he could dazzle us with his creative displays." First Sergeant had left me to do the dirty work of pressuring Davis so she better not be implying I should have done something differently. "Stuff is missing, but I haven't seen any proof that it was stolen."

She nodded as she pulled a business card from her pocket and handed it to me like it was a Willy Wonka golden ticket. "His name is Ted," she said. "He's good people." The card was simple—white with block lettering—and provided a beeper number and address for Ted's Taxis but nothing else. This must be her friend the Vietnam vet.

"Thanks," I said.

As she moved to leave her nose wrinkled. "No offense, ma'am, but I'm going to have Washburn run a mop in here this afternoon. Something stinks, and it's not just this inventory."

NO GUTS, NO GLORY

Friday night, after the longest-three-day week in Army history, a rickety yellow cab pulled up in front of my apartment building, its horn wheezing like the old smokers after PT. Earlier that day I'd cornered Shumacher at the motor pool and she'd murmured that her period still hadn't started. We agreed that the catfish fry at the VFW by Hunter Army Airfield would be a good place to strategize. Actually, the fried food was her idea, but the middle of a contentious inventory was nowhere to talk, so I'd agreed.

I grimaced at my face in the mirror. Mascara and eyeshadow made me look ghoulish, but it was too late to swipe it off. I grabbed my wallet and gave Rambo a guilty pat on the head. "We'll watch lots of movies this weekend, buddy, but I've got a couple things to do first." Rambo was as sleek and sharp as obsidian, a present from Shumacher when they'd found an abandoned litter of kittens in the motor pool last year, to thank me for helping her get promoted. Rambo and I were a team—in my opinion, anyway. Like his namesake, Rambo tended to keep his more tender emotions in reserve. He left for his evening patrol of the apartment complex without a backward glance.

"Thanks for taking me all the way to Hunter." I opened the front passenger door so that Ted, of Ted's Taxis, wouldn't think I was the kind of officer who expected to be squired around.

"I don't mind," Ted said as he moved a box of cassette tapes off the seat and shifted the column into reverse. "I've got friends who spend a lot of time at that VFW by the airfield."

I took quick stock of the shiny-faced hippy whose hair had leaked from the top of his head into the wispy beard clinging to his chin. Would my father have looked like this now? There's no way my mother would've allowed it. "How do you know First Sergeant St. John again?" First Sergeant was a closed book. Formal. Dark-skinned. A woman. I couldn't picture her hanging out with some middle-aged bean-sprout eater, but the most unlikely people bonded in GI towns.

"I played baseball with her cousin when we were in high school." Ted looked over his graying ponytail and waved his way into Friday evening traffic. "Our families didn't get to be friends, exactly, but cordial. Nodding acquaintances, like you do in sports."

I hadn't played organized sports growing up except for one disastrous season of softball, my mother yelling from the bleachers too loudly and too often, Jack having snuck into the games with her Coke. I'd gone back to playing Annie Oakley and Sacagawea in the woods by myself. It was less embarrassing.

"And then Indigo came by to talk to me when she was thinking about enlisting," Ted continued. "That was back in '77 or '78—I'm not too sure because I was a mess back then. I think her mother sent her to me, half hoping I'd put her off the idea." He chuckled at the memory, chest thick with cigarette tar. "We forged a strange, ebony and ivory bond after that."

In Athens, the races stayed separate. When I was in high school Black kids parked in one section of the high school parking lot and rednecks in another—both at the back by the fence but divided by a lane that might as well have been the 17th Parallel. In an unspoken but ironclad rule, the spots closest to the building were left open for the rich White kids who came screaming into the lot right before the morning bell in the new cars they all got for their sixteenth birthdays. With no car, I didn't have to worry about where to park—with the rednecks because I was poor, or at the front because I wasn't outright persecuted by the popular kids—but it would never have been in the Black section of the lot. To be honest, I'd been a little afraid of the Black kids, segregated parking lots or no. They flung their arms wide in conversation. They laughed out loud and cut up in class. They made faces at the teachers' backs on their way to the principal's office. Their boldness astounded me. First Sergeant was quiet and confident and there must have been Black kids in high school who were quiet and confident, too, but I'd been too wrapped up in my own insecurity to notice them. I was jealous of the familiar way Ted talked about knowing First Sergeant's family. I'd been friendly with a few Black soldiers over the years, but never friends.

"That's cool," I said, for lack of a more insightful response.

"Sports and war—they cement relationships," Ted said, granting permission to enter the conversation that we both knew was the real reason for the cab ride.

I took a deep breath, the inside of the cab suddenly feeling as claustrophobic as a confessional. Beside me, Ted exuded calm. First Sergeant hadn't advertised him falsely—he seemed like good people, groovy appearance notwithstanding. But what did I know about combat? What right did I have to pepper him with questions about the taking of life when I spent my days aggravated by mere paperwork and personality conflicts? I watched so many war movies that collateral damage had become an abstraction when what I wanted to understand was the reality of it. People *died*. My father must have died and that had reversed the tide of my entire life. This taxi driver had seen things I couldn't imagine—not just on a screen, but in terrifying, Technicolor life. His experiences would have been virtually the same as my father's, but as desperate as I was to understand them, did Ted owe it to other people to talk about how he squared his actions with his morality? And did I have the right to demand this from him? Combat veterans possessed the information I craved, but whenever I had one at my disposal I froze up.

It had been easier to talk to teachers. My high school librarian helped research my father's unit and I wrote letters to people who were in his platoon, although no one ever answered. The career counselor invited military recruiters, and my history teacher hosted guest speakers. A few of my college ROTC instructors had been to Vietnam, but aside from listing rote battlefield information none of them dug into the details of what I wanted to know, which had more to do with internal injuries to themselves than the physical damage they'd inflicted on others. No one wanted to talk about what combat did to a soul. Drill Sergeant Gallagher had taught me that blood made the grass grow, but the real lesson was that blunting affect, dehumanizing others, was both an offense and a defense. A joke you told with the noose around your neck.

No guts, no glory, though. "I already know about 'We took hill number blah blah during the height of the monsoon season,'" I said, fingers bracketing the space between us.

Ted's laugh was as mild as the summer air blowing past the open taxi window. By day Fort Stewart was an inferno but being serenaded by swamp frogs and listening to the lullabies of birds as the evening turned to night made summer almost bearable. "Talking about firefights is as far as a lot of guys can go without tripping their own personal wires," he said. "Monday morning quarterbacking is as analytical as they can get."

"Sometimes TV shows and movies tell you more than people do." In college, I'd taken a regular babysitting job so I could watch *China Beach*, four seasons of a show about nurses near Da Nang that my mother turned off whenever it came on at home. I'd had to sneak to the movie theater to see *Apocalypse Now.*

"Well, I don't watch TV or any kind of war movies," Ted said. "Hollywood usually gets it wrong. Books, you gotta figure the writers have taken more time to think things through."

"Most books are still pretty surface level," I said. "A lot of facts and figures about military campaigns. No soul-searching." We'd all read *Platoon Leader* in college and there was some soul-searching in that one, but also a lot of talk of guys walking into booby traps and getting medically evacuated and that was just that—poof. Gone. I refused to believe they'd left no emotional trace.

"Brain stuff—not so much heart." Ted nodded.

"No soul," I repeated, warming up. "Although, I'm not a hundred percent sure what it is I want them to say. None of them tell me what really goes through the mind of a combat soldier." Not just any soldier—my father. The feelings he shared in his letters seemed to have incapacitated him. He was troubled by his actions and those of his soldiers. He'd waded so far into the heart of darkness it had clouded his judgment. It impacted his ability to lead, and ultimately, to survive. I winced as Ted examined his conscience in silence. I was pushing too hard. There's no way Vietnam wasn't a painful subject.

We talked baseball for the rest of the drive around the perimeter of Fort Stewart, sticking to safe topics like whether Ted thought the Braves would make it to the World Series again. I'd like to have heard more about First Sergeant but couldn't think of a way to bring her back up.

Just as I was mentally rehearsing a question about leadership, which seemed like a less fraught way to approach the topic of combat, Ted pulled into a dirt parking lot and cut the taxi's engine. "I'll walk you in. It's not a rough crowd but somebody might look at you funny for being here." He didn't act disappointed that I hadn't dug very deep with the Vietnam stuff.

I smoothed the long cotton skirt that hid my bug-bitten legs and tugged at the hem of the R.E.M. concert T-shirt that showed off the only tanned part of my Army anatomy, my forearms. Most of my meager wardrobe was on its way to Korea and girly clothes always felt like a costume, anyway. Even as a child I'd been more comfortable in Toughskins and T-shirts ordered from the backs of cereal boxes. Yes, I was a single woman alone. That was a vulnerable way to walk into any bar. But sturdy girls like me and Shumacher should fit right in at a VFW. We weren't veterans but we were active duty and that should count for something with this crowd.

The parking lot was full of pickup trucks, interspersed with Jeeps and motorcycles and the rare sedan, but Shumacher's red Toyota was not among them. My heart sank. Alone, as always. "It's a free country," I said to Ted. I straightened my spine and squared my shoulders, feigning bravado like I always did. "Come in if you want to."

EQUAL OPPORTUNITY

Shumacher was there, sipping a soda in front of a basket of curly fries, at home among the Formica table-tops, bad perms and acid-washed jeans. No one in the room was paying the least bit of attention to her although people cast quick glances my way when I entered with Ted. "There's my friend over there," I told him. Shumacher wasn't my friend, but Ted wasn't fact-checking. "Can I call you later for a ride home?"

"Sure thing, doll. You have my card—call me any time." Ted sauntered over to the bar and clapped a man on the shoulder. Several other men turned in his direction—tall and short, White and various shades of golden and brown, thin and alcohol-ravaged, and one so top-heavy he had to throw a leg out like a kickstand to stay propped on his bar stool. All of them somewhere in their mid to late forties—although they could have been teenagers still, clustered around a tap on somebody's wooden porch in the country after a ball game long ago.

"I'm sorry to keep you waiting." I slid into the booth across from Shumacher. "How's it going?" Shumacher was a tall girl, fair-skinned and dark-haired with nondescript, even features, from the middle of nowhere in the middle of the country. Middle of the road ASVAB score, middle of the pack in her maintenance class at Aberdeen Proving Ground. Nothing in her file to indicate potential greatness as she sat in the chair next to my desk in the personnel office at Battalion last year, holding tight to her grimy mechanic's fingers—claiming she was being overlooked for promotion to specialist.

What set Shumacher apart was that she wasn't tentative. She wasn't trying the Army on for size as so many other soldiers were and because of this, unlike with most women, I actually felt better about myself around her. She was rock-solid. I'd helped her study for the Soldier of the Month board and after she won, I'd guided her promotion paperwork through all the right inboxes. Mediocre male soldiers made rank all the time. There was no reason Shumacher shouldn't have been promoted, and a couple of chromosomal reasons why she hadn't. We set things right for her and I felt more than usually invested.

"It's going okay I guess." Shumacher picked up a fry and examined it from several angles before popping it into her mouth. "I'm fine at work, but when I get back to the barracks in the afternoon I start to feel queasy. Maybe because I have time to pay attention? I don't know."

"Have you been on sick call yet?"

Shumacher chewed slowly but the expression in her hazel eyes was equal parts defiant and waiting for the axe to fall. I expected to hear one of the many excuses soldiers concocted when they hadn't done something they'd been told to do. *I didn't have time . . . The sergeant wouldn't let me go until . . .* Shumacher swallowed. "No, ma'am."

Did Shumacher even want this baby? She hadn't said. "Forgive me asking, Specialist Shumacher—but it *is* Private Washburn's, right?"

Shumacher's head pulled up from the French fries. "Lieutenant Mills."

"Sorry, sorry." I wrapped a hand around my neck to hide the telltale flush. Other females in the barracks might have needed paternity tests, but that was not Shumacher's way. But in spite of my embarrassment, I had a sudden, driving need to know this baby was wanted. "Are you guys going to get married? Are you thinking about getting out of the Army?"

Shumacher picked up another fry and set it down. "I have no intention of hitching myself to a disaster, ma'am."

Washburn had tried to keep me from walking into the cross hairs at my assumption of command ceremony. Had that only been a week ago? It felt like a lifetime. But he'd also laughed when Sergeant Davis—with Shumacher's participation, actually—doused me in diesel smoke during training. Washburn wasn't strong enough to resist the pull of characters like Davis, but he wasn't heartless. He'd probably like being involved with his own kid. Hell, he was only nineteen years old himself. He had recent experience. "Not everyone has to have a picture-perfect, two-parent family," I said. But I'd craved a two-parent family with an almost physical hunger for most of my life and I had definite opinions on mothering while strapped for resources, formed during the years I'd watched my mother struggle. Maybe Washburn was trying to duck responsibility. Maybe Shumacher *didn't* want this baby. It angered me to think of any child alone in a house, cold and hungry and waiting for an adult to come home. And on some days, putting a key in the door after school and dreading what she might find on the other side. Some kids were fine growing up with one parent, but some kids were not. My hand moved to where my father's letter would have been had I been wearing a BDU blouse instead of a concert T-shirt.

"Have you considered . . . uh . . ."

"Have I considered *what*, ma'am?" Shumacher's eyes blazed against the light of a random strand of illuminated red chili peppers hanging from the ceiling.

"You know," I stumbled. "All of your . . . options." My religious upbringing had been haphazard, but the hippy Catholic school I'd gone to planted some beliefs about abortion in my conscience. Not everyone was conflicted, though. Maybe Shumacher had no intention of raising a child, with or without a father. I had to ask.

"Oh." Shumacher waved a hand in dismissal. "That's not for me. But you know Sar'n Davis'll want me straight out of the motor pool as soon as he finds out."

I pictured Davis flinging the Styrofoam cup across his office. First Sergeant's displeased face; the mechanics watching through the Plexiglass window. The Watergate salad, the diesel smoke, the temper tantrum about his inventory. Davis was more than a little bit on my shit list. What he didn't know—for the moment, anyway—wouldn't hurt him and it might give Shumacher a little breathing room. A female soldier ought to be in charge of the decisions concerning her own body. "Okay. But you should have gone on sick call by now. Sergeant Davis or no Sergeant Davis, it's not good to be around all those fumes in the motor pool."

"Please, ma'am." Shumacher's face changed from defiant to pleading. She'd had to scrap hard to be taken seriously in the motor pool. But what was she asking for? For a pregnancy to pause while the Army learned to be supportive of motherhood?

I'd be long gone before Shumacher started to show—not that I was keeping quiet about a pregnancy for anything close to three months. Three days, more like. Babies made me nervous. I was an only child of only children, and my house hadn't been the one in the neighborhood where all the kids dumped their bikes and stayed to play. I understood why people liked babies—they were cute with their open-eyed, solemn faces and sticky fingers, waving like anemones to attract their prey. But I hadn't developed the baby skill set. My childhood had been a lonely one, wandering in the woods and keeping company with the creek.

"Get your ass to sick call, Specialist Shumacher."

"Yes, ma'am. I will. I promise. First thing Monday—oh, wait—we have inventories."

Motor pool inventory would go on for a couple more days, then the soldiers had layouts for their personal equipment. I sighed. "The very *first* morning after the inventories are over, you are to go on sick call to get this pregnancy confirmed. In the meantime, don't do anything that might hurt you or the baby."

"No, ma'am. I would never."

In the movies military leaders barked orders at soldiers and they scrambled off to do their bidding without question. In real life, soldiers didn't always do what they were told, let alone what was in their own best interests. It wasn't entirely clear what Shumacher had agreed she'd never do, but I didn't ask the follow-up question. As with Ted, I'd pushed enough.

Shumacher took a thoughtful slurp of her soda. For someone who may or may not be pregnant she was mighty cavalier about taking care of herself. Not worried about breathing in toxic substances in the motor pool, blithely munching on junk. "Shouldn't you be watching what you eat?" I asked.

Shumacher's forearm inched around her basket of fries. "Let's change the subject."

The Army wormed its tentacles into every corner of a life like kudzu vines bringing down the porch of a house, but I could let Shumacher make some decisions about her own body, even if—or maybe in retaliation for the fact that—the Old Man was micromanaging mine. "Okay, let me get a drink," I conceded. "Then there's something I need to ask you."

I wanted something to eat but everything on the VFW's menu was deep-fried, so I ordered a Budweiser from a woman with acne scars and gentle brown eyes. While I waited I tried to eavesdrop on Ted, absorbed in conversation with an older Black man. They punctuated their jokes with jabs of the cigarettes they held between their fingers, the president's indoor smoking policy be damned. The other man wore a ball cap with Korean War-era dates and the name of a ship embroidered on it. I was tempted to lurk until I got absorbed into their orbit, but Shumacher was waiting for me across the room.

"So," I said, squeaking back into the vinyl booth. "I need you to be straight with me."

Shumacher shook her head, apologizing for what she thought I was asking. "Nobody's talking about the puking anymore, ma'am. Now it's all about the inventory, but the guys will get on board eventually. The fact that you came out to training and did the preventive maintenance on your own vehicle—people respect that."

"Whoa," I said. "That's not what I was asking about, but okay." My neck went blotchy, but I forced myself to acknowledge progress.

One big swing to the negative (of course the soldiers had talked about the puking—what did I expect?), one creeping increment forward. Any officer who turned up to training and did their own preventive maintenance could expect the same. That was Leadership 101. "What I want to know is what's going on between Sergeant Davis and First Sergeant. You've been around the two of them longer than I have. What's the deal?"

"Ah. Yeah." Shumacher cast her eyes down and ran a finger through the condensation on the outside of her waxed soda cup. She hunched her shoulders forward like she had something to protect. It was a strange question for an officer to ask an enlisted soldier, but I didn't have time to wait for the universe to reveal itself and First Sergeant was not forthcoming. "I guess Sergeant Davis thought the colonel should have made him first sergeant instead."

I blew into my beer bottle and it whistled like an incoming round. The Old Man had wanted an NCO from outside Headquarters to step in after the last training exercise failure. "I don't want any of these Headquarters sergeants jostling for promotion but ducking responsibility," he'd ranted to Captain Williams during a staff meeting. I'd jotted that line in the margin of my notes in sheer amazement. It took one to know one.

"But that was a while ago," I said to Shumacher. "Sergeant Davis is still mad about it?"

"Well, there's more to it than that."

God, I hated gossip. "If it's keeping Headquarters from moving forward, then I need to know. I can't fix this company if the two of them are squaring off, however below the radar they're trying to keep it."

"Okay," Shumacher said. "Okay. But this is just my opinion, right? If you want the whole story, you're going to have to talk to Sar'n Davis and First Sergeant yourself."

"I did ask her about it and she didn't deny there was an issue," I said. "She didn't want to go into detail, though. And she sure didn't mention that this had been going on all this time."

Shumacher waved her hand like a white flag. "I don't know if Captain Williams knew how much the two of them were at each other's throats, but he let things go way too long."

"Soldiers don't tell officers everything, you know," I said. Captain Williams was not the kind of person soldiers confided in. Drink with, sure. But bare their souls? Davis might have bitched to him, but First Sergeant wouldn't have gone near his office.

"It's not like they're openly at war. It's not a war when one person starts the whole thing. Sar'n Davis thought he should be first sergeant and he went to the colonel and said so. But the colonel brought First Sergeant St. John on anyway. And in the beginning most soldiers followed her just fine, because what she was saying made sense. But Sar'n Davis made an issue about everything. He said she should have just waited until Captain Williams left instead of triggering the IG. Stuff like that. And because he's so loud about it, some of the other mechanics are starting to talk." Shumacher stopped. Davis was floating more or less peacefully on the Army's waters, below which his feet kicked and flailed and dragged others down with him. Maybe one of those people was Washburn, which would explain Shumacher's waning interest in him. And it sure explained how Davis stood primed to undercut me if I didn't handle things in a way that pleased him. "Anyway, Sar'n Davis said that First Sergeant went to EO on him, but I don't think she did. She'd have known that EO never fixes anything."

The Army's Equal Opportunity program was there to support soldiers who struggled at work for various reasons—race and sex being two of them. But programs that thrived on anonymous reports—Social Work Services, drug and alcohol counseling, Equal Opportunity— were guerrilla organizations in an Army whose business was direct confrontation. And no matter which way the battles were fought the same people always won in the end. Everyone learned this, sometimes the hard way, about five minutes after coming on active duty. It was pointless to deny it.

"And he keeps saying it," Shumacher continued. "His theory is that the colonel had to put a Black woman in that position to meet some kind of requirement on a briefing slide, and that she's running over to EO to report on him every time he questions her ability to do the job."

"Shit," I said, more to myself than to Shumacher. To keep the two of them from dragging the whole company down, I was going to have to wade into those waters myself. No matter who was right, the Old Man did not like an alarmist.

"Anyway, that's pretty much it," Shumacher said. "First Sergeant knows what he's saying but can't do much about it. She probably thinks you won't be able to get him under control, either."

I bristled. First Sergeant wasn't just sitting around doing nothing, was she? She was probably biding her time. And I hadn't caved to any of Davis's complaints yet. I was doing my job, no matter how uncomfortably. "First off, First Sergeant St. John is perfectly capable of taking down a dirtbag. The example of Captain Williams comes to mind. Second, I'll be just dandy at getting Sergeant Davis to comply. I started this morning and plan to carry on first thing Monday." I prayed for the fortitude to pull this off. I was nowhere near as strong as First Sergeant.

"Ma'am?" Shumacher stopped swirling her finger around the surface of her drink cup. "There are more people involved than just Sar'n Davis."

"I won't let it backfire on the rest of you." Everybody had things they wanted, right that minute. People were going to need to get in line. "But I have to start somewhere, and I'm already starting from behind. Can you understand that?"

Shumacher looked down at her cup.

"I have to start somewhere," I repeated. I wanted to fix Headquarters Company, not prop up a false front and call it a working store. Better leaders might have known how to perform the surgery that healed an organization from the inside, but I didn't have any other tactic but to start with the regulations, with the skin of the thing, and work my way toward the heart. "There's not much time before the field exercise."

"Yes, ma'am." Shumacher sighed as though she were picking up something heavy and placing it in her own path.

"Which reminds me, I don't want you to do all the lifting and carrying for the equipment layouts, either."

"Lieutenant Mills." Shumacher's jaw hardened as she took a long, last slurp from the soda. "I appreciate your concern, but I don't need you to hover over me like I'm some fragile thing."

"You're not—" My insides writhed like I'd swallowed a cauldron of boiling helplessness. Why did everything have to be so hard? Why was everyone trying to run while shooting themselves in the foot? "Neither one of us is especially fragile," I said, hearing the tone of false camaraderie that the Old Man used when he was manipulating someone. I hated myself for it. "We're a lot alike, you and me."

Shumacher pushed her French fry basket away. "No offense, ma'am, but we're really not. People who've been working their jobs for a few years may know a thing or two about how best to do them. People who've lived in their own bodies for more than twenty years may have some ideas about what they're capable of."

"You're right." My words tumbled out in a hodge-podge of responses I'd crafted to previous slights but never delivered. "Maybe the average specialist has been doing her job for longer than the average lieutenant. And of course you know your own body better than I do. Nevertheless, I have to make decisions about what's best for all of Headquarters."

"*Nevertheless.* I guess you can make me do whatever you want at work." Shumacher's cheeks were bright red and tiny drops of sweat plastered dark hair to the skin around her temples. "But your reasons have nothing to do with what's best for the company."

For a wild second I thought Shumacher knew about my failed weigh-in. But she couldn't know that. What she and everyone knew was that I was a temporary commander, that I was there to do a job and then split. I would have loved to blast Shumacher with all my pent-up frustration, but she didn't deserve it. She'd given me a kitten. I'd thought we had kind of a bond.

"I'm gonna go." Shumacher stood up. "Is that your cabbie over there? I wonder if he'd give me a ride back to post."

"You didn't drive?" The answer didn't matter. I wanted Shumacher to sit down, for the two of us to have a heart-to-heart about how to be real friends without the rank difference sprouting like an impenetrable hedge between us. If Shumacher walked out of the VFW, Storey would be my one remaining ally at Headquarters Company, and Storey, the brown-noser, didn't count. I'd have no one.

"I'm having a little trouble with my pickup, but I had to leave it at the barracks to keep people from talking, anyway." Shumacher examined the vestiges of motor oil in the dry creases of her hands. Sloppy in her T-shirt and khaki shorts, but so strong in her person. "It's better if we're not seen together."

I caught my breath. Frustration made me cry and I would not cry there. "His name is Ted," I said, waving at Ted's back and remembering how First Sergeant had waved his business card at me the day before.

Ted held a finger-phone to his ear as he followed Shumacher out and I nodded, miserably. Next time I'd ask him all the things I wanted to know about Vietnam but hadn't been brave enough to, friendless chickenshit that I was. I finished my beer then picked at the fries remaining in Shumacher's basket. Oh, to have a friend as solid as Shumacher, who ate and drank and said and did what she wanted. I carried the empty fry basket, soda cup, and beer bottle to the bar and sat myself halfway onto one of the stools. "Do y'all have any 333 Premium Export?" I asked the woman with the kind brown eyes.

TO US AND THOSE LIKE US

I woke at 0530 the next morning like I always did, even though it was Saturday and I'd only gotten home from the VFW a few hours before. I slumped into the kitchen, started the coffee, and put my head straight under the tap, drinking like I'd just crossed the Sahara and not the beige carpeted expanse from my bedroom. I collapsed onto the folded blanket currently serving as my couch. My few sticks of furniture were in storage since I'd thought I was heading to the bachelor officer quarters in Korea. I leaned my head against the wall and closed my eyes, but the ebb and swell of the room drove me back to the air mattress. I slept. At 0730 I got up to pee, still too dizzy to stand in the shower, so I went back to bed, dreaming about 333 Premium Export, which the Vietnam vets called "Ba Ba Ba," although of course the VFW didn't stock it. We'd left a platoon of empty Budweiser bottles on the bar instead, and when I went to pay for it all at the end of the night my credit card got declined.

Shocked awake by the memory, I opened my eyes. I was rancid with the smell of secondhand smoke over old perfume and makeup. I held my head in my hands while I sat on the closed toilet lid listening to the bathtub fill, a position that was both a prayer and a way to keep my thoughts from spilling all over the floor. Beer was a terrible drink. It was a truth serum, an unlocker of confidence I did not possess in social situations. It made me believe I was funnier and more insightful than I was. Under beer's influence I bought rounds of drinks and dazzled random conversation partners. God knows what I'd said to Ted's friends. I remembered arguing with an older man—well, arguing wasn't the right word. We'd hollered over the blaring jukebox, agreeing heatedly with each other. He was warm with the smell of Old Spice, his face a blur except for his skin, oily and purpled with rosacea. I held forth on the Stanford Prison experiment, a psychological study in which student "guards" were given authority over student "prisoners." The researchers had to call the experiment off because the student guards adapted to their roles much too enthusiastically, while the prisoners became cowed and subservient to the point that real abuse occurred. The drunk veteran and I talked about the My Lai massacre. The guy said that the officers were to blame, that the soldiers would have been too caught up in the moment to disobey orders no matter how wrong. I'd had to drain another entire bottle while I thought about that. I decided not to bring up Operation Speedy Express, the action in the IV Corps tactical zone that my father had been part of.

I'd never wanted to experience the Army firsthand—to immerse myself in the megalith that swallowed my father whole—until I researched My Lai for a psychology paper in college. After turning the paper in I'd gone straight to the Army building on campus and signed up for ROTC, which flipped my mother out, but I was determined. I couldn't comprehend the kind of organization that produced both cowards and heroes, sometimes in the same person, but hell if I wasn't going to figure it out. The plan was to do this from somewhere far in the rear, though. Somewhere I'd have access to records and information, where I could read and think. Fat lot of good this stupid personnel job had done me in that department.

I soaked in the tub until the water turned cold, trying to dissolve the night before. The jokes were no longer funny, and the psychological commentary felt ham-fisted. No amount of bath water could reinflate my wallet. I should have called my mother to ask about the declined credit card, but I knew how that conversation would play out—there'd be an innocent denial or a hot defense, or a claim that whatever was purchased to take the card up to the limit again was something for me. Putting my mother on my card was supposed to help make ends meet; her widow's pension wasn't much, and she had a hard time finding and holding a job that meshed with her personality. But she spent too much money on the wackiest things, especially when she was feeling her worst. Better to skip the call and wait to talk to the bank on Monday instead.

I splashed tepid water on my face and took my time standing up. I reached for a towel, imagining I'd left some weight behind in the tub but knowing that an indeterminate number of Budweisers hadn't done me any favors. Maybe I *had* asked if anyone at the VFW knew about Operation Speedy Express. Anyone who'd been in the Mekong Delta in 1969 would have heard of it. I'd have remembered their reactions, though, and I didn't remember, and that weighed on me.

Damp, in clean sweats and back on my air mattress, I considered the telephone. I had to go back to the VFW to pay my bill. If I called Ted to take me out there it'd cost another $15 each way, plus what I owed him from the ride home last night—then I'd be broke for the next week until payday. But if I drove out to Hunter myself I'd enter the VFW alone, and I wasn't sure I could walk into that wood-paneled room without Ted and the beery cloak of the previous evening to protect me. Ted was right; I was an outsider there.

A different voice, not Ted's, answered the phone. "This is his day off." The voice was gravelly with cigarettes. Rough but kind. "Can I help you with something?"

I almost said no but decided that old soldiers—Ted's drivers were all veterans—would recognize a coward if they heard one on the phone. "Can I leave you my number? I need to go somewhere but it has to be Ted to take me."

"Okay." I pictured the driver reaching for a notepad, curious but too professional to ask. Five minutes later the phone rang.

"I need to make things right." The urgency in my voice traveled the wires between us. I needed to get back in his taxi to ask my most pressing questions before I sobered up enough to wimp out again. I needed to go back to the VFW to finish my conversations while all our drunken memories were at least somewhat intact.

After we hung up I went to the cash machine then stood outside to wait, the unrelenting sun baking my sluggish thoughts. In less than two months I'd be trudging through the Fort Stewart training area with Headquarters Company, uniform stiff with dried sweat, covered with mosquito bites, slapping at sand gnats and keeping an eye out for copperheads. I'd be getting shot at by blank rounds guided by lasers and our "water buffalo" would ride on a trailer, full of potable water for brushing teeth and refilling canteens. It was all tedious and a bore and none of it remotely resembled my father's experience. I wanted to lie down on the hot sidewalk and sleep forever.

Ted opened the cab door from the inside and moved his box of cassettes out of the way again. I pulled out my wallet, but he shooed it closed. "Your money's no good today."

"But I owe you from last night." I'd withdrawn the last hundred dollars from my account and was prepared to fight. I wasn't a charity case. Ted had come back to the VFW after dropping Shumacher off and listened to my inebriated rambling as he carted my drunk butt home without delivering a lecture—and I hadn't even paid him for the ride.

Something about the way I gripped the twenty dollar bill must have told Ted I wouldn't relent. He took it from my hand. "Okay, boss. For last night. But I'm off duty now, and I'm going out to Hunter to say hello to my friends anyway. Might as well take you along."

"I'm not okay with this," I grumbled as I climbed in. People kept score when they did nice things for others, so it was best never to let it happen. Doing the giving, even if it meant I had to do everything myself and pay for everyone around me, was a protective measure against obligation.

Having settled my debt and buckled in, I looked at the box of cassettes now resting in the well by my feet. I wasn't in the mood for chit-chat and didn't know how to launch the real talk. "Should I put some music on?"

"Sure. I don't much care for what they play on the radio nowadays, but you might find something you like in there."

I'd been a teenager in Athens in the '80s and we listened to every kind of music. Current pop music wasn't all that bad—in fact, Alanis Morrisette was a goddess. And the soundtrack of my childhood was in that box. Geezers didn't have a lock on the good stuff. I ran my hand over the jumble of cases, turning them this way and that so they all faced the same direction.

Ted laughed. "Indigo does that whenever I give her a ride somewhere."

So First Sergeant had sat in this seat, too, organizing Ted's collection. "I still can't quite picture you two as friends."

"I'm a little older than she is. I'm sure you've noticed." Ted glanced over as if expecting me to protest that he didn't look old. Instead of responding I went back to tidying the cassettes; people got so cranked up about their age.

There were a dozen or fifteen steel cuff bracelets in the box, making it difficult to line the cases up straight. Each cuff was engraved with the name, rank, branch of service and date that a serviceman had gone missing, most during the Vietnam years. It was trendy to wear these in uniform and I'd thought about getting one with my father's name on it but didn't want to have the conversations it would provoke.

Ted examined his reflection in the rearview mirror. "Anyway, it's weird but it works. We grew up in different sections of town at different times, but we talk shop about the Army. Life and death and all its mysteries—that kind of thing."

This statement shimmered in the hot air of the front seat like a single spider's thread cast into the sunlight with nowhere to attach. Even in the Army, where everyone dressed the same and got paid the same and lived next door to whomever the housing office put you next to, racial misunderstandings happened all the time. Maybe the Army helped bigoted soldiers get over a few things, but there were still plenty of obstacles to peaceful coexistence.

I picked out a cassette and slid it into the tape deck. I knew this one from a lazy summer evening when I was about ten. My mother had been on an energetic upswing, and we were lounging around, singing to records on the old hi-fi stereo. "I picked up a Simon and Garfunkel today," she said, and put on the *Parsley, Sage, Rosemary and Thyme* album. When the song "7 O'Clock News/Silent Night" had come on, my mother stopped singing. I thought she'd been listening to me sing "Silent Night," but now, hearing the lyrics coming through Ted's speakers was like hearing the song for the first time, and through my mother's ears. Between and around the harmonizing a news reader reported on the protests against the war in Vietnam. It ended with Nixon declaring that protests were un-American and that the only way forward was to escalate. I hadn't paid attention to that half of the song when I was a kid, and stuck to the hot seat of Ted's taxi, it made sense that after the 1993 Senate Commission concluded that there was no chance that any American POWs were still alive in Vietnam, and had declared my mother officially widowed, she'd taken her whole record collection to the Potters House thrift store in downtown Athens and left it by the door with that album right on top. I popped out the cassette.

"It ain't Christmas, is it?" Ted's laugh was throaty but sad, like a longtime smoker who'd given up too late. "And that ain't a Christmas carol."

"No, it is not." I rifled through the box and pulled out a Creedence best hits album. "Fortunate Son." "Who'll Stop the Rain." "Run through the Jungle."

"There's a lot going on in that box," Ted admitted.

"It is kind of morbid." I neglected to mention that the Fort Stewart librarians called me every time they got a new book about Vietnam and that I spent most nights on the sofa with my cat watching Oliver Stone movies.

"The dead walk among us," Ted said. "Or ride alongside us, whichever the case may be." He made the turn onto Georgia 204, weaving the cab through lanes of other drivers on Saturday shopping errands. His free hand swooped through hot air currents out the open window, and he cast a quick glance at me. "Although some of us are more accepting of that fact than others, it would seem."

This was it then. The roll and loop of my hangover was gone but my brain floated behind me like a helium balloon on a string. "My father went missing in Vietnam." It felt right to say it in that claustrophobic taxi, full of its old-car smells.

Ted darted his eyes at the box of cassettes and bracelets, his cardboard shrine to those who were lost and left behind. "That's rough," he said. "That leaves too many questions unanswered."

"I haven't had a single question answered." It came out frustrated when, really, I had no right to complain. My mother and I weren't the only ones. Some American remains had been returned over the years, but thousands hadn't and almost no bodies of missing Vietnamese soldiers, north or south, had made it back to their families. "I've made calls and written letters, and, other than the original notification telegram and letter from my father's commander, we don't have one solitary fact about what happened."

"That's rough," Ted repeated. In a war that had been so televised, so covered by journalists, so written about by historians, in which so many men served, it *was* unfair that no one knew anything about my father. On the other hand, soldiers clammed up when the story made them—or the Army—look bad. During the trial of the soldier in charge of the My Lai massacre, Army leadership had closed ranks, admitted no wrong, and everyone escaped justice. I assumed that if there had been something good to say about my father someone would have said it. His letters made him look too sensitive, too affected by what went on. I wanted to know what kind of person reacted like that. I wanted to know, I guess, if I was that kind of person.

"I mean, it's ridiculous at this point to think he might be alive." Saying this aloud served two purposes: first, it established me as a rational adult—in contrast to my mother, who still believed those Rambo-type movies where long-forgotten POWs got rescued after twenty years. And second, it offered Ted, as the expert in the car, an opportunity to say whether he thought there was any foundation for the theory that there might still be POWs alive in Vietnam. It made no logical sense, but there would always be that *what if.*

As usual, feather-light hope got smashed by reality's brick. "Yeah, there's no way," Ted said. "That guy who's been on the news? The one who says he's John Hartley Robinson? It's total bullshit. Maybe a few guys got left behind—guys kept at smaller prisons, say—and that's tragic. But there's no way they'd still be alive after more than twenty years."

Ted was right. It had all been so violent and so out of control, and so long ago. If someone presented me with a box of bones after all this time I'd half believe they belonged to someone else. Still, I hated to hear the truth spoken so plainly. "He went missing in the Mekong Delta during night operations. The official notification said 'Body not recovered,' but it didn't say whether he'd been shot or was bitten by a snake or went rogue or deserted to an opium den or got abducted by aliens—nothing."

"I'm sorry, doll," Ted said. "That's really, really rough."

If anyone else on the planet called me doll I'd have cleaned his ever-loving clock, or at least fantasized about it. But Ted was like a tough-talking uncle, and it was a relief to speak to someone who'd been in more or less the same place as my father, under circumstances I assumed were similar. He could call me doll. "I know it's stupid to hope, so I don't," I said. "Not really. But I'm trying hard to understand—not just what happened to my dad, but that whole war."

"Oh, I'm not sure any of us can understand that." Ted's laugh was quick, dismissive. He turned the taxi into the rough sand of the VFW's parking lot and cut the engine. "If you weren't there during one of those firefights you wouldn't be able to get your head around it. Hell, I *was* in plenty of firefights, and I'm not sure *I* know what went on over there. The VC understood us better than we did them, but nobody's got a lock on the whole story. Certainly not a bunch of drunk old grunts."

I sat for a moment, listening to the engine tick and settle. My temples throbbed from clenching my jaw. I wasn't the world's most confident person about anything else except this quest to understand Vietnam. It didn't impact anyone except my mother and me. That being the case, why would anyone stand in the way of it? I wasn't about to be dismissed as some girl who could never comprehend. "I have to try," I said.

We slapped through the screen door, and I walked straight to the bar. I'd pay my bill first. As for the rest—talking to any vets who might be there—I'd launch straight in before I lost my nerve. Ted underestimated how deep a hole my father had left behind. I had some basic facts to skitter down into it, but they barely covered the bottom. From counting up the times he'd mentioned enemy contact in his letters, my father had been on at least 129 patrols and search-and-destroy missions before he went missing. He hadn't wanted to go on any of them but was consumed with guilt about sending anyone else. He'd been covered in mosquito bites and got lightheaded when he had to pull leeches off himself. The Mekong River smelled bad even in the pouring rain. But I wanted to feel what he had felt. I wanted to crawl inside his skin and calm his pumping heart when he was afraid. I wanted an unflinching discussion with ground-pounders, to glean more information to add to my small trove. Had it been like the movie *Platoon*, where NCOs killed indiscriminately and turned a blind eye to rape? Had soldiers gone after the ones who were stone-cold killers, like Charlie Sheen's character did? Leaders who rubbed their soldiers the wrong way sometimes ended up fragged. This was a fact, not just something from movies. The thought was terrifying to contemplate, but it might explain why no one ever answered my letters asking for more information about my father. This was one leaden fear I didn't want to drop into the well. The splash it created would have overwhelmed me. But it was too heavy to keep carrying around.

"I'm Minerva Mills," I said to a man on the other side of the bar who was cutting limes and piling them into a highball glass. He had spiky black hair that was graying at the temples, olive skin, and dark eyes with deep shadows under them. He smiled, puzzled, and shook his head. "I have a tab from last night I need to settle?"

"Hey, Hector." Ted came up behind me. "How're you?"

"Hey, Ted." Hector reached over the counter and clasped Ted's hand. "What's this about a tab?"

Ted explained there should be a chit with my name on it while I stood there, mute with annoyance. Had my explanation been so hard to comprehend? Did I need a man to translate for me? I didn't like to be talked around like I was some kind of lamp.

Hector lifted the cash register drawer and rooted around until he found the note about the shortfall from the night before. "Here we go. That'll be fifty-seven dollars, ma'am."

I swallowed hard and handed over three twenty dollar bills with what I hoped was the confidence of a person who had plenty more where that came from, when in fact it was just about all I had left after giving Ted his cab fare. The times I'd seen Captain Williams at the officers' club he'd snapped at bartenders to get their attention, ordering everything with a flourish, and everyone acted like that was perfectly normal. He'd never hunched protectively around a stash of money. I was a stranger to that kind of swagger.

"Let me buy you a drink," I said to Ted. "And another one of whatever this gentleman's having." I pointed at a man sitting alone on a bar stool. He might have been the one I talked war crimes with the night before.

The man looked up. His cheeks were purpled with veins and his nose was bulbous. His hands trembled as he polished off a glass of something the color of topaz. "You're that girl officer," he said, and my heart beat faster. If I didn't handle this just right, it might be ages before I found other Vietnam vets to talk to.

"Yes, sir." I held out my hand to shake although I didn't want to touch him. His hair was wet, and he smelled of cheap aftershave, but also of something distilling from deep within. I knew the signs of a body sloughing alcohol, one whose anatomy had switched from regular metabolism to the breakdown of itself.

"I ain't no 'sir.'" His handshake was weak, and he let go to polish off his dregs and accept the fresh glass Hector pushed to him.

"Oh, sorry," I said. "I should have known—"

"Her father was MIA in Nam," Ted interjected, and again I squelched my irritation at being spoken for while I was standing right there. "So why don't you say thank you to the lady, Jeff?"

"To us and those like us." Jeff raised the glass, and his posture relaxed a fraction of an inch. Ted cocked his head at me to sit on the stool next to Jeff but raised his finger to his lips. He didn't know that me and this guy had traveled a few miles of road together already.

"Damn few left." Ted took a wax cup of soda from Hector and raised it to me. He settled on the next seat over and both men drank thoughtfully. "Although, guys like us aren't in short supply," Ted said. "The three of us might even be over strength." Jeff snorted. Logan had used the same term to describe me to Pettit that first day in the latrine, so that made four of us in the bar, surplus to requirements. A half squad of replaceable soldiers, pinned down by memories of a war that went nowhere.

"Soda's free for designated drivers," Hector explained. "But that'll be three dollars for the whiskey. You want anything, ma'am?"

"I'll just have a glass of water." The smell of the VFW was hitting me in the most vulnerable part of my soft palate. Alcohol was out of the question and besides, I was down to my last ten dollars after the bar tab and tip and standing Jeff another round. I waved to indicate Ted's drink. "You can't have even one beer if you're driving?"

"I'm just over a thousand days sober." Ted said this matter-of-factly, although he dug a 5.56 brass round out of his pocket and set it next to his cup with some effort. "I'm finally getting to the point where I can sit at a bar with these assholes and not want to drink them under it."

"You left that job to me." Suddenly animated, Jeff winked at Ted. "Somebody had to fall off the wagon when you climbed on."

My head thumped along with the jukebox in the background, a reminder of all the time and money I'd wasted the night before. I hadn't caught on that Ted was in recovery although he said he was a mess when he met First Sergeant. I knew about problem drinkers but nothing about people who'd quit and made it stick.

"Heavy is the head that wears the crown." Ted twisted his soda around on the bar top. No need for coasters in a place like this.

"Nah, it's good you quit," Jeff said. "I should quit. My liver would thank me for it. But we did have some times, didn't we?"

"We did, indeed." The three men paused to recollect their wayward pasts.

Hector smiled and took a breath in preparation for what I hoped would be a war story. Instead he said, "Remember when we crashed all them Bicentennial celebrations in '76?"

"We was shitfaced at all the fireworks shows," Jeff laughed. They'd probably reminisced about this a thousand times, but nineteen years fell from Jeff's ravaged face when he considered it anew. "We ruined a lot of picnics."

"Only red, white, and blue I touched that year was cans of PBR," Hector said.

"We might have wrapped a few flags around ourselves," Ted said. A fresh gust of laughter returned both Jeff and Hector to their youth.

"Holy shit, man. That time you streaked at the beach?"

"Middle of the got-damn day. Families eating buckets of fried chicken, and there you was, nekkid as the day you was born."

"Somebody had to show some war-hero pride." Ted chuckled and took a sip of Coke, enjoying himself.

"That ain't all you showed."

"I had flag everything in 1976," I said. My mother had bought me a T-shirt with an iron-on flag decal that I'd put back on as soon as it was washed and came off the laundry line. She'd sewn an embroidered flag patch over a hole in my jeans.

"A real little patriot." Jeff reverted from merry young man to sullen drunk at the mention of earnestness. "Stars and Stripes forever and all that?"

"I mean, I was just a kid." I didn't have unlimited courage or the cash to keep buying rounds of drinks, so I had to shove the conversation along. "Flags were cool because it was the Bicentennial. The country must've been looking for something positive after all those years of war, huh?"

"Where was your dad in Nam?" Hector's smile absorbed Jeff's contentiousness. He must have picked up on the past tense that Ted used to refer to my father and was nice enough to ask, to open the door like a gentleman. He didn't realize he was also blocking the entryway. Jeff and I had primed this conversational pump last night and I was ready to pick up where we left off, even if—or because—Jeff was in a confrontational mood. We could get right to business.

"He was a platoon leader with the 9th Infantry in the Mekong Delta, but he disappeared on patrol one night. In 1969, during Operation Speedy Express." I hoped the others were familiar with that time and place, the purpose of that combat action. I didn't want to have to explain what happened there, the free-fire zones, the assumption that everyone was an enemy, the extreme numbers of casualties among the South Vietnamese population. The way civilian body counts were added to inflate the kill ratios. It was like My Lai every day for months. The men shifted on their seats. They knew. Speaking it aloud, I grew uncomfortable. "An action like that, seems like it'd have an effect on you."

"It would be easy to lose a body in Nam, especially at night." Ted built his sentences word by word. They came from far away, and he placed them with effort. "It was so incredibly dark. It messed with your mind sometimes."

The other two men nodded but didn't speak.

"I was in the mountains, not in the Delta, but there was this time that one of our squads got ambushed. Some of the guys got so rattled they ran off and left casualties behind."

Jeff huffed into his glass. He'd obviously heard this story before. "Fuckin' cherry lieutenant."

"We was all new at one point," Hector said. He looked from me, gauging how much I could handle, and back to Jeff. "Be honest. Patrolling was some scary shit."

"Anyway, a day or so later the platoon took more guys out to the same spot to see if we could find anybody, but Charlie had cleared them all out by then." Ted paused and Jeff looked ready to speak but Ted cleared his throat and continued. "The point is, we could go looking for bodies if something went wrong, because we were mostly in jungles or up in the hills. If you lost a body in the Delta, it stayed lost."

My heart sank and I had to work to keep a neutral expression on my face. Of course a body would stay lost in the dark, in and around all that water. Of course it would. *Goodbye*, I said to my father for the millionth time. But with a mixture of unease and stubbornness I added, *I will still find you.*

"You learn to do a job out there, and you get good at it, or you die." Jeff spoke in the present tense, hypnotized by the swirling of his glass. "Like Patton said—you make the other bastard die for *his* country." His bleary eyes scrutinized me. "You seen *Patton?*"

"Of course I have." Black cover, gold block letters on the spine— before it got packed off to Korea, *Patton* stood at attention on the far left of my shelf of videos. Except for the idea that Patton believed in reincarnation, it wasn't my favorite war movie. World War II, with its straight-forward, good guy-bad guy narrative, didn't interest me all that much unless it was a discussion of moral decision-making. *Judgment at Nuremberg* got way more play time with Rambo and me than *Patton* did. "I guess you can't think too much about the other poor bastard, huh? Might drive you off the deep end."

Hector's face clouded over and Jeff stared down the bottom of his glass one more time before tipping it toward himself. "Nope." He passed the back of his hand across his mouth. "Thinking makes you hesitate. Might get you killed, or get your soldiers killed. No offense, but an officer needs to be decisive or get the hell out of the way."

I watched Jeff, how his mind's eye seemed to be viewing a specific film clip just as he'd replayed the scene of Ted streaking, wrapped in the American flag. And as quickly as Jeff's soldierly bluster vaporized I was huddled in a faraway foxhole with him, ankle-deep in dirty water. The skin of my feet rotted in my boots and the air stank of someone who had shit himself out of pure terror. Those were real bullets ripping through the understory, the aim of which was to take my face clean off. This was not a theoretical exercise for these guys, or for me, at that moment. It would have felt that way to my father. It would have felt like the most natural thing in the world to run from a firefight like Ted's cherry lieutenant had, or to keep your head down to survive one more night.

"Hey Ted?" It was almost a whisper. My lungs couldn't seem to grab enough air around my quick, shallow breath.

"Yeah, doll?"

"I'm ready to go." Because the fact was, these guys were willing to walk back into danger for me. I saw it in Hector's frozen smile, and in the resolute way Jeff hunched over his glass. They stood ready to help a daughter of one of them, but I was the one who was too scared to go any further. It was an emotional state I had to relearn every time I encountered it—I was the one who went catatonic with fear. I seemed to forget this lesson every time I ran away from it, while these guys, and my father, had kept pushing through.

Outside, Ted put the taxi in gear and pulled onto the road. "That didn't go the way you wanted."

I'd hoped these men would be generous with me, and maybe for the most part they were still hiding behind liquor, easy answers, and a refusal to acknowledge what some soldiers had done—and not just to Vietnamese people. But they were inching out of their comfort zones for me, and what I had to confront—again, always—was my cowardice on the precipice of understanding something. Some doors were meant to stay shut because once opened, you had to examine the contents of those closets at close range. It took more strength than I had to confront the heart of a soldier's sorrow. Ted was right. It could probably never be done. Not by me, anyway.

"You okay?" Ted glanced away from the road, and I shook my head. A crowd of critical thoughts was gathering along the sidelines, but he didn't know how quickly the voices in my head reached a crescendo. How they screamed away any fledgling confidence I managed to muster. How they sounded like the crying that came from the other side of my closed bedroom door when I was a kid, barricaded inside with library books and a sleeve of reduced-price cookies to block the noise.

At home, the light from the answering machine blinked from the floor of the empty living room. "Hey, honey! I had to use the credit card to pay the mechanic for the quarterly maintenance on your father's car, in case you're wondering what that charge is when you get the bill. Hope you're having a good day! Love you!" My mother's message bleated to a close. She left messages when she thought I'd be out, especially when it was about money, and we squabbled over why my father's old Mustang had to be kept tip-top. About why we couldn't sell it to raise much-needed cash instead of draining away funds to ensure it would be ready for a soldier who was never coming home. I longed to have a real conversation with my mother, but even though our fingers were intertwined so tightly, our palms rarely touched. I sighed and erased the message. One more thing to get a handle on.

"Hey, you ole pole cat." Rambo emerged from the bedroom, and I shifted my keys to the other hand to scratch behind his ears. His purr sounded disappointed. "I know, I know. We're both starving." I set my wallet on the empty counter and opened the cupboard. There wasn't much in there except for some cans that were so old the labels had slipped off, and a big stack of cat food. I dumped one into Rambo's dish and the smell of tuna filled the stuffy kitchen. I flipped the thermostat to start the air conditioning, washed my hands and rooted through the human food options. I was at the stage of emptiness where hunger goes away, leaving nothing but anxiety and a headache. It was too hot to warm anything up on the stove and the coffee had gone cold, still in the pot from when I'd made it and then forgotten it hours before.

I pulled a beer from a lone six pack in the fridge. I hadn't had a proper meal since lunch yesterday so I could indulge in a cold one—the diet of champions. The package store had just started carrying 333 Premium Export, because what better way was there to hail the recent normalization of trade between the US and Vietnam than with the clinking of bottles? The expensive beer had been a present to myself, a balm to cool the sting of my delayed assignment to Korea.

The cat worried the last scraps of food into the edges of his bowl, and I found a half-empty carton of ice cream behind a bag of peas in the freezer. How had I forgotten that? I couldn't usually coexist with sweets in the house. I took the carton and a spoon and the beer bottle to my folded blanket sofa and turned on the TV/VCR that Army Community Services had loaned me after I put my stuff in storage. Jeff, the bleary-eyed Vietnam vet, had said an officer needed to be decisive, but I was faltering, emotions and options flapping around me like wet laundry in the wind.

The cat, smelling like a ball of furry fish, settled beside me for a bath. I had nowhere to go and no money to spend and I was brain-dead after the trip out to the Hunter VFW. The shelf of men who never disappointed—Martin, Sylvester, Charlie, Francis—had been left out of storage for this very situation. Rambo sniffed and then refused a spoonful of freezer-burned ice cream while I considered which war would distract me from my heavy heart. I needed to think through everything happening at work and the intense conversations I'd just had, but none of these movies facilitated quiet contemplation. They just drowned things out.

I got up from the blanket and went to the hall closet, where the old cardboard boot box sat alone on a shelf. Everything else was in a storage unit or on its way to Korea. Only the few things I would have needed right away, or couldn't bear to have out of easy reach, remained. I pulled the box down and went back to the living room. Rambo ignored the ice cream carton on the floor as I began to read.

LETTERS

I picked from the front of the box. Not the very front because those were transitional notes, written from Travis Air Force Base in California and Subic Bay in the Philippines, reporting on palm trees and tropical fruit as though my father was going on an extended vacation and describing the different sights and smells—observations on the novelty of being out of training at last and on the eve of something bigger. My parents were both asking what they could do for their country in those days. I'd read through these letters many times in high school and college, touching the paper my father had touched like a blind person, trying to derive a connection from the feel of his writing as much as its content. Everyone said I looked like him, but because of his time in-country, he'd concluded that he didn't want anyone like him to be brought into the world.

The first time I'd read those words I banished them to a different box, my box of worst things—a music box whose ballerina no longer twirled, filled with notes from boys who wanted to break up, conversations I'd transcribed of mean things people said about my mother or me, a photograph of the paternal grandparents I'd met as a baby and sometimes talked to on the phone but didn't really know. The Letter resided underneath all that because it was my foundation. Even after I threw the whole shitty box of worst things out, The Letter had come with me into the Army.

My father had written on pale blue Army notepaper, still available in the stationery aisle of the PX. All the envelopes had been slit carefully at the top as though my mother were prolonging the opening of them—uncertain whether their contents were the literary equivalent of a pair of earrings or a severed ear. The envelopes had grown tired from their long journeys and in all their years waiting in the boot box—their edges browning, the ink bleeding on the addresses, and in the corners where the word *FREE* took the place of a stamp. I'd trawled these letters many times, looking for clues. Now I approached them like tarot cards, pulling a random sample to see how they would speak.

I told you I wouldn't hold anything back, honey—but I'm not sure I can or even want to tell you everything about combat. We were in our first firefight today—or I should say, I was in my first firefight. Only a couple of buck privates were as green as I was out there. I'm lucky to have some tough old bastards in my platoon, but they were the ones who did the leading. If I could earn their respect—and after today I'm not at all sure that's a possibility— we'd be okay. When I say okay, I mean keeping these soldiers as safe as possible while bullets are flying overhead.

His nerves jangled over the miles and years. I wondered if he'd used the word *overhead* to make my mother feel better or whether that was for himself.

I can hear you remind me that I promised to keep myself safe, and I will.

My eyes craned to see around the corner of his words, my thoughts a calendar of peaceful images: sailboats in Cam Ranh Bay, the green geometry of rice fields shaped to hillsides. This was the Vietnam I'd see when I was finally there, every bit the miracle of recovery from war as the German cities the Trummerfrauen rebuilt, brick by shattered brick. My father had been more of a natural coward than a destroyer, and he hadn't destroyed fast enough to survive. There was a lesson for me in that, but it was outside my intellectual grasp, a lucid half-sleep insight that disappeared in the blazing Georgia sun. I reached for it as it receded, as those thoughts always did.

My father signed off with a paragraph about how much he missed my mother. He'd left just after their first wedding anniversary, so he made oblique reference to what a special memory that was for him. In later letters these closing sentences became more graphic and I was glad this spin of the epistolary bottle hadn't produced one of those. The only thing my mother ever said about their relationship was that they were completely, totally in love—she was second only to his Mustang, she joked to the other widows who believed they were still wives. I felt like a normal kid for a second, embarrassed by my parents. It was momentarily comforting.

I replaced the letter in the boot box, keeping them in order by the dates inside, not by post marks. I'd discovered when I read them the first time that ordering by postmark didn't guarantee perfect chronology. Some letters were dated well before they arrived, but I wanted to read them in the order my father had written them.

I pulled another one, this time from slightly less than halfway through. When I'd discovered these letters in the moldy box in the trunk of the Mustang, after I got my license in high school and harbored the misguided notion that my mother would let me drive my father's car, they were in a jumbled pile along with his reeking old uniforms, a pair of black boots and a shoeshine kit, spare change, unused stationery in a plastic pouch, a rusted razor, and two touristy trinkets—a tiny hula girl with straight black hair and a pair of sandals made from old tires. I'd stared at the mud stains on the uniforms, so very like Georgia red clay, and been amazed at the sheer number of letters as I put them in order—two or three, sometimes four a week for almost six months, all on the faded blue paper tucked into matching envelopes. The return address was a kaleidoscope of acronyms and numbers. I'd have a similar foreign military address if—when!—I got to Korea.

The disordered state of the trunk's contents indicated that my mother had wanted nothing to do with any of it once the US pulled out of South Vietnam in 1973, leaving her husband behind. She must have thrown his letters into the box and slammed the trunk like it was her own container of worst things, keeping one prewar photo of the two of them enshrined on top of the TV. She never talked about the nitty-gritty of his disappearance. She never used the words *death* or *dead*, not even with the other widows. Not that I'd ever heard.

My father's second letter was from two months into his rotation and was infused with sadness and disillusionment, his upbeat mood as long gone as the beaches of the Philippines:

> *The people we're supposed to be helping hate us, and I can't really say I blame them. Here in the Delta we're surrounded by VC sympathizers but there's no way of knowing who the real ones are. Our only tool is to treat everyone as the enemy, and we have to assume they're lying when they beg us not to turn them out of their homes as we clear and burn villages where VC have been operating. It makes tactical sense but in my hooch at night I can't stop myself from thinking about you as one of these women, left alone at the mercy of men like us.*
>
> *Write to me about the tulips you planted this year, and what you wore to church on Christmas. I need to picture something pretty.*

I stopped reading to picture a village being cleared of its inhabitants. Elderly farmers arguing; children standing in for the men and women off fighting. No one succeeding. Drill Sergeant Gallagher had taught us to regard "the enemy" as a sawdust opponent, and Hollywood's version of death and destruction made the plight of ordinary Vietnamese people seem like an unfortunate but expected outcome. In contrast, real boots-on-the-ground survival meant being ferociously aggressive and must have required powerful mental defense mechanisms. Probably by this point in his tour my father had been paranoid. Superstitious. Thinking about a blooming flower on the other side of the planet would have been easier than believing he could ever fit back into civilian life—take up residence in our little house, sit behind the wheel of his car, be a happy husband and father when he'd deprived others of that possibility. I'd done the mental math; it was too early for news of my mother's pregnancy to have reached him at that point. And in The Letter, which my mother received a few days after this one, he'd written that a child was an indulgence, a liability even, in a world where everything and everyone was a ticking time bomb. That was the letter I carried in my breast pocket. My insurance policy and a perpetual reminder never to get a big head about anything.

The first time I'd slipped The Letter from the envelope, I was hiding in the crowded closet of my childhood bedroom. I was hoping, as I did with each letter when I read it for the first time, for a physical description, a dumb joke, some dad-like detail to refine the mental statue I was carving of him and found . . . something else. The breath had caught in my throat and my heartbeat slowed as I realized that he hadn't dreamed of the possibility of me the way I dreamed about him. Not at all. Once I'd read The Letter all the prior moments of my life snapped to attention like a line of soldiers. All the hurts and slights and inability to connect. He hadn't wanted me to be born, and it all made sense.

I mean, he would have loved me if he'd met me. Parents couldn't help but love their children, right? But still. Nothing in the rest of the letters indicated that he knew my mother was pregnant, so she must not have told him. Maybe she was keeping the news until she saw him on rest and recuperation leave, halfway through his tour. But once I'd eaten that fruit from the tree of knowledge of good and evil, I couldn't rid myself of it. There was nowhere outside myself to stash that information, so instead, I tucked it next to my heart. Ingesting a little poison every day strengthened a person.

I got up and walked to the bathroom for a wad of toilet paper, more to press the tears back than to wipe the few that had leaked out. I'd allow myself a good cry at some point, but emotions belonged in their proper places and this was not one of them.

On the way back to the couch I narrowly missed stepping on Rambo, sniffing around the carton of melting ice cream. "It's fucking unacceptable, isn't it, buddy?" I said. He growled in agreement, at least about the ice cream. He wasn't much for wallowing in self-pity. I picked up the carton and went to the kitchen to throw it out. I took a second beer out of the fridge, snapped the cap into the open trash can, then returned to the blanket. I removed the last letter in the box, the one dated three days before my father went missing.

Hey, honey, it's late here but I can't fall asleep, so I thought I'd drop you a line to let you know I'm thinking of you. There's a break in the downpour and the frogs are hollering, and it's reminding me of the peepers down by the creek.

He meant the creek behind the house in Athens. The peepers sang all summer and I fell asleep to their music through my open window whenever I was home.

Only four more weeks in the bush before I'm done with my platoon time, and I can see you on R&R. I feel guilty about the fact that platoon leaders rotate out after six months—the grunts stay in the bush for their entire year. It's an unfair policy and they're right to bitch about it. I told the commander I'd stay with the platoon for longer, but the soldiers won't be sorry to see me go when it's my time. It's nothing personal. I've already told you how Igoe, the one we call Smoke, says I'm too soft, and I'm sure he and the other NCOs are hoping the next guy won't slow them down with so much thinking. It'll make them feel better to bad-mouth me after I've gone to some cushy admin job in the rear.

And now I can hear you telling me it's time to let someone else take a turn in the fight, so here's my answer—yes, ma'am. Twenty-seven days and a wake up.

And that was it. My father's letters showed him in opposition to his NCOs, since he was the only one openly wrestling with the morality of what they were being asked to do, and at war with himself since he did what he was told anyway. He talked about Smoke in several letters, about what he'd done to Vietnamese villagers and how he'd called my father a weak link—with, as he put it—all of his pansy-ass navel-gazing. By Smoke's logic, the only way to do the job was to be a stone-cold killer. That was the gist of what Jeff had said, too, staring into the oily depths of his whiskey on the VFW bar stool. My father had only half-assed tried to earn his soldiers' respect and cooperation because he couldn't fully commit to what his commanders had asked him to do. He agonized over the competing demands of keeping himself and his soldiers alive with the taking of other lives, but in the end his scrupulous conscience hadn't spared him. Sometimes I wished my father had been better at compartmentalizing his actions, walling off the things he had to do. Maybe if he'd been able to do that he would have made it to his own bar stool like the old soldiers lined up at the VFW, drinking away his memories.

My own efforts to win over the Headquarters soldiers were also a sham. First Sergeant had been right when she said throwing the book at them would be ineffective at creating real change, but the patient approach hadn't worked with Davis and the motor pool like she said it would. The modern Army seemed trite and superficial compared to the real, hard things Jeff and Ted and Hector and my father had had to endure, but it was what I had to work with. There had to be a way to protect my own vulnerabilities, but cowards hid behind their regulation-reinforced desks, and behind walls of senior NCO advisers. Somehow or other it was time to lead from the front of Headquarters Company.

NAPALM STICKS TO KIDS

Bright and early Monday morning everyone turned out to the parade field. Birds gathered on power lines along the perimeter to watch the proceedings, snifters of scorched grass and sand and pine needles held to their beaks. The soldiers' muttering ceased when I rounded the Headquarters Company building and recommenced as I walked onto the field. Even the Old Man had turned up to physical training, creating another hush among the rank and file.

"Good morning, sir." I said, acutely aware of everyone's eyes on me. It was hard to exude professionalism while wearing shapeless gray PT shorts, especially when your butt was too big.

"Lieutenant Mills." He gave a little chop of a salute and looked around at the soldiers, half of whom were whispering furiously at the other half to tuck in their T-shirts and demanding to know why the hell they hadn't shaved. It was rare that they gathered for unit physical training at all. Having the Old Man there was unprecedented. "Good turn out."

"Yes, sir—I'm winning all the popularity contests this morning." I bounced on my toes, wishing I had somewhere to put my hands. "I had First Sergeant call down the roster to tell the soldiers we're not doing the honor system for PT anymore."

"Good thing I'm here so I don't get on your bad side," the Old Man chortled, but from behind his jolly commander act he gave me a penetrating look, perhaps realizing I wasn't as docile as he'd assumed.

First Sergeant formed the soldiers up and I took over. "The push-up!" I called. Rather than stopping at ten pushups, I led them through twenty. A push-up deficiency could only be fixed with liberal doses of more of them, and according to the training files, Pettit, Reyes and Robinson struggled with them on PT tests. To be respected, a woman had to be able to knock 'em out like a man. Pushups were hard currency in the Army, and this was my morning to fling money on the bar.

Do you see me, Dad? It wasn't a prayer exactly, but a stray, wispy thought I sent into the otherwise cloudless sky. If he'd been here, he might have admired my straight back, my strong arms. I hoped he would be proud, although if he'd survived, maybe I wouldn't have been on that parade field at all.

As Headquarters Company down-up-down-upped in unison, I scanned back and forth between First Sergeant and Shumacher. Their push-up form was good; they could handle it. Lieutenant Logan was hanging in there, too, but her hair had started to snake out of its French braid. The corner of my mouth twitched into a smile at this first sign of struggle.

"We got to break you down," Drill Sergeant Gallagher had said at Basic Camp, again and again. "Broken people make the best soldiers."

"The Mountain Climber!" I announced after the pushups were done but before I brought them up from their positions parallel to the earth. "Starting position, move!" Broken people didn't fixate on every firing neuron. They learned to channel the pain.

Legs tucked under chests then churned back and forth in cadence. We did twice as many Mountain Climbers, too, and the ranks of grimacing faces, including the Old Man's, waited for my next command. I was out of breath and lactic acid hummed through my arms and chest, the sun already uncomfortably hot on my back. No. Today was the day to prove myself in everyone's eyes, the Old Man's in particular. My weight might not have met his standards, but I could do some damn PT.

I held them in the front-leaning rest position, breathing my way through the first minute of a plank and into the second. *Mind over muscle.*

I wondered what Logan and Pettit would say about me in the personnel shop later, then shoved it out of my mind. Working through pain led to higher PT scores and higher self-esteem. Burning lungs and muscle fibers were a catalyst for change. PT would help us all develop discipline—me, to lose my extra weight, and the company to pass the training exercise.

A few backsides tented toward the sun and five seconds before I called time, Davis collapsed onto his belly. He shot me a disdainful look, as though his lack of endurance was somehow my fault. I hopped up and brushed my palms against my shorts, removing his weakness along with the loose grass. *Ain't nobody hiding behind a stack of paperwork on this parade field, buddy,* I thought.

I had them pair off for sit-ups and Logan stood alone, without a partner, until one of the mechanics reached up to her. Somebody on the ground said something I couldn't hear, and laughter rippled along the ranks of motor pool soldiers. When the sit-ups were finished I divided them into work sections for relay races, and any team whose energy lagged got switched over to pushups. Let motor pool laugh about that. To finish off, all thirty-seven of us lined up in single file. We shuffled around the track while, one by one, the soldier at the end of the line sprinted to the front.

I sent the Old Man up first, his face red and unsmiling. Had I gone too hard? Bad things happened when you embarrassed your boss, this one in particular. The Old Man chugged like a rusty train engine, but he made it to the front of the line, maybe because the soldiers adjusted their speed. *Phew.*

Storey ran past. "Great PT, ma'am," he panted. He'd need to lay off the cigs if we were going to maintain this level of training intensity.

Davis struggled to the front of the line. *Here we go*, I thought, waiting for whatever comment he'd pull from the bottom of his lungs. He didn't say anything but the sweat pouring off him fairly boiled with resentment. There *was* a solid element of retribution in this workout aimed squarely at him. I was his boss now, and the sooner we both got our heads around that fact, the sooner I'd get the job done and be out of his hair. He could try to push my buttons while he ate my dust.

"Great PT, ma'am," said soldier after soldier as they ran by. Washburn, because he just had to be different, sang:

"Flying low across the trees,

"Pilots doing what they please,

"Dropping frags on refugees—"

The soldiers, Davis's voice loudest of all, joined in on the last line. "'Cause napalm sticks to kids!"

That song. It was written by dissident draftees as a criticism of the war in Vietnam but had morphed into a tongue-in-cheek cadence for unit runs all across the Army, gallows humor mixed with unshakable belief in American military superiority being some funny shit. I craned my neck to see how Logan was reacting. I'd never given the cadence a second thought until there was a soldier of Vietnamese descent running around the track with us. I caught a glimpse of lifted chin and cheekbone that I hoped meant she was not taking it personally.

First Sergeant glided by without a word, barely breathing, and giving me a look so fleeting I might have imagined it. Too quick to understand. When she caught up to Washburn she popped him on the head. He winced and pretended to be hurt and everyone laughed again. *First Sar'n dropped a frag on Washburn.* Laughter and pain brought soldiers together.

I was the last runner, sprinting far ahead to the side of the track to minimize the opportunity others had to marvel at how my backside powered me around. There were always comments, though, and today was no different.

"Get it, LT."

"Go, speed racer."

"Let me hitch myself to that ride."

You had to laugh it off and outrun it.

When everyone else formed back up I turned them over to Storey for stretches. He looked happy in front of the formation. Ecstatic to be overworked.

"Air Assault!" he said, freckles massed into reddish-brown blobs on each cheek. A hoo-ah went up from the company as I returned to the rank of officers and senior NCOs at the back. My muscles were tight and I felt self-conscious but redeemed, like I always did after a decent workout. My endorphin bump was tempered by the displeasure rolling off the backs of Davis and the Old Man, and by the possibility that Logan was upset. I would have liked an uncomplicated victory, but no battle was won without casualties.

Storey dismissed the formation for chow and the Old Man gathered his keys and canteen from the grass and patted my sweaty shoulder. The weight of his hand was everyone smearing my uniform with Watergate salad two Fridays before. "Welcome to the new Headquarters Company, sir." I hoped I sounded convincing.

"If you keep this up, we're all going to lose our love handles, Lieutenant Mills." The Old Man's lips pressed into a tight smile; apparently he intended for me to work off my own love handles, not his. No doubt after this he'd be supporting me from behind his desk, leaving me without visible command oomph at morning PT. No wonder the Headquarters PT averages were so . . . average. No wonder enlisted soldiers bad-mouthed officers.

As the Old Man and the rest of the company limped to their cars, someone retched behind the bleachers and I found Shumacher in the aluminum shade, wiping her mouth on the shoulder of her T-shirt. "You need to go on sick call, Specialist Shumacher." I kept my voice low but decisive. "You need to tell everyone what's going on, and then we need Sergeant Storey to put you on pregnancy PT."

"Please stop hovering, ma'am." Shumacher's whisper was fierce. "I actually started to spot this morning."

"What? Just now? Because of PT?" I'd gone entirely too gung-ho if I'd caused a freaking miscarriage. "Are you cramping?"

Car keys jingled. "You all right, Specialist Shumacher?" First Sergeant's sweaty face gleamed like the tannic waters of the nearby Canoochee River but no litany of complaints about her knees and back crossed her lips. She was rock hard.

"I'm fine." Shumacher avoided First Sergeant's eyes. "It's just hot out here."

"Okay, then. Drink some water," she said as she took her leave. "See you in the office, ma'am."

Did that mean we needed to talk? Nervousness swirled its way up from deep within me but I kicked at its weedy tentacles, still high on my own badassery. Of course we needed to talk. A new company commander and her first sergeant needed to talk and talk and talk. Sure, if she had overhead me and Shumacher I'd have some questions to answer, but the bulk of the company's problems had to do with training, paperwork, and equipment accountability, and I was a whiz with paperwork. And I was First Sergeant's supervisor, not the other way around, dammit.

I turned back to Shumacher. "Go. On. Sick call."

"I'm fine," Shumacher insisted. She raised the hem of her T-shirt to wipe her face, exposing a strip of muscled abs that I couldn't help but covet. "It can wait a couple more days until we're done with the inventory. Plus, maybe my period is starting after all."

"Two more days, or I'm telling everyone myself," I said.

ME LOVE YOU LONG TIME

A man, most of a man, empty trouser legs folded under him, pulled himself along the ground on a small wooden cart. He smiled up at Logan and said, "Pink panties are my favorite," and she couldn't respond because

1. her Vietnamese was virtually nonexistent. It was the language of stilted phone conversations to relatives and friends in California. The language of you're-so-headstrong-I-don't-know-what-to-do-with-you. The whisper of songs and stories into her hair at night when she was a little girl. But mostly she and her mother spoke English.

2. she was too shocked by this man's appearance to utter a word. She, who never met a social situation she couldn't bludgeon her way through, would not open her mouth because, while his lips were pulled back on bare gums, her teeth glinted with braces and rubber bands. Gross men were everywhere but she'd never been in a city like this, so crowded, so teeming with motorbikes and cyclos and cars and people who both looked like her and also bore no resemblance to her whatsoever. Her mother had been back to Vietnam, but this was Logan's first trip, and it was kind of cool but also kind of freaky that for once in her life she

didn't stick out, not really, even with her light hair, and she wasn't going to let this perv ruin it for her. She wasn't about to open her mouth and reveal that she was, in fact, as much of a tourist as that old guy ten feet away with the Army baseball cap, sweating like a monsoon downpour.

And now there was another man—a boy, really, smiling up at her saying, "I'll hold your feet, ma'am." It was the curse of the new kid to be abandoned and Logan was fresh meat. A new second lieutenant whose perimeter needed to be probed, as they said, even though she was an officer. When Lieutenant Mills told them to pair off everyone had found their usual sit-up partners. That girl Pettit had flown to the side of another female soldier, leaving Logan alone. She didn't want some random guy touching her, but she couldn't act like pairing with an enlisted soldier was beneath her. Even though they were, literally, scattered around her on the ground.

"Come on, then," she sighed. "Hold my ankles tight."

"I got you, ma'am." The soldier's pimples glowed hot pink against the flushed skin of his face as he braced himself against her knees, hands hard against her insteps. He was right there when she raised her torso, but he was a gentleman—he turned his face away. She was lying on an ant hill and felt the colony's bite as her back smashed away at their house.

"I'll hold you tight, ma'am." Another soldier, somewhere off to her right, mocked the one holding her feet. These morons thought they were funny. Her mother had told her story after story about the GIs she'd rebuffed, men infinitely more battle-hardened and psychologically strong than these over-eager children. Other women fell for this shit, the disrespect men claimed as admiration. But not her.

On the vertical, Logan paused to look for some sign that others had overheard. Lieutenant Mills was at the front of the formation, eyes on her stopwatch. A tall girl had stopped doing sit-ups to glare at a soldier whose close-cropped hair was so blond it was white, two pairs away. Logan had expected a man who looked like that, grinning and blond, when she'd met her father—but got a somewhat beaten down, balding guy instead. She and her mother had been politely disappointed. He was kind enough, though. He sent her a card every year for her birthday.

The tall girl didn't say anything to the blond soldier, and the colonel, three pairs away on the other side, didn't react since that wasn't the kind of comment he'd find problematic. But Logan wasn't the least bit cowed by weakness masquerading as humor. On the contrary—it fueled her rage. She, who'd arrived in America twenty years ago, and had therefore been here longer than some of these punks had been alive.

Down up, down up, she smashed the ant hill.

"Ooh, me love you long time." The soldiers around her brayed with mirth. The soldier holding her feet gave her a quick, embarrassed smile. Whoever said this, if confronted, would swear he'd said it to the soldier holding her feet, not to her. She, whose first words, according to her mother, were the swear words that crowded her current thoughts but rarely exited her lips, disciplined as she was to speak and act correctly. These fuckers didn't know who they were fucking with.

"You're too *beaucoup*," she said through gritted teeth while pumping out the reps. They'd know that scene from *Full Metal Jacket*. She'd gotten a lot of mileage out of that line.

"Fifteen dollah," somebody laughed. At her, who was an officer in the Army of her father but also of the enemy. These spoiled babies had zero experience with how much you had to put up with to get where you wanted to be.

THEY SAY THAT IN THE ARMY THE CHOW IS MIGHTY FINE

The Monday inventories were just like Friday's except hotter. Davis barely spoke, and Jones was silent but for the soft tocks his ballpoint made against the clipboard. It took all my strength to keep marking down the missing items, knowing that the soldiers standing sullenly by the vehicles might have to pay for them. The urge to turn a blind eye to it—to wave my own pen like Captain Williams had, to make it all go away on paper, was overwhelming. The buck had to stop somewhere, though, and I was the jerk holding up a hand. Just a bit more than two months to go.

After the day was finally over, with its promise to repeat itself the next, I peeled my uniform off and left it hanging in the latrine like a skin. I put on my dirty PT shirt and shorts, threw my ruck on my back and ran home instead of driving. Two-a-day workouts would blast all this extra weight, and the steady rhythm of feet on concrete would shake the events of the day into manageable boxes.

In college I'd come across the work of the psychologist Carl Rogers, who said that a person of integrity could help people if you came at them with genuine love in your heart. But the principal of unconditional positive regard was hard to pull off when you worked with guys like Davis. I was going to have to drag him to the finish line—an endeavor that would leave my tank depleted and my social currency low.

A Silverado slowed as it passed me, window rolled down to reveal a shorn head and scowling face. "Move that ass!" the man said and rolled the window back up. His bumper was covered with American and Confederate flags, and in the rear window of the cab a black and white POW/MIA sticker reminded someone—certainly not the missing soldiers themselves—"You are not forgotten."

My face flushed hotter, and I stopped dead in my tracks, lungs suddenly empty of air as though the guy had driven straight over my chest. In my mind's eye I charged down the sidewalk after the retreating vehicle. I threw down my Alice pack and hurled myself into the bed of the truck, pushed that stupid little back window open and grabbed the man's ear. I imagined that the barber's razor had left the sides of the man's head bare but that his ears were small and delicate, like curls of fancy pasta. I yanked his head around by one of those ears until he faced me and demanded, "Just who do you think you're talking to, Mr. Big Expert on POWs? Here's something you should never forget: You can't talk to a woman—any woman—like that."

Instead I doubled over, bracing myself with my hands on my knees. I gulped the thick afternoon air but gagged on it. I couldn't breathe in this place. The Old Man would probably have said the guy was just trying to motivate me to improve.

The truck turned the corner and thundered off post. I pushed up slowly, like an old woman, and swiped at my face with the shoulder of my T-shirt, still pungent from the morning's PT session and now soaked through with fresh sweat. I began to run again, my feet thudding like cinder blocks. I was starving. I hadn't eaten anything since a granola bar at lunch time, and the cupboards at home were bare. It seemed pointless to shop and cook for one anyway. Everything seemed pointless. Eat. Sleep. Work, work, work. Get paid, spend the money, repeat. Pointless.

I still had the ten-dollar bill left from the VFW, though, so after I cleared the main gate I turned onto General Stewart Way and ran the two blocks to Lucky China. I stood outside with my heels hanging off the curb to stretch my calves and looked around. Runner's high couldn't make the surroundings more attractive. There was a rent-to-own furniture store, a payday loan office, a nail salon, and an Army-Navy surplus shop in the same strip mall—typical GI town businesses. Completely different from the steel and glass high rises of Seoul and the street markets full of new sights and smells. Just a bit more than two months if all went well. Never mind that I'd actually be stationed at Camp Casey, way north on the DMZ and by all reports cold and absolutely miserable. Anything had to be better than Hinesville, Georgia on a sweltering Monday night in July.

I entered the cool blast of Lucky China and studied the menu hanging behind the register. I'd have the stir-fried vegetables, no meat or rice, and fill in the gaps with water. It wasn't just about the calories. Whenever I stood at a cash register I thought of my mother, tightening her financial belt notch by irresponsible notch. Even a tiny indulgence like a fancy six pack of beer or a takeout dinner filled me with guilt.

"Hey there, Lieutenant Mills." The good-luck bells on the door jingled and Logan entered, fresh in soft cotton trousers and espadrilles, hair hanging poker-straight to her shoulders, wafting with perfume. Through the glass I saw Logan's candy-apple red Mustang parked in the spot closest to the restaurant door and was glad my seven-year-old Civic wasn't there to be compared. Lieutenants were famous for plunking their entire paychecks into payments for hot cars, but because of the guilt thing, I'd bought used.

"You can call me Min," I sighed, beyond hunger or caring what Logan called me. Sure, Logan was on battalion staff, so I was her company commander, but that was an administrative technicality. It was fine for us to use first names even though we weren't exactly equals. Logan was clean and pretty. She had a cute new car and a cushy office job and had gone to Cornell. She'd probably been all over the world while I'd barely left Georgia.

"Oh, right. Min." Logan tucked her hair behind one ear. Her smile seemed genuine. "You ran over here? That's hard core after that PT session this morning."

My cheeks flushed at the mention of the morning's PT. How could Logan drop compliments when Washburn had sung that asinine song about napalm sticking to kids? I should have apologized right then. If I'd been a good person, if I was even remotely able to feel unconditional positive regard like Carl Rogers, I'd have called Logan to see how things were going. Now it was too late. "Did you have a good first week in personnel?" I gritted my teeth to get the question out. *Observe the niceties.* Love a person, even if you were half embarrassed, half seething with jealousy in their presence. While I'd been rolling the stone of Headquarters uphill, Logan would have been flipping through files with fingernails as delicate as shells from Tybee Island, judging my work and gossiping in the battalion break room with the other staff officers. I sniffed and flexed my ankles to show I didn't care all that much about her answer.

Logan's nostrils fluttered as the odor of my T-shirt reached her. "The colonel took me to lunch at the O Club today," she said. "He's nice, don't you think?"

She looked out the corner of her eye like she was asking a loaded question rather than flaunting her favored status, but I ignored it. The Old Man had never taken me to lunch at the O Club, not just the two of us, until the day he told me he was canceling my orders to Korea. Had it been almost two weeks since I'd wiped Logan's face with a cupcake? I felt bad about the napalm song but I wasn't sorry for the cupcake. "Oh, he's a peach." I turned to the clerk at the register. "Can I just have the steamed vegetables, please?" Even stir-fried vegetables were too caloric. I'd rather starve to death than order too much food in front of Logan.

"I'll have the pork-fried rice, please, and the wontons." Logan simpered over her shoulder, "I'm so bad. I already had a giant sandwich for lunch. And my mom would be so embarrassed that I'm ordering American Chinese food."

My mother would have objected to Chinese food on the grounds that it was fattening, but I guessed that wasn't what Logan was talking about. "Do your parents own a Vietnamese restaurant or something?"

Logan's smile faded. "My mother is a real estate agent."

Shit. I couldn't seem to say anything to Logan without making a fool of myself, so I wasn't about to ask why getting Chinese takeout was embarrassing. "Not that there's anything wrong with running a restaurant!" I glanced at the woman behind the counter packing up our orders. "But don't you worry about the fried rice. I'll run it off you at PT tomorrow." I moved to the cash register, neck blotchy.

"The colonel told me at lunch that staff officers don't have to go to PT. Not the ones who max the tests, anyway." Logan's face brightened again, like a fantastic idea had just occurred to her. "But I can keep coming if you need the support?"

"It would be awesome if *all* the staff officers came to PT," I spluttered, my passive-aggressive comments eroding my stomach lining like pure hydrochloric acid. "Lead by example and all that."

"I can do that." Logan said this like she was granting me a favor, and I marveled at how quickly two female soldiers could develop a history with each other.

The woman behind the counter handed us our bags—mine small and light, Logan's full of deep-fried goodness. I loitered in front of the Army-Navy store until Logan's Mustang thundered out of the parking lot, then turned to trudge the last humid half mile along the shoulder of the road. I should have played the charade out to the end and asked Logan to give me a ride, but I didn't want her to see my apartment complex in case it wasn't as nice as where she lived. Logan was a constant, bitchy reminder of everything that was deficient in me. As I walked I indulged in a large helping of loathing for her. I was no Carl Rogers.

My apartment was still and dark, just like the Headquarters Company building except for Rambo slinking wraithlike from the bedroom. "Hey, Sly Stallone." I picked him up and gave him a hug and a kiss. "At least somebody loves me." He wriggled out of my arms, only wanting to be let out on his evening stroll. I sighed, open the door for him, washed my hands, and rooted through the takeout. A greasy paper bag rested on top of the carton of vegetables—the lady at Lucky China had given me Logan's wontons by mistake. Or maybe she was one of those nice, nurturing people who wanted to feed the world. Maybe she'd seen more than I was giving her credit for, observing how I'd run to her shop and ordered the skinniest menu possible. Maybe she was the kind of person who would accept me without trying to re-shape me. The possibility made my eyes sting with tears.

I popped a wonton in my mouth and bit down with a satisfying crunch. I could've called Logan to say I got part of her dinner order; I'd updated the battalion recall roster myself, right before I handed over the reins of personnel. But I was hungry and couldn't stand Logan. *Take that*, I crunched. Skinny people could eat what they wanted, but I could not. *And that.* I ate every bit of the evidence of Lucky China's mistake and then ate my vegetables. I was dying of thirst but instead of drinking a glass of water, I pulled one of the last three beers from the fridge. I'd already blown my diet with the wontons so why the hell not.

The first beer went down easily so I cracked another. I opened my fortune cookie and ate it even though it tasted like folded cardboard. *Remember this date in two months!* the slip of paper said. *Your life will change!*

"You're damn straight it will," I said to the empty apartment. I opened the cupboard to see what else there was to eat.

A GREAT ARMY DAY

The phone rang next to my head and I rolled to answer it, the air mattress groaning under my weight. The room was pitch black except for the glowing blue face of my alarm clock that read two thirty. This could not be good.

"Lieutenant Mills," I croaked, still feeling the effects of my weird binge from the night before.

"Good morning, Lieutenant Mills!" the Old Man's voice boomed in my ear. "Thought I'd start Tuesday off with a random piss test. Activate your recall roster and I'll see you at the gym ASAP."

Shit. Usually a battalion commander let company commanders know ahead of time if an alert was coming down the pike. Not at zero-dark-thirty along with everyone else.

"What's the uniform, sir?" For all I knew we could be peeing into cups and then walking onto a C-5 Galaxy, on our way to Yugoslavia and the hell with my Korea plan.

"Just PT uniform." He hung up.

Shit shit shit. My body moved in all directions at once. My hands reached for my discarded T-shirt, shorts, and running shoes. I cursed living out of a duffel bag and having to wear a smelly PT uniform even as I pulled the company roster from under the phone and dialed.

"First Sergeant? It's Lieutenant Mills. Can you call the NCOs? We have a urinalysis. Uniform is PT and we're meeting at the gym."

"Yes, ma'am." First Sergeant's voice went from drowsy to focused in an instant. We hung up and I began to call the staff officers, starting with the S-1.

Logan's phone rang and rang—where could she be at 2:32 in the morning? Was she a super-deep sleeper, or spending her nights elsewhere? Had she been on her way to a date when I saw her at Lucky China? I didn't have time to worry about her, though. Lieutenant Perfect could answer to the Old Man about why she couldn't be reached during a battalion recall.

I phoned the S-2, S-3, and S-4 staff officers, waking wives and kids in the process, enduring the mild swearing. I couldn't reach the S-3, either. Oh, well, that made two officers who'd get called on the carpet later. I threw my wallet and shower stuff into my kit bag. I grabbed my keys and started for the car, almost tripping over Rambo coming up the apartment complex stairs after night patrol.

"Got-dammit." I turned to let him into the apartment. "Sorry, buddy." I locked him in, blocking his reproachful face because I didn't have even a second to pat him on the head. He'd figure out why I was apologizing when he went to his cat bowl and found nothing but dry food. He'd let me hear about it whenever I made it home that night.

Then I remembered I'd left my car on post the day before.

"Fucking A," I moaned. "Fuckity, fuck, fuck." I could have run back upstairs to call First Sergeant or Storey, but I could also double time it toward post and snag a ride from someone driving by and probably get there faster. I hoofed it into Hinesville, trying to distract myself from the panic of being late and the fullness of my bladder. I'd learned not to pee when woken for a urinalysis. It was hard enough to fill the cup with another soldier watching.

A dirty gray sedan pulled over onto the shoulder ahead of me and I tensed, waiting for some clever comment about how I should be moving my ass every morning before dawn. A head with a high and tight poked itself out the window. "Remember that scene from *Rambo* where he's hitching a ride into Jerkwater, USA?" the head asked, smiling.

It wasn't Brian Dennehy but a sergeant who worked in one of the maintenance companies. "Little early for a ruck march," he said as I buckled in.

"It's gonna be a great Army day," I grumbled. Usually I was the annoyingly perky one during a recall, but the Old Man had caught me off guard with this one and the best I could do at that moment was to shift away from the seatbelt and pray I could hold my bladder until we got to post.

We pulled into the parking lot in front of the Corkan gym, a holdover from Fort Stewart's origins in the buildup to World War II. Paint peeled from the wooden exterior; extractor fans roared like angry giants in a vain attempt to cool the inside air. I liked to think of the legions of soldiers who'd come before me, the ones who'd lain on the same duct-taped weight benches and shuttled back and forth on the squeaking basketball court. Those who'd run up the bleachers and pushed down against the floor boards. I was among the uniformed multitudes who'd swung through the door of that gym. This was a place I'd made a mark, and crappy as it was, I loved it.

I thanked the sergeant for the ride and inhaled what would probably be my last cool lungful of air for the day, faintly seasoned with salt from the far away ocean. A mockingbird trapped in a nearby holly bush sang its heart out instead of trying to escape. The need to pee was too overwhelming to appreciate any of it and the random nature of this urinalysis had me paranoid. A urinalysis was an inspection and the rulebook was clear—you couldn't search just one soldier's car, or barracks room, or bladder, on the suspicion that he was up to no good. A commander was on safer legal ground to piss the whole battalion to catch the one dirtbag who'd smoked more than cigarettes in Savannah over the weekend. I wasn't a dirtbag, but I tended to feel guilty for things even when they weren't my fault. And the Old Man hadn't told me this was coming.

Logan stood next to the door to the female latrine cradling a clipboard in her arms. It was three o'clock in the morning, but her

French braid was neat and she looked polished in her PT uniform. At least she had puffy bags under her eyes. "What's up, Logan?" I asked. It was clear what was up—Logan had known about this ahead of time. That was why she hadn't answered her phone. I yanked on my sweaty ponytail to tidy it up.

"The colonel has me observing the female soldiers," she said. "You want to sneak in first before everyone else gets here?"

She handed me a sample cup wrapped in plastic and waved me into the latrine. I was grateful not to have to perform in front of one of the gruff female NCOs from the maintenance companies, but hoped since Logan was new, she might let me pee in peace. Logan kept the stall door open (correct procedure) but propped herself companionably against the frame, which was entirely unnecessary.

"You know what you're doing, right?" I had enough working against me. The last thing I needed was to have my sample swapped with the one from GI Johnny Pothead.

"Of course I do," Logan said.

I was embarrassed at the warmth of the cup when I handed it to her and at how quickly I'd filled it. Logan, oblivious, busied herself writing the last four of my social security number on the outside. "They kept some of us at Fort Lee for a couple of months after our Basic Course," she went on. "I got trained on all the extra duty that new lieutenants get stuck with—urinalysis, running firing ranges, a bunch of stuff."

Washing my hands reminded me of the last time the two of us had shared a latrine. Logan was different this morning than she'd been at Lucky China, and different than she'd been with Pettit the day I took over Headquarters. Nervously chatty instead of cocky. I could try to be friendlier. New day, new opportunities and all that. Now that I'd made my deposit with Uncle Sam, I could pitch in—maybe run PT for everyone else while the urinalysis team finished up with the performance-shy. "Oh, the glamorous life we lead, huh?" I said.

"Should we knock out your weigh-in?" Logan released the clip on the stack of forms and began to flip through them. They were height and weight logs.

"Oh." I stood still, holding a soggy paper towel. "You're weighing people?"

Logan's cheeks pinked but she squared her shoulders and looked me in the eye. "The colonel told me to weigh all the females."

"Well, that's just fucking great." Steamed vegetables and two bottles of 333 Premium Export had only been the appetizer to my "dinner" the night before, in addition to the fortune cookie and Logan's fried wontons. I'd needed something else to grind my teeth on, to chew through the day I'd survived with Davis and Master Sergeant Jones and First Sergeant and Logan herself. Line 'em up and knock 'em down—that's what I'd done with the mystery cans of food in my cupboard. I'd rinsed their dusty tops and opened them one by one. I ate a whole can of peas and a can of shoe peg corn. The can of tomato paste was too thick to swallow on its own, so I swished it down with the third and final beer. I didn't like tomato products and I'd only bought any of those canned goods because they were the kind of food normal people were supposed to have in their cupboards, but I didn't let that stop me. I was not a normal eater.

Logan led me around to the corner of the locker room where the scale was and stood, feet planted wide, determined instead of nervous. I slipped my shoes off and stepped onto the platform. "You're still five feet, eight inches?" Logan looked up from her checklist and the two of us locked eyes.

"Leann." I made no attempt to keep the sarcasm from my voice. "My height has not changed. Which is a good thing, since I don't think you're tall enough to measure me anyway."

Logan giggled but there wasn't anything funny in that latrine that stank of sour mops. I broke eye contact first. I slid the weight to the right and flicked left to adjust. The arm on the scale stilled. Click, click went the ballpoint. I stepped off and zeroed it, then stepped back on, adjusted all the weights again until the arm balanced. *Got-dammit.*

"So that's two pounds up from last time." Logan peered at the scale and then at the weight standards chart under her checklist, and cross referenced it with my height. "Oh," Logan said as she clicked the pen one last time to write. "Oh."

"Yeah," I said, neck heating up. "'*Oh*.'" Logan was the last person I wanted to know this fact about me.

Logan straightened and jutted out her chin. "This is on me. I was talking to the colonel last night and I mentioned that I saw you at Lucky China. That's what gave him the idea for a surprise urinalysis and weigh-in."

"You were talking to the colonel? About me? On the *phone*?" If Logan had any scrap of decency, any loyalty to other junior officers, she'd have known not to mention that she'd seen me eating fast food. It didn't sound like Logan knew I'd been flagged for weight but I didn't feel like being fair. "You told him I was at Lucky China?"

"No! He called me. He just—"

I snatched the clipboard and pen out of Logan's hands and wrote my weight in big, inky block numbers next to my name, for Logan's ease of reporting that I was a lardass to the Old Man. "Did you happen to mention that all I ordered was steamed vegetables? Or did you just narc to him about me eating at all?"

"I had to get him to stop—" Logan's face was bright red but not in the least supplicant. "I'm weighing you because he told me to. All I said was—"

"Is someone here to do body fat percentages or are you a guru on that, too?" A trained sergeant measured the body circumferences of soldiers who hadn't made weight. Soldiers who carried a lot of muscle sometimes failed weight but were satisfactory with the tape measurement standards. Shumacher failed her weigh-ins but always made tape. I'd made tape last time, too, although failing on weight hadn't satisfied the Old Man's personal standards for officers.

"I'm sorry, Lieutenant Mills." Logan's fists rested on her hips. She didn't sound sorry at all. "We can ask out in the gym if there's anyone who can tape you."

"No, we do not need to make an announcement in the gym,"
I said. "And I think you've done quite enough already. I'll handle
this." I shoved the clipboard back at her and stalked out of the latrine,
impressed with myself for making a scene. It was the middle of the
goddamn night—the perfect time for blowing one's cool. It was quiet
and we were alone, and it was surprisingly easy to unload on Logan,
even with her pushing back. I'd never known another woman to argue
instead of going underground with gossip and in a weird way it made
me trust her, but I prayed she'd keep her mouth shut about my weight
until I could talk to the Old Man myself.

The latrine door squealed in protest and I almost barreled into
the battalion training officer, Jackson Bennett, his dark brown face
gleaming with sweat even though it was still early. He stopped in his
tracks. "Hey, Min." He'd always been more Captain Williams's friend
than mine, but he was an okay guy. Less of a player than some of
the other unmarried male officers. "How's it going? I'm looking for
Lieutenant Logan. Soldiers are starting to turn up and they need to
pee."

"All good." I hoped the low light masked how pissed off I was.
"And Logan's in the latrine. You can start sending the females in." I
paused. I hadn't talked to any of the other staff officers since I'd taken
over Headquarters. "How are you?"

What I wanted to ask was whether he'd heard from Captain
Williams. I'd have loved to unload on him like I had with Logan,
and not in a way that built trust. The dude had saddled me with a
nightmare. I hadn't seen him since the Friday the IG inspection results
were announced, but even the Old Man couldn't throw a captain out
of the Army—he'd have had to stash him somewhere.

"Busy morning," Jackson said, raising a stack of files, and we both
grimaced by way of a smile. He'd have a lot to do to get ready for the
summer field exercise. "How's command treating you?"

"Kicking my ass a little, but I'm kicking it right back." I neglected
to mention that I needed someone to tape me because I'd just failed my

weigh-in. Again. "I'm supposed to be doing inventories this morning."

"Ah, sorry about that. We threw a wrench in the works with this piss test."

"You knew about it, too?"

Jackson adjusted the weight of the files and didn't meet my eyes.

"Man, the staff officer mafia is letting me down," I said. This implied I'd ever been part of them to begin with.

Across the gym, waves of soldiers stood up from their seats in the bleachers. The Old Man had entered. "Sorry, Min." Jackson patted the top of the stack. "Gotta scoot. We should get a beer some time."

"Payday's Friday," I said, but I was never ingesting another calorie as long as I lived. I crossed the gym floor to greet the Old Man.

"Two pounds up, sir," I said. It was better that he heard it from me instead of Logan, and better if I accepted the consequences without sniveling or making excuses.

His face—jolly as he bounced across the gym—clouded over. "As I recall, you were over the max last time, Lieutenant." He said this as if he were informing me of a grave situation that would never have occurred to me otherwise.

"Yes, sir," I said. "I was just talking to Captain Bennett about getting taped." I rationalized the lie because I *had* told Logan I'd take care of it, and I intended to. Those two pounds were bloat from eating salty canned vegetables. If I fasted all day I should be able to shed them before close of business.

The Old Man rested a paternal hand on my shoulder and settled into lecture mode. "Eating out at fast food restaurants is not the example you want to be setting for soldiers, Lieutenant Mills. Not when you're on weight control."

"Yes, sir, I know," I said, trying to sound penitent instead of furious. Logan should have kept her damn mouth shut. Even if she hadn't told the Old Man on purpose, her offhand comment about seeing me at Lucky China was the entire reason Battalion was having a piss test that morning—to catch me in the act of being fat. "I'm as surprised and disappointed in myself as you are, sir. I've been working out really hard." There was no need to share my erratic eating habits with him. I could tell the truth without telling the whole truth.

"We need Headquarters back on its feet. It might be more critical than ever that our units are fit to fight. Don't make me regret my decision to put you in charge of this company."

"No, sir," I said. Here was another hint that something was happening with Yugoslavia. Also, he seemed to have convinced himself that he'd given me Headquarters as some kind of reward and not used it as leverage against my assignment to Korea. Had he forgotten about that? "My weight is a nonissue," I babbled. "I'll be back on track by close of business. We're doing inventories again today, and we've already started addressing training deficiencies. Headquarters is going to be squared away in no time, sir."

"See that it is. Brigade is breathing down my neck about that accountability mess." The Old Man's attention wandered. He'd caught sight of Jackson with his armload of files.

"Yes, sir." I pictured myself tearing through an entire pizza, followed by an ice cream sundae containing all thirty-one flavors. What luxury it would be to eat without commentary. "Headquarters is going to crush the field exercise and it'll all be tied up with a pretty bow for you by the end of the summer. Then I'll skippity hop right to my assignment to Korea." *Skippity hop?* I was rambling like a jackass, but the Old Man wasn't listening anyway. Maybe if I'd been a thin person, the kind of person who could eat giant sandwiches and fried rice, he'd have listened to me. Maybe he'd hear the question behind what I was saying and tell me the Korea plan was still in place.

"Yes, yes—have an outstanding day, Lieutenant Mills," he said as he turned to take his leave. Either he was suffering from selective amnesia or selective hearing. "This command is an opportunity for you to prove yourself as a leader, so for the love of god get your weight squared away. I don't want to have to counsel you for this again."

"Yes, sir." Had this been a verbal counseling? "No, sir." I needed to get on his calendar for a time of day he wasn't distracted by a thousand other things. I had to starve those two pounds off and get Logan to weigh me again at the end of the day. Ugh. What I needed was to get out of Headquarters and away from these people. For good.

CYA

My head hurt and I was tired. So tired. My cheek rested against something hard and cool, my arm wrapped painfully around the top of my head. Someone's hand was on my shoulder but I was reluctant to rise, limbs aquatic and heavy. My ears popped as I drifted, two voices pulling me upward even though I wanted to sink back down into the silt, to bump along the murky bottoms, pulled this way and that by the tides and river traffic, forever.

" . . . she's so mad at me and got all up in my face. But the colonel's been calling me and calling me . . . had to tell him I'd already been to dinner to get him to give up . . . And then he got huffy and said he'd make me supervise the whole . . ." The voice belonged to Logan, tightened by the whine of near-tears, but Logan was not a crybaby. Logan was ruthless.

A second voice murmured words that meant to soothe but I couldn't make all of them out. "You don't have to let it wash off you, ma'am . . ." Like water, smooth and fast-running. "The lieutenant and I can help you report—"

I blinked against the weight of my eyelids and the hand on my shoulder began to shake it.

"I think she's coming around!" Logan's voice pitched up and her face came into focus as I opened one eye. I seemed to be lying on a linoleum floor with Logan crouched next to my head. Why was Logan talking about me again? She needed to shut her trap. "Can you hear me?" Logan asked.

"What the—?" I untangled my arm and pushed myself up into a sitting position. I was behind a treadmill in the cardio room at the gym, with Logan next to me and First Sergeant huddled half a squat over. Quite a few after-work exercisers were trying unsuccessfully to mind their own damn business on other machines.

"Easy, ma'am." First Sergeant and Logan each took an arm and hauled me upright. "Paramedics should be here any minute, so you don't need to be rushing off anywhere. You came off this thing pretty hard."

I pulled my arms away from them. After slogging through a full day of inventory at the motor pool and drinking nothing but black coffee to make me pee, I'd sucked up my pride and called Logan to ask her to weigh me again. First Sergeant, so quiet in those damn soft-soled boots, had overheard. She insisted on coming along—to have a witness, she said. To keep the Old Man from thinking I'd pressured Logan into fudging the numbers—as if I would ever do such a thing. But considering all the stuff that had gone missing from the motor pool and from the supply room before that, and Davis's complaints that First Sergeant was reporting him to EO, she had a point. I had to cover my ass. At the moment it was hanging out for all to see. I wanted to throw a dumbbell against a wall.

Shumacher's face shimmered into view from earlier in the day when I'd cornered her during the urinalysis to tell her to go straight from the gym to sick call. "I actually lost a pound from all the puking," Shumacher laughed. She'd have to be taped, as usual, but her mood was buoyant. "And because my period started after all—no more bloat." So that was the end of the pregnancy scare and lucky for Shumacher. I was the one Headquarters Company soldier under the microscope for my weight and now everyone knew it. I'd been running a quick three miles on the treadmill for penance as Logan entered the cardio room. I guess I passed out.

"It looked like you were cooling down and then you just . . . collapsed."

Logan's ebony eyes were concerned, which I was too fuzzy to fight against at that moment. Military women competed against each other in the Cool Girl sweepstakes and I'd caught Logan in that power play again, this time trying to preempt First Sergeant while I was unconscious. Telling some sob story about the Old Man calling her at home. Logan was trying to ease her conscience while sabotaging my reputation in the process. Masterful.

"My head hurts." I put a hand to my forehead and all the nerve endings on the knot I found there lit up at once.

"Yeah, you, uh—" Logan scooped her arm out in front of herself, then back toward her heart. "You kind of fell forward and then slid off the back of the treadmill. I think you hit your head on the end of it. The paramedics can take you to the emergency room to get it checked."

First Sergeant crowded in, smelling like tropical suntan lotion and stress. "Your pupils look all right, but you should probably let them rule out a concussion, ma'am."

The buzzing in my ears was fading and I was ready to stop making a spectacle of myself. "I can't believe you called an ambulance," I said. "I'm fine." The Army scrutinized and judged my flawed body at every opportunity, and I'd never been happy as the center of attention. "Can we just go down to the locker room and be done with this endless fucking day?"

"You sure?" Logan asked. "You weren't out that long, but it's better to be safe than sorry."

"I have a hard head," I said. "And I don't have time to be an invalid, so you can quit it with the Mother Theresa act." I struggled to get my feet underneath me. Again, much to my annoyance, the other two had to help pull me all the way up. The floor of the cardio room tilted away, and my vision started to tunnel, but I took a deep breath and closed my eyes. This was the same reaction I had the first time my mother put me on the Cabbage Soup Diet, both of us mistaking dizzy spells for weight loss. "We're going to make you as pretty on the outside as you are on the inside," my mother had said. That first time, I'd been optimistic.

I knew better now. I wasn't hurt from my fall—I just needed to eat something. I needed to eat, and to drink about a gallon of water, and then I'd be fine. And I did not want to talk to these two skinny-bones about fasting all day—I wanted to get weighed and go home. No. I'd have to go to the commissary first because there was absolutely no food in the house. I could buy a jar of Ragu and some pasta with my last few dollars. It was either that or cat food.

First Sergeant went to meet the paramedics from Winn Army Hospital, then rejoined me and Logan in the locker room. Hands trembling, I peed and took my shoes off, and fifteen hours after the phone call that had started the day the drama was over. Wherever those two stray pounds had come from, they'd left and taken one of their friends with them. Logan entered this weight on my PT card. "I started you a new one," she said. "I transcribed everything over from your old card except what you wrote this morning. We can assume your tape from last time is the same, or even better. So technically, you're compliant."

"Not according to the colonel." I was mortified that any women at all, especially these two, were in possession of the number upon which my future hung. First Sergeant never talked, but she judged plenty from behind those tight lips and quiet boots. And scratch my earlier feeling—I didn't trust Logan farther than I could throw her. But everything hurt, from the lump on my forehead all the way through my entire midsection. My legs wobbled, and not from relief. I was so hungry I felt weepy. "I guess I should tell him I'm a pound closer to my goal weight." I wasn't sure I could make myself move in the direction of the Old Man's office.

"He's in meetings with Captain Bennett," Logan said. "Or at least he was when I came over here. I can leave him a note when I get back to Battalion if you want. I won't tell him what happened, just that you're back on track."

What was Logan's game? Was she putting on an act because First Sergeant was there? Some women were diabolically good at rallying every other woman to hate you. But I couldn't control Logan's mouth, and I

had to let her do her job. "Thanks," I said ungraciously. "I appreciate it."
I needed food, and to go home and check on Rambo. But I was going
to talk to the Old Man, and very soon, to make sure he heard the Lucky
China story the way I wanted to tell it and to remind him that he'd
promised I could leave Fort Stewart the minute we aced the field exercise.

"Lieutenant Mills?" Logan asked. She shot a glance at First Sergeant.

"Call me Min," I sighed.

"Oh, right." Logan's laugh was not that of a schemer, but one with
a favor to ask. "Min. Uh, First Sergeant St. John said you could help
me with something. A company commander thing."

SMART BOMBS

"**S**mart bombs." Leann's mother paused in front of the television to scoff at the nonstop coverage of General Schwartzkopf. To sneer at the so-called surgical precision with which the tidy little war was being waged. "There's nothing smart about a bomb." She was carrying Leann's acceptance letter to Cornell, and the documents offering her an ROTC scholarship to pay for it, into the kitchen. Leann wasn't sure whether her mother was going to read them over the phone to someone or set them on fire.

She agreed with her mother about the bombs, thinking about the guy with no legs in Saigon and other Vietnamese people, young and old, the absence of limbs more noticeable than intact appendages. She thought about the buildings and villages still creeping toward restoration, and how people couldn't go exploring or till their own soil without encountering the destructive forces that had rained from the skies or been emplaced and left behind so many years ago. Bombs were never smart. But Leann liked Norman Schwartzkopf. He reminded her of herself. There would always be wars, so it was better they were run by people who stood up straight and took up space, who weren't afraid to speak their minds and who, by the force of their presence, made other people feel safe.

America didn't see Leann that way. For the third grade play she'd demanded to be Oz, the Great and Powerful. Not the wimpy guy behind the curtain at the end—she was going to be the one with the dry ice and booming voice. She'd been enraged when Mrs. Chandler cast her as fucking Toto. Her mother apologized to Mrs. Chandler when Leann refused the part using those exact words. She waved her hands as if to say, "What can you do with such a stubborn child?"

"Lots of children want to be the wizard," Mrs. Chandler had said. When Leann stuck out her jaw Mrs. Chandler said, "But you're so cute. You'd make an adorable Toto."

Leann looked away, arms folded, unrelenting.

"But you can be Oz if you want."

"Not the one behind the curtain," Leann said, like she was the one granting favors.

It was Mrs. Chandler's turn to throw up her hands.

Laughter bubbled up in Logan's chest to think about it, even now.

At home her mother had said, "You did right, my girl. You are no one's little dog." They still said this to each other when the world underestimated them.

CLOSE ENOUGH FOR GOVERNMENT WORK

Two days later Storey and I took the soldiers to the training area to practice land navigation—the mathematics of azimuths and pace counts and the art of deciphering terrain features on topographic maps. At Fort Stewart this consisted of stomping through hills of fire ants, getting cut by saw palmettos, and trying not to lose a boot in the sucking mud while also trying to find rusty can lids nailed to loblolly pines in the thousands of acres outside of main post. Beetle Bailey hadn't called it Camp Swampy for nothing, and if the results from the last field exercise were any indication, we were going to lose a few soldiers to the swamp.

"What a waste of time," Davis complained. "If we go to war we're just going to be in a shed somewhere, fixing broke shit faster. Instead we're out here playing Last of the Fucking Mohicans." I pulled a small green notebook from my cargo pocket and scribbled a note. Enough of trying to convince Davis of my ability to hammer down. It was time to start documenting his lack of professionalism.

"Everybody needs to know how to navigate with a map and compass, Sergeant Davis." First Sergeant said. Her patience with motor pool drama had worn thin. "It's a life skill, and a metaphor for this whole company right now." It was so unusual for her to address Davis directly that he shut up. It was probably only temporary, but I'd take it.

The soldiers practiced their pace counts between two trees on a sandy tank trail, then I handed them slips of paper with a series of grid coordinates to find and sent them on their way. After a few minutes, Storey and First Sergeant faded into the woods to give the less skilled soldiers a hand if they needed it.

I sat on the tailgate of First Sergeant's military Blazer slapping mosquitos, glad to have Davis's angry, anxious face out of my line of sight for an hour or so. Since the inventories, none of the motor pool soldiers had been cooperative. Even Washburn had begun taking attitude cues from Davis, although his demeanor changed from sullen teenager to whipped puppy whenever Shumacher was around. In a complete switch-up considering how adamant she'd been about staying in the maintenance bays, Shumacher had volunteered to take over the tool room. Maybe she was putting distance between herself and Washburn, and if it kept motor pool equipment from going missing, who was I to say anything? I had bigger fish to fry.

At the gym on Tuesday, Logan had asked me to lodge a complaint against the Old Man, whose invitations to lunch had escalated to calling her at all hours. Sexual harassment wasn't something I could turn a blind eye to even when it was our mutual boss who was doing the harassing. Logan was a Headquarters Company soldier and I'd support her—but with my assignment to Korea teetering in one direction and a possible mission to Yugoslavia in the other, this was an especially precarious time to be pissing the Old Man off.

"You're sure you want to do this?" After Logan had apologized for telling the Old Man she saw me at Lucky China, the temperature among the three of us in the latrine had shifted toward the slightly more chilled—but I was still nervous. An EO complaint would make all our lives harder. "You realize if you go public, they'll take you out of your job, right? We could make it anonymous."

"He's the one they ought to remove from his job," Logan fumed. She'd only told the Old Man she'd already eaten—"Lieutenant Mills was there, sir. Ask her!"—to deflect his dinner invitation. And Logan wasn't, as it turned out, going to be trifled with. "For once, I want to make a guy uncomfortable."

First Sergeant nodded but her lips made a straight line. After all of Davis's pot-stirring about her reporting him to EO she must have had some thoughts on the current situation, but as usual she wasn't sharing them. "Let's give that office some actual business," she said, her voice resigned and her arms clamped tight around her ribcage. "Although I'm with Lieutenant Mills, ma'am. Your life is the one that'll get hard if you confront the colonel head-on. We can still make him sweat with an anonymous complaint."

Although Logan wanted to bring down big heat, I made the call on her behalf and asked to withhold her identity. We hunkered down in anticipation of a storm but so far the Old Man hadn't even clouded over. He was spending a lot of time with Captain Bennett, running scenarios for the field exercise and the possible humanitarian aid mission to Yugoslavia. None of us had been called into his office. He was leaving Logan alone.

So, to spend a morning in the woods was a welcome reprieve from that source of tension, even if the bugs and Davis were more obnoxious than usual. There was something supremely satisfying about carrying what I needed on my back, the quiet of trees and nothing but the click of ants' jaws to interrupt the shush of my boots through pine needles. When I was the adjutant I used to volunteer to pull overnight duty in the tactical operations center during field exercises, even though I could have avoided going to the field altogether. But today felt like I was crawling under barbed wire on my back, watching the arc of tracer rounds dip closer and closer to my nose. There would be repercussions with the Old Man. He'd be even less supportive, just for starters, and even more "motivating" in his comments about my body, and more publicly. His behavior around Logan might both escalate and burrow further underground—a passing hand on her shoulder, her waist, her ass—of such subtlety as to be vociferously deniable.

Logan was in danger, yet my feelings toward her were as tangled as the scrubby undergrowth. There'd been too many times that women or girls tilted the mirror onto a view I never imagined possible. An endlessly distorted funhouse I couldn't find my way out of, much less my one real reflection. I couldn't remember a single time when I felt sure of my place among those who should have been my own.

When I was six my mother had taken me to a father-daughter dance. I stood by a punch table in another school's cafeteria admiring the clusters of pink frosting flowers in each corner of a giant sheet cake. "Brownie Troop 41 Father-Daughter Dance May 1975" was written across the top in flowing pink script, which I studied so I could practice the cursive later. The F looked like half of an anchor. I swirled the full skirt of my dress back and forth to make the petticoats swish underneath, the pale blue skirt shimmering in the overhead lights. I pinched the iridescent fabric like my mother had in the store and rubbed it between my thumb and forefinger like my mother rubbed the bills when she'd opened her wallet at the cash register. "Why don't we put this on my card?" she'd said, suddenly and cheerfully, to the lady behind the counter, who smiled for the first time since we'd come in. My mother had asked a lot of picky questions. When she did that she usually left without buying anything, but on this day, after she announced that she'd be using her new credit card, she bought me the most beautiful dress in the shop and a pair of patent leather shoes with real high heels. "A girl going to her first dance ought to wear heels," she said. The lady wrapped the shoes in tissue paper and handed me the box like a sacrament. My mother signed the receipt with a determined flourish, bearing down hard on the pen like I did when I was trying to do my best handwriting.

The punch tasted like Hi-C, not that we ever had that at home. I wondered when the Brownie leader would cut the cake. I wondered what my mother had gone to check again in the ladies room. She'd brought a large garment bag with two hangers poking through the top and had been down to the bathroom twice already to make sure it was still there, each time leaving me to "make a new friend, Minerva." I was too shy to talk to the other girls. My mother's relationships with the wives of missing soldiers were forged in shared experience and she was perplexed that I didn't have a circle of friends but didn't tell me how I was supposed to go about making them except for bringing me to this other school, this other Brownie troop, even though I was a year too young. I was worried about lying about my age but hoping to find at least one other girl who was allowed to whittle sticks with a pen knife, who liked to climb trees and play in the creek. A party for prospective scouts might be the place to meet someone like that, away from the pressures of flavored lip gloss and pretending not to be good at the monkey bars of my own school playground.

A group clustered around a girl and a man I assumed was her father since they had the same walnut-brown faces and both wore long vests. The mumble of their conversation changed tenor and my grip slipped on the plastic cup as my mother emerged from the bathroom wearing my father's old Army uniform. She must have altered it with her sewing machine, because my father was a tall, big man—a fact she mentioned whenever she lamented why I was so big for my age. It wouldn't be long before I weighed more than she did, my mother had said as she tugged at the waist of my new dress, but at least in this case it might help me find some friends. Her words were light when she'd said this; it was preferable to be small and delicate. Maybe I'd be more like her when I grew up, petite and popular.

My mother's polished shoes squeaked on the linoleum as she swaggered toward me. Heads leaned together and hands raised to shield people's mouths, but I only had eyes for her. When she was halfway across the hall I could see she had painted a curly mustache on her upper lip, like a cartoon villain. She was giggling so hard her eyes watered, and in that moment I forgot I was an outsider. I felt sorry for the other girls, whose fathers were boring instead of birdlike and endlessly amusing.

One hand was in my mother's pocket but she removed it and held it, palm up, bowing in front of me. "May I have this dance, my lady?" she said as the opening piano notes for "Lady," by Styx, came over the speakers. I giggled too and put my cup down and we sashayed to the middle of the room.

"It's the perfect song for you!" my mother called over the music. Other girls and their fathers joined us on the dance floor, but heads turned toward us. My mother held our hands up so I could spin. My skirt was beautiful under the lights, and I had the best mother, a mother who would sign me up for scouts because she knew I wanted to be like Juliette Gordon Lowe, the first American Girl Scout. A mother who bought me a GI Joe to date my Barbie and let me pull down branches from the trees in our yard to build my own hooch. One who pretended to twirl her mustache and waggled her eyebrows to make me laugh. Singing with my mother was our special, private pastime, and for the moment it didn't matter that I didn't have a father. My mother gave me all the love I needed.

After that song was over we stayed on the dance floor because the troop leader in charge of the music put on "Boogie Shoes," by K.C. and the Sunshine Band. Some of the fathers tugged their daughters to the sidelines, but my mother and I had come to show each other off. To be with each other was our favorite thing, and those fathers didn't even know the words.

My mother said she was thirsty after the second dance, though, when the music changed moods yet again. Feeling grown up, I suggested she try the punch.

"Good idea." Without thinking, my mother swiped at her sweaty upper lip and her mustache smeared. Her eyes had lost their sparkle. "I don't like this song."

A lady I didn't know was singing about saying a little prayer, and the Black dads and girls came out onto the floor just as the White dads were leaving it. This Brownie troop was made up of girls from several different schools and there were more Black people in the cafeteria than I'd ever been in the same room with. There were only two Black girls in my whole school and although one of them and I played football and other rough games with the boys, the two Black girls ate together at lunch. It seemed natural that the Black dads and daughters have the dance floor to themselves for a song. Fair.

I'd lost my punch cup but my mother got us new ones and she didn't even scold me about being wasteful. We sipped reflectively as the Black fathers and daughters sang to each other. They looked happy to be together, and although moments before I had lacked nothing as I danced with my dressed-up mother, resentment tugged at me. These girls had fathers and I did not and that was *not* fair.

"I need to powder my nose," my mother said when the song finished. She'd gone a few steps when the walnut-brown man I'd seen earlier, long vest swinging, walked over and laid a hand on her arm. He ducked his head to look my mother in the eyes. He wasn't angry, but he wasn't smiling, and I held my breath. More than a few necks swiveled to watch a Black man approach the White woman dressed in a cut-down uniform.

"We just finished evacuating the Marines from the Embassy two weeks ago," the man said. Diamonds of sweat sparkled in the curly hair at his temples. There was no question mark at the end of his statement but it was still a question.

"I am aware." My mother glanced down at his hand on her arm and he dropped it. It had been six years since my father went missing, my whole life. I didn't understand what the man was saying except that when adults talked about Marines, it was about Vietnam. My desperation to hear overrode how unprecedented it was that in 1975, in this cafeteria-turned-dancehall, a Black man should address a White woman with confidence. Not deference; not aggression—although that was the source of fear that swept through the cafeteria as soon as he left his circle of friends and walked toward my mother. That fear slammed into my heart—but this man exuded a quiet assumption that he had the right to speak, which rendered everyone else speechless. "We should be proud of trying to help for as long as we did," my mother said, chin lifted. "And ashamed about leaving so many of our own behind."

"I'm very sorry for your loss, ma'am." His eyes flicked over the patches and insignia on the uniform jacket and then to me. He wasn't lying about being sorry, but there was something he knew that my mother did not, and I waited to see if he would say what it was. I didn't know any soldiers, only the wives of missing ones. I hadn't thought there was anything wrong with my mother dressing in my father's uniform until that moment. She was mother and father. She was everything. "I was there," the man said. "I lost some good friends. But the Vietnamese people didn't want us there. And they didn't need us to tell them what to think."

"My husband is not lost." My mother began walking toward the ladies' room. "And you're a disgrace to democracy if you think my husband's service, and yours, were for nothing."

His face flushed and his eyes showed an emotion that was new to me. They were sad, but also hurt and angry as he watched my mother march across the gym. His shoulders were squared and so were hers.

I swirled my punch cup and the Hi-C splashed down the front of my dress. I dabbed at it with a napkin but that made the stain sink in more.

"Don't worry, honey," the troop leader behind the punch table said. Her voice was shaking. I was only six, but I felt the tension swell in the cafeteria, and then ebb—slightly—as my mother walked out of it and the man returned to the group of Black families. "Get your mama to pour some club soda on that when you get home."

"Yes, ma'am." I was going to be in so much trouble. My mother would say I was making a spectacle of myself, which I knew was bad even though I didn't wear glasses.

"Would you like the first slice of cake? It's a corner piece."

I'd lost my appetite but accepted the plate the troop leader handed across the table, setting my cup down to balance the little plate on one hand while I ate with the other. It was a big piece, prime cake real estate with all the pink roses clustered in the corner. I wasn't used to sweets and my throat closed around the first glob of frosting.

"Is your mother a man?" The girl who matched the man who'd spoken so boldly to my mother came over with a herd of other girls for their slices of cake and stood with her hands on her hips. In contrast to my dishwater-blond wisps, this girl's hair was thick, parted down the middle and twisted into plaits fastened at the ends with bright plastic balls. What I'd thought was a deep red maxi skirt was long, flowing trousers. I felt babyish in my full skirt with the polyester petticoats. Juliette Gordon Lowe would have worn elegant trousers instead of some baby dress. I could see why this girl was the boss of the cafeteria that smelled like smashed green beans. I swallowed hard against another ball of cake. I shook my head no.

"Then why does she dress like one?"

I had no idea what to say to this girl who might as well be from another planet. I wanted to tell her that even if my mother was silly, at least my father wasn't unpatriotic like her father was. I didn't trust myself to say "unpatriotic" around my mouthful of icing. I wasn't even sure what it meant, only that it was bad. As I shrugged, my overloaded plate wobbled, then tipped. I tried to catch it but the corner piece of cake with its top-heavy pile of flowers fell onto my dress and slid down the front, then landed frosting-side-down on the floor. Girls backed up all around me like I had rabies. My cheeks and neck turned as scarlet as the girl's trousers.

"Good lord, Minerva, what have you done?" My mother arrived in the middle of the group, made a quick assessment and concluded that I was at fault. She was back to wearing the plain wrap dress she'd come in, but a gray shadow of mustache remained on her upper lip, and I was embarrassed for her as much as I was for myself. As my mother knelt next to me with a wad of napkins, there was a smell of something stronger than perfume coming from her, like unwashed glasses left in the sink overnight.

"I dropped my cake, Mama," I whispered. Mercifully, most of the girls had turned back to the punch table but the boss girl was still staring. I hated them all. I hated Brownies and never wanted to come back, not even to go camping with these girls who probably just wanted to sing stupid songs around the fire and not learn how to be real scouts.

"I see that," my mother snapped. "And you've ruined this brand-new, very expensive dress."

"Yes, ma'am." In that moment, I hated my mother, too, for dressing up and pretending to be a soldier and for bringing me to this place where we could be laughed at. I hated the walnut-brown man who didn't look like a soldier but was one—or had been one. I hated him for knowing something true about my father but not saying what it was. I hated that he was there, and my father was still in Vietnam. Mostly I hated myself for being the wrong kind of girl in every way. My arms were not willowy and my ribcage was too wide. I wasn't interested in the right things and could never think of the right thing to say, not that anyone was listening. I'd been proud to think of myself as my mother's special girl, had taken solace in our zany orbit of two, but now I was ashamed.

And now, twenty years on, my relationships with other women were still prisms and kaleidoscopes with no clear views. Negotiating male-dominated spaces was to tiptoe through a minefield—except the obstacles I approached most cautiously were other women. I got the definite sense Logan was disappointed that I'd watered down the complaint to EO, but we might have caught glimpses of each other's true selves in the latrine the other day and neither of us had run away screaming. She hadn't laughed, or tattled, or been weird. I'd stuck my neck out and she hadn't lopped off my head. It was a start. A twinge of optimism like a mosquito bite, quick and itchy.

When it came to First Sergeant I still didn't really know what I was looking at—only that there was stuff going on that I was supposed to be seeing but just wasn't. I tended to figure out where things stood after I fell over them in the dark. She was right when she'd told Davis that the skills for finding one's way around a forest or swamp were a metaphor for life, and I kept stumbling forward. Before the soldiers had gotten in the trucks that morning, I addressed the rumors about an impending trip to the Balkans. I admitted I didn't know if the rumors were true but promised them I wouldn't keep information from them as I learned more. The concern on their faces indicated they were taking the rumors seriously. I hoped that translated into them finally taking training seriously.

I waved gnats from in front of my face as cicadas screamed in the background. I never thought about cicadas until I was somewhere enclosed, like the inside of a vehicle or an office, then my ears rang with the vibrations of their wings.

Twigs cracked off to my right and Washburn walked out of the woods. Pine branches weighed down with Spanish moss bent to shake hands over his head, the light filtering through them yellowish on his skin and accentuating the shadows under his eyes. "How's it going out there, Washburn?" He'd failed land nav the last time the company did the course, so I'd given him my personal, high-speed compass instead of an Army-issue one.

"It's going." Like Davis and some of the other motor pool mechanics, Washburn had been neglecting to call me ma'am. I didn't know why he was being disrespectful—he wasn't going to owe any money because of the inventories. He drove First Sergeant's military Blazer and of course nothing had gone missing from that. "I even found a few of my points."

Appearing between the trees behind Washburn with a thermos cup in one hand, serene among the mosquitos, First Sergeant cleared her throat. She'd told me that morning that I needed to address how lax the soldiers were in my presence. Passive-aggressive anger at being held to Army standards, and chummy familiarity when speaking to an officer, was a bad combination in her book. I didn't disagree. I'd walked the talk with these soldiers for two weeks now, sweat alongside them at PT, stayed late and come in on weekends to complete paperwork. I was scratching bug bites during Sergeants' Time while every other officer stayed back in the climate-controlled comfort of main post. Officers shouldn't demand customs and courtesies before they'd earned them, but I'd paid for my honorifics and it was time to remind the soldiers of that.

"It's going, *ma'am*," I said, trying to be gentle.

Washburn's blue eyes, offset by those white eyebrows and his sunburned face, blazed. "It's going, MA'AM!" he barked. He unfolded his soggy sheet of grid coordinates and slapped it down on the tailgate, smacking my compass on top of it. He walked over to a fallen log that served as the seating area for the land nav course, propped one boot on it and dug in a cargo pocket for his cigarettes and lighter.

Adrenaline zoomed through my bloodstream, and I wished I had a corner piece of frosted cake to smash into Washburn's face. I was sick of smartasses. *Breathe*, I told myself. *Don't let one stressed-out soldier get under your skin.* Washburn was only a kid. Maybe Shumacher had told him to take a hike and if so, he'd be upset. I reached for Washburn's score sheet, hand shaking only a little, and checked his answers against the master list. "Good job," I said. "You got all but one of your points. Somehow you missed Juliet, which wasn't far from Mike, where you landed. You still wound up here. That gives you a satisfactory score."

"Close enough for government work." Washburn flicked ash off his cigarette. "When I saw the port-a-potties I knew the end was nigh." The grunts hadn't had sky blue toilets to scout for when they were in the Saudi desert or the jungles of Vietnam, but at least Washburn had improved on his last attempt. First Sergeant cleared her throat again.

Washburn's bolts did need tightening, but he had tried to keep me from being pelted with pink food. I attributed his mood swings to misguided loyalty to Davis, and to how thoroughly Shumacher was blowing him off. I could cut him some slack. "Fill your canteen?" I gestured at the five-gallon can next to me.

He tipped the can to get some water as Private First Class Robinson, one of the cooks, walked out of the tree line. She'd missed one of her points, too, but I gave her credit. On the field exercise it would be me and the senior NCOs who navigated and made decisions. It wasn't necessary to be a perfectionist as long as the junior soldiers' performance was good enough. You had to pick your battles, and this wasn't one as far as I was concerned.

Soldiers trickled back and after thirty more minutes Storey sounded the air horn to summon the stragglers. He handed out bag lunches we'd picked up from the mess hall. "Plain baloney on white." Washburn opened his sandwich to inspect it. He'd taken his Kevlar helmet off and his crew cut stuck up at odd angles. "The Army hates me."

I opened my mouth to tell him he ought to be grateful there was such a thing as a free lunch in the Army—I was so tired of pasta and Ragu, a plain baloney sandwich sounded fantastic. And it could have been worse. I could have trundled out a case of MREs like Captain Williams had. Before I could think of how to scold him, First Sergeant walked over to Washburn and popped him on the sweaty head. "You need to square yourself away, Private." Without waiting for a response she went back to her seat in the cab of her Blazer and took a self-righteous bite out of her own sandwich.

The rest of the company, sitting on logs or on the sandy ground around the vehicles to eat their lunches, burst out laughing. Shumacher had to lean against the tailgate of her two-and-a-half ton truck, holding a hand to her lower belly to support herself. Even Davis laughed, happy to let Washburn take the heat for the pot he'd set to boil.

Washburn's face turned red, and he dipped his head just far enough to wrench my heart. I snuck glances at him as he chewed fast, thinking of all the meals I'd eaten with shame as the condiment. Washburn wasn't a super-soldier but he'd done okay on the morning's task. Wasn't that good enough for a nineteen-year-old? Or maybe I was being too even-handed in my judgment and Washburn *was* playing his whole life for jokes. I needed everyone to be serious, but that swat to the head spoiled my appetite and the fledgling goodwill developing between First Sergeant and me.

I rolled my lunch bag closed, threw my apple core into the underbrush and gathered up the score sheets. Land navigation didn't matter. Disrespect didn't matter. Getting away from Fort Stewart—that was what drove me through the day. To my way of thinking, First Sergeant was picking the wrong battles. But sometimes you didn't have to pick a battle at all. And for the moment, I was tired of fighting.

WIND STORM DARIA

The wind had a different destination in mind for Indigo than the payphone on the corner, but she tacked against it and pulled the door open with effort. The Criminal Investigation Division would be monitoring her home phone calls until she left Germany for the States. Not because they didn't trust her, the chief and the commander were quick to say. It was for her own safety, and for that of the community.

"They're making it seem like I was involved, Wolfgang." She'd been trying to reach him for more than a week. "Even though I went to them with what I know, they're turning it around on me."

"Involved in what, Schatz?"

"Please don't play dumb." Indigo raised her voice over the wind outside the booth. "We don't have that kind of time."

"No one was hurt," Wolfgang said, testing the waters.

"Actually, a couple of careers are going to be obliterated," Indigo said. "One of which is mine if you don't tell them that I had nothing to do with any of it."

"But you brought me to a military function." His voice reached through the receiver and stroked her cheek playfully. "You were most definitely involved."

"Not intentionally! Wolfgang, please—"

"I have been thinking about doing some traveling," he said. "It sounds like this would be a good time for it. But I'd like to see you before I go."

Indigo put another Deutschmark into the phone. "It's better for both of us if you don't," she said. What if someone saw him entering or leaving her house? Everyone on her street peeked around those damn lace curtains. "Besides, the wind's kicking up. It's not safe for you to be out on a motorcycle."

The coin bounced its way down into the machine. "Are you at a payphone, Schatz?" Wolfgang feigned hurt. "We are at the point where you can't have any trace of me in your life?"

Indigo spoke fast for fear he'd hang up on her. "Did you do it?"

Wolfgang didn't respond and Indigo imagined him cocking his shaggy head to look at her, to gauge where she was going with this.

"It's just for me, for my own peace of mind," Indigo said. "In a weird way I'd feel better knowing it was you. I would think there was some deeper meaning behind it than the obvious message of hating women."

"Yes." Like a foot stomp.

"Yes what?"

"Yes, it is good for people to heed the lessons that history provides us. Yes, it is good for women to feel powerful. Not necessarily powerful in the ways men define it, but yes, to claim their aggressive nature as an equal half of the human animal species."

It was Indigo's turn to pause. How much had he deliberately played her and how much had he just gotten lucky? When she hung up she knew he'd come anyway, so she fished another coin out of her pocket and dialed the desk sergeant. She should have known better than to ever, ever trust this man. She'd never be such a fool again.

SQUARED AWAY

First Sergeant sent the soldiers straight to motor stables, telling the other NCOs to release them for the day as soon as preventive maintenance was squared away. "They did pretty well out there on the land nav course," I said to her shadow as it passed by my office door after formation. The shadow paused as if deciding whether I was qualified to evaluate soldier performance and then, having completed its calculations, stepped into the frame.

"The past couple of weeks have been hard on them, and we aren't out of the woods yet. Pardon the pun. But yes, ma'am, the soldiers are starting to come around."

"Can you sit down for a minute?" It felt like inviting a new neighbor in for coffee although I was the new neighbor, the wall between our offices plastered with awkwardness. "I'm on the colonel's calendar for this afternoon and I'm nervous," I admitted. "I keep waiting for the hammer to fall."

She sat down lightly on the edge of the sofa where it would be easy to eject if her phone rang, or if the conversation got too difficult. She took a cautious sip of her coffee. "You're bringing up the complaint?"

"No!" I said. "No way. Maybe he'll want to talk about it, but I'm not bringing it up first. I need to ask him about something else."

We examined our respective coffee cups. First Sergeant was too polite, or too disinterested, to ask what I was discussing with the Old

Man if not the EO complaint. "Were you okay out there today?" I asked. Had she been a mean girl growing up, or just comfortable putting others in what she thought were their places? "I'm not saying he didn't deserve it, but you were kind of tough on Washburn."

"It takes a lot more than a few moody soldiers to get under my skin, ma'am," she said. "You have to expect the wheels to make noise even though we're starting to gain some traction." She stopped short of saying that apathy was giving ground against my pushing, but the words hovered at the end of the sentence.

"I guess so." I didn't smile at the almost compliment. No one liked when an officer took credit for what had been a combined effort.

First Sergeant made a noncommittal sound.

"Is there something else?" I'd spent a whole winter when I was eleven or twelve, feeding and creeping ever closer to a deer that lived in the woods behind my house. It took patience of minute increments to earn the trust of something—or someone—so naturally skittish.

"Yes, ma'am, there's something else." The midday sun filtering through the blinds lit her face, a chiaroscuro of fleeting vulnerability. She took a deep breath. "Soldiers are supposed to seek out opportunities to lead, but I'd stopped thinking I'd make first sergeant when the colonel approached me about taking on Headquarters."

"It's amazing to me that you had to wait so long," I said, not amazed at all. Only amazed at how loud my voice sounded. There were many reasons why she could've been overlooked for leadership, most having to do with her skin color and sex. I'd read her personnel file for crying out loud. There were reasons.

"Well." First Sergeant knew the reasons, too, not that she'd let on. "Like I said, I'd pretty much given up the possibility of making rank before retirement. And I'm grateful the Army has left me here at Fort Stewart for so long, to be closer to my family."

"Where's your home again?" Too late I remembered that officially, I didn't know where she was from, and she gave me a strange look, trying to remember whether she'd shared this information before. *Shut up and listen, Minerva*, I thought.

"Sunbury. It's off the beaten path in Liberty County, down closer to the coast. A couple of signers of the Declaration of Independence are from the same area." She didn't stray from facts we'd all seen in the welcome packet to Fort Stewart. "Sunbury used to be a port town a couple hundred years ago, but it's silted up now. You might have seen the road signs."

What she didn't say but I'd read in a library book of local history was that people who worked on the nearby rice plantations had been stolen from rice-growing areas of Africa. Because of their technical expertise, they didn't get sold away as often, and the Black communities that grew up along the Georgia and South Carolina coasts secreted themselves into private, intact townships after emancipation. A lot of African traditions remained in those communities, having morphed into their own uniquely American versions of African culture. I didn't know what those things were, only that the areas around Darien and Riceboro, the sites of former plantations, were completely different worlds than the north Georgia I'd grown up in. It was an uncomfortable but intriguing situation to contemplate, how and when First Sergeant's family might have established itself outside of Fort Stewart.

"Anyway—I've been planning what to do after retirement." She spoke slowly, thoughtfully, then sped up, like she was trying to outpace the need to discuss her personal life. "It may be a few years away, but I've been thinking about it."

"I can't imagine you retired." She would not fit in on a bar stool at the VFW with Ted's crowd, that was for sure.

"People say that." Her eyes stopped wandering the room and trained on me, causing me to shift in my seat. "But I can picture myself other places. I'm a few credits shy of my master's degree for one thing. I've been chipping away at it for years, like I did with my bachelor's."

"I didn't know." Another emotion flashed across First Sergeant's face, a reaction to being underestimated even though it made perfect sense that a smart, hardworking woman of any color, especially a senior NCO, was putting the finishing touches on an advanced degree as she retired from active duty. It delighted me to know this, in fact; I just hadn't seen any transcripts in her file. But there was no way to say this that wouldn't reveal that I'd snooped. "That's awesome," I said, neck flushed with guilt.

"Thank you," she said, with an almost imperceptible roll of her eyes. Whatever she needed from me, it wasn't my approval. "So when the colonel asked me if I'd like to take the first sergeant job it was a tough choice. I knew Headquarters would be a challenge and I wanted to take it on, but I needed to be able to get to class a night or two a week. And I volunteer at my old high school for an after-school program, teaching history that's not covered in textbooks. The colonel said he was fine with that. He'd support me doing both."

"Ah." What history did she teach that wasn't covered? I was immediately curious, but that was a conversation for another time.

"The high school kids are out for summer, which gives me time to get the company through the field exercise. But I'm watching Division gear up for this humanitarian aid mission. Nervous isn't quite the right word, but . . ."

"Ah," I said again, panic seizing my heart. She wasn't talking about a few extra hours to do school work. She wanted to bail on the same troop movement I did. I forced a smile onto my face. "How can I help? I'm assuming that a jaunt to war-torn Eastern Europe might derail your plans." My mouth formed the correct words but I wanted to snatch them back. "Do you need me to drop a hint to the colonel about his promise to you while I'm over there?"

"Yes, ma'am." First Sergeant's grip on her coffee cup relaxed, her shoulders lowered a full inch and she spoke in a rush. "I'll work my tail off until Headquarters goes, but if there's any way I could be in the rear detachment, I could finish my degree on time. I'll talk to him myself, of course, but he needs a bit of . . . softening up."

Well. I knew that. And now that she'd explained it, I *could* see her in slacks instead of BDUs, sitting on the edge of a desk and holding a roomful of teenagers in thrall. She'd have to unlearn her habit of popping smartasses on the head, but she'd be a great teacher. I could also see Headquarters falling apart without her at the helm, especially if I was heading toward Asia instead of to Yugoslavia with them. First Sergeant had put in her time and deserved to start thinking about her future. But we couldn't both stay out of the humanitarian aid mission. There was no way the Old Man would go for that.

"Consider it done. Although—" The Old Man wasn't a giant fan of either of us. This situation required extreme finesse. "Do you want to go with me to the colonel this afternoon to make sure Lieutenant Logan is all right? And to remind him what you said before, about Captain Williams and the missing equipment? We could double-check with him about the Yugoslavia rumors and his promise to you about graduate school while we're there." I exhaled. If she remembered that I was supposed to be leaving for Korea after the field exercise it had slipped her mind.

"Forget what I said about getting to the bottom of things with the missing equipment, ma'am. You and I both know the colonel isn't going to do anything about that. Let's get the paperwork squared away, request a Report of Survey and let Brigade decide what to do about the money. We've done our part by asking the questions. As far as my master's goes—just play that one by ear. If it comes up, and the colonel's not on the warpath about the EO complaint or any of the other issues, float it past him and see what he says. Otherwise we'll pick a better time."

Oh, it was going to come up all right. "Roger that," I said. But I didn't trust myself to pull this meeting off. Not one little bit.

KNEE-DEEP IN HAND GRENADES

The Old Man had a secretary, a civilian named Patsy Klein, not that anyone dared call her that. She was Mrs. Klein, or messages you left for the Old Man never reached him. God forbid some hapless staff officer sing "I Fall to Pieces" in her presence. But me and Mrs. Klein got along. We shared a loathing for country music and a habit of not being friends with just anybody, and I was sorry she wasn't there when I arrived at Battalion headquarters. I could have used her crusty presence as I entered the Old Man's office since I was the bearer of inconvenient information, and discomfort made the Old Man difficult to deal with. He'd promised Korea to me and graduate school to First Sergeant and might scrap his promises to both of us if I didn't handle this just right.

In Mrs. Klein's place—since Mrs. Klein left every day at four o'clock on the dot—Logan sat filing her nails and humming to herself, not looking at all like she feared reprisal from the Old Man. Her BDU sleeves were folded crisply to her elbows. There was no trace of dust on her boots as she pivoted out from behind Mrs. Klein's polished wooden desk, far nicer than my metal desk in the old World War II barracks of Headquarters Company. I'd left my web belt and Kevlar behind, but there was no removing the red clay from my jungle boots or the machine oil from my cuticles, residue of the preventive maintenance that Reyes and I had done on our Humvee during Motor Stables. I'd been outside in the coastal Georgia heat all day and the swamp had lodged itself in my armpits.

A gargoyle of a smile stretched Logan's features. "I'll let the colonel know you're here." She walked to the door of the inner office and rested her hand lightly on the frame, the scent of flowers accompanying her movements. "Lieutenant Mills is here to see you, sir?" As though she was puzzled and couldn't for the life of her remember that I'd asked to be put on the Old Man's calendar after she revived me on the floor of the gym on Tuesday. As if we weren't the ones to call EO to complain about him right after. I didn't care for playacting as a rule, but Logan's performance was virtuoso. This chick had brass balls.

"Come on in, Lieutenant Mills!" The Old Man's voice sounded like a carnival barker, calling out to roll a skee ball instead of preparing to discuss financial losses, training exercises, humanitarian aid missions, or his own abuse of power. His Army was a caricature of the one Logan and I were serving in. A parallel universe.

"Thanks, sir." The door closed behind us with a carpeted hush. I perched on a leather armchair, sweaty palms on my knees to keep the jitter of my boots under control. The Old Man propped his feet on top of his mahogany desk. This nudged the blotter and calendar forward and they, in turn, knocked his nameplate off the perpendicular. Between my hunger headache and the overpowering inclination to straighten his desk items, I was going to struggle to focus on the task at hand.

But before I had a chance to begin he swung his feet down. "Should we ask Lieutenant Logan to make us some coffee?"

"Uh, I'm okay, sir." An adjutant was not a secretary. I needed to teach Logan how to disappear in the late afternoon. It was a survival skill for staff officers.

The Old Man pressed the intercom and summoned Logan anyway. His chair groaned as he settled back. "So, how bad are the inventories?" he asked.

"There are a lot of things missing, sir." I shook my head and my tired brain scattered the takeout menus in my empty kitchen drawer at home.

One more pasta dinner before payday then I could buy some proper food. Maybe once I'd eaten a square meal I could organize my thoughts. "It's not any one huge, missing item but a lot of small things that add up. My mental tally so far is running into the thousands of dollars."

The Old Man grimaced. "Yes, yes. There's been some sloppy accounting. I'm waiting for the logistics folks to make their recommendations."

From the chair to my right, I swore I heard First Sergeant clear her throat, although of course there was no one there. "Sir, this is the same sloppy accounting that was brought to your attention before Captain Williams left. And now all these additional items are missing. He's left a bunch of soldiers holding the bag." I pictured Davis's angry, sweating face. The set of Shumacher's jaw. "You might be hearing from *them*."

"You know . . . " The Old Man paused when Logan entered carrying a fiberglass tray, on which was balanced three thick, white ceramic cups—unrefined touches compared to the opulence of the rest of the surroundings. A nicer set of china stood on a sideboard in Mrs. Klein's office, but Logan had opted for chow hall crockery.

She plonked the tray down on a corner of the Old Man's desk and helped herself to a cup without serving anyone else, then sat in the brown leather arm chair to my left. I looked from the other two cups to Logan. Her movements were so gleefully angry I wondered if she'd melted Ex-Lax into the Old Man's coffee and was hanging around to watch him drink it. I was glad I'd declined any.

Oblivious, the Old Man smiled his thanks and reached for a cup. "Where was I? Oh, yes—I'm all for scrupulous accounting. It's important that you're holding everyone to the highest standards. But NCOs are pretty good at making equipment layouts work, if you know what I mean. Borrowing from Peter to pay Paul. Putting a wrench here one day, over there the next. Your motor sergeant must not be very experienced with this."

On my right, the imaginary First Sergeant blew on her imaginary coffee like the softest of rattlesnake warnings. The ghost of my father settled on the arm of First Sergeant's chair. Great—the committee of my conscience was assembled.

Logan arranged her smile as though she were as curious about my response as the Old Man was. Personnel people didn't give a crap about command inventories. I sure didn't, but I was too famished to interpret the monkeyshines of both real and imagined witnesses. "Well, I haven't given the NCOs reason to think I'm messing around, sir." I was leaving these chumps far, far behind in a couple of months—mere weeks, really—but we'd be playing Army by the rules until I did. This was what the Old Man wanted from me, right? "And I don't mean to give you the impression that it's only a wrench here and there. There are bigger things. Any half-decent bean counter would notice they were missing."

"Like what?" Although I was irritated by the interruptions, Logan was asking the questions the Old Man glossed over. Her confident delivery demanded a response.

"Things from the supply room, like web belts and canteens. There are also some gas masks missing, and a jack assembly for a two-and-a-half ton truck—from a temperamental deuce and a half at that. I don't want to be stuck somewhere with that thing broken down and not have any way to get under it."

The Old Man's shiny bonhomie vanished. "Somebody pilfered a jack?"

"I'm not saying that either." Like First Sergeant, I couldn't prove anything had been stolen. "Only that it and other items can't be accounted for. And not just in the motor pool and supply room—the chow hall too." I glanced at the tray on the corner of his desk. Nobody cared about missing chow hall stuff.

"Well. There goes my speech about going easy on hardworking NCOs. I'll sign that Report of Survey paperwork as soon as it hits my inbox. It sounds like we need to make an example of some people." The Old Man's gaze trained on the middle distance, the thousand-yard stare of a man in danger of bringing heat down on his own position if news of substantial material losses reached the ears of the brigade commander.

If an example was going to be made I hoped it was Captain Williams with his finger-snapping, profligate ways, or Davis, but I worried about everyone else. I glanced at Logan, curled into the leather chair, staking her stubborn claim in the belly of the beast.

"Sir, is there enough documentation to lay the financial burden on Captain Williams's shoulders? It seems wrong to make the soldiers take the heaviest fall." Where the heck was the guy, anyway? Why hadn't the Old Man kept him around until the paperwork was straightened out?

"Well, if they wanted to stay out of hot water, they should have said something about the irregularities before now." The Old Man's mask slipped just far enough to peek over the top, but he probably didn't intend for me see a nervous expression flit across his face. He wasn't used to being held accountable, certainly not by lieutenants. We were supposed to be cowering in his presence, not the other way around.

"Sir, First Sergeant St. John brought the issue of equipment losses to your attention months ago. It was what triggered the IG inspection." I kept my tone free of supplication or flirtation or other nonsense, but my nerves were firing in every direction. I had reason to stay on the Old Man's good side and needed to move the conversation onto more important topics, but out of the corner of my mind's eye I saw First Sergeant nod. Logan was practically incandescent in the next seat over. I had people to support.

The Old Man didn't give up. It was frustrating, trying to have an adult conversation with someone who refused to drop the act. "I do not need a reminder, Lieutenant Mills. I've made several personnel changes at Headquarters Company, one of which was appointing you to lead it when it became clear that Captain Williams wasn't suitable. It's not a difficult thing to remove someone from command when he—or she—isn't working out."

Oh, shit. I sat up straighter, as if this would absorb the impact of what he might be about to say. Would it matter if he took me out of command? Would the Army send *me* to some out-of-the-way desk while they decided what to do with me? It wasn't easy to put someone straight out of the Army. God knows, I'd counseled many officers and senior NCOs in their attempts to separate soldiers who weren't cut out for military life. There had to be a reason, and it had to be well documented, and military lawyers had to be involved—and even then a battalion commander could hold the door open but needed help to boot someone through it. "You should do what you think is best for the mission, sir." It wasn't what I believed. I believed the Old Man should do what was right, which was to find Captain Williams and sock it to him. Also, he should lay off Logan. And let me go to Korea. And let First Sergeant stay in the rear. But the Army followed no rule book, not really. It more often than not ran on the whims of random lieutenant colonels, and that bitter pill made me sick to my empty stomach.

The mirage of First Sergeant shifted, and opened her mouth as if to say something. The Old Man waved a hand. "Now, now," he said, back to playing Mr. Magnanimous. "No need to be hasty. I'm very pleased with the progress you're making. We always knew this period of reform would be painful for Headquarters. I've had to do some unpleasant things to get us to this point, and now it's on you to lead your company the rest of the way. You and your first sergeant are knee-deep in hand grenades, Lieutenant Mills. Initiate that Report of Survey, and let's give the system a chance to work before we go stirring up more trouble."

"Yes, sir." I wanted to slap him awake, to knock him from his comfortable axis. Real people's ability to pay their bills hung on Brigade's decision and I wasn't sure this man who spent his days starring in the role of battalion commander understood that. But I couldn't think of what to say that would dissolve his soft, carpeted fantasy.

The Old Man's smile geared into reverse and he stood up. Logan and I rose with him, and I spoke quickly. "Sir, have you heard any more rumors about Division going on the humanitarian aid mission to Yugoslavia?" I had no opportunity to ease into it, but First Sergeant and I were going to get our questions answered one way or the other. "If the rumors are true, does that mean we'll go with them?"

The Old Man pursed his lips, no longer hiding the fact that he'd had quite enough of me for one afternoon. "We don't have official word, but I've sat in a few meetings where the verbs are becoming more . . . active, shall we say. And yes, if Division goes, the supporting units go. So it looks like you could get yourself a battlefield command, Lieutenant," the Old Man said. "What would you say to that?"

Shit shit shit. This conversation was a complete disaster. A humanitarian aid mission wasn't a battlefield command, but it *would* be good for my career to lead a company, even a small one, in a hot zone—if I cared about that kind of thing, which I did not.

"Thank you, sir." Lest he think I was agreeing, I added, "But I'm still planning to head to my Korea assignment after the field exercise." I held my breath and waited for his response. First Sergeant's retirement plans were a hand grenade, and my fingers toyed with the pull ring. Someone would stay back from the humanitarian mission. There was always a rear detachment, usually comprised of soldiers a unit could do without. It was a career risk to put oneself in that category but First Sergeant's career was winding up. She was beginning to think of herself as a free woman. I searched desperately for a way to bring this conversation off.

Hanging in the hushed, pleasant air, among the carpets, curtains and rich furniture, my ambition looked shabby compared to the glamorous alternative the Old Man was dangling. Logan's eyes locked on me. First Sergeant had risen and crossed the room and now lurked, arms folded and tapping her imaginary foot, over in the corner by the flag stand. I just wanted my damn spaghetti dinner. I wanted a shower, and a beer, and for once, someone to say yes without exacting a literal pound of flesh.

"You're still holding out for Korea?" The Old Man looked puzzled. Less jolly and not at all impressed. "Missions like this don't come along very often, Lieutenant Mills. You can go to Korea any time."

He hadn't nixed my plan outright. And it sounded like he was leaving the choice up to me, even though he didn't like what he was hearing. "Yes, sir. We'll get all the records straight and crush the field exercise, I'm certain of it. Everything should be squared away for the next commander." Make a decision and move out, that's how it was done, and I'd made my decision the minute Vietnam and the United States opened official liaison offices as a precursor to full embassies, back in January. I was getting stationed in Korea and hopping over to Vietnam whenever I could get a few days of leave to rub together. It was what I'd wanted from the minute I joined ROTC. I needed my boots on the ground of that country.

The Old Man's face didn't match his words. "I do appreciate all your hard work, Lieutenant Mills. I know I promised you could go to the ball after you finished these last few chores."

"Thank you very much, sir. It's important to me." Just another month or two of this grind then I'd go to Asia and grab that elusive whatever it was for myself, hold it in my hands and examine it at close range like Washburn studying my compass. If I was honest with myself, I was a tiny bit envious of the adventure everyone else would have in Yugoslavia. But mostly relieved—if relief was measured by the thinning of a stomach lining.

"First Sergeant St. John was telling me that she's almost finished with a master's degree in history." Another inelegant transition, but it was all I could come up with. "It got me thinking that I should go back for my master's. Military history. The Vietnam War."

The Old Man ran one hand over the flat oval of his hair and consulted his watch on the other arm. "There's not a lot of time for that kind of thing, Lieutenant."

"Oh, no, sir." My laugh was pure fakery. I flashed an embarrassed smile at Logan, who was looking at me, not in an admiring way, as if seeing me for the first time. I hadn't meant to say that about Vietnam. "The field exercise and getting the company ready for the possible mission are my first priorities. But I wanted to ask you about First Sergeant St. John. She said she'd spoken to you about doing some volunteering at a local high school in the fall?" Rushed and self-conscious in front of Logan, I kept to the point, but the Old Man's response loomed up before I even finished asking the question.

"Ah, yes, I remember." His lips pressed together. "It's the nature of these troop movements, I'm afraid. We disappointed a lot of people when we left for the Gulf, too, but the needs of the Army come first. Tell your First Sergeant she'll have to wait for next year to do her volunteering. From what I recall, it wasn't a required part of her degree, anyway."

"No, sir." All traces of relief evaporated, replaced with a straight injection of adrenaline. For one mad second I entertained the idea of sacrificing myself, of offering to go to the Balkans with the stipulation that First Sergeant be allowed to serve as the NCO in charge of the rear detachment. She deserved to prepare for her retirement years. And the Old Man was right—Korea was always an option for the oddballs who requested an assignment there.

"I'm going to need First Sergeant St. John with the company if I've got yet another new commander in there." No, he was not in a negotiating mood. "So, it might come down to a difficult decision."

This was my moment to do something noble, but my thoughts raced and misfired through my tired, hungry brain. The Old Man hadn't promised anything—his grip just as tight on my future as ever, pending Headquarters' performance in the field. But he was using stronger verbs too. We were all seeing a satisfactory outcome to everyone's hard work taking shape on the horizon. We *would* get to the point where a decision needed to be made between First Sergeant's goal and mine. And I was not a Medal of Honor type. I was going to keep my head down, just like my father had. It was a terrible fact to face about myself, but I wasn't going to sacrifice my dream for someone else's. Unlike my father, I was going to survive. "To be honest, sir, any officer will do fine in the job as long as First Sergeant St. John is in charge," I jabbered. "She can run that company with one hand tied behind her back."

Logan set her mug on the chow hall tray, head turned so I couldn't see her face. Next to the flag, First Sergeant threw up her hands in disgust and vanished, taking my father with her. I wished with every fiber of my traitorous being that I could follow them.

"I think you're selling yourself short, but you're not wrong, either." The Old Man looked at me more shrewdly than I thought him capable. Perhaps he could assess selfishness in others even though he was oblivious to signs of it in himself. "I'll keep this in mind in the event we're tasked to go."

"Yes, sir." My mind flicked through my handful of successes. The soldiers were doing better on physical fitness. They'd improved on land navigation, and I'd be there to make sure we aced that portion of the field exercise. Davis was the last angry gasp of the old Headquarters Company, but even he'd been shut up by the inventory hanging over his head. Pretty much, anyway. Headquarters had outgrown the need for me, not that they'd ever really needed me in the first place. I could leave them in good conscience as long as First Sergeant stayed in charge—but there would be no way to make my actions look less self-serving when I told her about it. She was too smart to be fooled by officer words, anyway.

"Finish your inventories and initiate that Report of Survey," the Old Man said. "We need Brigade's decision on that ASAP."

"Yes, sir."

"And keep your weight down, Lieutenant."

"Yes, sir. Thank you for your time, sir." I saluted and left without saying goodbye to Logan. Instead of elated I felt empty—empty of morals, drained of any possibility of joy. I'd talk to First Sergeant after I ate something, after consoling myself with horrific war movies and a few hours of sleep. The only good thing in my life right then was pasta and Ragu.

LOGAN, ALONE

There were no confessionals in the Fort Stewart chapel. That would have been too overtly Catholic in a space used primarily by Protestants, and Logan preferred face-to-face anyway. She met the priest in his office, where awards and decorations covered the wall, but mystery novels were mixed in with the Merton.

She minced no words. "I need something to do with my anger, Father."

Also not one to spew platitudes, the chaplain's eyes glinted. "Anger seems like an appropriate response in this situation," he said. "You were right to report your supervisor's behavior. But it doesn't feel like enough?"

"I reported him for the right reasons—to keep him from hurting people. Other women. Me. But I have this need to . . . dominate, especially people who I think are trying to get over on me. It's like I explode on the inside. I don't stop to think—I just *do*. I don't understand this about myself." Logan explained to the chaplain that nothing was happening with her report—that nothing *would* happen, but what she found most frustrating was that no one was even talking about what the colonel did. She'd made statements and spoken to representatives and received responses that were more like verbal pats on the head than reassurances that justice would be served, and the colonel hadn't said one word about it. There'd been no dust-up, no confrontation. No one's reputation was being tarnished, his or hers. Her nerve endings jangled with lack of resolution.

"This silence from your leadership—it's making you second-guess your decision to report?"

"No." Logan gripped the armrests of the chair, needing to put pressure on something. "And yes. I'm not sorry I reported him, even if he never gets in trouble." She wouldn't say his name even though the conversation was protected. She wouldn't dignify him with an identity since he'd worked so hard to deny hers. "Even if he gives me some bullshit, passive-aggressive evaluation when it's time for my OER. If he's felt even one second of discomfort, I'm glad. But I'm left with all this—" She loosened her choke-hold on the armrests. Spread her fingers wide. "Stuff."

"Well." The chaplain cleared his throat. "You didn't deserve what happened to you—even if, or even *because* you have a strong personality. So what I'm going to suggest is not penance, not for anger that's righteous. Do you understand that?"

"Yes, Father." Her eyes stung at the idea that anger could be justified. By itself, this was an absolution for all the times she'd apologized for being how she was.

"But there are some things you could do with your anger. You know the Vietnamese families that live out by Hunter?"

She did. She'd scanned the regular faces at Mass, if for no other reason than to make sure the colonel wasn't there. Most belonged to nuclear families with young children, the severe haircuts of the male soldiers a dead giveaway, but their Sunday behavior subdued in comparison to the way they tore around post during the week in their trucks and secondhand sports cars, blaring music and cussing out the windows at friend and foe alike. The chest-thump that the world, or at least Fort Stewart, belonged to the combat soldier.

Her scan had paused on faces that looked like hers and she'd crept closer to the pews those families occupied as the Sundays went by. In Vietnam people remarked on her golden-brown hair and fair skin, but so did her American relatives and acquaintances. It was controversial, being mixed, and the people at Mass were the families of South Vietnamese helicopter pilots who'd come to the area for aviation training in the early 1970s when Nixon was first attempting to extricate American soldiers from the quagmire. Then these pilots returned to the community outside of Savannah after Saigon fell, bringing their families—the heat and humidity and rice fields familiar, if not particularly homelike. They were fervent Catholics and anti-Communists. More American than anyone native-born. They spoke to her in Vietnamese and she responded in English, solidifying their opinion of her. But yes, she knew them.

"Let's put some of that excess energy to work then," the chaplain said.

FOR WHAT I HAVE DONE AND
WHAT I HAVE FAILED TO DO

Before PT formation the next day I told First Sergeant what happened in my meeting with the Old Man, my words slowed and stuttering as the expression on her face deepened into outrage. I left out the mental math I'd done in my attempt to sway him; she could deduce how badly I'd miscalculated without an explanation.

"And when he told me that at least one of us would have to go on the mission, he and I agreed that with all of your experience it would be better if it was you." At this lame attempt to be complimentary, the corner of her lip locked into a curl and she cut her eyes as if to survey the many times she'd pretended to believe an officer's falsehoods. "Because you've been to Europe," I continued. The coffee-induced bravado I'd mustered flew away from me crazily, like a deflated balloon. "And because the soldiers listen to you. They look up to you."

When I mentioned the prior tour in Europe, First Sergeant's eyebrow raised like a battle flag. We didn't talk about personal stuff; we hadn't discussed Germany. My breath caught as I waited for the accusation but all that squeezed from between her teeth was, "All right, then." She patted the side of her PT shorts as if checking for cigarettes, although there was no pocket there and she'd just as soon shoot the smokers as join them. "I've got a safety briefing to give these soldiers before the weekend."

I tried one more time to say the right thing, recognizing even as the words left my lips how ridiculous I sounded. "It's not for sure that anyone's going," I stammered. "But if you do, the mission will be the better for it."

She was halfway out the door but she turned, fingers splaying her keys like a weapon. "Ma'am, in my experience, when somebody says something is for the good of the mission it's usually what's good for them personally."

Shumacher had thrown that old chestnut back at me too. Neither of them was wrong. As long as I got my weight under the limit and Headquarters passed the field exercise, I was going to Korea. For the moment my battle was all but won. But First Sergeant held the moral high ground and that was the ultimate advantage in war.

She stalked into the day room where a group of soldiers clustered around the TV, smoking and watching CNN and waiting for formation. I followed at a remove.

"See, all them Yugoslavians've been at each other's throats for a thousand years," Washburn was explaining to the others. The soldiers nodded sagely as the pictures cut from the International War Crimes Tribunal in The Hague to scenes of people fleeing from towns in eastern Bosnia. This, although there was a nominal cease-fire. "We got no business going over there."

First Sergeant picked up the remote and the screen went blank. "Smoke outside," she snarled. "And I better not find a single butt on my grass."

"Yes, first sergeant," the soldiers mumbled. They made motions to leave.

"No butts on the grass!" Washburn said. He was trying to lighten the mood, but I shook my head. The kid never missed an opportunity to step in shit.

First Sergeant faced him, lips pulled back from her teeth. Only an idiot would have taken it for a smile. "Furthermore, Private Washburn, it's a brand-new horror every day in that country. If you paid any real attention to the news reports, you'd have seen that the Serbian army is killing thousands of unarmed civilians while the world watches. If we don't intervene, it won't stop."

Washburn stood stock-still. Soldiers loved to hold forth on subjects they knew little about, but it was unusual to be knocked off the overly simplistic soapbox. "So if you don't know what you're talking about," she continued, "I'd suggest you keep your uninformed mouth shut."

"Yes, first sergeant," Washburn whispered. No one moved until she slammed out of the room, then they meekly gathered their keys and their cigarette packs and followed her out. I remained, alone. I crossed the room and picked up the remote and turned the news back on. This time, talk of a massacre. People taken from their homes and shot; women raped. I turned the TV off. I didn't know how much time passed but somehow I was back in my office with another cup of coffee. I was missing the safety briefing and PT but couldn't make myself go. Not only had I not jumped on a grenade for First Sergeant, I'd been the one to lob it into the perimeter we'd started to build around our relationship. My father had also wrestled with the devil, at least on paper in his letters to my mother, coming across so morally preoccupied but he'd still done what he needed to do. If he and his soldiers had been ordered to cleanse Bosnian villages instead of Vietnamese ones, they'd have done it—or, wringing his hypocritical hands, he'd have sent someone else to do it. He'd have done anything—or nothing at all—to get back to his beloved wife. And in the end, feeling terrible about what he'd done, or failed to do, neither saved him nor wiped his slate clean.

GAS, GAS, GAS

E yes screwed tight and holding my breath, I bent over the ammo pouches hanging from my web belt. I slipped the butyl rubber of the gas mask under my chin, cradled it to my face, drew the straps over my head and yanked them tight. I pulled back the hood and forcibly exhaled to clear the mask—feeling, as I always did about chemical gear, more than a little claustrophobic—then pressed my hands over the filters and inhaled to seal it. It was less than a month until the field exercise and the Old Man had ordered us to add nuclear, biological, and chemical training to the line-up.

"Seven seconds." Under the shade of the tent we'd practiced setting up the day before, Storey clicked his stopwatch and the soldiers clapped politely.

They put their masks on and after Storey timed them, First Sergeant and I walked around to check the seals. My relationship with her was icy and purely professional, and the rest of Headquarters took their cues from our uneasy détente. The tension in the company ratcheted up with each day that we didn't hear back from Brigade about the Report of Survey, but Shumacher was still working in the tool room, so no more equipment had wandered off the motor pool inventory. Everyone was on eggshells and Logan was cutting me an especially wide berth. As the days dragged on, I'd told myself again and again that it didn't matter if no one bounced out of bed in the morning to get to work. We all had jobs to do, and after I was gone everyone would be happy again. The company looked better on paper and, however joylessly, was performing better on the ground. I took a grim measure of satisfaction from that.

The Old Man climbed onto the M88, where Shumacher was ready to fire up the smoke generator to simulate a gas attack. It galled me to take a page from Davis's training book, but the Old Man was as pleased as the mechanics to play with his fifty-ton toy. And more than ever, I needed someone to be pleased.

"Your hair is keeping your mask from sealing." First Sergeant tugged on Robinson's mask. Rob had gotten a sleek bob of braids put in after the last payday. She smiled as they brushed her dimpled cheeks while she jogged during PT and as she served food in the chow hall. True, they didn't strictly adhere to the regulations, but they were neat looking and cost a lot to put in, and they brought Rob pleasure. We could afford to be a little flexible now that good order and discipline were more or less restored—that was my thinking. But since First Sergeant had brought it up, I had to say something.

"You'll have them out before we go to the field, right, Rob?" I kept my voice low to prevent the sparks of conflict between me and First Sergeant from fanning up in front of the Old Man.

"We can't make exceptions for female soldiers, ma'am." I couldn't see First Sergeant's face underneath her mask but wondered what it cost her to have to come down on one of the few other Black women in the unit, especially for an issue as fraught as hair. Her head swiveled from the Old Man on the M88 to Davis, checking mask seals on the mechanics, before turning back to me. "You don't want to give anyone a reason to say you play favorites."

From the hatch of the M88, Shumacher gunned its smoke generator, and the Old Man watched the thick white clouds roll out the back of the vehicle. "This is great hands-on training, Lieutenant Mills!" He raised both thumbs in the air.

Still masked, I gave the Old Man a salute, glad he couldn't see how irritated First Sergeant and I were with each other. My face streamed with sweat. "Have them out before the training exercise, Rob," I said. Rob, eyes wide inside her mask, nodded. "The men already give the women a hard enough time, so I don't see why we should add to it. Women should support each other."

"Should they now," First Sergeant said.

Everyone walked through the M88's smoke to test their seals, and when I gave the "all clear" signal the Headquarters soldiers gathered under the tent again. "This concludes the training on donning your M17 protective mask," Storey announced. "What are your questions?" Army training was delivered in call and response. It let everyone know what had happened and what was coming next. It circumvented some of the endless, unproductive wisecracking.

There were no questions. Everyone was barbecuing inside their charcoal-lined chemical suits and ready for a break. "If there are no questions—" Storey began again, but was interrupted by a hand in the air. "What's your question, Private Washburn?"

"No question, sergeant." For once, Washburn looked serious. He turned his mask over in his hands and fiddled with the straps, looking from Shumacher, over on the M88, back to Storey. It was sad that Washburn was obviously still so hung up on Shumacher, who no longer even gave him a passing glance. "It was good training. I couldn't hardly smell the diesel with my mask on. Chemicals can fuck a body up."

"Pardon your French," Storey said.

"Spring Butt," Reyes chided, and a chuckle waved around the group. A spring butt was a soldier who bounced up with one more question when everyone else was ready to be done.

Storey opened his mouth to speak but the Old Man broke in from astride the M88. "Chemical training is important." He announced this like he'd invented the idea. "Saddam Hussein gassed his own people, and our country might be walking into another unknown situation—one where the bullets have not stopped flying." The brass casings of the Balkan bullets hadn't even cooled. Serbia had refused to give back the ground they'd taken in the safe zones of eastern Bosnia. News reports on the massacre in Srebrenica were grim. NATO peacekeepers had been taken hostage on more than one occasion, and pressure was mounting to begin tactical air strikes against the Serbian military. The day room was full of soldiers every morning before PT now, paying sharp attention to developments.

"I know the rumor mill has been churning extra hard," the Old Man continued, silhouetted by the sun. "And it has some truth to it."

The soldiers looked around the tent with fresh eyes. Logan and the personnel shop had set up a table to help soldiers update their Dependent Care Plans, a required part of readying to leave the country for people with families. I'd also sweet-talked a sergeant from JAG into being there for will writing, and to go over the various types of powers of attorney to leave with spouses or trusted friends. All this paperwork was required, all of the time, but as it dawned on the soldiers that this was more than an annual drill, they pressed out of the tent and toward the Old Man.

"NATO is negotiating another cease-fire among the warring factions," the Old Man said. "After they work out the specifics, they'll almost certainly be tasked to provide more peacekeepers, so it's likely that Division will be tasked in turn. We need to be ready to go."

Headquarters was quiet for one eerie, stifling moment, and then hands shot into the air.

"Sir—is there any indication when—"

"For how long?"

Off to the side of the group closing in on the Old Man, First Sergeant stood with her arms crossed. I'd have given a lot to know how the confirmation of the rumors was affecting her. She'd had time to get her head around the fact that she'd be going on the mission, but I shriveled inside at the part I'd played in it, even as justifications rallied to my defense. She'd been in the Army seventeen years. She knew that when the job was to clear a path, sometimes there were casualties.

The Old Man held up his hand and the soldiers shut up, the only sounds the rub of chem suit sleeves crossing and uncrossing themselves, and the whine of cicadas rising and falling on waves of sultry air. The five second span of time between when the Old Man's words fired through the collected synapses and back out of the soldiers' questioning mouths encapsulated the worst of war—uncertainty and chaos.

The Old Man served me up to the soldiers with a wave of the same hand. I flexed my fingers, gathered my thoughts, and stepped into the line of fire. The role of a leader was to remain clear-headed in the middle of the maelstrom. "We don't know when, or even if Headquarters is going for sure—just that it's likely. I promise you, the second the colonel gives me the order, I will let you know." The faces of the soldiers were sweaty, anxious, unconvinced. "Until then, we have to take the rumors seriously. So. Let's have single soldiers form up at the JAG table, and those of you with dependents start with personnel."

Logan and Pettit waited behind the personnel table, French braids smooth and tidy in the muggy August air. They'd weaseled out of the gas mask training to set up shop. "I've been to NBC School," Logan reminded me as she right-angled a stack of papers in front of herself. Of course she had.

I turned to First Sergeant as the soldiers broke apart then regrouped into two lines. "First Sergeant, can you make sure all the single soldiers sign in with JAG? I don't want anyone slipping through the cracks."

She fixed me with a gaze, a silent callout for performing for my boss. "Please," I said, and she nodded and turned away. Feeling like a trained monkey, I thanked the Old Man for taking part in the morning's activities as he left with all the staff officers except Logan.

I walked back to the personnel table, trying not to appear too interested. I'd processed my fair share of Dependent Care Plans, but some people were making the switch to banking electronically via the World Wide Web and this was another option Logan and Pettit were offering. It seemed odd and insecure, but it might be the most reliable way to make sure my mother didn't fall behind on her bills if I was half a world away in Korea. I wanted to ask about it but hated to admit that Logan knew more about something than I did.

Davis nudged Shumacher out of the front spot of the line that was forming on Pettit. Shumacher was chewing on a cuticle and looking hot and frazzled. "You're in the wrong line, Specialist Shumacher," I said. "Single soldiers are talking to JAG first. And anyway, dependent care plans are only for people who have children to square away."

Shumacher opened her mouth, then closed it. She moved out of Davis's way but remained, hovering, by the personnel table. "Move out, Specialist," I said. This was not a situation where Shumacher, at least, knew better than me what to do.

LOGAN, THE GREAT AND POWERFUL

Logan scanned the crowd of soldiers under the tent, forming two lines in front of the tables on either end. Satisfied that people were where they needed to be, she and Pettit took their seats.

A sweating, scowling man leaned over the table. "Shumacher and I have to get back to the motor pool," he said, less than a foot from Pettit's face. He'd diagnosed Pettit as the weaker of the two of them, a classic bully tactic. "Her truck has a Class III leak, and we need to get it ready to take to Third Shop before everybody comes down for motor stables." Logan cleared her throat to signal a warning. If this guy thought he could muscle up on her clerk he was very mistaken.

Pettit pulled back but didn't bat an eyelash. She didn't need to— Logan had prepped her for the onslaught of excuses people would use to avoid dealing with their financial obligations. She'd be ready for guys like this to get loud, but his propensity to dominate everything around him would also cloud his judgment, as so often happened with people who hadn't had to learn to control their impulses. "Just keep your cool," Logan had warned her. "Blowhards back down if you don't react. And if somebody starts something, I'll be right there. I've got your back."

And this asshole? She'd seen him in action already. He thought no one heard what he muttered about female soldiers while he was supposed to be doing PT. Logan was born ready for this moment, and suppressed a smile as Pettit flipped through folders until she found his, then fixed her eyes wide. The picture of innocence and professionalism. "We're missing documentation to show that you have an emergency fund, Sergeant Davis. There isn't a direct deposit form or a bank statement."

"I can take care of my family, Specialist." Davis's face, already flushed from the heat and from his gas mask, turned heart-attack red. "If I say I can cover emergency expenses while I'm away, I can."

"Also," Pettit said, as though Sergeant Davis hadn't even spoken, "You'll need a power of attorney for your wife."

"I ain't giving my wife no power of attorney. If she had access to the emergency fund she'd blow it on a shopping spree." Sergeant Davis looked to the men around him for support but the soldiers within earshot quickly craned their necks to study the roof struts of the GP Medium or to gaze at the M88. They consulted their wrist watches or examined the parched grass of the parade field being trampled under their chemical boots. Sergeant Storey, the handsome supply sergeant who was sweet on Lieutenant Mills although she seemed utterly oblivious to his attentions, turned to scowl at Davis from all the way across the tent at the JAG table.

Logan made eye contact with Lieutenant Mills. This Davis was slowing her and Pettit down and it would be a fantastic time for Lieutenant Mills to do her damn job. For once, Lieutenant Mills caught Logan's drift. She took hold of Davis's uniform blouse between her thumb and forefinger and pulled him out of line.

Davis looked down at his arm and Lieutenant Mills let go of his sleeve. "Sergeant Davis, you are out of line," she said, and Logan pushed down another laugh. "Stop giving Specialist Pettit a hard time. *Start* setting a positive example for the soldiers of this company. Your attitude is unbecoming." Out of the corner of her eye Logan saw First Sergeant St. John leave the group of single soldiers at the JAG end of the tent to make her way toward Lieutenant Mills and Sergeant Davis.

"Wouldn't nobody *have* an attitude if I was first sergeant." The canvas peak of the GP Medium both muffled and amplified his voice. "Wouldn't nobody have to pay for missing equipment, because it wouldn't have gone missing in the first place. Us men are watching this place fall to shit with females in charge. All this cutesy paperwork?" He waved his grubby hand to encompass the personnel table. "Is just window-dressing for incompetence. A soldier's word used to mean something. Now you gotta have paperwork to support every damn thing you say."

The soldiers under the tent stopped breathing. Pettit and the JAG sergeant kept their eyes fastened on their work; their heads and hands still. Logan watched it all, head up.

"Take your file from Specialist Pettit and have it completed and on my desk by close of business," Lieutenant Mills said. Her voice, too, was quiet yet audible to everyone under the tent.

Logan nodded. Close of business was a reasonable length of time, although Davis was barely clinging to reasonable. The women weren't the ones who'd lost equipment and let training slide. None of the women broadcast their feelings about their hard lives at the top of their lungs or grumbled under their breath. What might be perceived as weakness had more to do with the women's complete lack of interest in the nonstop bullshit spewing from the mouths of the men, especially this one. Logan waited for Lieutenant Mills to say something to this effect. She clapped a lid on the anger that boiled up from her guts and thought about how the Catholic chaplain was teaching her to funnel her rage. She thought about the Vietnamese women the chaplain had introduced her to—their living rooms, the cups of tea, the halting, laughter-filled lessons in Vietnamese and English. The way she was helping them understand new forms of American banking so they could better direct their family finances. The way they reminded her of her true self, the one completely outside of the Army. Logan took a deep breath. Positive action could only dissipate so much negative energy.

Sergeant Davis reached over and grabbed the manila folder out of Pettit's hands. He tore it in half, right in front of Lieutenant Mills's face, and then slammed the two halves down on the table. Without another word, he pivoted to walk away. Heads swiveled his way and then back at Lieutenant Mills, then just as quickly back to whatever it was they were supposed to be focusing on.

Lieutenant Mills froze, but as usual anger had the opposite effect on Logan. It rendered her eloquent instead of tongue-tied. She sprang to her feet, Oz, the Great and Powerful. "As you were, Sergeant," Logan demanded. "You will speak respectfully to Specialist Pettit, not least because you really don't want to piss off the people who handle your paperwork."

The mouth of the bully opened and closed like a mute marionette. Logan was right, of course—this blowhard wasn't used to anyone—and certainly not someone who looked like Logan—getting in his face. He'd have been one of the soldiers her mother mocked—one of the support guys who stayed in the rear of the war, partying at her bar and trying to convince the bar girls to have sympathy for his pampered plight. Until the girls rebuffed him and things got ugly, and her mother had to have the MPs throw his ass out. It wasn't that combat soldiers were more important than support soldiers—the problem was people misunderstood who really held the power.

Someone, maybe Sergeant Storey at the other end of the tent, coughed back a laugh, which created the interval Lieutenant Mills needed to jolt to life. She strode around the stunned sergeant and held up a hand. "When you're ready to act like an adult, Sergeant Davis, report to my office with your supervisor. And bring that file you just tore up." There was no other possible response. When a soldier had been so blatantly disrespectful it had to be smacked down hard. Lieutenant Mills had to match his anger with her own; that was the only reaction this guy would understand. Lieutenant Mills was finally starting to get it.

First Sergeant St. John closed the gap between them and her face, too, was grim.

"Get your soldier," Lieutenant Mills said to her. "And meet me in my office in thirty minutes." First Sergeant St. John hauled Davis from under the tent, and Pettit and Logan tucked their stray hairs behind their ears, tidied their papers, and resumed their work.

DEATH BY A THOUSAND PAPER CUTS

I looked at my watch as I left Storey in charge of the tent. It was 10:33. My goal to survive Headquarters Company one day at a time was now breaking down on an hourly basis and this next hour was going to be the most brutal yet.

It took two minutes to stalk across the parade field, shedding chemical suit layers as I went. When I entered the day room I paused a moment, letting my eyes adjust to the gloom. The TV in the corner told a quiet story to itself of Bosnian men herded from schools and warehouses where they'd been kept by Serbian soldiers, and into nearby forests and fields. It flashed pictures of women sobbing through bad teeth, their head coverings too reminiscent of Iraq, their solemn children too ragged and brown and far away to engender sympathy in an American heart. The world had overlooked the mass genocide in Rwanda the year before; there wouldn't be outrage over this, either. American soldiers would go, the ticker tape commentary running under the newsreel images informed me, but they wouldn't understand their role, and neither would the American public. The Army intervened without asking enough questions and never woke up to what was required of it until we were too deeply involved already. Same as it ever was.

My office clock read 10:37 as I creaked down into my chair and pulled a small green notebook from my middle desk drawer. I opened a document on my word processor and began to type.

At precisely 11:03 there was a sharp rap on the door jamb and Davis, accompanied by First Sergeant, reported as ordered. His hat was blocked and rested on his outstretched forearm, fingers cupping the brim. I put the two of them at ease and they locked into parade rest, everyone playing their parts by the numbers. To still my shaking hands, I took a swig of the coffee that had been sitting on my desk since early that morning, then spent a long moment studying Davis's face. All the defiance from earlier had settled into something calmer but hard, and I took from it the emotion I needed for myself, which was a certain stoic acceptance in front of a firing squad. Should I have felt more unsure, facing these two sergeants who each had reasons for hating me? It was my finger on the trigger in that moment and I surprised myself by realizing that I was perfectly capable of squeezing it. Davis a hundred percent deserved what he was getting. I did *not* feel unsure of myself. Not one bit. This certainty was itself unsettling and I would need to think about it. Later.

"I have in front of me a letter of counseling, Sergeant Davis." My hands rested on either side of the paper and my palms were damp, not from nervousness but from the lightning speed with which I'd retrieved my notes, typed, and printed the letter in triplicate—one for Davis, one for his file, and one for safe-keeping since counseling statements were sometimes made to disappear. As Logan had warned him, Davis should have known better than to mess with an Army administrator. I might have wobbled with Headquarters in the beginning and maybe Davis thought he could exploit what he perceived as my weakness, but by god, I knew paperwork. His actions under the tent were glaringly wrong. No one would think I was being too harsh to counsel him. I probably wasn't being harsh enough.

"It includes dates, times, and locations of three occasions of insubordinate behavior—two in the motor pool—the time you doused me with diesel smoke, and the time you questioned my authority during the inventories. Your lack of professionalism culminated in your outburst this morning, which is the third incident I have listed.

I could have included several more." I paused but Davis was still staring straight ahead. One droplet of sweat trickled from his temple toward his cheekbone. Judging from the grayish white skin around his ears, which contrasted with the rest of his sunburned face, First Sergeant must have taken a battery-operated razor to his hair before she brought him in. "You are allowed to believe whatever you want, of course, but your opinions are to remain inside your head. Your sidebar commentary and criticisms are detrimental to the good order and discipline of this unit. You are *not* to vent to other soldiers about what displeases you anymore, nor are you to discuss your displeasure unless it is to me or First Sergeant St. John and done in a professional manner. Your attitude and your job performance will improve substantially by the end of next week or the pressure on you will increase." I didn't elaborate on what that could look like. His balls were in a vise and he knew it. "First Sergeant?"

"Yes, ma'am." First Sergeant had been standing at a less tight position of parade rest behind Davis while they both listened, but now she, too, shifted into sharper focus. Her face was a mask as always, a dark pool gleaming over Georgia red clay, but I didn't detect anger there—just dislike, which I'd earned fair and square, and respected her for.

"Sergeant Davis will supervise motor stables as normal this afternoon," I said. "But after motor stables you and Sergeant Davis will write a list of concrete action steps to address his lack of professionalism. Some of those steps must specifically address his attitude toward female soldiers." Davis flicked one resentful glance my way. In the letter of counseling I'd outlined that all the soldiers he criticized were females. Let him snivel about that to his buddies. It was an objective, documented fact, and it felt powerful to hold the worst part of his behavior over his head without the need for the Equal Opportunity office at all—and to remind First Sergeant that I did, in fact, support other women. Recent events to the contrary. "You will put the entire action plan on my desk, signed by both of you, before you leave today. I will meet with both of you at 1700 on Monday, Wednesday, and Friday of next week to document Sergeant Davis's progress. The first action he will take will be the completion of all administrative paperwork required for a possible mission to Yugoslavia. As I said on the parade field, I want it completed by close of business tomorrow."

Her whole career she'd run orderly rooms and personnel shops of her own, so my precision would not come as a surprise to her, although my expectations were laid out more clearly than was typical. Her facial expression was an appraisal, an assessment of whether she thought I'd follow through on this tough talk. I hoped she understood how deadly serious I was—she was still gagging from having her own throat cut, after all. She moved to speak but I held up a hand. It was done. "What are your questions?" I asked.

Neither had any questions. They read and signed the three copies of the letter, and Davis folded one and slid it into a cargo pocket. I dismissed them for lunch and Davis saluted, pivoted, and left the office without another word. First Sergeant followed after casting one more inscrutable look over her shoulder.

PERFORMANCE PLAN

I sat at my desk for a long time after Davis stomped out, thinking about how, when my mother was either in a super-enthusiastic, super-organized, super-controlling phase or completely disengaged and lost, I used to crunch into the woods behind our house, breaking fallen branches into smaller and smaller twigs until the world became more manageable. Would my father have felt something similar, wading through the leeches and snakes of the Mekong Delta? Up to his sternum in misery and fear, trying to keep an eye on his soldiers while they held their rifles overhead until their shoulders ached? Sodden boots and packs pulling them down and backward at the same time? Had my father had the same recurring nightmare I did lately, of low-crawling through muck and progressing by mere inches? Today I'd taken a hill, but I might have to relinquish it tomorrow. I wondered if my father would be proud of me for hammering down on Davis or ashamed.

I sat in the dim office with nothing but the hum and drip of the window air conditioning unit as background music. My words to Davis were both a key and a heavy iron chest to drag. My stomach growled and the fuzz in my brain reminded me that I hadn't had breakfast because I'd been too revved up before the morning's training session to eat. I could have gone to the food court at the PX now that there was some money in my checking account, but I didn't want to encounter the stares or frightened courtesies of the soldiers who'd been under the tent with me.

I couldn't risk being seen in proximity to fast food, and anyway, eating seemed like such a routine thing to do, all things considered. Patton never stopped a battle so he could snarf a sandwich.

Ignoring the emptiness in my heart and in my gut, I walked into the deserted day room and downed the dregs of the coffee pot without so much as pouring it into a cup. I rinsed the scorched carafe then walked to the motor pool to supervise weekly maintenance.

Caffeine kept the hunger pangs at bay and the vehicles were serviced in record time. Storey took a team to the parade field to break down the tent and I had First Sergeant dismiss everyone else early. The soldiers slunk away without thanking me; they knew I hadn't given them time off because I was pleased.

Back at my desk I drummed my fingers and reread the commanders' guide to the Uniformed Code of Military Justice. I reviewed the company's improving training statistics and flicked through finance regulations, looking for a loophole to thread all the responsibility through Captain Williams's paycheck, wherever he was, for whenever the decision about the Report of Survey came back from Brigade. I drank coffee until the lining of my empty stomach sizzled, all to the murmurs coming from First Sergeant's office as she and Davis worked on his performance plan. I sat, chest rising and falling, and looked at the bulletin board across the office with its memos and SOPs tacked up at right angles, still there from Captain Williams's command. My signature block wasn't on the bottom of the papers that fluttered as the fan oscillated over their surfaces. My command would be an invisible blip in Headquarters history. Try as I might, I couldn't find it in my heart to care. None of it—not me, not any of it—mattered except right-angling the whole unit into place then leaving.

The memos curled away from the cork and drifted back into position in rhythm with the fan. I closed my eyes and imagined myself at home, propped against the wall on my folded wool blanket with a cold beer in one hand and the TV remote in the other. Unable to hold my head upright, I laid my forehead on my folded arms, keeping an ear out for the voices to stop next door, on alert for First Sergeant and her quiet boots.

The sound of a clearing throat jerked me awake and I bolted upright, swiping at a damp cheek. First Sergeant held out a typed sheet of paper and I took it, trying in vain to cover the puddle I'd left on the blotter. There was no way to pretend I hadn't been dead asleep on the job. "I don't want him to apologize to me," I said after glancing over the draft of Davis's plan. "I want him to apologize to Pettit for giving her a hard time today. And I want him to apologize to you. This company would be an absolute disaster if you weren't the first sergeant."

"Well. . ." First Sergeant hesitated. My words sounded too much like something the Old Man would say and she never fell for manipulation in any case, but at the moment her uniform lacked its usual starch. The shadows under her eyes were dry and deep, like she carried the weight of her session with Davis there. "He's already apologized to me."

"He did?" Davis hadn't looked particularly contrite earlier.

"He did, and I apologized to him."

"You *what*? You've put up with an unbelievable amount of shit from him, First Sergeant. He ought to be licking your boots and begging for forgiveness. He's treated you like some . . . some . . ." Words failed me.

"I asked you to let me handle the NCOs in the beginning, and you have, ma'am. So I'm handling this mess." She looked less defiant than utterly spent. "But if you must know, I apologized for not asking him why he's so mad all the time. I should have been a big enough person to at least ask that question."

My mouth fell open. Here I was, finally getting tough on Davis, and there was First Sergeant, digging to an even deeper level of leadership than I'd known possible. "And why is he so mad all the time?" I could hardly bring myself to ask it. I didn't care.

"Maybe you should ask him that yourself, ma'am."

"Not today, First Sergeant. Maybe not ever." It wasn't noble of me, but it made my wicked heart sing that Davis was suffering for a change. Anger was cathartic and more than that, I was right to be angry. Wasn't I? I was. First Sergeant could go ahead and be the hero.

After another round of revisions the document was completed to my satisfaction and signed by all of us. I was packing my kit bag to go home as the brass doorknob at the front of the building clicked behind Davis. Softly. "I think you've got him going in the right direction, ma'am." First Sergeant used the word *you*, but the muscle in her voice sounded sore and depleted, like she'd been pushing Davis uphill with it for the last two hours.

"I did what needed to be done." I slung my web belt over my shoulder and laid my wallet on top of the kit bag. I had no juice, either, not even to accept this tiniest of palm branches. I'd been selfish to put my needs first about Korea, but she hadn't made the last month easy on me.

"He's got a lot going on at home," she said. "It doesn't excuse his attitude, but he's got a little boy with special needs and a wife who doesn't handle it so well."

My head shot up. So this was what they'd been talking about for so long. "I don't remember seeing his name on the list for EFMP." The Exceptional Family Member Program provided therapeutic services for children who needed extra support. The full program only existed at larger Army posts, so sometimes soldiers didn't enroll their children because it limited where they could be stationed. Soldiers like Davis might have withheld information just to be ornery.

"No, ma'am." First Sergeant's tired eyes narrowed slightly. Always with the appraisals. "He told me in confidence, although I've been thinking there was something going on with him for a while now. I'm only telling you so you don't think he's a complete dirtbag."

"It's going to take more than one sob story to make me change my mind about Sergeant Davis, First Sergeant. Is this also his excuse for treating women like shit?"

"No, ma'am." She looked out the window. It was the best time of a summer day, escaping into the arms of a sun that had loosened its grip. "Well. Maybe."

"You and I need to stop taking our frustrations with each other out on the soldiers," I said. Everyone was working at cross-purposes to everyone else, and if everyone in the Army was as sleep-deprived and underfed and over-caffeinated as I was right then, it was a wonder anything ever got done. "Poor Robinson. She got caught in our sights today. I think we scared those plaits right off her."

First Sergeant huffed. "Private First Class Robinson is tougher than you're giving her credit for, ma'am. Having hair that complies is not the hardest thing she'll have to face in the Army."

I blinked my eyes to reset the cranial hum that always accompanied hunger pangs. I shook my head. First Sergeant was not the kind of person who made it easy to agree. But even if she was digging in her heels like her own balky sergeants, the entire company was going to have to acknowledge that posturing fooled no one. Not me, anyway. Not anymore.

REPORT OF SURVEY

For the next two weeks Davis was quiet, and uncharacteristically supportive of Pettit, who was getting better at the copious amounts of pushups Storey and I administered. I counted the passing days by the number of lonely granola bars I ate at my desk before work call formations and during my solitary lunches. I accepted the Old Man's accolades at the Unit Status Report briefing for, among other things, the fact that Davis had gotten the leak on Shumacher's truck repaired so quickly. The Old Man didn't berate me for the equipment shortages I was required to report, and Davis marched through the other requirements on his improvement plan. Probably my strong-arm tactics were what the company had needed all along. Life was not joyful, but everyone's performance was improving, and my time at Fort Stewart was drawing to a close.

I was brushing granola crumbs from my lap on a Friday afternoon at the end of August when the front door of the deserted Headquarters Company building opened and closed and boots that were too heavy to be First Sergeant's marched down the hallway. And anyway, she had dismissed the company for a well-earned long weekend for Labor Day then followed them right out the door.

It was Master Sergeant Jones, the senior sergeant from the battalion logistics office who'd helped me with the motor pool inventories, holding a large envelope.

"Sorry to interrupt, ma'am." Jones smiled like he had good news and I attempted to return it, surprised by how much effort it required to push my face into that unfamiliar position. Then he wrinkled his nose. "Begging your pardon, but it smells like socks in here."

"It's the ghost of Captain Williams," I sighed. "I can't quite banish it."

A dimple appeared in one of Jones's cheeks and he laid the envelope on my desk. "Speaking of which, we thought you'd like to be the first to see this."

The office symbol on the outside of the shotgun envelope, so-called because of the holes that perforated it, was from Brigade. "Has the colonel seen this already?" I asked. If it was coming to me from that level it should have routed through the Old Man's office first.

"Yes, ma'am. He's the one who asked me to bring it to you personally."

I slid the enclosed memo out, holding it gingerly so as not to leave granola bar smudges on it. It was the decision on the Report of Survey from the missing inventory items. "What the hell?" I said as I scanned it. "They're writing it all off? I mean, I'm glad the mechanics aren't being held responsible, but they're writing *all* of it off? Even Captain Williams is getting off scot-free?"

Jones's dimple disappeared. His mouth flattened out and formed no expression I could read. "I don't disagree with you, ma'am," he said. "It sets a bad example when a soldier doesn't get so much as a slap on the wrist. But I'll put the decision in context if you can keep a lid on some news."

"Of course." My words cracked like bullets. Apparently any good-time guy could run an organization into the ground and get away with it. It wasn't fair.

"NATO is bombing the Serbs in eastern Bosnia," Jones said. "The Joint Chiefs are revving up in anticipation of a pretty big troop movement to support the peace effort. You've probably seen it all on the news. Division will be in go-mode by the time we finish the field exercise, and Brigade isn't in the mood to hunt down a few thousand dollars of equipment losses. In fact, they're using the upcoming mission as justification for replacing everything with no questions asked." He paused, anticipating that I'd have something to say. "It's the end of the money year anyway. Our funds need to be spent or we'll lose them. Nobody gets hurt."

"Well, shit." I stood up and threw my granola bar wrapper into the trash can. It was happening. "I can't believe Captain Williams isn't getting punished for being slack at best." *And maybe outright stealing*, I thought, although I'd never found proof of that.

I could feel Master Sergeant Jones's eyes on me as I read the memo more carefully. The office symbol was from the Brigade logistics office and was dated the day before. The memo itself was short and to the point, although the enclosures still in the shotgun were lengthier: photocopies of the inventories and of the Report of Survey itself. My eyes halted at the bottom of the cover page, where the field grade officer in charge of Brigade logistics had signed her name. In the bottom left corner was a long list, in rank order, of all the officers and senior NCOs who'd been furnished a copy. Among the captains listed was a name I recognized—a captain assigned as an assistant logistician to the Brigade S-4.

Captain Curtis Williams.

"What the fuck, Sergeant Jones." I said, so shocked I left the "master" off his rank.

He made no more attempts to treat the contents of the envelope like a cause for celebration. His face was a naked admission that he'd known all along that Captain Williams was tucked away at Brigade, that he and the Old Man had known the decision that would be handed down before I sweated through all the inventories and painstakingly assembled my report. Before I'd made an enemy of Davis and the entire motor pool and First Sergeant and all of Headquarters in my effort to get the paperwork right. My chest grew tight, forcing heat up my neck like a thermometer.

"There was nowhere else to put him for a month or two until the colonel could get him a new assignment," Jones said. His forehead was a lighter brown than the rest of his face—soldier tan lines he'd earned standing in the unrelenting sun of the motor pool inventory, too, although it didn't make me feel more charitable toward him in that moment. "Brigade needed an extra pair of hands, and the S-4 is a good place for a maintenance officer to cross-train."

"A maintenance officer who can't keep track of his own equipment?" I was flabbergasted, although I shouldn't have been. I should have known the Old Man didn't have it in him to discipline Captain Williams the way he deserved. I should have remembered that well-liked male officers always failed upward. My cheeks flamed and my grip on the memo tightened. "That's the last place you ought to put someone like that."

"It wasn't my call, ma'am." Jones shrugged, and I shook my head. Except for First Sergeant, I seemed to be the only Headquarters soldier who grappled with the morality of waste. I looked down to where I was white-knuckling the paper and wished I was holding my M16. I wanted to beat my desk with the butt of a rifle right about then.

"Well. I guess I should be glad for the soldiers who aren't going to have to pay for anything, but mostly it irritates the shit out of me." I gagged on the words. Forced them down like a glob of frosting made of pure sugar and Crisco that I might vomit right back up.

A few thousand dollars was nothing compared to, say, the cost of an M88 armored recovery vehicle, or the millions of dollars it would cost to replace the broken Abrams tank it could haul out of a training area swamp. But a few thousand dollars would mean a lot to someone like my mother, or Sergeant Davis, or any one of millions of Americans who lived close to the bone. It wasn't a sum that most people could just wave away with the stroke of a pen. Jones, and the Old Man, and the Brigade S-4 had decided it didn't matter that Captain Williams lost that much money. Worse, they'd given him a soft place to land while I mopped up his mess. While sergeants and soldiers organized rooms and buildings full of stuff, laid it out by the numbers and counted, filled out paperwork and sent it all up, argued with each other in the blazing Fort Stewart sun, tossed and turned with worry that they might be responsible for repaying it, and wrecked their relationships with each other. According to the brass on high, none of it was worth bothering over. It pissed me off to the core, but there was nowhere for the anger to boil except up my neck to my face and back down to my guts.

I set the paperwork down on the desk then placed a shaking hand over my midsection as if there were any possible way to calm myself. "When can I tell the soldiers about Yugoslavia? I promised I'd tell them as soon as I heard anything."

"Not yet, ma'am." Jones's face was serious, no longer apologetic. "I'm out of line telling you as much as I have. I'm just trying to keep you from getting wrapped around the axle about an issue that's out of our control."

"I can't even tell First Sergeant St. John?"

"No, ma'am." Jones shifted like he was squeezing his big frame into First Sergeant's boots. No senior NCO wanted to have information withheld from them. "Let everyone have their long weekend. Let the colonel inform all you company commanders first, then you can tell Headquarters however you want to."

Damn. It wasn't a theoretical troop movement anymore. First Sergeant was going on this mission and I was forbidden to tell her. I'd either have to lie through my teeth or go out of my way to avoid her, which was impossible. Time slowed down as I thought about two weeks in the field, everyone living cheek by jowl with nowhere to go at the end of the day with their anger and resentment except one cot over in a GP Medium. "The colonel needs to make it official ASAP. You know how fast the rumor mill is going to spit this out." Everyone would know about it by work call formation on Monday, anyway, even if no one said an official word.

"Soon, ma'am."

"Roger," I growled. Just when I thought company morale couldn't get worse. "I appreciate you being straight with me, but you need to get out of here before somebody sees you. If people start to speculate I'm not going to be able to keep my mouth shut. Sorry to be so blunt."

"No offense taken." Jones raised his hat in a half salute and nodded curtly. "Have a good weekend."

Right. Like I was going to hit the town with this earth-shattering news hanging over my head. Like I could put on a happy face about the Report of Survey decision. Captain Williams needed to pay for missing tools and parts; that was the simple truth. And Davis—he spent so much time being mad at the world he didn't see all that equipment disappearing from under his nose? Hell, maybe he'd even taken some of it himself, justifying it because of his family situation. I slapped the desktop and sat down hard in my chair. No one cared. I'd just be one shrill voice, alone like a madwoman in the wilderness, trying to stop the Army from writing off a few lost field rations and canteen cups. The important stuff would be replaced; the rest was inconsequential because the Army was about to dump millions of dollars into moving Division across the ocean to keep Serbians and Bosnians and Croatians from killing each other. Struck in that light, the missing jack assembly from Shumacher's truck *was* a paltry nonissue. I had to get my priorities in order. I had to at least redeem myself with First Sergeant, ASAP.

Across the office, the fan ruffled the SOPs hanging on the bulletin board, then turned to cool the sweat that had broken out across the bridge of my nose. It lifted the hair from my forehead, then passed over the bulletin board again. The metallic shine of something small caught my eye and, feeling like I weighed a thousand pounds, I pushed up from my chair to investigate.

It was a key hanging from a chain of paperclips, one more stupid thing that needed to be sorted out. I snatched it from behind the memorandum and threw it on my desk, picturing some jackass— probably Captain Williams—snickering to himself while he strung paperclips together for me to unhook later, a metaphor in office supplies.

I looked down at the calendar on my desk to remind myself what was happening after the long weekend, absentmindedly yanking the clips apart and putting them into the dish next to my computer monitor. When I was done, I held the key up to the dim light and examined it more carefully. It was the wrong kind for the filing cabinets out in the orderly room, and anyway, those keys hung in their proper places in the key box now.

This key was thin, silver. Not a bronze Yale door key, but too thick to go in one of the flimsy metal wall lockers we used for supply cabinets. My gaze slid down to the lock on the inside edge of my desk, next to my knee. The one I hadn't been able to open since the day I took over the company.

I pushed the key into the lock and turned. Bingo.

The large file drawer at the bottom of the desk popped open and the smell, always unpleasant in that office, jumped out and grabbed me by the throat. A plastic takeout bag from Lucky China filled the bottom of the otherwise empty drawer.

Holding my breath, and with the thumb and index fingers of each hand I pulled the top open, not sure if a rat had crawled in there and died after having eaten ancient egg fried rice. But it was a PT uniform, wadded up and mildewed, and running shoes. No wonder the office smelled like socks. Captain Williams, in his hurry to vacate when the Old Man was throwing him out, had left me a bag of nasty, unwashed clothes. At some point he must have changed out of his T-shirt and shorts and forgotten the bag was in there. Or maybe he'd panicked with the Old Man standing over him and forgotten it. Or forgot that the key was half-obscured behind the memos on the bulletin board. Or maybe he'd thought it'd be funny to leave his stench behind.

Using the same two fingers, I pulled the bag out of the drawer. "Disgusting," I said to the fetid air. I'd need packs of those stick-up air fresheners.

Coins rattled as I set the bag onto the floor. Nostrils flaring, I dumped his uniform and shoes straight into the garbage can. A handful of change remained on the bottom of the bag, along with a crumple of papers. Gross as it was, I couldn't make myself throw away money, so I scooped out the quarters and dimes. I took the papers out and smoothed them on my desktop. Once a paperwork person, always a paperwork person. I couldn't throw them away without looking at them, either.

One slip was a receipt for Moo-Goo-Gai Pan, thankfully long gone. The other two were pale yellow receipts, customer copies of a three-ply form from the Army-Navy store in the strip mall next to Lucky China. Receipts for uniforms, shelter halves, tent pegs. Receipts for cases of MREs, canteens and mess kits. Ammo pouches. Field jackets. Multiples of all of them, and both receipts with the signature of Curtis Williams at the bottom. Not from having purchased the items—these were bills of sale.

"Holy shit," I said.

ACT OF CONTRITION

The road map wouldn't zig-zag back into a neat rectangle, so I gave up and flung it onto the passenger seat, covering the plain manila folder. First Sergeant hadn't been exaggerating when she said Sunbury was off the beaten path, and I'd been mistaken to think I could just mosey into the rural enclaves around Fort Stewart and find a house I'd never been to, even with the address I copied from her personnel file before I took off.

Cicadas loud in my ears, I turned onto an unpaved road that was marked with a faint line on the map, but no name. My tires rolled over sand, creating more sand from the oyster shells they ground beneath them. Tall pine trees crowded the trail and the occasional gap between them made room for small houses with deep porches like half-hooded eyelids. Vague human outlines fanned themselves behind their screens keeping watch; dogs napped in the shade the porches cast.

Here, lost somewhere between Liberty and McIntosh counties, I couldn't ask for directions. I'd inserted myself into a private place, a place others had created for themselves in throwaway pockets of swamp. This was not an Army community where all skin tones worked together more or less professionally, if not always harmoniously. This was coastal Georgia, where hurt and angry ghosts and current residents alike startled at the sight of an unfamiliar face. They'd look on me with as much trepidation as I was feeling, and not just because I was out of bounds. I must have been very close to Sunbury and First Sergeant's home, but I was trespassing just the same. And the contents of that envelope, while not exactly dangerous, were going to cause a ruckus.

I nosed into a driveway and imagined that rocking chairs paused as people leaned forward to peer at my license plate, cautiously curious as long as I didn't get out. I backed onto the sandy trail and turned around, then drove all the way back to Hinesville.

"Can you take me to First Sergeant St. John's house?" Ted was playing Spades with one of the other drivers, both of them shiny-faced under the ceiling fan of the glorified shed that served as his taxi stand, while Joni Mitchell sucked the remaining energy from the room from a boom box on a plywood shelf.

"You mean Indigo's apartment?" Ted asked. He scooped cards toward himself and recorded his score like he had all the time in the world. "Or her mother's house?"

"Her mother's house, I guess." It was odd to think of First Sergeant living in an apartment. Probably she had proper furniture, nice things she'd collected in Germany. She wouldn't live like a warrior-nun like I did with my empty refrigerator, makeshift sofa, video collection, and books. "The recall roster said she was going out to Sunbury this weekend."

"All right, then." Ted turned his cards over and stood, boosting himself like an old man with his hands against his thighs. He was only forty-something. He didn't need to pretend that it was his advanced age slowing him down when actually it was my revving nerves.

Once we were underway, Ted handed me the box containing his collection of Vietnam protest music. "This far into the cattails we're only getting gospel," he said. "Can't even pick up the ball game except at night."

There were fewer MIA bracelets jumbled in with the cassettes. "Have you sold some?"

"I don't sell 'em, doll. I just give them to people who need them. I almost offered you one last time." A steel POW/MIA cuff would have been an announcement, an admission, a shiny hair shirt for all to see—or maybe a gleaming door knob to open a conversation. I pulled a bracelet from the box and slipped it sideways onto my wrist. Clark Devereaux, an Air Force first lieutenant who went missing in 1967. Almost certainly a pilot, but had he been a husband? A father? Or a treasured son? Maybe he hadn't been treasured by anyone. Maybe nothing was left of him but his teeth and no one thought of him at all. "Looks good." Ted flicked a glance at my wrist, and I was grateful he understood without having to be told that those bracelets were more than righteous accessories.

"Thank you." The silver gleamed against my tanned forearm and felt heavier than a narrow band of stainless steel should.

"So tell me why we're going to Sunbury?"

"I've got something I need to show First Sergeant St. John. It's important." The manila envelope held proof that she'd been right all along, that Captain Williams had stolen Army equipment and sold it on the side. I didn't want to wait until everyone was back at work after the Labor Day weekend to show her—I needed to take her the receipts now, then to the Old Man to demand he go after Captain Williams for payment. First Sergeant and I might never be bosom buddies but maybe I could salvage our working relationship if I finally followed through on that.

I was bringing news of the deployment too. I didn't care if I got in trouble with Master Sergeant Jones, I was telling First Sergeant what was going on. I tightened the bracelet on my wrist until it pinched, bracing myself for the blast of anger I might have to endure.

The smell of salt and dry grass and boat fuel got stronger the closer we got to the Sunbury Channel and the Medway River. Sandy roads leading into thick woods bordered both sides of the two-lane highway, and I put in a Cat Stevens tape even though it was too hot for "Moon Shadow." A lone pine tree bent over the road like an elbow, and we drove under it. The tree was so close to the shoulder that road crews had paved around it, which pleased me. That tree had done its share of adapting already. "I missed this before." My voice was loud over the music and the sharp oven air blowing in the window. "In Athens, there's a tree that owns itself."

"Do what?"

"That's what it's called—the Tree that Owns Itself. A man deeded the land that surrounds a white oak on his property, to the tree, in his will."

"Huh," Ted said. "I like that." And because we both liked trees and were the kind of people who understood that even a tree might want a measure of self-determination, I calmed down a little. But my feet still jittered against the footwell.

The taxi turned left at a sign that read, "Old Dirt Road," which was paved. A fresh wave of anxiety washed over me as we left the main road and entered the jaundiced light filtering through tree branches, raining with sheets of Spanish moss. The tires grumbled over a crushed-granite driveway where a dozen cars lined one side. Hardwood trees punctuated an open, flat lot behind a house, with a deep pine wood behind that. Crepe myrtles struggled on either side of a screened-in porch, gone leggy stretching for the sun, their fuchsia blooms unapologetic against the lapis-blue shutters and porch trim.

A tall Black woman let the screen door bang shut behind her as she crunched across the gravel, drying her hands on her apron. The previous Thanksgiving my mother had met me at the door of the Athens house, wearing a half circle of ruffled eyelet still creased from the package and wielding a bottle of white wine she claimed to be basting the turkey with. The turkey was raw at the bone and my mother had refolded the apron and taken it back to the mall the next day under the frenzied cover of Black Friday. But this woman was not in costume. This was an honest-to-god working apron.

She stopped in front of the taxi and Ted stuck his head out the window. "Hey, Mrs. St. John."

"Ted!" Her face relaxed, erasing all doubt as to her relation to First Sergeant. She had the same direct, intelligent way of looking at a person. "I didn't expect to see you out here today. Who's that in the car with you?"

I took a deep breath and got out of the cab, barricading myself behind the open car door. "Hello, ma'am, I'm Lieutenant Mills. I work with your daughter?"

Mrs. St. John's smile faded. No doubt she'd heard about me. But before I could speak, the wooden frame of the screen slapped again and First Sergeant herself came out. "I'm sorry to drop in unannounced," I said. My eyes darted between the two women and around the front of the house. Based on the number of cars lining the drive and the murmur of voices competing with the cicadas, Ted and I had interrupted a gathering, and there was nothing more gauche than turning up at a party to which one hadn't been invited. I should've figured that families would be cooking out all weekend. "I found something in my desk that I thought you should see. But it can wait until next week." I clutched the folder, unsure whether to hand it over.

"You're welcome any time, ma'am." No matter what she said, the doors were not swinging wide to wave me in—someone not from Sunbury, and an officer, and the selfish kind at that. She reached for the folder, even more formal in front of her mother than she was at work and opened it to scan the flattened documents. "Well, what do you know." Her voice lacked the triumph I was hoping for. "What are you going to do with these?"

So. She had not snapped into action, galvanized by proof she'd been right about Captain Williams. My sins were too great and those wrinkled scraps were no dispensation. I hadn't been absolved, not that I'd really expected her to throw her arms around me at last.

Mrs. St. John leaned her head into the cab window. "Y'all want to come around back for a plate?" That *y'all* was Ted, not me.

"You probably have customers to get back to, don't you?" I gave Ted a pointed look. I hadn't delivered a bolt of lightning after all, and now I wanted to be back in the taxi and driving away.

Mrs. St. John skewered me into position at the side of the cab. It was her house and she'd invite who she wanted. Party crashers didn't get to call any shots. "It's quiet at the ole taxi stand today." The annoying lethargy returned to Ted's voice. "I'd love to stay if there's a slice of key lime pie in it for me."

"You know we've got way more than that. Just leave the cab right here." Ted put it in park, threw the keys on the seat and trailed behind Mrs. St. John around the corner of the house. Their footsteps crunched away over the gravel and First Sergeant handed the envelope back to me.

"I should have looked harder for proof he was stealing," I said. First Sergeant was watchful, still. "So for what it's worth, I'm going to take these to the colonel. I can't believe it, but they've had Captain Williams working at Brigade all this time."

"It doesn't surprise me." She crossed her arms, holding back as always.

There was no point pretending that an elephant wasn't standing there in Mrs. St. John's front yard. "First Sergeant, I need to apologize." Tears pricked at the back of my eyes, but I blinked them away. Female soldiers couldn't cry in front of the males, and I sure as hell couldn't cry in front of other women, especially not this one. "You tried to keep me from learning everything the hard way, but I was too much of a knucklehead to listen. I'm sorry."

First Sergeant's feet shifted on the loose rocks. She looked away, then back at me. "I appreciate you saying that," she said.

"It gets worse," I sighed. "NATO is bombing the Serbs, and Division's going to mobilize after we get back from the field. I'm not supposed to be telling you this, but I thought you deserved to know."

Her nose wrinkled like something smelled bad, when in fact the smoke wafting from the back of the house carried the rich scents of chicken fat and charcoal. Saliva filled my mouth. I'd planned a juice fast followed by a triumphant weigh-in after the long weekend. It was time to check those last lousy pounds off the list although I always forgot how miserable fasting was. Days of weakness, crankiness, and sheer desperation, trying to make it to the end. Just thinking about it made me want to eat the world. "Do you want me to tell the colonel I'll go to Yugoslavia?" I asked. "Would that make it better between us?" Asking for forgiveness seemed like overkill. But seeking to be reconciled was different, and maybe within reach. I held my breath, praying to be strong enough to deal with everything, including her response.

"No, ma'am." First Sergeant shook her head. "It's a nice gesture, but you going would not make anything better. What's done is done, and if there's one thing you told the colonel that's true, it's that the company is better off with me. I've got myself talked into it, anyway. A humanitarian aid mission is important work, and this'll be one last adventure before I retire. Kids will keep needing history teachers. They can wait one more year for me."

She had barely blinked at the news that Battalion was mobilizing. My goal of going to Korea looked and felt cheap in the light of her sacrifice for the greater good. "You're a better person than I am," I said. My neck flushed and I squirmed, searching for integrity and finding little. I wanted to go to Asia for good reasons and I'd done what I needed to do to get there. My overwhelming feeling was one of relief, which meant First Sergeant *was* a better person than me.

She barked a laugh. "Are you Catholic, ma'am?"

"I am," I said, surprised. My mother was a garden variety Protestant, but she'd raised me Catholic as a concession to my father's family. "I mean, not a good one. Why?"

"Because I'm starting to feel like your priest, and I don't want to hear any more confessions right now. And I don't usually do anything unless I want to."

"Let me grab Ted and get out of your hair." I'd done what I needed to do and felt somewhat better—and also worse. I raised the file like it was a scale to balance. "I'll take this to the colonel. I just wanted you to know I found your proof."

"Nothing's going to come of taking a few receipts to the colonel, ma'am. Brigade's writing the losses off and the colonel's focused on this mission. They're not going to do anything about Captain Williams. Let's just get through the training exercise in peace."

"It's all so unfair." I was the source of some of the unfairness, but now that I'd admitted it I wanted to go after the other perps.

"That's life." First Sergeant's lip tightened in one corner of her mouth, not exactly a smile. Her gaze snagged on the metal cuff, bright on my wrist, and she exhaled audibly. "And so is the need for lunch. You want something to eat before you go?" She wasn't making an overture of friendship; she was just being polite because of my tragic backstory. But the smell of the barbecue overrode my embarrassment at having so many things I was hungry for.

I followed her to the backyard, inhaling as we passed the porch and thinking how an old screen smelled like rain. I grew up in a house wrapped around the dregs of whiskey and secondhand smoke, but the slap of that door and its rusty screen relieved the tightness between my shoulder blades. I hadn't found my place in the world yet, but when I did, I hoped it looked something like this. I longed to collapse on the musty old sofa on Mrs. St. John's porch with nothing to do but listen to the drone of bees. That felt like its own kind of goal. Maybe something to do after Korea. Maybe something to do with my mother, but maybe also not.

Behind the house in a large open yard a couple dozen people, every shade of brown found in the natural earth, sat and stood in friendly groupings. "Food's ready!" First Sergeant clapped her hands at a cluster of people in lawn chairs. "Y'all come eat." This wasn't the kind of gathering at which people waited for others to go first. There was no chance the food would run out, so no reason to hang back. Parents chivvied their children toward two picnic tables, behind which Mrs. St. John and a handful of other women inspected the contents of their Chinet. I put myself at the end of the line like a good officer. I'd eat a little to be polite then slip away with Ted. But everything looked so good. Green bottles of Kroger lemon-lime soda stood at attention. Plastic cutlery formed a geometric pattern and the pink plastic tablecloth fluttered in a faint breeze. It was a picnic version of my mother's Pink Tea, except people seemed genuinely happy to be there.

"Baby, take some more potato salad," one of the women said when I got to the front. I was less startled to be called *baby* than I was to be invited to eat more. There was a smile in the woman's dark eyes, although the rest of her face was guarded. She must have picked up that I wasn't exactly a family friend.

"Other people's cooking is my favorite food," I said shyly. The woman laughed as I spooned up more potato salad. What I'd been craving for months—maybe for my whole life—was permission to eat. Her laugh was a gift. I wouldn't go all gung-ho, I'd just try to have a normal lunch. Big pans of macaroni salad and banana pudding weren't out to get me. They weren't plotting my demise—they were there to feed these people, to ground them in the ritual of a Saturday afternoon among friends. I could allow myself these small, nice things.

Mrs. St. John cleared her throat, and I realized a half-dozen people had gathered behind me while I admired the baked beans. I took a napkin and fork and moved out of the way. The beans reminded me of being ten years old and running through the sprinkler with my cousin Jimmy—who wasn't my cousin. My mother was an only child and my father came from St. Louis, so I rarely saw that side of the family. My mother and Jimmy's mother got together every Memorial Day, and then all the hot summer Sundays, to smoke and drink and talk about their husbands as if they were deadbeats instead of just dead. My mother listened to Jimmy's mother bad-mouth her missing husband so she'd have another adult to drink with. My mother would pretend to agree; I'd observed this behavior in many women and girls. Eventually our mothers would feed us hotdogs and beans, and because Jimmy was there, I'd be allowed a second helping.

"Don't let my mother scare you." First Sergeant interrupted my thoughts. From behind her table Mrs. St. John rearranged chicken pieces into neat rows of wings, drumsticks, and thighs. "She always gets snappish when she's got people over at the house. Especially today since it's my cousin Janine's shower." She pointed to a woman who, like many of the women at the picnic, was tall and thin. The woman carried her pregnancy like a basketball tucked low into the front of her shorts. Her hair was tied back in a scarf printed with small squares of gold and orange that made her head and neck look like they were carved from rich teak. If I were pregnant I'd love to be elegant at it but would probably just swell indiscriminately like I had after I ate all the canned vegetables. I could barely allow myself to imagine having a child someday, much less be surrounded by a happy, chattering crowd, all there to shower me with love.

"I am so sorry for turning up like this." Ted had settled in an Adirondack chair next to an old woman wrapped in crochet, although it was sweltering even under the trees, and as I looked around the yard I saw the pink table cloths and tired balloons bobbing in the heat with new eyes. A girl. I would want a daughter. First Sergeant said I apologized too much. I buried the impulse to want anything too much. I wondered if this was the feeling my father had when he'd said he didn't want children.

"Don't worry about it." She leaned toward the group of women that was coalescing around Janine, who sat down near a table loaded with gifts that I'd also overlooked in my preoccupation with not being a bother. I'd been thinking of First Sergeant as a loner like me but as it turned out, she didn't need Army friends. She came equipped with an entire support system.

A few men lurked on the periphery of the circle around Janine, but most gathered at a card table under a tree several yards away. Ted excused himself from the old lady and moved to stand with his forearm propped against the trunk like he'd grown there, like he could take root and stay there all day. Janine was handed a gift, and she turned the box over in her hands, admiring the wrapping and bows. She slid a long, manicured finger under each piece of tape and handed the undefiled sheet to a little girl with spiral ponytails and wearing a yellow sundress, who stacked the paper neatly. The slow ritual made me desperate to leave. I wanted Ted to get bored. I wanted Janine to rip through the paper to create a polite interval through which I could escape.

Janine held up a miniature pink baseball glove and a pair of cleats so tiny I could have worn them on my thumbs. The crowd erupted with approval, and I almost did too. Part of me was pulled in the direction of the women but the stronger force pulled away. Ever the electron, never the nucleus. "Thank you for lunch." I wiped my mouth and prepared to leave. First Sergeant gave me an absent-minded smile and went to join her family, leaving me awash in envy.

OH, LORD, I WANNA GO HOME

ndigo walked for hours on the beach at Tybee Island, kicking piles of detritus and filling her lungs with the wet, salty air. It was still winter everywhere, but this was not the kerosene-smelling basement apartment in Germany. Seagulls played on the softening air currents. Retirees gathered shells without staring at her although you didn't see a Black person at Tybee every day, and the sound of the waves drowned out, for a time, the sound of Wolfgang's motorcycle disappearing into newly-opened Eastern Europe. The waves gathered and crashed, carrying the Atlantic bilge higher up the tideline but never to the same spot.

One day Ted appeared, and as Indigo looked up a wave caught her running shoes. "Hey," she said, and kept on walking, hands in her jacket pockets, shoes squelching around cold feet. She couldn't stop, and Ted was the last person she should have been around. She wanted to strangle him with the long strands of his hair that fluttered like seaweed in the ocean air, just enough like Wolfgang's to ruin everything. She didn't want to hear one word about philosophy or politics or religion. There was nowhere to go that some well-meaning White person didn't show up, trying to help.

"Hey," he said. "Mind if I walk with you?" They were not a pair of anything, not by any measurement, but they'd always been comfortable around each other. That was the most precious thing Wolfgang had stolen.

"I need to be alone," she said. Ted smiled. Smiled just a bit, and nodded, and wasn't at all ingratiating. He just got it and left.

Time gathered and crashed. Every now and again Ted turned up and Indigo minded it less and less, sometimes in the tiniest increments imaginable. Flipping through a photo album—prewar Ted among the groups of smiling boys. Driving by his taxi stand and no longer having to suppress the impulse to ram it with her car.

Sometimes a bigger wave rolled in—two whole innings of a ball game they both happened to attend, both pairs of eyes on the field but Ted telling her he'd gotten sober and was working his way through the steps. He never snuck up, though, and always let her make the call. Eventually they grew easy in each other's presence again, higher and higher up the tideline as the years passed.

BUT THEY WON'T LET ME GO HOME

Instead of a box of cassettes on the passenger seat I had a zippered pouch of CDs, and I was blasting Joan Armatrading to drown out Rambo's protests. "Sorry, buddy," I said to his cat carrier between songs. "You could be living a free and feral life in the motor pool, but instead you're stuck with me—and with grandma for the next few weeks." Staying with my mother was hardly cat jail. The last time I went to the field my mother had gotten in the habit of spoon-feeding him yogurt.

"His favorite flavor is strawberry," she'd crooned, tickling him under the chin. Always with the pink food.

"For god's sake, Mom." But I was grateful. At work, everyone with kids was scrambling to figure out child care for the two-week field exercise, and now also for the year away in Yugoslavia, or Bosnia as we were starting to call it. One car ride with a yowling cat was a piece of cake in comparison.

A little after suppertime I hauled Rambo's carrier from the car and banged through the door of the low ranch house. "We're here!" I announced. It was comfortable, if not exactly good, to be home. The familiar scents of secondhand smoke and sour wine instantly conjured memories of escaping into the woodsy surroundings when I was a kid. I'd climbed trees and wandered to the creek with no one to accompany me but birds and bugs and books. I used to pretend I was my father, alone and forging his way in the Vietnamese jungle, until I started

reading military history and watching war movies and concluded that
he couldn't possibly have lived long enough to do any of those things.
The house breathed sadness—I forgot this the longer I spent away from
it. I wondered if my mother stayed because it was the only environment
to which her lungs were adapted anymore, like she'd never be able to
function on dry land again.

My mother looked up from her recliner and self-consciousness
flitted like headlights across her face then disappeared just as quickly.
She jumped up, setting aside the Dixie Chicken tumbler she used as a
wine glass. I put the cat carrier down and Rambo, who had been quiet
until we entered the dingy living room, began to complain again. "Let
him out! Let him out!" My mother waved a hand toward the insistent-
sounding box as she held her arms open. "I didn't expect you so early."

I surveyed the room over my mother's shoulder as we hugged.
The television was turned to the evening news, the ever-present scenes
of war in the Balkans. A Marlboro Light burned in the ashtray (since
Dunhills were saved for special occasions) and library books littered the
coffee table. What looked like the beginning of a poem was scribbled
on the envelope of what looked like the financial planning information
I'd sent at Logan's suggestion. It wasn't the worst I'd ever seen it, not
by a long shot. The thick layer of dust was as gone as the 1980s.
No aluminum trays of TV dinners decomposed where they'd been
set down then forgotten. No sullen, pudgy wraith peeked around the
corner, the after-image of the girl from the Brownie dance.

I unlatched the wire door, and the cat was a black blur as he bolted
for his favorite closet. I straightened, hand to my low back. "You want
to sit down, honey?" my mother asked.

"No, thanks. I've been on my ass for four hours." My mother coughed
low in her chest as the cuss word slipped into the cigarette smoke.

"All right, then—how about a drink?"

We moved into the kitchen where the mismatched Corelle dishes
occupied their usual place, piled into the sink. Crumbs dusted the
counter in front of the toaster and the bread bag was open next to it.

The old house would always harbor a few flying cockroaches, ready to ambush when the kitchen lights were turned on at night, but at least my mother was eating. A thought flashed through my mind about what it would be like to be a person who forgot to eat, but I banished it just as quickly. I wanted to eat. I wanted the rest of my life to be a backyard barbecue where I could choose from all kinds of delicious food with no one casting a sideways glance at my plate. I didn't want to be out of control with food, but I didn't want to starve myself for the rest of my life, either. My mother was small and I was not and that was life. I wasn't cured of wishing I'd been born tiny, and others would continue to consider it a personal failing that I hadn't. I'd probably always share that opinion on some level. It was too ingrained. But within reason, or until I got panicky again, I was going to be a person who did not forget to eat.

While my mother broke ice cubes into glasses, I set up a litter box and brought my overnight bag in from the car. The only nonalcoholic drink in the refrigerator was a pitcher of homemade iced tea, packed with sprigs of mint from the patch by the water hose outside. Otherwise the shelves were crowded with wine, vodka, and mixers—increasing priorities over the last two years. There was food, though—a minor miracle. My mother was better stocked than I was in my Hinesville apartment.

The hallway leading to the bedrooms was narrow, tight with the memory of my mother on the telephone in 1993—sliding down the wall to the floor with the receiver still in her hand, legs that had held her up for more than two decades buckling under the news that her husband had been declared Killed in Action, Body Not Recovered. Finally, officially. Irreversibly. I just happened to be there that day, and after the phone call I'd sat in the same cramped hallway and traced patterns on the ancient, nubbed green carpet, waiting for my mother to open the bedroom door she sobbed behind, alone. Praying that my father's death was killing her for the last time.

"So, when are you coming back for our boy?" Rambo had come out of hiding and positioned himself under my mother's hand in the kitchen. His purring warbled into protest when she stopped rubbing his head, so she bent back down. "You're in the field for two weeks?" Of course she was already calculating the number of days until my next visit.

"Yes, but we're not leaving just yet. We'll be super busy until then, though, so thanks for letting me bring Rambo up now. I should be back at the end of September, beginning of October if that's okay? I'll call you with the exact date when I have it."

"You know you can leave him forever if you want to, honey. For that year you're in Korea or whatever." My mother's tone indicated that it was my leaving, not the prospect of keeping the cat, that displeased her. For once, the only pressure was on the space between Rambo's ears. Good. Rambo released his vigilant, upright posture and sank onto his side like she'd cast a spell cast on him.

I paused, collecting the words I'd assembled during the four-hour car ride. "Speaking of which." I told her about the possibility that Fort Stewart soldiers would spend a year in the Balkans. I kept it clinical and fast, like the reporters still audible from the other room. It didn't affect me. It wasn't about me. But my mother was going to have something to say.

"The Balkans? But that's a war zone, Minerva." My mother stood up and Rambo bleated in protest. Her eyes fell on the silver cuff on my wrist, shining in the fading light of the kitchen window.

I put my hand over it, remembering how I promised her when I joined the Army that personnel people were always in the rear with the gear. That's how we both wanted it, although my mother didn't want me anywhere near the Army at all, really. "There was a cease-fire," I said. "Division is going as peacekeepers, not combatants."

"The Serbs aren't exactly honoring cease-fires, are they?" My mother had been working on that Dixie Chicken tumbler of wine, but her words came out unmuddled. "We've all seen the coverage of the massacres, and the stories about the peacekeepers who were taken hostage." She held a hand out, palm up.

Without a word I took the cuff off and handed it to her across the kitchen table, windows open to the breeze and the evening air full of the last fluty notes of a wood thrush and the first flickers of lightning bugs. "Do these things mean what they used to mean?" she asked.

She'd melted to the hallway floor, weeping. It had been two years, and twenty-four before that, but my mother's wounds were still raw and too easily reopened. "I'm not wearing it as any kind of statement. It's just for me." I should've known not to wear the bracelet here.

"Well, it's a terrible reminder of what can happen when the US military sends its best young people overseas without thinking it through. That is a terrible, terrible thing to carry on your arm. I don't know how you can stand it."

"I know a guy who carries a whole box of them around in his car." It was an ineffective argument, either for or against the bracelets. For or against sending soldiers to war—or to peace.

"What your friend lugs around in his car is his own business," my mother snapped. Our quick back and forth was always the same— exchanges of fire but no battle either of us could claim victory over. Scuttling backward through the vegetation to avoid direct contact. A body count of words with no progress, just a deepening of the mire.

"Well, Division is going to the Balkans. *I'm* going to Korea." My goal of going to Asia felt like the easy way out compared to what the others were doing, but my mother was holding both options up to the cylindrical bulb that ran over the sink and her scrutiny diminished them both. "I mean, maybe. My Korea assignment isn't official yet. Maybe I won't go anywhere." The kitchen walls squeezed in. I took a half step back, in search of the front door, an escape hatch, oxygen. First Sergeant could happily spend a long weekend with her entire extended family, and I couldn't even be in the same building as my mother for fifteen minutes.

She was unconvinced. "They'll send you. They'll send all of you to this place where we have no business involving ourselves, and then not put enough resources into doing the job properly."

"The scenario is more World War II than Vietnam, Mom. The bad guys and the good guys are more clear-cut." I broke one of the rules of engagement, the one where you didn't mention that country by name. My mother's face froze but I plunged on. "Anyway, peacekeepers don't engage. The job is to enforce the cease-fire agreements, whatever they end up being."

"Military advisers are allowed to return fire. That's how it escalates. You and your father, you think I don't know how the military works." My mother slipped into present tense, referring to my father as though he were there, which of course he always was. "A politician will say whatever he needs to, to convince the American public that his only recourse is to put our children in harm's way. Not his own children, mind you. Other people's children. *My* child. Those people don't need us. Europe should take care of itself."

Out in the living room atop the TV console, my parents smiled from a photograph identical to the one I kept on my desk at work, leaning against the same Mustang that was parked in the garage. The photo of my father was perpetually young and smiling. His uniform was blank of ribbons, with only the bars on his shoulders and the crossed rifles on the collar points to brighten his Class A jacket. One arm rested on the roof of his car, the other was draped over my mother's shoulder, a whisper pregnant with me—our only family portrait. Their patriotism was pure back then. They believed America had a role to play in the world.

"I'm not going, Mom. And the soldiers would rather have someone else in charge, anyway." This was easier to admit than I thought it would be. The Old Man had used me to bully Headquarters into doing their jobs and would say I was the reason for low morale once I left. It was the same situation my father had written about with his own soldiers. "They don't need anyone and especially not me. It's the story of my damn life. And the colonel decides where I go. I get no say."

My mother fixed me with a hard look. "You are very necessary," she said. "I don't understand where this self-flagellating is coming from. And I'll bet you have more of a choice than you're letting on."

"I'm not at all necessary." I never had been. When I'd found the box of letters in the trunk of my father's car—when I read The Letter for the first time—my life had suddenly made sense. Instead of confronting my mother with the information, though, I'd walked straight to my bed and slept for sixteen hours, one hour for every year I'd been alive. "Nobody wants me there. I'm over strength."

"Honestly, Minerva. You always know exactly what not to say." She walked to the refrigerator followed by a hopeful Rambo. She released the cork from the neck of a bottle of Gallo Gold over his incessant cries for a treat. Those motions would be familiar to him, the sight of a woman reaching for a drink. They were certainly familiar to me.

"Hush." My mother's words reached for the cat at her feet. "You hush now."

She took the bottle and her tumbler and closed the bedroom door in Rambo's face. I picked him up and hugged him, then went back to the kitchen and gave him a can of wet food. "Don't worry," I told him. "She still loves you." But he didn't care. Cats didn't require rapprochement as long as someone was feeding them.

The key hung by the door that led from the kitchen into the garage. I unlocked the door and stood in the entrance, inhaling the smells of machine oil, dry-rotted upholstery and uncirculated air. A hot garage smelled a lot like the Army. I returned to the fridge, ignoring the glass of iced tea still on the counter where my mother had left it for me. I opened a new bottle of the Gallo and poured myself a glass, then pulled the chain to the overhead lightbulb in the garage. I tugged open the Mustang's trunk and rooted around until I found my father's blue infantry stationery. The bucket seat sighed as I settled in. There was no way to do my job—no way to exist in my life—that didn't end up displeasing or damaging my mother or someone else. It would have been such a little thing to run a tube from the exhaust pipe into the stuffy interior of my father's car. So poetically perfect. If I'd been writing the script of some schlocky melodrama, that's what I'd have had my tragic heroine do.

But I was a self-preservation type and could find another way to connect with a mother who refused to engage. I ran my hand over the plastic cover of my father's stationery.

ARMY TRAINING AND EVALUATION PROGRAM (ARTEP)

After a mutually hungover cup of coffee with my mother the next morning I said, "I'll see you in a month," and blocked Rambo from sneaking out the door with me. My mother gave me an extra squeeze and it looked for a moment like she wanted to say something, but she held back. We were okay and not okay, just like always, as long as we never talked about anything head-on. My mother saw and heard only what confirmed her already-held beliefs and used that unrelenting focus to maintain the shape of her reality.

She stood in the driveway, cracked in three places from tree roots growing underneath it, and shaded her eyes, then waved. In the rearview mirror I watched as she ran a hand over the stiff crest of her hair and walked back into the house.

At work it was a weary couple of weeks of packing trucks and last-minute briefings about the ARTEP schedule. I relayed the information to the NCOs and even Storey trudged away from meetings with resignation in his ordinarily bouncy step. Training was looking good. We might even ace the evaluation, but everyone was waiting for me to be done and gone. Even though the pressure of paying for missing equipment had been removed, motor pool still blamed me for making an issue of it in the first place.

As First Sergeant had predicted the Old Man showed no interest in the receipts from the Army-Navy store. "Brigade has written these losses off," he said. The papers looked crummy and insignificant even to me. "They're giving a promising young officer a second chance, so why can't you?" It was pointless to argue. When I finally parked my car at the company the morning of the convoy to the training area it was both a relief and a last, insurmountable obstacle. At least I'd be spending the next two weeks in the woods, and trees forgave everything.

At the bivouac site, the female soldiers raised a GP Medium under the supervision of First Sergeant. We accounted for its guy lines and dressed them all right, then heaved the center pole as the tent stood and rearranged its heavy canvas skirts. Panting from the exertion, Logan and I brushed pine needles and sand from our palms, moving aside as the others busied themselves with tent pegs. "Are you bunking in the Operations Center?" I asked. She'd be the only female in there if she did that, but she'd be with the other staff officers.

"No." Logan watched as Pettit tied the knots off. "Are you having a GP Small for yourself?"

"No, I'll just set up a cot in here with y'all." Neither of us wanted to seem too good for communal living so now we'd be under the same roof for two weeks.

Once the structure was secure the women unfolded cots and threw out sleeping bags, and First Sergeant ducked through the tent flap door. "Two straight rows," she said. "We ain't having a messy female barracks." Reyes and Robinson rolled the side flaps to let air circulate but it remained in green shadow. Logan, First Sergeant, and I placed our cots on one end of the tent, and there we were—all the women together. How hard could that be?

After the bivouac site was set up to the Old Man's satisfaction, with trucks parked under camouflage netting and the water buffalo next to the Tactical Operations Center, the cooks went to rustle up some chow. I unrolled my sleeping bag and laid my toiletries, pogey bait and notebook across the top, removing the packet of light blue infantry stationery from my duffel bag last. I was going public with my bag of peanut M&Ms just like everyone else, dammit, and that stationery wasn't a holy relic. Those sheets of paper served no purpose desiccating in the stifling heat and cold winters of my mother's garage. Maybe it was cruel to drag a reminder of the past into the infection-dissipating light, since my mother's usual response to painful emotional input was to shut down, to hide behind a door, to anesthetize it. But seeing First Sergeant surrounded by a family of supportive women had been a revelation, and I wanted a sliver of that for myself. A letter could be personal but still keep some distance, like spaces between cots.

Hi Mom, it's me.

Our last conversation didn't end all that well and I want to do better. I'm sorry if seeing Dad's old letter paper for the first time in a quarter century is upsetting, but using his stationery helps me feel closer to both of you, like this is something we can all share. I'm looking for him in all the ways I can think of, and if my doing that causes you pain, I'm also sorry for that. I can keep my thoughts about him to myself if it's too hard for you, but I have to do this for my own sanity. I can't keep pretending that he's out there somewhere, trying to find us, when it's only us who are looking. I will always be looking, though. You should know that.

I also want you to know you have a place in my heart and in my thoughts, and that you're welcome in my world—even though I don't feel welcome in the Army most of the time myself. Which is not that big of a deal. I'm not planning to make a career of it or anything. I hope you see that it's all going to be okay for us. I love you.

The words bounced around, like my thoughts. I wasn't really making sense, but the letter said what I wanted to say.

Soldiers buzzed in and out of the tent, too busy and self-sufficient to pay much attention to me, sitting on my cot and blinking back tears.

It felt stupid to go from apologizing to my mother to talking about how hot it was, even in mid-September, to asking how Rambo was, to reporting which disgusting flavor of MRE I got stuck with because I let the other soldiers pick first. I left it at that, sealed and stamped the envelope, and wrote READ THIS ONE FIRST under my mother's address. I pulled out a new sheet of paper.

> *I'll never admit it in the company of other soldiers, but I sort of like the dehydrated pork patty. There, I said it. Ha ha. I'll explain it to you later if you don't know what I'm talking about. I'm told the C rations Dad had in Vietnam were not as bad, although I'm sure they're all awful. Our cooks have a field kitchen going here, so these MREs are only for days we're on a firing range, or days like tomorrow when we're getting graded on land nav (navigating our way around the woods) and will be gone from the bivouac site for most of the day.*

This letter stumbled over itself, too, and I was back in the woods of my youth, creeping ever closer to the timid deer. But here on the ARTEP I had to be decisive. I'd been given a choice about what to be graded on and when, so I'd opted to get our weakest event over right away. If land nav went well we could ride the wave of success forward. If we bolo'd it, there'd be time to try again toward the end of the two-week exercise.

To my surprise, Logan joined us on the land nav course. "Lead by example and all that, right?" she said. We wanted to dislike each other, but sometimes we couldn't help but agree—like we had about the importance of bunking with the other women.

"Roger." I still looked forward to seeing Logan's shiny boots caked with muck, that perfect French braid all messed up and sweaty. It wasn't noble of me, but the woods were my turf, dammit. Logan didn't get to be great at everything.

Dear Mom,

While I was stomping around on land nav today, I got a little off course. Okay, I was lost. Completely, utterly turned around, and I wound up at a small, unmarked cemetery instead of at my next point. There are a quite a few cemeteries out here in the training area from old towns that got bought up during World War II when Fort Stewart expanded, but this one looked like no one had been there in more than fifty years. I'm not going to lie—I was panicked about being lost and failing the training task, but I couldn't help looking around. It's morbid to admit—I didn't want to see the graves of children or think of them as scared and sad and left behind by their families but couldn't stop myself from doing the math on those grave markers.

Anyway, of all the soldiers to get lost on the course it had to be me, the commander. The one with the fancy compass. The one who's supposedly so good at land nav. Everyone else did fine, even my driver who has bad eyesight, and especially this new second lieutenant who I'll tell you about some other time. Grrr. I got back to the company area two hours late, mortified and sure we'd blown the whole field exercise on the very first day.

The colonel was all set to jump on my case—he made some "joke" about not sending a lieutenant to Korea who couldn't find her way out of a paper bag—but I think the graders could tell I felt bad enough as it was. They said to make up for the failure, they were putting me in charge of navigating the whole battalion out of the training area and back to main post on the last night. It's a fair way for me to redeem myself. The punishment fits the crime, so to speak. We'll just be following major tank trails to get out of here, anyway. I'm trying to tell myself it'll all be fine.

Anyway (x2!), I'm just rambling, like I was on the course, and I'll self-correct now like I did then. I'm hot and tired but wanted to let you know that even though I'm not fine it'll all be fine, and that I love you. Give Rambo some pink yogurt for me.

I wrote from my cot, after evening chow and after I'd been given our operating orders from the graders for the next day. I told First Sergeant what needed to be done and she took it from there, everything ticking along like my tactical wristwatch, no one mentioning my land nav failure, although they were probably talking about it behind my back. I breathed. I wrote. I wrestled with the terror that Headquarters would fail again and that I'd never get out of the Fort Stewart woods, literally or metaphorically. I had nothing else to do but sit and write my fears to a mother who couldn't talk back.

Later that night, Logan told a ghost story while the rest of us lay on top of our sleeping bags, sweating even with the canvas sides of the tent rolled up. "You've probably never heard of the Trưng sisters." Logan pitched her voice low and mysterious in the dim light. On the cot next to her, Pettit giggled. "But they were two Vietnamese warrior women who raised an army to beat back Chinese invaders during the Han Dynasty."

"Badass." Shumacher's eyes were closed, her voice drowsy, a pair of white granny underpants hanging from a support pole over her head like the moon. It must be nice to be the kind of person who could sleep soundly anywhere. The first night of the training exercise she'd fallen asleep as if she'd been enchanted, while I'd been kept awake by the mosquitos and the creaking of the aluminum bones of the cots as everyone tossed and turned in the heat.

"After two years of a just and peaceful rule, the Chinese Army again invaded the Trưng sisters' realm." I strained to hear Logan over the noise of Washburn at the water buffalo, singing softly to himself around his ablutions. "Flying low above the trees, pilots doing what they please. Droppin' frags on refugees . . . " His singing was stream of conscious, disconnected from the physical world. But still. I swung my legs over the side of my cot to go talk to him.

"Shut the fuck up, Washburn." A voice I didn't recognize interrupted the song about napalm sticking to kids. It was Robinson, the shy, dimpled cook, now sporting a short natural hairstyle instead of her braids. I'd barely heard Robinson speak aloud before, much less drop an f-bomb. Inside and outside the tent the bivouac site went silent.

"Sorry," came the sheepish reply. The lyrics turned to the vigorous sounds of brushing teeth—Washburn taking his embarrassment out on his gums.

Logan cleared her throat. It was too dark to see her reaction to the song. "Rather than allow themselves to be captured, the sisters bit off their own tongues and flung themselves into the Hát Giang River." Logan's voice rose in confidence as she spoke the river's name, her accent completely American but with some words dropping off at angles different from the slurry Southern speech all around us. I wondered if a person missed it, not being able to speak a mother tongue, and how many other people, places, and memories Logan's heart had to hold spaces for. "Another fierce woman warrior, Phùng Thị Chính, had given birth on the battlefield. When they were facing defeat at the hands of the Chinese she killed her baby and committed suicide as well."

Shumacher sat up on her cot. "No," she said. Her pregnancy scare had been months ago but must have affected her more than I realized. Shumacher's silhouette was sharp as she faced Logan. "No, ma'am."

"Oh, yes." Logan had recovered her ghosty, storyteller voice. "Some say their restless spirits still roam the forests and mountains of northern Việt Nam, wreaking vengeance on those who enter their territory. Those whose intentions are not good."

I shivered despite the heat and slapped a mosquito on my forearm. Was Logan thinking about the Old Man, or just telling a story? On the cot closest to the door of the tent, First Sergeant shifted onto her side to listen. Her eyes gleamed in the weak light from Washburn's tactical flashlight as he returned to the tent where the male mechanics were bunking.

"Anyway," Logan intoned. "I'm not telling you a story about the Trưng sisters. *Their* ghosts are not the ones who haunt *these* forests." Pettit laughed out loud and was shushed by the others. I hadn't been invited to many slumber parties when I was a kid, and if someone's mother forced her to invite all the girls in the class I had to bring blankets and a pillow because I didn't own a sleeping bag. My mother was awkward around all the parents who hadn't been wrecked by war. Once I overheard a mother call me "poor thing" to her husband as I was creeping up the stairs to ask for a glass of water. Instead I crept to a bedroom phone and called my mother to pick me up. But I was a little in love with the women in the tent that night. Even though my cot was on the end of the tent with First Sergeant and Logan, I felt I was inching toward membership in a group.

"I found an old cemetery in the woods today," I said to the darkened tent, paying the entry fee to the club by putting myself in a one-down position. I hated to do it, but it was a requirement among women and the closest I could get to admitting I'd screwed up on land nav. From the pause that resulted, it was clear the others knew why I'd been late getting back. "I saw the graves of babies."

"No, *ma'am*." Shumacher sounded close to tears.

"No watery graves for those babies," giggled Pettit. My heart went cold in the muggy night, thinking of the desperate women of Logan's story. Of my father's own probably watery grave.

"The old folks in my family say if a person isn't sent off properly after they pass, their spirits will wander until they are." First Sergeant raised herself on her elbow to speak—to deflect from Pettit having gone a little too dark. She was still in T-shirt and BDU trousers, hair still neatly pulled back. She hadn't been disheveled in front of the rest of us even once yet.

"We say the same." Logan claimed the *we*. I was outside the circle that Logan and First Sergeant were drawing around themselves but fought the impulse to feel sorry for myself. I wasn't quite the social outcast I had been. I was in the tent with the others, wasn't I?

"They say you've got to leave them some food at their graves," First Sergeant went on. Her teeth were white under the pitched roof of the tent, and her voice smiled in Logan's direction. "Some of their possessions, and favorite food and such, or they'll keep coming back to your house, looking for them."

"I don't want to hear no more ghost stories," Reyes said. "Y'all are freaking me out."

Laughter rippled around the tent. "Quiet down and get some sleep," First Sergeant said, sitting fully upright on the edge of her cot. As I drifted off she pulled out a small green notebook, flicked on the red tactical lens of her flashlight and hunched over to write.

Sometime later I woke. Logan and First Sergeant were outside the tent flap, talking quietly and slapping mosquitos.

" . . . left behind but used her connections to get us out in 1975."

I angled my head so I could hear over Shumacher's snores.

" . . . found my father, which was fine, but disappointing. I mean, once she got us reconnected . . . no interest . . . had to do everything on her own, anyway."

Logan was talking about her father? And she'd found him, but it hadn't been what she expected? I was wide awake in an instant.

The night rendered First Sergeant's voice fuzzy. "Never say never, ma'am, but . . . doesn't make you any less than one hundred percent American."

"No," Logan said. "I know. But . . . "

Logan mumbled something, and then First Sergeant spoke again. "How about the rest of it? Has the colonel stopped . . . ?"

"Backed off some," Logan said, "nothing I can't . . . " The two voices paused as soft whistling approached, then receded on its way to the perimeter, web belt rattling. The blithe spirit of Washburn, never at rest.

"Anyway . . . since the minute I got here . . ." Logan's voice dropped out of range. I wanted to leap out of my sleeping bag and plonk myself next to the two of them, but other people's stories didn't automatically belong to me. I understood that now. And I couldn't cobble together any real information from eavesdropping or snooping in Logan's personnel file, not that I was going to do that kind of thing anymore.

If Logan or First Sergeant or the vets at the VFW wanted to hold their stories close, that was their right. I walled myself up with personal information, too, although I was beginning to find it lonely inside my fortress of facts. Isolating myself didn't help me understand anything or anyone, but I didn't know how to break free. Not yet.

Logan and First Sergeant were completely at ease outside the tent flap, bonding in a way I never would with either of them, and I just had to deal with it. I fell back to sleep and dreamed envious dreams.

Hi Mom,

This morning the colonel came peeling up to our bivouac site in a spray of sand and red clay dust to tell me that an armored personnel carrier had gotten stuck in the muck. An APC looks like a small tank and is used to carry soldiers into battle, and apparently some grunts were hotdogging around on the tank trails and got themselves in trouble—this happens a lot when they're let loose in the woods. It seems like every Fort Stewart unit is out here playing Army one more time before being sent to Bosnia—we still don't have official word, but we know it's going to happen. You've probably seen on the news that NATO is still shelling the Serbs. It's a paradox, but it's the only way to get them to the negotiating table. Anyway, the training area is alive with these guys and their APCs.

So the Old Man saunters down from his truck like John Wayne fresh from the Aqua Velva factory. He must be going home to shower—maybe even to sleep. We're only twenty miles from post, so I guess he's taking advantage of his rank. The rest of us smell like we've been in the woods for almost two weeks, which isn't pretty, but it breaks down the barriers. You can't be too formal around people when it's obvious you're just a bunch of animals after all.

"We're gonna need the M88, Lieutenant Mills," he says. M88s are tankish looking vehicles, too, but strong enough to tow real tanks. The maintenance companies' M88s were all out

on jobs since the infantry guys are going hog wild out here. But our M88 was all the way back in the company area, locked in the motor pool because it's just a bonus toy we have. We weren't supposed to need it for this exercise.

But I guess the infantry commander called our Old Man, asking for a favor, so he told me to send somebody back to fetch it. I couldn't say no because he's holding my Korea assignment over my head until the bitter end, but also, we had the time to do it. Since my snafu with land nav, the company's done pretty well on all our other training tasks if I do say so myself. And I was happy for an excuse for the motor sergeant to run back to post to check in with his wife and kid. He could drop off and pick up mail while he was there. The Old Man told me I could go back with the motor sergeant if I wanted, to run to the gym for a shower, but I wanted to stay with the soldiers. Not to hold anyone's hand, just to watch them do their jobs and be proud.

(quick break for chow—now I'm back)

So there we all were, in a circular clearing among the pine trees, baking in a patch of mud just big enough to hold an M113 Armored Personnel Carrier. The head of the APC driver kept popping in and out of the hatch, listening to instructions then submerging to steer. No one wanted to throw a track while they pulled it back onto the tank trail. It would be an extreme pain in the ass if an APC couldn't roll on its own after being recovered from the swamp so far from main post.

For the first time I understood what it meant to have my heart in my mouth while I watched everyone work—my motor sergeant inching this fifty-ton M88 backward from the sink hole, with a female mechanic named Shumacher standing next to it and guiding him away from trees. The motor sergeant is kind of a jerk, but he's calmed down some over the last couple of months—maybe that phone call to his wife cheered him up. Long story. I'll tell you another time.

Shumacher, unapologetically taking her place in the scene and every bit of a match for the clanking rhinos that surrounded her, had guided the M88 back onto the tank trail while I fidgeted, tapping my fingers against my upper lip. The September afternoon was swelteringly hot, and I imagined these two hulking vehicles melting into pools of molten metal, seeping into the ground water and poisoning everything around them. Rice grew in the flooded fields from the Georgia coast all the way to Vietnam. Food grew from slime; slime was enriched by the humans and animals that returned to it. An animal or vehicle or human could disappear into the stinking grasp of this swamp with nothing or no one to pull them out and they might be gone in one sense, but their molecules, good or bad, remained.

I blinked. The heat was messing with my head. But eventually the swamp relinquished the APC with a slurping pop and a shout from the soldiers in and around both vehicles. "Next time, stick to the trail, soldier," First Sergeant admonished as the infantry team remounted the APC and drove away. The grunts beamed and cursed and boxed the air, dripping decomposing vegetation as they lumbered past. The name stenciled on the side of the vehicle was *Apocalypse Now.*

"Charlie don't surf!" the driver shouted back. Had he seen Logan, propped against a pine tree, examining her filthy fingernails, before he quoted that line from the movie? The thing Robert Duvall's character said before they swooped around shooting Vietnamese people to the Wagner-infused soundtrack?

"We're doing good, LT." Storey, appearing next to me, had remained unflappable with every about-face we were asked to make by the Old Man and the graders. The giant urns of coffee that Robinson and the other cooks kept topped up day and night helped, but still.

"We are, aren't we?" I turned to look at him. There were shadows under his reddish-brown eyes, made darker by a combination of sweat and camouflage paint that settled in all our pores even after thorough washing at the water buffalo. I could have kissed him for using the word *we*. "Those APCs make me nervous," I said. "Bunch of cowboys riding wild like Valkyries all over the ranges."

He nodded. "We've just got to keep it together for a couple more tasks. Then we get our people the hell out of here."

BUT ONLY SAY THE WORD AND I SHALL BE HEALED

Covered in swamp muck from the APC recovery, the soldiers swaggered back to the bivouac site. The voices around the perimeter were full of energy; they contained smiles. "Let me talk to a guy I know out here," Storey said. "He can hook us up with a trip to the shower tent."

"We've only got one more night in the field." It wasn't practical. We could suck it up for just a little longer. But oh, my god, my skin craved soap, hot water, steam. Baby wipes were not cutting it anymore.

"A shower would pump up morale before we hit that convoy." There was a question mark in the depths of Storey's penny-bright eyes. The freckles across the bridge of his nose had multiplied under the relentless sun and I was overcome with an impulse to run a light fingertip over them. "And it's not against the regs to make your boss happy, is it, LT?"

"I guess not!" I said, a ridiculous trill in my voice. Besides the fact that it would never occur to me to do something to make the Old Man happy—please him, sure—but make him happy? On purpose? The thought sickened me. But was I flirting with Storey? Because for some non-Army reason Storey wanted a piece of my true self and that was the hardest thing for me to give. I was easing up with the others but until this moment I'd been inclined to buckle tighter with him. "Thank you," I relented. Sort of. "The soldiers will love that."

There was a small changing area at the entrance to the shower tent, a perk one of Storey's buddies had rigged up for senior leaders and anyone else lucky enough to be owed a favor from him. Headquarters cycled through in groups, and the females had a fifteen-minute block of time to get in and out. We reverted to Basic Training skills—strip, scrub, dress wet into minimum acceptable uniform, figure your hair out later. I averted my eyes from First Sergeant's wiry nudity. From Rob's curves and from Reyes without her glasses. I gritted my teeth against Pettit's refusal to share a shower head while her conditioner stayed on for three full minutes before rinsing. I would not—not!—compare my body to Logan's.

I kept my head down and prayed that everyone would be too self-conscious to notice that although I'd settled into a relaxed pattern of eating meals with the company, and that my uniforms were looser from all the sweating, I would always be, as my mother used to whisper to friends when she thought I wasn't listening, a little "broad in the beam." That comment had always made me feel like a barn. A barn wrapped around a cow. So I broke a land speed record getting dressed and out of the shower tent, then returned to the bivouac site while everyone else went to chow. The cooks were serving one more hot meal before they broke down the field kitchen in preparation for the convoy back to main post—chili mac and peach cobbler. The soldiers were beside themselves with glee.

Back on my cot, I attempted to braid my wet hair without the benefit of a mirror. My shoulders ached; I couldn't think what I'd done for them to be so fatigued. The silhouette of First Sergeant appeared in the doorway to the tent, holding her green notebook and a pen. "You going to Mass, ma'am?"

The aluminum side piece of the cot dug into the back of my legs and the cot groaned as I twisted to look at her, arms still raised as I jabbed bobby pins into my skull without the benefit of a mirror. "Say again, First Sergeant? Mass?"

First Sergeant waved her notebook. "They announced it in the first sergeants' meeting. Something Lieutenant Logan set up. One of the protestant chaplains is holding a service in the operations center, and the Catholic chaplain is saying a combat Mass out in the tree line. I thought, since you're Catholic and all, you might be going."

I shook my head. "I'm not a practicing Catholic, First Sergeant," I reminded her. "Is it even Sunday?" All the days had run together in a muddy mess.

"It is indeed, ma'am."

I didn't enjoy going to Mass. It took too long, and standing shoulder to shoulder with a bunch of other hypocrites made me impatient. But what the hell. "Well, I just had a shower. I may as well go wash away my sins." I tortured my French braid with one more bobby pin and stood. "Hopefully I won't burn up on entry."

In a small clearing among the trees outside of our Headquarters perimeter, a full bird colonel in BDUs and Kevlar, sleeves rolled down to his wrists, stood with his back to a stump on which he'd placed an olive green bag. His branch insignia was a stitched black cross. The name on his tape was Marcantonio.

"Don't stand too close together." He smiled at us—Logan, Washburn, me, and a handful of soldiers from the maintenance companies. The last Army priest I'd encountered made it a point to kiss every woman as they left the chapel, even going so far as to block the doorway so we couldn't pass. That chaplain drove a new Saab, a shiny refutation of his vow of poverty, but this guy exuded calm like a quiet breeze. He seemed at home with a stump for an altar. "Give yourselves plenty of space. We can't have the enemy take you out with one tight cluster bomb." It was a tactical Mass; we raised our arms to shoulder height and spread out like it was a PT session. He did not invite us to sit.

We bowed our heads and he spoke softly and rapidly over us. We responded in kind, maintaining noise discipline. I might have gone to Mass more often if it was always like this. I didn't need a folk choir or a ten-piece band or a tambourine section. Just trees, and quick, quiet devotion. In lieu of a homily the priest thanked Logan for inviting him and she beamed, an expression of pleasure more genuine than I'd ever seen on her face. The priest had been a chaplain in Vietnam, he said, hopping on and off choppers into the bush and onto remote fire bases. He was glad to revisit an experience that had been so meaningful for him.

Other than that he didn't elaborate on his war experiences. Maybe my father had been among the units he'd prayed with and for, sent to do a terrible job, lonely and heartbroken and halfway around the world. Maybe I should talk to this guy—as a true searcher, not a researcher. The very thought struck fear and hope in my heart—a little more hope than fear.

Father Marcantonio raised his arms. "Peace be with you," he said.

"And also with you," we murmured. As the priest removed a small flask of wine and a container of consecrated hosts from his green bag, the rest of us crossed the clearing to shake hands as an offering of peace. This was the only part of Mass I truly enjoyed, a moment of realness that broke into the ritual. A chance to breathe, to make things more right in the world. I eyed Logan. She'd kept her head down for most of the service and wasn't looking my way, but before I could make an overture Washburn walked over to her. I couldn't hear what he said, everyone was so hushed and spread out, but at the end of whatever it was, Washburn stuck his hand out to shake and instead of taking his hand Logan pulled him into a hug. Washburn returned to his place among the trees, cheeks bright pink, and Logan ran a finger under her eyes. She must have felt me looking her way because she finally raised her head, cocked it, and flashed me a peace sign, a tiny smile pushed into one corner of her mouth. I peaced her back.

SITUATION NORMAL, ALL FUCKED UP (SNAFU)

We spent the next morning tearing down the bivouac site and repacking the trucks. All around me soldiers moved at tempo, filling duffels and Alice packs as I rolled my sweat-soaked sleeping bag. We'd performed well and all that stood between Battalion and home were a few small training tasks and one last tactical convoy.

Just after lunch, the graders sprang some mock medical emergencies on us. Having been prepped beforehand, and with great dramatic flourishes, Davis pretended to have a heart attack. Washburn simulated jamming a screwdriver into his leg and Logan "broke" her wrist. "You must have been typing too fast," I said while splinting it, but my joke fell flat. We'd exchanged peace signs, but a genuine friendship took time—time I didn't have. But I could still try.

"Your vehicles will be moving through an area known to have experienced chemical weapons attacks," the head grader intoned during the final operations order. I looked around the cluster of company commanders to share an eye roll. We were in the back forty of the largest Army post east of the Mississippi river. We stood on swampy, sandy ground usurped from indigenous people first, made prosperous off the backs of stolen people, then commandeered from disgruntled towns in the run-up to World War II. The training area might have been peopled by dirty soldiers and angry spirits, but Saddam Hussein was not hiding among the branches of a live oak, getting bitten by sand fleas, finger twitching on the detonator of an ACME chemical warhead.

I'd plotted the route for the convoy along the main tank trails to keep everything as simple as possible. I was a little anxious about the outcome, but all this playacting resulted in soldiers taking training less seriously, not more. Instead of smirking at the theatrics, though, the other company commanders, all captains except me, scratched busily with stubby pencils into their green notebooks. I was due to get promoted pretty soon if the Old Man stopped making such a big deal about my weight, but I'd have to do something to stave off the lobotomy that seemed to accompany pinning on captain's bars.

As night fell we fired up the engines and the trucks hitched forward. I peered into the gloomy void where trees glowed like tall, straight ghosts and wasn't sure if what I was seeing was real or whether the blackout lights of Shumacher's deuce and a half, creeping along in front of Reyes and me at the end of the convoy, had wrecked my night vision. Although the flimsy vinyl doors of the Humvee weren't much of a barrier to start with, I unzipped the window to merge with the world of darkness, relying on sound to calculate nearness. The cicadas formed a one-note symphony against which the engines of Battalion's vehicles played. The maintenance companies were whole klicks ahead already, leaders interspersed among the many kilometers of vehicles as we made our cautious way out of the training area and toward main post. The Old Man was doing his thing up at the front, but Headquarters Company brought up the rear. I wanted to make sure every last vehicle made it back.

We were all in our MOPP suits, ready for the chemical attack, and our canteens were full because even after sunset it was eighty-something degrees and 90 percent humidity. As Reyes hunched over the steering wheel, concentrating on keeping the correct combat distance from the back end of the deuce and a half carrying Robinson and Shumacher, I thought with longing of the six pack of 333 Premium Export I'd left in the refrigerator in my apartment. I didn't care if the convoy took four hours and recovery operations took another four hours after we got back to Headquarters—I was cracking one of those bad boys open when I got home. Sweat drained in a steady stream down my temples and between my shoulder blades. It pooled around my waist and into the seams of my last pair of clean underwear, into the thick socks under my jungle boots, which were themselves inside my rubber MOPP overshoes. I wanted an ice-cold beer and a shower and to sleep for twenty four hours straight. First things first, though.

"What's that hanging from Shumacher's bumper?" The blackout headlights cast an otherworldly light against the dust cloud raised by the convoy and illuminated a large white something fluttering from the back of Shumacher's truck. I'd told everyone to attach something light-colored to the back of each vehicle to make it easier to see in the moonless dark.

"I don't know, LT." Reyes leaned even closer to the windshield, the dark, dust, and her poor eyesight putting extra pressure on her. She spoke reassuringly. "It ain't one of Lieutenant Logan's ghosts." The Humvee's engine bucked quietly as we rolled over the sandy trail, and Reyes wiped under her eyes as if to clear the murk from her vision. She didn't take her eyes off the white blob and the dim red lights, themselves pulsing like tired eyes from Shumacher's bumper.

Suddenly the space between the two vehicles filled with a thick, grayish-red smoke that turned blackish-red. The deuce came to a complete stop and even as careful as Reyes was, she barely managed to slam on the Humvee's brakes to avoid ramming into the back of the truck. The smell of diesel fuel seeped into the crack where I'd unzipped the window. "What the hell?" The white blob was right in front of us. It was a pair of Shumacher's granny underpants.

I met Shumacher trundling around the corner of the truck, enormous in her MOPP suit and scowling beneath her sweaty camouflage face paint. "Nice warning flag," I teased, worried that one stupid snafu would dismantle the convoy that was supposed to be anticlimactic. I needed to navigate Battalion home with zero mistakes. I was making up for my land nav bolo and couldn't screw up now.

Shumacher snatched the underwear off the bumper and threw it at me. "Stupid Washburn." She untied the canvas flap covering the truck's contents, lowered the tailgate, and pulled out a roll of wrenches and a nontactical flashlight.

"You're not going under there?"

"The heck I'm not." In the dim red of my tactical lens Shumacher's face settled into familiar stubbornness. "Those liars at Third Shop said they'd fixed that leak. We just blew a seal or I'll eat my gas mask."

The air was thick with a humid sludge of swamp rot and diesel, and Shumacher wriggled into god knows what with nothing but a roll of tools to protect herself. Could a handful of soldiers at the back of a convoy jack this truck up in the dark if we needed to? We did have a new jack assembly. The ground was so sandy, though.

"Specialist Shumacher, get out from under there," I said to her MOPP boots.

"There is no one else." Davis was ahead of us somewhere, in the tree line with the M88, counting the convoy vehicles until we'd all passed and it was time to fire up the smoke generator. Since we'd brought the M88 out into the field, I decided to use it to camouflage our departure, the icing on the cake of our performance. So Shumacher was right— there wasn't anyone else available to trouble shoot the deuce. I turned back to the Humvee and reached for the radio. Reyes's head was back; I let her sleep. We were all bone-tired.

I pressed the handset. "Elias, this is Taylor." Why had I suggested we take names from *Platoon* for our call signs? It sounded ridiculous in the swampy night, like I was becoming one of the other captains already, taking genuine, stupid pleasure in playacting our Army roles.

"Go ahead, Taylor," First Sergeant's voice crackled. Good. She wasn't out of radio range yet.

"Elias, stop the convoy. We've got a situation back here."

"Roger, Taylor." The handset went dead, and I pictured First Sergeant telling Washburn to slow her military Blazer to a stop, giving the other vehicles time to halt safely. She'd walk down the line, making sure everyone had their NBC equipment at the ready, thinking my radio message had something to do with the chemical attack we were told was coming. I'd set her straight in a minute.

Shumacher scooted her way from under the deuce and a half, grunting and exasperated. She hauled herself to her feet and held her thumb and forefinger up. "Some idiot plugged a leak in the oil pan with Bondo instead of replacing it. All the oil's drained out, so the engine's probably gone." She took a deep breath and laid her hand on her stomach.

"What's wrong?" What was wrong was that Davis should have inspected the deuce's repairs before he agreed to pick it up from Third Shop.

Shumacher paused, then exhaled, answering for herself and not the truck. "Nothing. I probably ate too much chili mac last night." Quite a few soldiers had overdone it at chow—the port-a-potties that morning were proof of that.

"Unsnap your jacket." I handed her a canteen from my web belt. "The graders can dock me points, but if they call a gas attack you are not to put your mask on." I prayed Shumacher wouldn't be a knucklehead about it, but she nodded and drank deeply from the canteen.

"We're gonna need a tow," she said when she lowered the canteen.

"All right." I was thinking as I spoke. "Okay, that works, because Sergeant Davis is around here somewhere. He can tow you with the M88. But, shit—he doesn't have a radio."

MOPP boots crunched over sand and a red pinpoint bobbed in the dark—the tactical lens of another flashlight—followed by Washburn moving at an encumbered jog. "Hey, ma'am," he panted. "When you didn't give the signal for gas, First Sar'n told me to come back and see what was up." He caught sight of Shumacher curled around her midsection and moved toward her, but she twisted her torso away.

"Have you seen Sergeant Davis and the M88?" If there was something wrong with Shumacher, Davis would need Washburn's help. I took a deep breath of the fetid air to steady myself. One thing at a time. "We need to scrap the smoke generator plan and get y'all to tow the deuce back to the company."

Just as Washburn raised his arm to point down the tank trail in the direction from which he'd come, a familiar Cummins engine flared, then changed pitch. Where the dust had subsided in the wake of the other vehicles, thick white smoke began to roll. The sound of something large and heavy clanked not far away and I felt like I was submerged in a sensory deprivation chamber in the humid night, but somehow also overwhelmed by competing inputs. Was Davis moving toward us with the M88 rather than staying put as he'd been instructed? I had no way of contacting him, but it was risky to be free-wheeling out here in the smoky dark. He should have stuck to the plan.

"Ma'am." Shumacher's voice was a pained gasp. She was holding onto the deuce's bumper with one hand and hunched over and cradling her stomach with the other. Washburn put his arm around her.

I pushed Washburn away from Shumacher. "Get First Sergeant on the radio," I said over the noise of the approaching vehicle. "Tell her the deuce is having engine trouble. We're going to have to tow it, but we've got it under control." Washburn, being a mechanic, would know how to phrase this in a way that didn't freak the Old Man out if he was still in range and listening to the chatter.

Shumacher needed attention, but I had to figure out which direction the M88 was coming from so I could stop Davis. I raised my head and listened. Had Washburn been about to say that Davis was just a little farther along the trail? The smoke was coming from about fifty meters ahead. So why did it sound like the M88 was blundering toward us through the trees to the side of the two halted vehicles? Why was the hazy smoke brightening as if illuminated by nontactical headlights?

I turned to look, but before I could see, before I could process what was happening, brakes squealed, and treads strained against their forward trajectory. A tracked vehicle did not turn on a dime when hemmed in by trees. Washburn had climbed into the passenger side of my Humvee to get on the radio and he and Reyes—awake now and likewise silhouetted against the brightness—were turned toward an armored personnel carrier that burst from between the trees straight at them.

Bright lights made a fuzzy arc in the smoke, then the APC plowed into the vinyl side of the Humvee. There was a sickening crunch, the sound of armor hitting the thin, metal-framed doors. The Humvee lurched forward into the back corner of the deuce, pushed by the much larger vehicle. The deuce moved, too, then halted the Humvee's momentum.

I froze. It took a full five seconds for the cicadas to recover, to begin screaming into the night, although an engine fan was still running somewhere. Those five seconds were so dense I could hear the Brownian noise of molecules struggling for space. Then someone was screaming in a language I didn't know. Maybe Reyes? Screaming in Tagalog? Robinson emerged from the cab of the deuce and stumbled toward me on the trail, but I motioned her back. "Lay on the horn," I said. "Fuck light and noise discipline. Turn on the headlights and don't stop blasting the horn until somebody turns up."

Rob gaped for one interminable second at how the side of the Humvee had wrapped itself around the undamaged front of the APC, then scrambled away. More light and noise, and I was moving and speaking in every direction while everyone else held still. "Please please please," I prayed. "Fuck fuck fuck." I pulled open the driver's side door of the Humvee and Reyes fell out, sobbing, into my arms.

"Are you okay?" I didn't mean to scream but the cicadas were so loud in my ears. Reyes nodded, then heaved like she was going to vomit, and I shoved her toward Shumacher. "Help each other." But I didn't know what I expected them to do. Reyes could be hurt, too, for all I knew.

The deuce's horn stopped blaring and I didn't have time to scream at Rob to keep it up because I was already screaming at the driver of the APC as he emerged from the hatch. "Back the fuck up!" I wasn't going to be able to pull Washburn, who was making alarming, inhuman noises of his own, over the rectangular drive tunnel that ran between the front seats of the Humvee. I couldn't get him out of the mangled wreckage on the other side unless the APC got out of the fucking way. *Fuck fuck fuck.*

The sound of more MOPP boots, this time running over the sand, brought voices, and then Davis was there, breathing hard. "What happened?" he asked. I'd have liked to know the same. I fired off words, praying that something would hit the right target.

"Get this fucking APC off Washburn," I said. I pulled on the shoulders of Washburn's MOPP jacket but it was no use.

More loud voices and swearing, then an engine thrown into reverse. *Please please please.* I ran around the Humvee. Washburn was crumpled in the passenger seat, hooked around the bent door and pressed into position by the drive tunnel.

"Back. The fuck. UP," I screamed, but the APC was already in motion. Once there was space between its front bumper and the Humvee I squeezed my way in, praying that the heavy vehicle didn't jolt forward again and pin me. It continued to reverse and the Humvee door popped open. I caught Washburn falling forward and eased him onto the ground, untangling his legs from bent metal and shredded vinyl as best I could. He didn't make a sound, but a perfect circle of something dark stained the torso of his charcoal NBC suit and it was spreading.

I knelt in the sand and ripped through snaps, feeling for a pulse at Washburn's carotid but couldn't be sure what was happening since my own heart was thumping so hard. I turned my ear to Washburn's mouth but couldn't see his chest rising and falling. The headlights cast strange shadows and there was so fucking much gear all over him.

"Get First Sergeant St. John on the radio," I barked at Davis. "Get the Old Man. Get someone. I need a working vehicle! Or you know what—" I looked up at the APC driver, whose face flashed from worried to defiant, as if there were some justification for a combat arms soldier to hotdog through the woods and plow into whatever support convoy he wanted to. Sweaty camouflage streaked like blood down the sides of his face. "Get on your radio to your unit. Whoever can get me and three passengers to the hospital the fastest wins the fucking training exercise."

SINS OF OMISSION

A s Hollywood as it would have been to thunder out of the training area with everyone strapped to an armored personnel carrier, it ended up being Davis who drove us to Winn Army Hospital. "It's my mechanics," he said, including Shumacher for perhaps the first time. First Sergeant pushed the keys to her Blazer into his hand without a word.

At the hospital, EMTs and doctors bent to the ballet of stretcher, crash cart, and forward momentum; speaking and moving efficiently with me but gently with Reyes and Shumacher. They were grave and respectful with the limp form of Washburn, who'd stopped responding to our attempts to keep him talking as Davis sped over tank trails and then through the dark streets and every stop sign of main post. We picked up an MP escort after we ran the third red light, alerted by the smudged white flag of Shumacher's underwear I waved out the passenger window.

The doors to the restricted area flapped then stilled, signaling their own surrender, and I stood, wanting to follow but unable to move. Adrenaline swirled through my bloodstream and pooled in my brain. I needed someone to rally me, to get me to charge, to do anything other than stand upright in that no man's land of a waiting room. The automatic doors shushed open and closed, admitting Davis.

"You found a parking spot?" What was I babbling about, of course he'd found a parking spot. Everyone else was on maneuvers, practicing for war in preparation for peacekeeping. Everyone else was having the regular fare of stress and sleep deprivation in the training area. Only I had left a trail of wrecked vehicles and bodies on my way to the Emergency Room.

"It's on the curb. I drove all around the parking lot then put it on the curb anyway." An alert, nervous energy replaced Davis's usual truculence. "The MPs are gonna wait with it."

I nodded, the immobility of my body a lie. All my muscle fibers hummed with concentration. I wanted Davis next to me, focusing on what was happening behind those swinging doors. Reyes was banged up and scared but probably fine; Shumacher was indestructible, whatever gastrointestinal issue she was having. My molecules sought the air for input from Washburn. I slowed my breathing. I listened. But the waiting room was cold and still, devoid of information.

The entrance to the parking lot opened like the doors of the command deck of the Starship Enterprise and I turned, ready with a clipped thank you for the MPs for allowing the Blazer to stay on the curb. Instead I was face-to-face with the Old Man. "Sir," I said, my voice drowned by the sudden scream of cicadas. After the doors closed again the only sound came from the hospital, the machinery keeping patients alive. I waited for him to tell me what a colossal disappointment I was. That I should get the hell out of there and go straight home and pack my bags for whatever purgatory he was relegating me to.

"I heard over the radio. Your first sergeant relayed a message up the convoy." The crease between the Old Man's eyebrows tightened with the effort of integrating so much information at once. I considered asking him if he could berate me later, in order to concentrate with me and Davis. And I wanted him to shut up so I could tell my side of the story—as soon as I could organize it in my mind.

"We brought them here ourselves." I tried, and failed, to sound decisive. "We didn't have time to wait for an ambulance to find us out there."

The crease between his eyebrows deepened at the word "them." Or maybe he was displeased I'd taken it upon myself to transport injured soldiers. He cocked his head to one side. "Ambulance?"

"I hope I didn't hurt Private Washburn." I spoke fast. The Old Man's arrival had broken a gap in my focus and invited self-doubt and recrimination, never far away under any circumstance, into the room. The best defense was a good offense, wasn't that the saying? I needed to tell him everything at once before he had a chance to ask the questions that would distract me from the task at hand which was—meditating? Praying? For my soldiers. I couldn't think and feel simultaneously, and god knows I didn't want to feel. "I know it's not a good idea to move someone who's been injured, but we were concerned about time."

"Injured?" The Old Man looked confused. "I heard about a mechanical issue, then that you were going to the hospital, which made no sense. Someone got hurt?"

His question hit me like a baseball bat. He might not have heard any radio chatter about Washburn. Washburn had been in the process of reporting the dead deuce, then First Sergeant would have called forward to other radios until she got word to the Old Man that there were problems at the rear of the convoy. Details would have overlapped and gotten garbled.

"What *happened*, Lieutenant Mills?"

I drew a breath. I was shaking, and not because I'd been in the unairconditioned field for two weeks and the waiting room felt like a meat locker. My molecules weren't vibrating to keep me warm; they were vibrating so hard my body was in danger of rattling apart. I had to pull myself, and the events of the last hour, together. I wrapped my arms around my torso but continued to shiver. It was going to take everything I had to keep my mouth moving but my attention trained toward Washburn. I groped with my heart for some sense that everything was going to be okay but again perceived nothing but the sterile hospital air. I ground my gears back into the room. "The last two vehicles were stopped, sir, with the M88 staged at the rear of the convoy." Before I had a chance to tell him that Davis had fired up the smoke generator to cover the convoy's exit, a woman not much older than me, with golden skin and dark hair cropped close and wearing a lab coat over her BDUs, slipped through the doors from the restricted area into the waiting room.

"How are they?" I crossed the space in one step, desperate for news. Under the fluorescent lights, captain's bars winked from the collar of her lab coat.

"We're going to keep PFC Reyes and Specialist Shumacher overnight, but they're fine. We gave Reyes a sedative and Shumacher's on an IV. All she needs are some fluids and some rest." From across the room, Davis exhaled.

"They're both okay?" I needed the captain to tell me twice.

"Well, those *three* are fine." The captain's smile meant to reassure, although a pulse of sadness blipped across her dark eyes, which puzzled me. "PFC Reyes is fine. And Specialist Shumacher and her baby are fine."

"Her *what*?" I spat. My head whipped toward the Old Man, then back to Davis. Blank stares. The Old Man raised his eyebrows so high they merged with his hairline. "Say again?"

"Specialist Shumacher is experiencing some mild preterm labor contractions," the captain explained. "It sounds scary, but she's not in danger of miscarrying. It might not have been such a great idea having her in full MOPP gear like that. She got pretty dehydrated."

"Miscarrying," I said. The Old Man stood mute next to me, questions winding up and bursting overhead like flares, lighting his target as they drifted down. Shumacher in the tool room; Shumacher driving the M88 rather than walking through the diesel smoke on training day. 'Miscarrying," I repeated. She'd never miscarried in the first place, back when she said she had. Holy shit.

The captain paused and the air thickened in anticipation. I felt like I was looking around the room, reaching for Davis while holding the Old Man at arms' length—there was no time to explain to him that

Shumacher might be fine now but that she was, in fact, in grave danger because I was going to kill her when I got my hands on her. "And Private Washburn?" It was my question to ask. I was the Headquarters Company commander—one in a line of disastrous commanders—but the commander in charge of this particular disaster.

The captain cleared her throat. "Was not so lucky, I'm afraid."

The Old Man's inhalation pulled the air from in front of me so that my head swam, and my knees began to buckle. The captain moved me toward the chairs where Davis had retreated, putting distance between himself and all these officers, watching the proceedings from the corner.

It was a short distance to the seat, but I felt like I was falling in a dream. Body falling from a helicopter over rice paddies, free falling. I waited for the relief of a hypnic jerk, something to bring me back to reality, but the grunt of cheap vinyl upholstery kept me in the room. "What do you mean, 'not so lucky'?" I prayed I hadn't understood or that the captain wasn't a doctor after all. Maybe she was just some administrator, not very knowledgeable about emergency medicine.

"His body took the full force of the impact." The captain's cheeks turned pink, and her eyes darted one millimeter away from direct contact. "We'll have to ask the family for permission to autopsy, to learn the extent of the internal damage, but he went into cardiac arrest almost as soon as you brought him in. We did everything we could, but we couldn't keep him with us. I'm so sorry."

"He's dead?" I'd stopped listening after the word "autopsy." I pictured Washburn lying on the tank trail in the stark shadows cast by the APC's headlights. I listened again to the horrible rasping as he labored to breathe. He hadn't been fine, but we'd driven as fast as we could, dammit. He'd been fine until that APC crashed out of nowhere. But as quickly as my anger flashed it disappeared, like heat lightening in the late summer—not enough to warm the ice at my core or the frosty air of the room, and not enough to hold back the gathering roll of sadness and self-blame.

"Yes." The captain's hand reached for mine. Her eyes were fierce now, honest and compassionate, and I clung to her gaze like someone floundering would to a life preserver. "He's dead."

The Old Man exhaled the oxygen he'd stolen from under my nose. I smelled the sweat escaping his layers of uniform, the scents of body odor, camouflage, and unbrushed teeth wafting up like air trapped in a mine shaft. "Oh, no," he said.

The captain turned to the Old Man, whose rank usurped every space. Soldiers thought they knew you when you opened your mouth from behind shining insignia. Assumptions were carried by both sides like shields, then raised during communication. "Yes, sir," she said.

Ice crystals floated through the air and my synapses fired to navigate around them, attempting to connect my brain with my heart, but my heart wanted to remain outside of this moment. Davis began to cry. In fact, he burst into tears, and his tears engulfed us all. His sobs melted the room, the aluminum frames of the chairs, the vinyl cushions identical to the ones in the Headquarters Company day room, the dog-eared, six-month-old copies of *Field & Stream* and *Soldier of Fortune* and *Reader's Digest*. They threatened to sweep me away. I looked to where my hand was anchored by the captain.

"I'll talk to Private Washburn's parents," I heard myself saying. I couldn't think of a thing I'd rather do less. There was Washburn singing stupid songs. He'd swung into First Sergeant's Blazer as we started the engines up for this last convoy, pure cornball and so alive. He'd tugged a garbage bag toward himself and hugged Logan at Mass and put his arm around Shumacher. There was his body on the dusty tank trail, the sound of engines winding down, and then it was on a hospital gurney. Wrecked. Still. I'd witnessed all of it, although I couldn't make myself believe it. "It should be me. He's my soldier." It was too soon for past tense, which made me think of my mother in her living room in Athens, reading a library book and smoking, or studying those financial literacy materials in the lamplight. I'd never asked her how she coped in the immediate aftermath of my father's disappearance. There would have been nowhere to hide from the onslaught of emotions if you were confronted with the worst possible news in the presence of strangers. It was absolute savagery to ambush a person in that way.

Davis's misery splashed around my ankles and crept up my shins. Thoughts hit my spinal column and bounced straight to the front of my mind. I'd need to go back over them like maps strewn across a desktop, study every inch of the tank trail, but time was strange in that waiting room. It lasted for eons as Davis cried and sea creatures developed legs and crawled onto the land surrounded by his tears. Time roared past like an armored personnel carrier. It sank like a woman to the floor. Washburn's parents wouldn't realize it right away, but it would be a mercy to receive that telephone call from someone who knew him. Had known him.

Before the Old Man could interject, I spilled the whole story, from the black smoke pouring from the deuce to the APC that burst through the trees. My words tumbled out as the waves of Davis's tears reached my shoulders. The pressure of them slowed and thawed me and began to weigh on the quick movement of my breath. I couldn't stop my hands from shaking as I scooped scattered truths toward myself.

"And the M88?" the Old Man asked.

"Was right where it was supposed to be, to mask the convoy." Chemical training had been his priority, right? The M88 was always supposed to be staged in the tree line. Davis had not had a radio but would have been counting vehicles, waiting for the last one to pass. He'd no doubt been tired, too, and must have thought we'd all gone by when minutes passed and he had no more vehicles to count. Someone would try to say that our two vehicles weren't visible because of the smoke from the M88, but the APC had already been rumbling off course toward us way before Davis flipped the switch.

In the corner, Davis laid his head on his knees as Washburn's death absorbed into him, causing him to shrink and tighten. Maybe his tears weren't all from sorrow. Davis had been under pressure to hustle the deuce through its repairs, just as the Third Shop mechanics would have been under pressure to kick the truck out the door so they could get ready to deploy. But if the deuce hadn't blown its engine, none of us would be in that waiting room. Davis *should* be blaming himself. He and those Third Shop mechanics were going to be in very hot water.

But Davis was my soldier, too, odd as that was to acknowledge, and I waited for the Old Man to bury me under the wreckage of the three vehicles now strewn across the training area tank trail. I wished it was Davis or me on that quiet hospital table. It would have been me, if I hadn't told Washburn to get on the radio. I swallowed a wave of misery and thought I might be sick on the Old Man's MOPP boots, from an overabundance of tears in my gullet and the screaming in my head. I was glad I hadn't died. I was a terrible person for thinking that. But—oh, god—I didn't want Washburn to be dead, either.

"Lieutenant Mills, why don't you let me handle talking to Private Washburn's parents?" The Old Man spoke his first coherent sentence since entering. His grimy face was shocked and sympathetic and something else I couldn't decipher. His eyes were more focused than I'd ever seen. "I have some experience with family notifications."

I needed everything to slow down long enough to think. Davis, his mouth wide in horror as he ran up on the scene on the trail. Me, barking a string of orders at him. For once he'd jolted into action, as he would to any voice steeped in authority. I'd reacted fast, I realized. I had not had a single moment of self-doubt out there, although I was more than making up for it now. So much so that I wish I had waffled. Maybe if I'd failed to act, that would have been what was needed to keep Washburn alive. But I didn't have time to sift through personal development bullshit just then. We'd left First Sergeant and Storey in a dusty cloud of dissipating diesel smoke backlit with red taillights. I had so many people to talk to, all at once, and so many places to be. The tentative connections I'd begun to build in the field, the delicate tendrils twining between brain and heart and confidence, had slammed into each other with full force.

"It is so . . ." The Old Man studied the backs of his hands where camouflage had settled into dry creases around his knuckles. He'd ridden my case for two-and-a-half months, but he'd also been out there getting dirty with us for the last two days. Soldiers made so many concessions for their leaders, even the ones who weren't that great. "It's a terrible thing to lose a soldier. That's the long and short of it."

My throat constricted; I wasn't sure I could speak. I didn't want to feel even a scrap of sympathy for this guy who was trying to take over this experience. This was not his show right now. And sorrow was rolling toward me, a whole ocean of Davis's tears, but I would not dive into its depths here. Not out of some preening sense of military decorum, or because it wasn't my show, either, but because it was monstrous and overwhelming, and also private and precious. I was going to have to swallow every awful mouthful of it—completely, thoroughly—but at the moment I was using every scrap of my considerable ability to wall it up. I didn't have the luxury of feeling just then and was terrified that if I succumbed to its full impact I'd never recover.

"This isn't the time to go into it, but you know there'll have to be another Report of Survey at the very least," the Old Man said. The captain rose to give us a moment to count the hard logistical nails, but I tugged her hand. I needed her to repeat the medical details so I could relay them to Washburn's family. I was hobbled and needed a crutch.

Inside the soft poison of my sorrow a seed of defensiveness began to harden. I was going to have to count and recount every mistake. Would judges and JAG officers—or parents of dead soldiers—think I was glossing over the faulty performance of Headquarters Company? This was what I'd always assumed was behind the lack of information surrounding my father's disappearance, although I understood now why my father's soldiers or Ted and his friends at the VFW might not want to talk about what happened. It hurt to face the whole, unvarnished truth. The truth was a many-headed hydra, impossible to wrestle into submission. Battles in the jungles of Vietnam must have been far messier than this training accident and everyone on that tank trail was going to have a different version of the facts. But the hard, irrefutable truth was that Washburn was dead. And his parents were going to want to know why. My heart felt like it had been ground under the treads of the APC.

The Army would make it sound like I'd been out of my depth as a leader in order to give the Washburn family someone to blame. I was no perfect person but the Army's need to grind everyone under its treads was what had killed their son. Washburn was dead because hoo-ah combat soldiers thought they were running the show when in fact they were the show's trained monkeys. If I were to be blamed for anything it should be for keeping my head down and mouth shut about all of this, for all this time.

"Sir, I should be the one to talk to Private Washburn's family." I might have to blubber my way through the conversation, but I'd do it to save them some pain. A shot straight to the heart. A mercy killing. "I've been on the receiving end of bad news. The family will want the truth. They deserve to hear it from someone who was there."

"Just what is it that you're planning to say?" The Old Man's eyes narrowed as though he expected me to be embarrassed, to fall over myself with apologies, but that seed of stubbornness was growing. I had screwed up, but there were things I'd done well, and my fear that I couldn't handle leadership under stress had not come to pass. I had not fallen apart in an emergency. In fact, all my training had kicked into gear when the APC burst through the trees. I wished like hell no one had been in the Humvee driver's seat when it did, but the final training task for the Old Man was whether he could see all the competing truths and accept them. Whether he'd let me tell Washburn's family the truth, my way, instead of regurgitating some pablum that Public Affairs gave me to say. There was no way out but forward, but my story wouldn't be loaded with platitudes or half truths, or words and phrases that were only trapdoors to deeper truths. I might have nothing left but my integrity after tonight, and all of us were going to have to suck it up and feel some pain. But I was going to talk about what happened and I was going to talk about the real Washburn—not the sainted, sanitized version, but the whole, dopey, sweet, intellectually incurious but *real* knucklehead that he was.

Had been. Shit.

Davis sniffed from his corner. The captain in the lab coat leaned in the direction of the swinging doors to the restricted area and I looked out the window. Out in the parking lot, empty except for the two military vehicles parked on the curb and guarded by the MP sedan, the Old Man's engine was still running. His driver smoked under a street lamp. The hospital machinery thrummed and beeped, supporting nothing.

"I'll include everything—times, mileage, who said what, all of it, when I write my statement." The way to deal with the Old Man was with some backbone. He recognized it in others even if he didn't possess one himself. "I won't leave anything out. I've made mistakes. I understand that you might decide to make an example of me. But the Headquarters Company soldiers were not the ones most at fault tonight."

Davis raised his head from his knees. There: let my future listeners use this fact to wiggle a finger under the tight edge of the story, to let the possibility of blame slide through. I *had* made mistakes early on but would not confess to wrongdoing for my actions that night, nor for those of my soldiers. If Davis had been paying attention—and I'm pretty sure the soldiers paid more attention than officers gave them credit for—he'd know I was shooting straight. He'd catch some hot bullet casings as they flew, but his mistake out there was not nearly as grave as that of the APC crew.

"Anyway," I said. "It's possible to be wound so tight you're ineffective. Things came together for the company when I calmed down enough to trust people. I think when you talk to the graders they'll tell you the soldiers did pretty well on the exercise. The enlisted soldiers are not to blame for any of this. This is a leadership failure. All the way up the chain, sir." With that, I sealed my doom. No way would the Old Man let me assign him any blame. He'd make me disappear to save himself and I doubted he'd find me a cushy, out-of-the-way desk job like he had Captain Williams. I'd spend the rest of my life on a bar stool, steeping my regret in booze. Or working at the bar and saving my tips to bankroll my own trip to Asia.

"I've talked to the graders, and they've already told me as much about your company's performance." The Old Man looked puzzled by my rambling. Did he really, after all those years in charge of things, still not get how humans worked? All humans, even soldiers? I pictured myself at the battalion personnel office, resigning my commission to Logan. It would be poetic justice, I supposed, but I could go out knowing I'd learned a thing or two about leadership that hadn't been a put-on, a way of grand-standing in front of a formation, whipping soldiers into a frenzy of unexamined patriotism. It wasn't about being a scholar of the regulations, quoting chapter and verse. It wasn't a physical performance or an intellectual exercise at all. It ran deeper than that. It acknowledged that soldiers weren't wind-up toys. They were, every one of them—even the dirtbags—fully formed, functioning humans with lives and families and hopes and aspirations that may have nothing to do with the Army. I couldn't for the life of me think why no one had told me this before. It was so obvious. But I'd have traded every scrap of this new awareness if only Washburn would get up from that hospital bed and come whistling through the swinging doors.

"And who said anything about blaming anyone?" the Old Man said. Someone would have to take the blame, though. It was the Army way to find an inconsequential person to make the scapegoat, and no way in hell was it going to be the Old Man.

Before I could respond, the sliding doors shushed aside to admit First Sergeant.

YOUR ASS IS GRASS

The firefight was brief, ferocious, and entirely one-sided. "What in god's name were you thinking, turning on the smoke generator before all the vehicles had passed?" First Sergeant exploded across the waiting room at Davis without acknowledging the Old Man or me or the stunned captain.

Davis rose from his seat, an apology on his tear-streaked face instead of the usual thundercloud, but before he had a chance to say anything, the Old Man, ever the politician, tried to defuse the situation. "Now, then, First Sergeant St. John—let's all just take a minute. This is difficult for all of us."

"Difficult? What's difficult about it?" Her hair, usually every strand in place, was pressed from the Kevlar helmet clenched under her arm. "Count vehicles. Wait until said vehicles drive past. Start smoke generator. That's not the least bit difficult, even for this clown." She jutted her chin in Davis's direction, unwilling to speak his name. Her anger was a thing of beauty.

"How did you get here?" I craned my neck in time to see the taillights of a five-ton truck blink as it left the parking lot. "How did you even know—?" The woman intercepted information straight out of the air.

"Storey dropped me off," she barked. "And Robinson—you left her on the tank trail without a backward glance." She was furious at all of us, and rightly so, but I was desperate to get a word in edgewise. The news about Washburn would devastate her, but she was only getting started. "So what is *difficult* is that this man—" First Sergeant pointed a long, shaking finger at Davis, "Every time, just does whatever the hell he wants." I'd never heard her swear before. Under other circumstances I would have cheered out loud. Now, I needed to stop her before she said something she regretted.

"Hey, hey, hey." I rested my hands on her shoulders. There were visible bags under her eyes, creased with camouflage and sweat just like all of ours were, except hers carried so much more than everyone else's. She glared over my shoulder at Davis.

"Your ass is grass, Davis." Her voice cracked like she might cry from anger. "Like we needed one more mess on top of everything else."

"First Sergeant," I said. She must have been rehearsing this speech for as long as I'd known her, or longer; it came out so smooth, so impassioned, so perfectly righteous. But she had to shut up. Washburn waited for us behind those doors. "First Sergeant. You can say what you need to say, do what you need to do in a minute. But I have to tell you something."

"I have kept my peace for months, ma'am. *Months*. I will not be quiet. I will not let this man run roughshod over this company for one more minute. Do you hear me? I am done."

Davis stood there, arms by his sides. His mouth was closed but his jaw hung slack, no energy to talk back and no words to say anything.

"First Sergeant!" I gave her shoulders a quick shake and she released Davis from her death stare. "I have to tell you something."

FACING THE MUSIC

The sun was up and birds sang unapologetically. Somewhere a lawn mower chewed through the otherwise still air. "The grass is too wet," I said as First Sergeant, Davis and I climbed into the Blazer. First Sergeant shook with residual adrenaline and Davis was catatonic from its aftereffects so I drove, all of us struggling to ignore Washburn's Alice pack and duffel bag in the back seat next to Davis. The memory of Washburn—king of extra duty, champion mower of grass—cemented the fresh green smell onto my olfactory receptors forever.

Headquarters was deserted when we pulled up. The vehicles were locked in the motor pool, including the M88, so good old Storey must have gotten everyone else back to the company in one piece. There was no sign of the Humvee or the APC or the deuce, which was just as well because I had no energy to contemplate the looming investigation. I dropped First Sergeant and Davis at their cars and left First Sergeant's military Blazer in front of Headquarters building, right where the smokers always congregated. I drove home in my baking-hot Honda, choking on two weeks of rolled-up-window smells, tears drying on my cheeks as soon as they rolled down.

I skipped the beer and the shower and fell onto my air mattress still in my filthy uniform, my mind trudging up and down the dusty tank trail, on and off firing ranges and the land nav course, and all around the various training tasks. I had to fight to keep my brain from sliding into the well-worn groove of assuming Washburn's death was my fault. It was comfortable there; I wanted to wallow in self-blame. But people made mistakes when they were under pressure and in this case Headquarters had not been unprepared. There'd be an investigation and the Third Shop mechanics and especially the crew of the APC would be found at fault—that, I'd make sure of. If some Public Affairs spokesperson made a statement to the press to the effect that there was no clear responsibility for the accident, I'd resign my commission and spend the rest of my life like some wild-haired evangelist, standing at the intersections of major roads with a cardboard sign and shouting about how the Army continued to produce generation after generation of soldiers who did whatever the hell they felt like, then camouflaged themselves behind red, white, and blue when called to account for cavalier behavior. What purpose did it serve to pretend that an organization never made mistakes? Nobody among the rank and file believed in the Army's infallibility. As far as officers went, the more rarefied the air they breathed, the more intoxicated they became by the pretty fables—but it clouded judgment. Falling for the hype led to terrible outcomes. I had to put my own mask on in order to help the others around me.

I slid into a half-sleep limbo, dreaming about First Sergeant sitting on the side of her cot, writing in her green Army notebook. I sidled next to her and she looked up at me. Her eyes were dark with knowing that this was not the first time I'd invaded her privacy. I could not speak, my heart and mouth sealed with shame. But she didn't shield her writing and I could not stop myself from straining to read it in the gloom of that tent. There were things I just had to know. I would steal this knowledge if I had to.

She wrote with the stub of a chewed-up pencil in a language I wouldn't remember when I woke. She wanted to be a little girl again, to crawl under her mother's porch and play with a litter of kittens in the slatted sunlight. She allowed me to see her as this child, hair clacking with yellow Goody ponytail holders, walking with other children down the sandy drive to catch the school bus—then locked in a closet by the girls in her class for knowing too many answers. I saw her, older, almost grown, at the bedside of her own father, who was dying of cancer. It was a dream—I knew it was a dream—but she stood on a runway, shading her eyes against the sunlight's glare as an airplane carrying Logan took off from Tan Son Nhut Airport in Saigon. She was standing on a runway at Fort Ord in California to greet the plane when it landed, and she was also in the hallway as my mother sank to the floor, cradling the receiver in her hands. I could almost see—oh, how desperately I craved to see—what she had written about my father, but I couldn't decipher her small, cramped script. Dream-me screamed silently in despair that I'd never get another look at this information.

I searched, but there was nothing about working with Davis, or me, or anything about First Sergeant's time in Germany—just a tall man, fair-skinned and shaggy-haired, who loped like a wolf. The green notebook was a recounting of pain and sorrow and longing for home, but some events had not been worth recording. My dream self became aware of another notebook. A notebook that contained all of her life, not just the hard parts. The parties, her family, their smiles and laughter and pride. Wisely, she kept that one out of my reach. Only she was privy to her joy.

I hadn't thought I was fully asleep but woke to the sound of pounding on the door and the yowls of an unhappy cat. "You look dreadful," my mother said as she swanned past me through the door in a fragrant cloud, looking like she'd had a full night's sleep even though she must have been driving for hours and it was only—what time was it? For Chrissake—eleven in the morning.

I trailed after her into the kitchen as the mental ranks of hard conversations I was going to have that day began to form up. I was so tired my ribcage hurt. "How did you know?" I asked. I licked my chapped lips. Something was different about my mother.

She released Rambo and stood up. "Know what?"

"About . . ." I was still half asleep. I had a headache like a hangover. Bright sun on a blue soul was nauseating.

"You left me a message when you'd be back, and here you are. So here I am." She opened and closed the doors to my empty cupboards until she found a bag of coffee grounds in the refrigerator. "I thought I'd save you the drive up to Athens. Plus, I want to talk to you."

The way she said this made me lift my head from where I'd buried it in my arms on the breakfast counter. I knew that false, bright tone. It was the voice she used when she was trying to convince me to do something I didn't want to. Projecting for an audience that may or may not have been present in the room. She could save that crap for everyone else, though, because I'd outgrown it. "Holy shit—you changed your hair."

"Language," my mother said, folding a paper towel since I guess I didn't have any filters. "Although honestly, Minerva—the state of your stores. Disgraceful. And I don't think a simple haircut is all that remarkable." It was, though. She'd had it cut in flattering layers. It moved.

"It looks nice." There was a clean uniform hanging in the closet, and a pair of clean boots standing ready underneath it. I needed a shower. How long was my mother staying? Had she brought food for Rambo? Would she remember to set the cat box up? I had so many things to do besides have a klatsch and no energy for any of it, and my mother could talk her own ear off during one of her manic episodes. In my semiwakeful state I considered slipping out unnoticed, but of course I couldn't. "I have to go to work, Mom. There was an accident last night. A bad one." In this second recounting I only wobbled once, at the end—which, as far as I was concerned, lay on the tank trail. The rest of the night was a blur. "I've got to go and face the music."

My mother stopped her flitting to listen. When I finished there was only the burble of the coffee maker to break the silence, and the scratch of Rambo's claws on the front door as he, too, tried to escape the current situation. "Yes, it's time to face the music," my mother said. My story had brought the house lights up and her eyes, uncrazed by capillaries for once, looked straight into mine. She came over and wrapped her arms around me. "You have your shower and I'll take care of things out here."

"I might be gone for hours," I said, relaxing into her embrace. It had been a month and a half since I'd had a hug. "Can you wait here until I get back from work?"

"I know you're in a hurry, but I need to tell you something." My mother's voice hurried. "I've been driving since seven o'clock this morning because we need to have this conversation."

I dropped onto a stool, my curiosity barely polite. This would not be an uncomplicated visit, then. It hadn't even registered with her that I was dealing with some stuff here. That I might have vastly more important issues to deal with than, say, putting new tires on my father's car.

"Anyway." She braced herself against the other side of the kitchen island and reached for one of my hands. To my horror, her eyes filled with tears. It wasn't time for full-on crying yet and if my mother got going, I'd be a mess before I even got to work. As usual I was going to have to be the strong one, whatever it was she had to tell me that just couldn't wait. "When you were in Athens you said something about not being wanted or needed, or something like that. And then you said a few things along those lines in your letters from the woods."

"From the field," I said. I couldn't help it—I glanced over her shoulder at the clock.

She caught me doing it and straightened from where she'd bent over the counter. "And you wanted to know what happened to your father."

"This is what you drove all the way down from Athens to talk about?" Aside from how remarkable it was for her to admit that anything had happened to my father, I didn't understand why the conversation was suddenly so crucial. "This is nothing new, Mom. I've always wanted to know about Dad, but you would never discuss it. There's too much—" I shook my hand free. Too much, indeed. Too many tears shed behind too many closed doors, for too many years. Washburn would force a door open between me and Headquarters, but the one between my mother and me—that one was painted shut and would take something truly drastic to open it. "It's too hard." I squinted at a random stain on the Formica, trying to discern a shape but failing.

My mother turned away to pour us each a cup of coffee. "I hope you take your coffee black. You don't have any milk."

"I've been away for two weeks, Mom. Be glad there's no milk in the fridge." I didn't want to talk about milk, and as it turned out, I had something drastic right there. I unbuttoned the left pocket of my BDU blouse. "You probably haven't seen this in a while, so it's a good time to refresh your memory." I pulled the envelope from the plastic bag I carried it in, the one I transferred from one uniform to the next.

My mother pushed a cup of coffee across the counter and opened the envelope. The pale blue paper inside had been opened and refolded many more times than the other letters and I worried that she'd tear it. Instead, she passed a reverent hand over its fragile surface. I'd read it so many times I knew which words she was reading as her eyes scanned down the careworn page:

Hey honey,

This was the worst day yet. We cleared a few villages last week—I think I wrote you about how sad and awful that was— and that sector was considered "clean." The big bosses declared the area a free-fire zone, under the assumption that anyone left would be VC. Well, our company commander got word that VC had been operating near those empty villages and we were sent to do whatever mop-up was required. That's what they call it—a mop-up.

We got to the edge of what remained of one village and Smoke volunteered to take his squad forward to scout for any signs of activity. Most of the houses had been burned down when we came through before. It looked pretty deserted, and I hoped to god it was. I don't have the stomach left for any more firefights, not that I ever did.

So the rest of us hunkered down and waited for Smoke
to radio back, but the first thing we heard was the sound of
rifles—M16s and our own M60 machine gun. I know the sound
of an AK-47, and this wasn't it.

The rest of us ran forward to help, but all we found was an
old Vietnamese couple carrying gardening hoes. And a couple
of kids. All of them dead, lying on the ground, with Smoke and
his guys standing over them. Smoke didn't seem in the least
bothered by it—in fact, he was pretty defiant. "We thought
they were rocket launchers," he said, pointing at the tools. And
then looked at me like he was daring me to say something. "They
weren't supposed to be here," he said.

And I didn't say anything. This was the worst day, and this
is the hardest letter I've written to you yet. I'm a terrible person
and I should have known better than to send Smoke into what
was a tense situation. I should have gone myself, but I'm not
sure I would have done any differently if it'd been me reacting
to the silhouette of a person carrying something long over their
shoulders. Actually, knowing how I've been out here I probably
would have frozen up and the family would still be alive. Probably
they were just going out to work. It isn't like they can take their
rice fields with them when we move them away from their homes.

This is a terrible world we live in, my love, and I can't see
adding to it any more than I already have. Evil isn't something
that's confined to war zones—it's something we allow to take
root and grow in our hearts. It's something we pass along to
our children. And I know we've been told to do these things
by our leaders, and because of that some would say we're not
criminals, but I'm afraid of what kind of husband I'll be when
I come home. What kind of person spends any amount of time
rationalizing actions such as these? Or, in my case, allowing
them to happen without a word? I don't trust myself around
other people and I certainly don't trust my ability to raise a

child to be a good person. I don't think we should have children
in a world that considers them so dispensable.

I'm sorry this one is so heavy, but I promised you I'd tell you
everything about what happens here. And this is what happened
today.

My mother studied the letter for much longer than it took to read
it. "Ah," she said finally. "This letter. I'd forgotten how completely
truthful your father was." She used the word *was*. A past-tense verb.

"So," I said. I'd drained my coffee while my mother read, my eyes
never leaving her face. "You know where I get it from."

"Your truthfulness?" My mother's smile was wry. Neither of us was
particularly truthful although we liked to think of ourselves that way.
"Or this ridiculous notion of yours that you're somehow . . . what was
the phrase you used? 'Surplus to requirements'?"

"Over strength." I pretended to drink more coffee so I wouldn't
have to speak the word *unwanted*. "And the funny thing is, I've changed
my mind about that. I'm not unnecessary—not to my soldiers, anyway."

"Honey." My mother slid the letter gingerly back into the envelope,
like the precious and dangerous object it was. "Your father would have
thought the sun rose and set on you. He would've been gaga over you,
just like I am."

I couldn't look at my mother, not because I was afraid of raw
emotion but because I couldn't face even a hint of flippancy. Not one
twinkle to call her statement into question. My composure was as
fragile as the paper my father's letter was written on. "I know," I said.

"That's good." My mother sighed and searched in her purse. For
something to do with her hands? She pulled out a pack of Dunhills.
These were her special occasion cigarettes, and my guard rose higher.
"We didn't choose what happened to your father, but we can choose
how we deal with it."

"Right." I sensed we'd reached our limit, but my mother wasn't
quite finished. Why all this talk of my father? What was with the

haircut, and the cigarettes that were only for public consumption? "I've got to shower up and get to work," I said. "You should take a nap while I'm gone. We can talk more later."

My mother fidgeted with the cigarette pack. Clicked her lighter. "There's one more thing, honey," she said. "The thing I needed to tell you? There was another letter. One you never saw."

A COUPLE OF KNUCKLEHEADS

First Sergeant called a formation. My chin crumpled and my voice went thin as I spoke to the company, but I had to practice saying the words. Some of the soldiers cried and some cursed and punched the sides of vehicles. There would be drinking later.

Until then, we retreated to the motor pool and the arms room and the routine chores of recovering from field operations. I was up to my ankles in swamp muck when the Old Man and Logan, with the Catholic chaplain in tow, found me at the wash rack hosing down the five ton.

"It would be important to do this for the soldiers, and for Private Washburn's family." The Old Man was offering me the opportunity to organize a rousingly patriotic memorial service for Washburn, but the last thing I wanted to do was cobble together empty words and hymns and Bible passages to soothe the consciences of military leaders. The temptation was great to blast the Old Man like a high-powered hose, to tell him where to put his dog and pony show. This refusal could have been the final straw, the thing that made it easy to pin the training accident on me, and an excuse to deny my assignment to Korea. But I was too tired for cross-posturing with him today.

"I'm not sure I'm up to that task, sir."

"I can help," Logan said. Her eyes were wet, as were those of the chaplain. She didn't have a fleet of muddy vehicles to unpack, no weapons to clean or exhausted soldiers to send home on a three-day pass. "Father Marcantonio and I can organize everything."

"Thanks, Leann." I was lightheaded from my mother's strong coffee and weak-kneed from emotional overload. My uniform hung loose after two weeks in the field but rather than feeling good in my skin, it was like I'd signed out the wrong vehicle and didn't know how to drive it. To have someone lift one corner of the emotional wreckage would be an immense help.

The Old Man pursed his lips like a schoolmarm who'd pitted the girls against each other only to find them playing together instead. I fought my tendency to care what he thought. In my current frame of mind, the only bad outcome would be diminishing myself in front of the soldiers whose hearts were as damaged as the deuce and the Humvee. But units coalesced around grief. Even if the Old Man tried to pin the company's recent tragedies on me, the Headquarters soldiers and I would still have each other—at least until I got shown the door. We needed each other, and were going to keep needing each other, and that was no small thing to be grateful for.

After the vehicles and weapons were clean and First Sergeant sent the soldiers home, I found myself once again behind my desk with my palms on the blotter. This time, I stared hard at Shumacher's face, whose hazel eyes focused on the blank, beige wall behind my shoulder, her jaw set not nearly as hard as it usually was. Tears streamed silently down her face. She was flanked by Davis and First Sergeant.

"The first thing I'm going to say is for all three of you, then I need Specialist Shumacher alone," I said. We were all puffy eyed and not one of us was in the mood to argue, least of all Davis. He was on his fourth point of contact, knocked for a loop about Washburn and uncertain who'd be blamed for the poorly repaired leak in the deuce's oil pan. He and I were going to have some very uncomfortable meetings with the Old Man, starting right after this one. This counseling of Shumacher was chump change in comparison to what the next few days would cost him. "I've got a letter to put in your file, Specialist Shumacher, because not only did you endanger yourself, you compromised the safety of the entire company by lying about your pregnancy. I hope you understand how incredibly irresponsible that was."

"Yes, ma'am." Nope, not even Shumacher was going to argue with me that day.

"Did you volunteer for the tool room to get away from the exhaust fumes?" I remembered Shumacher's face, popping out of the hatch of the M88 instead of walking through the smoke, but she had also put herself between the M88 and the APC we pulled out of the swamp. Her actions didn't make sense.

"Yes, ma'am."

"Why?" My heart was hard after my conversation with my mother. "Why do that? And why keep this from everyone?"

Shumacher's chin wobbled. "You know why, LT." One reason stood next to Shumacher, but her disastrous lack of judgment was not entirely Davis's fault. Soldiers assumed they were immortal. That the other poor bastard would die, not them. "I thought I didn't need anyone to tell me what to do. Nobody wanted me to have this baby." In the hardest way imaginable Shumacher was learning the truth of collateral damage, but mostly her mistake was born of hubris and because of that, pure dumbassedness. It was the most Army mistake ever.

"This is a self-correcting situation," I continued. How could I, of all people, punish someone who wanted a child this much? "I hope you've scared yourself straight, and that you're going to take better care of yourself going forward."

"Yes, ma'am." Shumacher's knees softened a centimeter as it dawned on her that she might not have harsh punishment lobbed at her at the precise moment she needed stable employment. She sniffed and took a quick swipe under her nose and locked back into parade rest.

"So, I hope your physical response to overdoing it, and your hospitalization, and this letter of counseling are warning enough. I don't need to recommend anything stronger, do I?"

"No, ma'am." There was no reason to dog Shumacher out further. Plenty of people were getting away with worse and suffering far weaker consequences. Captain Williams wouldn't be reimbursing the taxpayers one dime of what he'd stolen from them. The Old Man hadn't experienced a moment of discomfort about the EO complaint. Davis and the Third Shop mechanics and the crew of the APC might have newspaper articles written about them and they might suffer from guilty consciences, but more than likely none of them would be held responsible for the accident. The Bosnia mission provided the perfect excuse to sweep even fatal training accidents under the vast Army rug. There was no need for me to do more than give one deeply remorseful soldier a slap on the wrist.

"Did Private Washburn know you were pregnant?" This question was for my personal benefit.

"Yes, ma'am." Shumacher's eyebrows drew together, and she flicked her gaze from the wall to me and back again.

"Was he happy about it?"

"Yes, ma'am, but—" I held up a hand as Shumacher's jaw tightened. She was in no position to assert that this wasn't my business. I felt bad, pushing her. She must have been a mess of emotions even if her feelings for Washburn had changed. But I wanted to know if Washburn had known. Shumacher's kid would want to know. As far as I was concerned, Shumacher better get used to answering the tough questions.

"That's all, Specialist. I'm not digging into your private life. Although I need your help with something, and you are going to do it without any back talk."

"Yes, ma'am." She looked down at me without moving her head from its straight-on position. "What's that, ma'am?"

"I need you with me when I call Private Washburn's family. They've had the Red Cross message, but they're waiting to hear from his unit. I am—and you are—going to give this family something to live for." Shumacher and I would hold hands as we went off this cliff together.

She swallowed hard. "Yes, ma'am," she said.

CALLED ON THE CARPET, AGAIN

After Davis saluted and left the plush quiet of the Old Man's office, I faced my boss. Just the two of us, with no audience.

"When the newspapers move on, is anyone going to pay attention to this new Report of Survey?" I'd washed vehicles and mopped the tears of soldiers and was now knee-deep in paperwork but had no intention of throwing my exhausted shoulder against the wheel of an investigation that was going nowhere. The anger I felt toward everyone except the Headquarters soldiers gave me power. It was odd to have the Old Man backed into a corner, but not uncomfortable. Anger could be useful.

My mind flashed back to my apartment the day before. There'd been a letter, my mother said, staring at the Formica countertop of my empty kitchen. "It came when you were still in high school."

"From Dad?" I banged my fist down. Hard. "And you never told me?"

"No, honey—no!" My mother's hand shook as it patted her hair but found that it was no longer a frozen j-shape. She tucked a strand behind her ear instead. "Of course not. I could never have kept that news to myself. No, this was a letter from one of your father's soldiers. His radio operator. He was answering a letter that you sent him."

Whoa. I slumped back onto the stool. I didn't trust my legs, or what I'd heard my mother say. "Someone answered one of my letters?"

"Yes." My mother took a shuddering breath and squared her shoulders. "It was a long letter. An apology. He was on patrol with your father the night he . . . died. He said what we already knew—that it was a firefight, and dark. He said they had to retreat but your father got . . . hit. Usually your father stayed right next to this soldier but somehow, that night, they weren't." My mother sighed. "They had to get out of there."

"You never told me," I said flatly. "You opened a letter that was addressed to me, and you never told me. Where is it?"

"I ripped it up," she said softly. So softly, to the Formica countertop. I pictured my mother in the '80s, when the drinking was heavy and the denial was entrenched. "And I burned the scraps. I'm so sorry, honey."

The Old Man cleared his throat, and I shook my thoughts back into the room. I honestly didn't care what his response was about any investigations. Nothing would ever surprise me again. "This could be serious for you, Lieutenant Mills." He tried one more time to be convincing but in the face of my stony nonresponse, he at last collapsed into the truth. "They're going to blow through this paperwork at speed," he admitted. "It'll be another write-off, and chances are good that nothing will come of it." There wasn't anyone in the room to back either of our statements up if anyone tried to hold us accountable for them. So, no reason to front. No reason to lie.

There were times to keep your mouth shut, it was true. The Davises of the world could have benefited from practicing some noise discipline. And I'd learned a lot, watching First Sergeant and Logan make judicious use of their words. But there were times that keeping your mouth shut was an act of cowardice. My mother and father and I had all self-immolated as a consequence of not knowing when to bottle up and when to speak.

On the other hand, there was something to be said for putting your body on the literal line. I'd always be proud of my father for volunteering to go to Vietnam. For trying, but also for asking himself the hard questions, especially when it became clear that what he was being asked to do was wrong. That he'd continued to follow orders was another issue, and I'd have given anything for him to have survived it all, to have been given the opportunity to spend the rest of his life wrestling with the fallout of both his inaction and the consequences of his actions. I was not going to squander the opportunity for myself.

"The company passed the ARTEP," I said. I squared my shoulders and took a deep breath. "They'll be more than ready to deploy, and I'm compliant on weight. I've actually been within the body fat standards this whole time."

The look on the Old Man's face admitted that he knew this. "I'll have Lieutenant Logan put in the request for orders for Korea for you."

And there they were—the vistas of green rice heads rippling on an errant breeze, then turning golden in the heat. Aquamarine water, white beaches, markets, spicy foods. The places my father had walked. But would being in Vietnam get me closer to feeling what he'd felt? Were there better places for me to learn what it meant to be a real leader of soldiers? As the Old Man had said himself, Korea would always be an option, but there were other routes to travel now. "I appreciate that, sir, but I've thought pretty hard about it and I want to go to Bosnia." My heart fluttered with nerves and my hand went reflexively to the pocket over my heart, to touch the place where a new letter rested next to the old one. I'd never been so sure of something, and so simultaneously heartbroken and terrified. "I want to go with my soldiers."

A HALLMARK MOMENT

It was the same pale blue paper, time-softened at the edges, the envelope addressed in my mother's careful, Zaner-Bloser penmanship. The letter inside had not traveled from halfway around the world, or even halfway across the state—my mother must have found the stationery on the floor of the living room among the post-field mess and brought it into the kitchen to write the note she left on the countertop while I was in the shower after our big blow-up. The paper buckled in places where tears had fallen, the ink gone fuzzy in the aftermath of writing, crying, leaving.

Honey. My darling Minerva. Min—

When I found out that I was pregnant with you I was the happiest woman in the world. I was really, truly . . . at that moment I had everything. A husband, a child, a future full of love. So please know that from the first second I was aware of you, you were most definitely, one hundred percent wanted and adored.

None of these feelings guarantee good motherhood, though. I know I put you through some terrible things, and not only because of what happened to your father.

One of the tear splotches blurred the word terrible, and I pictured my mother wiping carefully under one eye to keep her mascara from running.

I did the best I could, but I recognize that probably wasn't good enough.

But here comes the part where both of us commit to stop beating ourselves up for our so-called failings. This world is hard on women, and if you ever become a mother you'll understand even more how true this is. All of us—girls, women, more and more so the older we get—spend too much time bowing and scraping and just getting by. This is not about your father anymore, or any man, really. This is about what the two of us are going to do with the time we have remaining on this earth.

I, for one, intend to be a better mother, but I fear my window of opportunity is almost completely shut on that. All I can do now is not hold you back. To send you out into the world with both arms wide—not pulling you to me anymore, but always welcoming you home. Go have fabulous adventures, honey, whatever that means to you. Define life on your own terms, with my deepest love at your back and your father always in your heart.

I love you,

Mom

She wrote like I wrote—thoughts leaping over the abyss of deep emotion, trusting that our shared history would hold up the places where words faltered, but as the letter unspooled before my eyes I found my heart closing rather than opening. What a load of Hallmark bullshit. I shook my head as I read, and my heart tightened as I compared what my mother had written with the story of our lives. Why was I so grudging? Why couldn't I give her this easy closure? Was it all those hungry nights with nothing in my belly but unsalted cabbage soup? All the times I'd wanted a lap to climb into, even if it stank of cigarettes and wine, when my source of comfort had retreated behind a closed door? I wasn't a kid anymore. Now more than ever I knew grief was messy and my mother was human, letting it all hang out as she had. But writing a letter and then bolting from my apartment, avoiding the conversation that should have followed—that was my mother doing the same damn thing she always did, taking the easy route.

When someone was still so convinced of their own performance, though, sometimes the only thing you could do was take them at their word. I'd learned this from the Old Man, time and time again. And now my mother was saying, "Go. Have adventures." She was cutting the strings and handing them to me. Okay, then—that's what I'd do.

THE ARMY KEEPS ROLLING ALONG

I set my credit card on the bar at the VFW. "Whatever people want to drink," I told Hector.

"That's mighty nice of you." Hector reached for the card with a pause so slight I might have imagined it.

"I'm good for it." Hector didn't need to worry about my card being declined. I had extra money in my account since I'd been in the field for two weeks and hadn't had to buy groceries, only paying for an oil change and a tank of gas to drive my dad's car back to Fort Stewart after I chased my mother to Athens, and after a long, late-night conversation over iced tea, made easier in the darkness, lit only by the glow of my mother's cigarette butt and the promise of other such conversations before I left for Bosnia. After this first honest night I'd parked the old Honda on the curb in front of my mother's house with a For Sale sign on it and backed the Bullitt out of the garage. I had too much to do to stay longer this time. I needed to be with the Headquarters soldiers. But I'd be back.

"That ain't it," Hector laughed. "You cover your debts, LT. I just hate when a person's generosity gets taken advantage of, that's all."

"We need this," I said. "These drinks are an insurance policy." After the official memorial service for Washburn, after clamping my molars shut while listening to the Old Man drone on with his platitudes about Washburn's sacrifice, I'd taken the Headquarters soldiers aside and asked them to meet me at the Hunter VFW. No forced fun, I promised them. They didn't have to come if they didn't want to. But the NATO airstrikes had done their job on the Serbian holdouts and the diplomats were moving in to mop up. We'd been told to expect to spend a year in Bosnia, starting sometime around Christmas. Prep time was going to go fast. People had a lot to do, but proper mourning could not be put off. "You have a drink on me. And Jeff if he turns up."

"You're the boss." Hector smiled, wiping the counter with his rag. He laid the plastic rectangle on the ledge of the register. "It's a dollar a draft for the next hour."

"See? That's too easy," I said. "Give me a dozen to start, and a couple of Cokes."

It was nice outside, calm and sunny as if nothing momentous had happened or ever would, because it was an afternoon in early October and soldiers had gathered around weather-beaten picnic tables to drink. Davis had brought his wife and kid, and Mrs. Davis pushed their son on the swings while Shumacher hovered nearby, coaching him to kick and pump his legs so he could do it himself. It wasn't going very well but the little boy was laughing, anyway. There wasn't anything overt in his behavior or movements or speech to indicate any kind of disability, but what did anyone know about a person by looking at them from the outside? That's what First Sergeant had been trying to tell me months ago—that the soldiers wanted to be seen, and to know me as a person—not that she necessarily included herself in that number. Ah, well. She'd earned the right to her privacy, while I was still at the stage of having to give something of myself in order to earn it back.

Davis, wan from the memorial service, watched his family from a picnic table covered with cups and bottles. "You're crying enough for all of us," I said. I wasn't teasing him, or chiding. There was no way around some things—you had to go through them, and Davis had cried often over the past week, like a record needle stuck in a groove. Like a tired child.

I handed him a wadded-up tissue from my cargo pocket. "It's clean." We'd all worn our filthy field BDUs to the service as a tribute, and now I had only the new letter tucked in the pocket over my heart. In a weird way I missed my father's letter, but I needed to get used to this message from my mother. To start to trust its words.

Shumacher walked away from the swings. She ran a protective hand across her lower abdomen, then over the faded hood of my father's Mustang where it sat in the parking lot.

"You can stay back, you know," I said to Davis. We'd spent what felt like a thousand hours together while everyone else was home on a pass. We answered questions from Public Affairs to relay to the local press, and the story had gone national. Everyone from the Old Man through the brigade commander wanted to hear from Davis, again and again, about the deuce's repairs and his use of the smoke generator. They asked me about everything else. No one was going to do anything about the questions or the answers to the questions. Interest was already dying down, and after I got on that flight with Washburn's body, when I was out of uniform and sitting on his parents' sofa, I intended to tell them so. Or maybe I'd just tell them funny stories for now and save the harder things for later. I'd try to discern what they wanted to hear, and not just what I thought they needed to know. But maybe what they thought they wanted wasn't what they needed? Leadership was hard, especially when holding someone's heart in your two cupped hands.

In a quiet moment I'd shown Davis the receipts from the Army-Navy store to prove to him that Captain Williams was the bad guy, never First Sergeant. He'd accepted the news with resignation, another cross to bear, and apologized to her, but it was too late for all that. "Maybe it's better for you to stay back and help keep an eye on Shumacher," I said to Davis. Storey was going to act as first sergeant in Bosnia while First Sergeant St. John finished her degree in the rear. Storey was senior to Davis now that the Old Man was taking a stripe off Davis's rank, and Storey had squared away everything that any of us ever handed him. He was the better choice.

"Thanks, LT." Davis shifted his gaze to his family, away from the lone beer I'd set at the end of the picnic table for Washburn. "But we'll be okay. We've got a couple of months to apply for some programs to help my wife while I'm gone. Brigade is standing up this thing called a Family Readiness Group. Besides, I could use a peacekeeping mission to get my career back on track. I didn't get to go to the Gulf."

"Roger that."

We stopped to sip our beers, and Ted's taxi grumbled into the parking lot, pulling in next to my father's car. "Hot damn! Where'd you get this bad boy?" Ted, Logan, and First Sergeant emerged from the cab, arms piled with flat soda boxes of Lucky China takeout.

"I liberated it from my mother's garage." I was wearing Ted's steel cuff, half dreading the conversations about POW/MIAs that the bracelet and car would provoke, half eager to finally talk about my father with whomever was curious.

"1968 Mustang Bullitt fastback." Ted caressed the old car with his eyes, seeing a different vehicle than what I was looking at, like Shumacher had. "Mm, mm, mmm."

"And I get to drive it while you're gone." Shumacher gave the hood a proprietary pat. Even if Logan's shiny red Mustang had been next to it Shumacher and Ted would still have preferred my father's car, and that gave me a petty thrill. I had plenty of growing up to do.

"I'm leaving you the keys, but don't get ahead of yourself, Shumacher. My mother will come down here to smack you in person if anything happens to it."

"As if," Shumacher said. "I'll have this baby humming by the time you get back from downrange."

"Oh, god." I pictured Shumacher with an actual baby stuffed into a car seat, joyriding up and down the Fort Stewart corridor. "This is a sacred vehicle, Shumacher."

Ted's face was kind. "It was your dad's?" I nodded, throat suddenly tight, but he understood without requiring an explanation. "Hey, shove over so we can get this food on the table." Davis and I got up so Ted,

First Sergeant and Logan could unload all the cartons and bags. I moved Washburn's beer to the side so it wouldn't get jostled.

There were dozens of wontons, one of every flavor of fried rice from the Lucky China menu, vegetable and meat stir fries, and sweet-and-sour everything. "Gosh, thanks," I said to First Sergeant, trying not to calculate the total cost. I could afford it, and it was worth it to have this time together, none of which was ever guaranteed.

"Thank Lieutenant Logan. She paid." Logan smiled down at the carton top she was opening, hair flecked with gold falling forward over her eyes. She and the chaplain had taken Washburn's service from my shoulders, and now this.

Storey handed me a plastic-wrapped fortune cookie. "Penny for your thoughts, ma'am."

"Oh, I was just thinking what a badass Lieutenant Logan is." I kept my voice low so Logan wouldn't think I was being performative. I could go to her one-on-one like Washburn had at the combat Mass. Or I could give her reasons to trust me over the next year while we were in Bosnia together. "I have a lot to learn from people who give so easily."

"Say again?" For once, Storey wasn't trying to impress me and I wasn't second-guessing his motives. He was the next NCO I'd have to forge a bond with, and I meant to do better than I had with First Sergeant. "I've never met a lieutenant who works as hard as you do, or who cares so much."

"Yeah, well . . . that says more about the kinds of officers you've worked with than it does about me." I wasn't being falsely modest. Storey thought he knew me from my outward actions and because he saw everyone through his own generous lens. But I was miserly with my emotions. I wasn't good at prying my fingers from the tight grip they had on my own heart.

He cleared his throat but didn't contradict me. "Read your fortune," he said to change the subject. I broke open the cookie, read the slip of paper, and burst out laughing. Reyes, Robinson, and Pettit turned our way—they were sitting together and chatting quietly, Pettit not gossiping for once. I handed Storey the fortune. "Remember this date in two months! Your life will change!" he read. "What's so funny about that? Your life is definitely going to change in the next two months."

"It's the same fortune I got two months ago." I wiped tears from the corners of my eyes. I couldn't remember the last time I'd belly laughed. It hurt.

The Old Man's minivan pulled into the parking lot and Logan went to greet him. She must have told him we were meeting there because I sure as hell hadn't. "Fucking Logan," I sighed. "So full of forgiveness." Was one uncomplicated, sad afternoon too much to ask for? Logan was such a great human that she was moving past all the bullshit with the Old Man, too, apparently.

They walked toward the picnic table, and everyone was smiling and standing up, and Logan opened the green vinyl folder the Old Man handed to her.

"Attention to orders," Logan said, and everyone came to the position of attention. "The President of the United States, acting upon the recommendation of the Secretary of the Army, has placed special trust and confidence in the patriotism, integrity, and abilities of First Lieutenant Minerva Magdalene Mills." My mind side-slipped to the end of June, into the same unsettled state I'd been in when the Old Man was coming toward me in the day room with his plastic smile. It had been First Sergeant holding the guidon in her hands then, but this time she was holding silver railroad tracks to pin captain's rank on my grubby collar. She'd told me about a Sunbury ritual that might help me move on from the worst of the pain, after I'd given myself some time to feel it. She said I should throw salt over my shoulder onto Washburn's grave when we came back from Bosnia in a year, when I visited his parents again on my way to my officers' advanced course and wherever I was destined to go after that.

I shook myself to the present, to the warmth of the October afternoon, to the company of these broken but beautiful people—Ted, Logan, Shumacher, First Sergeant, and even Davis and Pettit and the

Old Man. I could still ask to go to Korea, and the Army would almost certainly grant that request. The pressure was off to go this minute because following in my father's footsteps now meant staying with these soldiers—voluntarily this time. My mother and I would call and write to each other from afar, and the seasons of the Army would cycle around again, the same and the same and the same, and yet farther forward every year, like waves creeping up the tideline.

ACKNOWLEDGMENTS

Deepest thanks go to my military friends, especially Colette Luscomb and Debbie Brown, who read and talked and read and talked some more about our own experiences and those of the characters in this story. Your insights and enthusiasm bucked me up more times than I can count. Thanks also to Debbie Brown, Randy Brown, Johnny Casella, Kat Cheeseman, and Jay Heltzer for weighing in on areas of military life I needed refresher training on. Robbie Ruth Smith read a draft so early it was paleolithic and didn't run away screaming—just smoked and cussed and quilted in the corner (as a Navy chief will do!), asked me some questions, and let me figure the answers out on my own. I love military people, especially all of you.

I also would never have had the courage to keep plunging ahead without the steadfast, boss-bitch friendship and camaraderie of my best writing bud, Kirsty Collinson. Thank you from the bottom of my heart for the millions of hours of writing time together ("Shall we crack on?") and countless cups of tea and bottomless wells of support in so, so many ways. Everyone needs a writing BFF like Kirsty and the moral support of other writers like the Subversive Mermaids and everyone in the #5amWritersClub if they're going to make it.

Huge thanks also to Kathleen Furin and Nita Collins for the toughest but most valuable of editorial love, and for the insights of Danielle Jones, Isabel Ngo, and Drew Pham that helped me beyond

measure in the writing of characters different from myself. A big slice
of key lime pie to my favorite native of coastal Georgia, Bruce Watkins,
for providing details on the civilian side of the Fort Stewart community.
I've done my best but any gaffes in description or characterization are
entirely the fault of a person who still has much to learn (that would
be me).

Lastly I want to acknowledge the unwavering and gracious support
of my family—Sam, Pallas, and Grace. Thank you for not minding all
the closed doors, or not minding much. Or at least for keeping it to
yourselves that you minded. You are the absolute best and I love you.

Milton Keynes UK
Ingram Content Group UK Ltd.
UKHW012243180624
444315UK00005B/567

Breaking UP Not Down

Your 7-Step Guide to Growing through a Break UP

By: Jeremy Sigal

Table of Contents:

Dedication:

This book is dedicated to all our x's, and all our nex's ☺. Thank you for always pushing me upwards, and know that I will always be there for you as my love for you is timeless. I pray you run forth with the power I instilled within towards your best being always ahead! Loving You Always, Jeremy ☺

Your 7-Step Guide to Growing through a Break UP – let's begin!

Breaking UP Not Down

Your 7-Step Guide to Growing through a Break UP

You know the whole it's not you, it's me thing...well the breakup is kind of like that.

Understand this one thing: **YOU ARE THE PROBLEM**, and that's a good thing, because you're the only person that you can fix. The good news? Well, as you fix you, you'll soon become the person for you that you could never have been for your past, where in that moment, happiness and success will find you.

It's much easier to blame everyone else for your bad relationships and that's why most everyone focuses on that one thing. The truth is that people are fundamentally weak where it's much more convenient to blame others for causing your problems, but the simple fact remains that the only person you can control is you. You can try to guide others, but if you fail to set boundaries and walkaway points on your partner's weaknesses, then you're either blind, weak, or in denial, and again, YOU ARE THE PROBLEM.

You are not your past. Your future will be defined ONLY by what you do next.

This book of power will drive home this single concept: **FOCUS ON YOU, FOCUS ON GROWTH**, and in that moment the world will bend to you! Your time to throttle up is now, so pull that knife out of your heart and continue your swan dive right into this 7-Step Program, because it's time for Breaking UP Not Down!

Before I hit you with that *"truth hurts"* BS, know this <u>One Thing</u>:

By the time you finish this quick read, you're going to feel more powerful, more confident, and more ready for greatness than you ever have throughout your entire broken past. **Trust me**. I'm not just some lame with a degree. I've accomplished more growth and success in rising to the top of arenas that most others could never even comprehend. I've acquired strength, strategy, and results that most others have never even attempted, so I promise you that Breaking UP Not Down will change you in ways you never saw coming.

I absolutely positively guaran-fuckin-te you that after reading this book, you're going to come out of this Break UP stronger, happier and more capable than you've ever been and that's because we're about to regain control of your path; a path you lost long ago when you settled into an unhealthy, unstable, unworthy relationship; #WTF were you thinking ☺.

The reason we're going to regain control of your path towards greatness, success and happiness is because humans naturally seek out comfortable rhythms/patterns, and once inside them, we stop growing. In your failed relationship, you stopped progressing towards your best being ahead, and as we stopped growing, we began to neglect ourselves and those around us which is the only reason we

4

ever fail. **The good news**: We're about to rapidly autocorrect ALL OF THAT!

Trust me when I tell you that I got you like no one else. So sit tight, hang on, and let's grow through this #together. Step-1 let's grow.

10/25/20 (x)Anniversary + Publication Date

Step 1: <u>Labeling It a Breakup</u>

"Your thinking can be no wiser than your understanding;
your actions no greater than your thoughts"

Oh you're sad, crying, thinking about dying being easier and what not...well **GOOD**, because that is EXACTLY where you're supposed to be as you **PROGRESS** into a Better Tomorrow!

I see you weeping like a child and I say to you, **CONGRATULATIONS** because your success, happiness and joy are ever nearer now!

You're only sad because you're focused on all the things you're missing and losing, where as your focus transitions to all the qualities, connections, and strength you're about to gain, you will become overwhelmed by the tidal wave of happiness as it consumes your every neuron.

Recognize that <u>Your x was Not The One for you</u>, and that's okay because as I'm about to show you, you weren't being the right one for you either. Understand that desperately wanting your x to be the one and them actually being the one for you are two extremely different notions.

"Love" is a chemical attachment in our brains to keep us connected to others for survival purposes, so it's important to recognize this primal instinct driving your desire to remain connected, and view it

6

as a driving force of chemical & emotion rather than logic and what's actually best for you.

Right now, you are the one torturing yourself as you fixate on your x's best qualities and equating that to who they are and who they were to you. STOP THAT RIGHT NOW! This is just a fatal flaw of evolution chasing connection for survival, but all emotion aside, your x broke you because they were broken themselves and YOU COULD NOT FIX THEM. If your x was truly the one, then why TF would they have abandoned you leaving you broken and unhappy?

When you're going through a breakup, you're probably consumed with "why's" and "what-if's," and although these responses are instinctive, the purpose of Breaking UP Not Down will teach you to transition to "**what now's**."

If you're like me and literally everyone else, you're probably in extreme denial that it's a breakup, and **that's NOT okay**. If you're like me and **literally everyone else**, you went through a complex relationship involving endless heartbreak, unhappiness, sacrifices, and an extreme lack of reciprocation.

It's for all these reasons that in Step 1 transitioning to "What Now," the single most important step you need to take is labeling this relationship "A Break-UP."

We'll get to the part where I'll show you all the things you could've done better to make it work, but for right now, understand that your partner didn't have the strength to make it work with you, and that's okay.

You deserve the world and although I'm going to show you step by step how to find that love from another, understand that you need a strong accountable trustworthy partner, and since you're growing through a Break-Up, recognize that <u>your partner DID NOT POSSESS the qualities you needed</u> in a "partnership."

Take for example that they dumped you because you were out of shape, depressed, lazy, or insecure. If they didn't do everything to motivate you into shape, healthy mindsets, productive abilities, or into trustworthiness of them, then your x did not have the strength you need and deserve. This would be your fault for failing to leave them sooner for another who was actually capable of your needs. If your x did do their best, then again, this is Your Fault and you could not be reading a better piece of literature for your progress into a better tomorrow.

For my recent breakup, we were miserable 70% of the time as we tolerated too much unhealthiness inside our relationship. When I say unhealthy, I mean that we were completely incapable of progressing through any disagreement through reliable solutions to the point that all we did was fight about fights. As I do for everyone around me, I spent endless time guiding her towards health, wealth and joy, and she returned the favor by destroying my peace and happiness every single day. Most of my frustrations stemmed from the fact that I felt my x was lazy, unaccountable to her word, messy, unaware, and more uncontrollably dedicated to false attacks than any other girl I had ever dated. The byproduct of our time was literally bringing out the worst in me which is how she remembers me to this day, but the one thing I did extremely well was clearly articulating my boundaries and continuously offering solutions to all our issues.

Knowing that I could not have done more for her in all areas, I was at a constant walkaway point where I would endlessly repeat: *"either give me peace or give me peace (out), as I'll take either."*

She took the latter and although I wanted her back as we all do, the single most important aspect was to realize that IT WAS DONE. We had already gone through countless other "breakups", and every single time she came back, I clearly labeled my boundaries and with her guarantee to respect those lines, she continued to fail us every time.

I was at a point where they say: *"It's better to be alone than to be with someone and wish you were alone."* I began to beg her to leave.

Step 1 to a Better Tomorrow is **Labeling This a Break UP**, as our only other option is literally sponsoring our own tragic unhappiness on a daily basis, and *THIS IS NOT WHY WE'RE IN THIS WORLD.*

Understand that comfort in your position keeps you exactly where you're at now. When it's time to grow, then it's time to embrace discomfort. Your single first objective in embracing discomfort towards change is Step 1 of this book: **Labeling it a Break UP**.

This book is not for those arguing inside a relationship. This book is strictly for those who are outside of that past and in need of a speedy recovery and progression towards their best being always ahead.

A typical breakup results in devastation and negative connotation, but the point is that here and now, you are making a **Decision to Grow** through this process rather than regress. So again, the time is now to make an agreement to yourself that this will be a <u>Breaking UP Not Down</u>. Here's the good news, when your goal is to avoid breaking down, admitting it's a Break UP starts you on your path to a better tomorrow, and now that you're identifying that path, it's time to shift into second gear and pick up some speed! Step 2, Soothe Thyself; Let's Begin!

June 28, 2020 - 3rd Date – Favorite x

Step 2: <u>Soothe Thyself</u>

*"we choose our feelings, so it's time to
choose to see some light in the darkness"*

The Break UP is real.

You're not eating, sleeping, or thinking clearly. You find yourself spending your days consumed with your lost love and you're starting to realize you're absolutely devastated. **AWESOME.** <u>You're exactly where you're supposed to be</u>, and now is your time for growth!

It's completely normal to go through these emotions in loss, but it's completely abnormal to allow these temporary feelings to define your trajectory in life and happiness. Unless you actually enjoy the misery, it's time to start picking yourself up!

If you want to Break DOWN, then continue isolating yourself, wasting your days, neglecting your body, embracing the sadness, and focusing on what-ifs.

Since your goal is to Break UP, it's time to let the healing being and it's time to begin **Soothing Thyself**. When darkness is all you see, darkness is all you'll have. Since it's time to start seeing some light, here are some of my single greatest tips to make it happen:

1) **Get Supportive + Positive People Around You:**

You know what they say about "an idle mind is the devil's workshop." You're too weak to be on your own with your destructive thoughts, and even though the last thing you may want to do is be around others, it's truly an important part of healing as others can help you process and make sense of things that you're likely unable to see or feel on your own.

Surrounded by others, you're much more likely to see things from other perspectives, and although you will likely be consumed with sad thoughts of your lost love throughout your interaction with others, it's massively important to make this effort and connect.

For starters, it's hard to lie in bed unshowered with a messy house if you have people over. Other people will hold you accountable to the bare minimum which is likely much more than you're doing at this moment.

Putting yourself around others will force you to not only clean up and nourish your body, but you're also likely to start absorbing their healthier energy as they're around you. Again, it's reality that you'll be obsessed with thoughts of your x during your interactions with others, and that's okay as it's probably going to be the main thing you choose to speak about anyway.

Here's the beauty about endlessly processing that topic: <u>you're about to be much more aware and capable of admitting your role</u>

in the problem **which is the only thing you can fix**. The more you talk about the problem, the more likely you are to have a shift in mindset from victim to victor.

2) <u>Drink Tons of Water</u>:

Your heart and brain are 73% water. You're likely malnourished from this state of loss, and as a result you're thinking is likely to be flawed. Even worse, when you're on the cusp of moving forward, then the last thing you'd want to do is be found at your worst.

Your time is now and your objective is **Throttling Up**, not Down. My favorite trick for drinking more water is using an open-top cup where you'll induce the gravity flow effect. Hamsters drink out of a little spigot, and unless you're trying to sip by the drip, start drinking massive amounts of water quickly.

3) <u>Protein Shakes + Smoothies</u>:

You're hungry, but you can't eat...sweet, drink a protein shake or smoothie. It's a great way to get your needed nutrition without the excess calories, and although it's best as a supplement, when you're failing to eat, protein shakes can keep you in the game. When you're really lacking in nutrient intake, you need to jack up your metabolism with movement. Although I recommend a quick gym session, even just heading out for a walk will start to get you going towards caloric intake.

Understand that the parts of your brain that take charge of emotional and physical pain sit closely together with the parts that dictate how we eat our food and its taste. As a result, this can lead us to believe that we no longer like the taste of our favorite foods. It comes down to your hormones where your body adjusts by suppressing hunger and slowing digestion so that eating doesn't need to be such a huge priority when you're heartbroken. Take comfort in knowing that your chemistry will adjust and you will recover from this.

4) **Stay Busy**:

You just left an unhealthy relationship where both they and you neglected your needs. When trying to avoid a Break Down, it's time to Progress Upwards and often times, these moments of tragedy can be our greatest push towards success and happiness in the future. Look at me, I'm writing this book in tears, but I know that moving forward and upward is my only option.

- Focus on new projects
- Learn new skills
- Connect with new people
- Work towards advancement in your career
- Cook your meals
- Clean your house
- Get your Dating Profile pictures ready for when you are
- Get on Dating Apps to see what's out there
- Start distancing your social media into a singles profile
- On and on, just STAY BUSY

5) <u>Watch Comedy Media</u>:

Although I absolutely discourage staying home alone, when you are alone and you're Breaking UP, it's important to watch things that make you laugh and smile over anything else.

The power of laughter is so strong that it has even aided in helping people cure cancer, no BS.

Stay laughing, stay smiling, and stay positive!

6) <u>Hit the Gym</u>:

I don't care how in shape or out of shape you were before your Break UP; at this point, the stress has taken a beating on your body. As a result, your metabolism is down and is quickly sinking to the same low level of your confidence.

Get to the gym. Get inspired by those around you. Start working out; Stop Breaking Down!

7) <u>Reduce Anxiety</u>:

<u>Fun Fact</u>: Although an antelope experiences stress as it runs from a lion, humans are the only animal that can actually create our own stress & anxiety. We sit in traffic, fume, and make a choice to be consumed by anxiety. We overthink about some situation we'll soon encounter (#FutureTrippin), and our heart just starts PUMPIN! When your mission is to rise, you're gonna have to learn to **Reduce Anxiety** and stress.

- **CONSTANT Deep Breaths:** Studies show that taking 5 deep belly breaths is equivalent to .25mg of Xanax. Deep breathing is the key to helping you control anxiety – because you can't breathe deeply and be anxious at the same time. This technique also involves holding your breath. It's called the 4-7-8 breathing technique, and it involves breathing in through your nose for a 4-count, holding your breath for a count of 7 and then slowly breathing out of your mouth for a count of 8. Do this at least twice a day. Also, remember to breathe throughout your interactions, especially while listening. Every single time I feel my anxiety rising, I realize that I've been taking shallow breaths for a while because I'm anxious. **#Breathe #Breathe #BREATHE**

- **Keep Your Hands Busy:** I regularly keep a bottle of water or a pen in my hands so I have something to play with. It's extremely soothing and allows you to relax your entire body as you enjoy simple rhythms.

- **Borrow Confidence From Your Abilities:** Never focus on your weaknesses. Fixate instead on all the strengths you have compared to others. Focus on <u>all the ways you maintain a winning position and that's it</u>. Remember, you can't control whether you win or lose; all you can do is fight the best possible fight and in that act truly losing is not an option.

- **Challenge Negative Thoughts:** Identify, analyze and challenge the automatic negative thoughts that underline your fear of the situation. You know your worth and the false beliefs

17

and attacks from your past will never define you; it's only what you do next that counts.

- **Focus on Others, Not on Yourself:** when around others, focus attention on them and remember that anxiety isn't as visible as you think. Focus on the present moment and really listen to what's being said. Focus on being genuine and attentive and release the pressure to be perfect.

- **Face Your Fears:** Don't rush into challenging your biggest fears on day one; be patient. Build your core strength and remember to use your skills to stay calm and connect.

- **Make an Effort to Be More Social:** take a social skills class or an assertiveness class. Work on your communication skills and go volunteer for something you enjoy.

- **Embrace an Anti-Anxiety Lifestyle:** Avoid or limit caffeine, drink only in moderation, get enough quality sleep, and quit smoking. Get more Omega-3 & Sunlight. Evidence shows that foods with Omega-3 can lower stress chemicals that can worsen anxiety. Sunlight: absorbing strong sunlight will raise your Vitamin-D levels which is thought to play an important role in your mental health.

- **Exercise:** Studies show that simple activity can deliver hours of relief to your anxiety, similar to taking aspirin for a headache.

- **Laughing:** Even a fake laugh can get you some relief from anxiety, according to EveryDayHealth.com. The laughing will trigger dopamine, a brain chemical associated with pleasure. The source says that "even anticipating a mirthful laugh" can reduce stress hormones (namely cortisol) that is shown to increase when you're most anxious.

- **Lullaby Yourself**: get into an easily controlled rhythm such as holding a drink for sipping, pen for caressing, music you can move to, rhythmic home cleaning, etc. These easily controlled rhythms become your Winners Effect where these small wins will give you your momentum towards comfort ☺.

8) <u>Hot Showers</u>:

Allow your senses to be overwhelmed with stimulus outside of your mind as you embrace the heat and water running over you. It's hard to take an amazing shower and feel worse afterwards.

9) <u>Remove Triggers</u>:

When your heart's in pain and your thoughts are consumed with your x, it's time to remove every trigger around you that places you back into the hurtful thoughts of them.

I simply throw any possessions left behind right into the trash chute. Donating is good too, but that takes time to organize and the longer it's around you, the longer your pain will remain.

- Take down pictures in the house and on your phone.
- Rid yourself immediately of their items.
- Avoid their music or songs tied to memories.

- Avoid people/places/things that trigger fond memories.
- Wash your bedding to cleanse them physically from you.
- Scrub the house down for a spiritual cleansing.
- Block their social media and avoid seeing or remembering them.

10) <u>Focus on Their Faults</u>:

<u>Never forget that your x made you feel horrible and left you broken</u>. It's important to focus on their negative qualities and how they mistreated you.

- Change their contact name in your phone to remind you of their worst. For me, my x was Unappreciative, she was a Liar, and she was consumed with unhealthy/unnecessary Chaos. Her contact name was changed to: Unappreciative Lying Chaos, and every time we spoke during the Break UP, that was how I remembered her...ACCURATELY! Stop torturing yourself by only remembering their best because if they truly were providing their best, you'd still be together.

- If you have a picture or video of them mistreating you, watch it. Remember those feelings instead of anything else.

11) <u>ReProgram</u>:

Face your triggers. If you had a special song or ringtone; assign it to another person and begin reprograming your moments. For example, the first girl I was in to after my Break UP immediately had her ring tone updated to that of my x. The song that was playing when my x came over for the first time is now the theme song playing as every new girl/memory arrives over for their first. Special outfit from your last; wear it for your next and assign a new memory to it. Rewrite your triggers, reprogram, and grow TF out of this and beyond!

Repetition: It will get easier. Your first few dates, nights in bed alone, going out without them; all these things become easier the more you repeat them. Begin to reprogram, add in endless repetition, and continue your ascend to your best being ahead.

Step 2: Soothe Thyself

As you begin to soothe yourself, you begin to take back control of your ill feelings and positive path.

Understand that no one should ever be mistreated; they should be made aware of their weaknesses and once it becomes apparent that it's untreatable, they should be dropped immediately!

Validate your Worth in Healthy Ways. It's not time for a revenge f**k- you'll only feel worse. What you're missing is being appreciated and loved, and that's not something that's quick to fix.

Recognize **that no one will love you more than you love yourself**. <u>START LOVING YOU AGAIN</u>! Start taking actions everyday towards happiness and as you do, your joyous life will become self-fulfilling. Step Two: Soothe Thyself.

11/30/20 Birthday & Book Signing

Step 3: <u>Admitting Your Role</u>

"the way you see the problem IS the problem"

Back to the introduction of this book; it's easy to blame everyone for everything. However, the greatest problem in this mindset is that you're failing to grow, and unless you desire the same outcome, some rapid change and new action is needed.

When we fail to grow, we become doomed to repeat our ill-fates, and that's what we call a Break Down. Take comfort in knowing that as you're reading this book, *This **WILL NOT** Be Your Fate*, and Step 3 is all about understanding your role as the problem so that you're able to blossom and embrace your best being always ahead.

As there's no comfort in growth, get ready to embrace some discomfort as we go through Step 3.

Cleary **<u>ADMIT</u>** the **things you could've done better** and areas you were slacking in. This exercise only works if you take your time with each question, **separate your emotion** from the issues, and answer as **unbiasedly** and honest as possible. Try to see the issue from how an outsider would look at your relationship. Check one box in each row depending on whether <u>you Provided that Quality to your x</u> or <u>Not</u>:

Your Quality	Provided (yes)	Unprovided (no)
In shape physically		
Mainly positive		
Motivating		
Assertive on your needs		
Sexually satisfying		
Maintained a clean body		
Maintained a clean home		
Supportive in their desires		
Accepting of their flaws		
Earning Trust		
100% Loyal		
Consistently Validating their strengths		
Choosing your battles to eliminate excessive arguments		
Outside your comfort zone for their needs		
Playful and Lighthearted		

Discussing more ideas than stories		
Didn't spend too much time with TV or video games.		
Accepting of criticism		
Respectful around others		
Utilized Anger Control		
Promoted Problem Solving		
Mainly Solution Oriented		
Understanding		
Mainly Promoted Peace		
Confident in self		
Secure in self		
Role Model to them		
Fighting Fair		
Not dependent on Them		

Not Hostile with Frustrations		
Never Physically Violent		
Not Controlling		
Humorous		
Intimate		
Present		
Appreciative		
Reciprocating		
Attentive		
Flexible in needs		
Eating Healthy		
Committed		
Drinking Enough Water		
Not dependent on drug or substance consumption		

Open to spontaneity and change		

If you checked **YES** in each box, then this breakup is entirely your fault as your partner was clearly unworthy and you should've found the strength to walk away long ago.

If you checked **NO** in 5 boxes or more, then **this breakup is entirely your fault** as you were failing to provide.

Either you were doing too much and were too weak, or **you were doing too little** and were **too weak**, where EACH OF THESE means YOU'RE THE PROBLEM. Trust me when I tell you that <u>this is the single greatest moment in moving forward</u> because guess what, **YOU Can Absolutely Change YOU!**

When you're failing to provide for the needs of your partner, then not only are you part of the problem, but in the end, you're either contributing solutions or you're contributing problems. Just know that <u>Contributing to the Problem IS THE PROBLEM</u>.

On the other hand, if you were doing so immaculate in providing solutions and still remaining in the problematic relationship, then that right there is the problem.

In my most recent relationship, I actually factually tried everything to accommodate her best and live with her worst.

I spent many years in prison for a troubled (and FUN) youth, and when I was finally released, I had become so aware of my person that I was truly able to offer everything and ask for nothing except presence and peace from others.

Infact, that is exactly what I explained to her on our first date; that her only job would be to soothe me. I've built numerous successful business, an incredible ever growing prominent social circle, and I maintain a plentiful use of free time void of pressure and urgency...cultivating a life of peace.

I have three amazing vehicles that I own outright, where she had access to a luxury vehicle fueled, insured and ready to go at her whim.

I own a luxury Highrise unit that with 75% perimeter of windows instead of walls promoting excellent lighting for mental clarity. She was able to enjoy the ease and beauty as she utilized amenities and slept as early or late as she desired.

As I paid for college as a personal trainer, I was able to help her quickly reach her fitness goals where I specialized in powerful 15min workouts for gain (video course on 15mins for Gains available at JeremySigal.com.)

Aside from physical growth, I worked on building her confidence in being assertive with others and in negotiating where I would pay her $100 every time she negotiated a discount on any purchase.

I also love to endlessly cook and clean, so her every desired meal was prepared on-call from scratch and cleaned for her immediately afterwards.

Although she had a side job doing digital marketing on her own at her convenience, her finances weren't great where I actually enjoyed contributing to her needs where reasonable, including purchasing all household items, some clothes and beauty products for her.

As I have a massively active social life with incredibly happy, positive and successful people, we were regularly on the go with exciting events, trips and dinners with interesting & inspiring people.

Knowing that she had a desire to own her own digital marketing agency, I began building her a website and always made sure to place her in front of experts in that one area so that she could learn, build, and grow into her dreams.

Massive Undying Loyalty to my people is the only reason why I have the life I live, as my lack in formal education and excessive criminal record should've devastated me years ago. <u>I've never once cheated on any girlfriend</u> nor have I engaged in any malicious act reducing my credibility.

Sex life: really great, healthy, and mutually validating. Although I'm sure each of us had enjoyed more physically attractive partners in our past, I absolutely worshiped everything about her and put in daily effort to ensure we were both happy and healthy intimately.

Not only did I provide endlessly, but on top of that, I'm an incredibly hilarious and effortlessly positive person always, where that in and of itself may be one of the greatest qualities any person can possess.

So I ask you, where's the problem? Why was she constantly attacking me with false positions and moving out almost every week? What I had at first thought were just bad habits and patterns on her part, I quickly began to realize that she could not get in between her emotions and her actions. Her emotions were stronger than her mind.

I was so stressed out from daily false attacks that I eventually implemented a $50/$500 rule for false attacks, where when I could show she was attacking me from a provably false position, she would have to pay $50, and if I were doing the same, I would happily pay $500. Not only did I never pay anything as I'm always very cautious, but she paid on her end 7 different times in a matter of a few weeks. Hoping the monetary aspect would be a trigger to help her get in-between her emotions was not working whatsoever. Nothing was reducing her insecurities and unnecessary stress load on us.

One thing I did really well was that I always set boundaries and walkaway points, and as she continued to break every single agreement, I began to push harder for her to either change or go.

She was obsessed with being right vs being happy, extremely irritable, endlessly distrusting, messy & lazy, and had begun coming off as the single most unappreciative person I have ever dated. She was obsessed with constant insecurity-based false-attacks and actually enjoyed testing how far she could push things.

When she eventually left and did not return, my heart was broken in ways I had never really felt before. This girl and I spent 24/7 together for months, with an absolutely jam packed schedule of growth & excitement and we were about to move forward into marriage and starting a family.

Step 3: **Admit Your Role**

My role was allowing the detriment to continue. I was weak in admitting that our relationship was doomed from the start. I was too disciplined and strong to be with someone who was lost, chaotic, unaware, and fundamentally weak.

It's time to **Admit Your Role** as **THE PROBLEM** so that we may begin to move forward on a better tomorrow. Your time for change and growth is now, and together, I promise you we will have it all!

Sept. 25, 2020 - 3month Anniversary (Favorite x)

Step 4: <u>Understand Their Role</u>

"The double-edged blade distributes harm from each direction."

Why have you not realized that your x's ONLY role was to drive you UP? I know it's counterintuitive to imagine, but the fact remains that you allowed yourself to be taken so far off path and beat down that you've now been shown all the areas you're about to build into being your best self ever!

It's definitely a Break UP, and when the mission is to avoid a BreakDown, it's time to understand the situation in full so that you're able to embrace healthy progress and success; always Onwards and Upwards!

Many times when we're trying to solve a problem that we're involved in, it's always easy to focus only on their faults which as we just covered is the wrong way to see it.

However, now that you're more accepting of your role as the problem, we can progress to their role which contributed to the unhealthy relationship and their soon to be visible role in your positive progress towards a better tomorrow.

Let's go back to our chart, but this time, let's focus on <u>qualities your x</u> either <u>did</u> or <u>did not provide</u> you in the relationship.

Again, separate the emotion from each issue. Take your time, and answer as fairly and as honest as possible. Focus on how an outsider would look at your relationship, and precisely admit their strengths and weaknesses here by checking each row once in either the Provided or Unprovided column:

Their Quality	Provided (yes)	Unprovided (no)
In shape physically		
Mainly positive		
Motivating		
Assertive on their needs		
Sexually satisfying		
Maintained a clean body		
Maintained a clean home		
Supportive in your desires		
Accepting of your flaws		
Earning Trust		
100% Loyal		
Consistently Validating your strengths		

Choosing their battles to eliminate excessive arguments		
Outside their comfort zone for your needs		
Playful and Lighthearted		
Discussing more ideas than stories		
Didn't spend too much time with TV or video games		
Accepting of criticism		
Respectful around others		
Utilized Anger Control		
Promoted Problem Solving		
Mainly Solution Oriented		
Understanding		
Mainly Promoted Peace		
Confident in self		
Secure in self		
Role Model to you		
Fighting Fair		

Not dependent on you		
Not Hostile with frustrations		
Never Physically Violent		
Not Controlling		
Humorous		
Intimate		
Present		
Appreciative		
Reciprocating		
Attentive		
Flexible in needs		
Eating Healthy		
Committed		
Drinking Enough Water		
Not dependent on drug or substance consumption		
Open to spontaneity and change		

If you marked more than 5 boxes of qualities that were unprovided for, then again, You're The Problem, and if your x was so perfect in so many ways and you failed them, then again, you're the problem.

The good news: **We already know the problem**. Now we can **transition to the solution** and begin by clearly identifying their role in your troubled past and your ever brighter future!

More than likely, your x failed you so badly as either they failed to bring you up, or they failed to climb up with you.

Either way, never underestimate the power and growth you're about to amass from this process, as I'm about to show you that this so called "Break UP" is likely the single greatest thing to ever happen to you.

Embrace this absolute truth, that "the road to success is always paved with failure."

Also understand that, "it's only a failure if you fail to grow."

That being said, it's time to grow and we're going to focus on how your x's role was filling voids you may not have even known you had. Understanding that as you identify your underlying needs that they were contributing to, you'll also begin to clearly identify the areas and needs that you'll need to start fulfilling for yourself.

As the biblical saying goes, **god helps those who helps themselves**.

Step 4: Understanding Their Role. We began by clearly identifying the qualities your x was not providing. I want you now to write that list of all their Unprovided Qualities here:

_____

_____

_____

_____

This is your task.
This is what you must do.

You need to start providing these qualities to yourself before you can ever expect another to provide them to you.

Understand that being in <u>a relationship is like having a puppy</u>. They're new, they're young, and <u>they require a lot of work and training</u> to make proper.

As you begin to amass these qualities, you will soon be able to go from student to teacher, at which point when your future partner is lacking, you can actually show them. Better yet is that as you were once a novice in these areas, who better to explain the process on progressing in each field. Perhaps the best part is that knowing success takes time requiring the constant embrace of growth and change to remain on top, understand that the single **greatest way to learn is to teach**.

That's why note taking and summarizing is such a powerful exercise, because you're internalizing outside information, processing it for your own understanding, and then organizing that understanding from the inside out as you detail it's structure for others. Your time to fix you as the problem is now. Read each quality and solution. Learn to become self-fulfilling first so you can eventually help others and receive it in return.

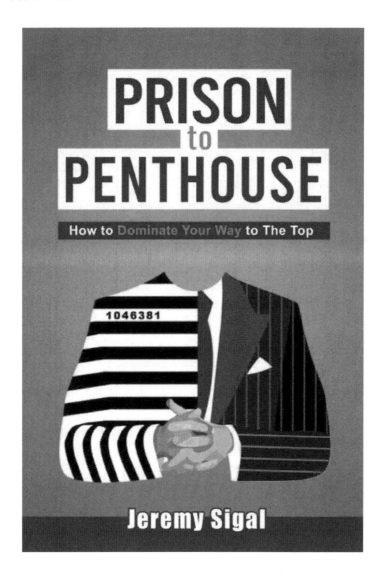

In shape physically	Were you? Get busy working out. Legs, Back and Chest are your biggest muscle groups and will induce rapid change fast.
Mainly positive	Embrace positivity. Become Grateful.
Motivating	Begin motivating people by example.
Assertive on their needs	Read my book <u>Prison to Penthouse</u> to learn how to become more assertive.
Sexually satisfying	Foreplay, endurance, strength, perception, rhythm, passion, feedback, research, and toys.
Maintained a clean body	Stay clean and ready for everything.
Maintained a clean home	Stay organized and cultivate a relaxing environment.
Supportive in your desires	Learn to build on your goals and invite others into your journey.
Accepting of your flaws	I have a rule of 3. I pick 3 issues I'm unattracted to and live with it. On #4, you're out lol.
Earning Trust	You gotta give trust to get trust. You CAN NOT micromanage their every affair.
100% Loyal	It's a must, as there's no coming back from this. If they weren't, what were

	you failing to provide? If you were, then why are you upset that your x was too weak to provide it in return? Onwards and Upwards!
Consistently Validating your strengths	You need to get good at validating the strengths of those around. As you build them, so too will your castle & empire blossom.
Choosing their battles to eliminate excessive arguments	You can be right or you can be happy, it's that simple. You have to let the little things go if you want to be happy.
Outside their comfort zone for your needs	Embrace discomfort in the growth of self and in the growth of others.
Playful and Lighthearted	Anyone can be serious and boring. Embrace the art of being lighthearted and playful as life truly is too short.
Discussing more Ideas than Stories	Stories keep us in the past. Ideas enable growth into an ever healthier future.
Didn't spend too much time with TV or video games.	Life is all around us. Avoid consuming life's beauty from in front of a screen.
Accepting of Criticism	If you can't grow into other's needs, you'll never be truly available for anyone. Listen, Process, and Pause. If you love that person, start truly internalizing their views and positions.

Respectful around others	What happens in private is yours, but if your chaos is in front of others, you're programming the circle around you to maintain disapproval of what could be and should be in your relationship.
Utilized Anger Control	Healthy frustration is everything. If you're escalating arguments into fights, then those angry fights will begin to define your relationship.
Promoted Problem Solving	Embrace problems and challenges with the mindset of working through them rather than in them.
Mainly Solution Oriented	Learn to habitually contribute solutions over problems.
Understanding	We're all individuals, and when we're joining a group, being flexible, understanding and accepting of your differences is everything.
Mainly Promoted Peace	Fighting every battle keeps us in misery. Learn to be accepting and begin focusing on peace.
Confident in self	It takes confidence in self to give confidence in relations. Grow your value. Gain your confidence.
Secure in self	To secure undying love from others, we must secure it first from ourselves.

Role Model to you	Be the role model. Focus on leading by example and promoting growth in others.
Not dependent on you	Structure and support to others requires self-sufficiency on your part. Embrace your independence and enjoy your times together.
Not Hostile with frustrations	Frustrations are part of every relationship, and you can't allow hostility to shut theirs down or you'll soon begin to shut them out.
Never Physically Violent	Like cheating, this massive action can never be undone. Focus on space. Understand that your answer in arguments is not more anger; it's stronger more articulate arguments.
Not Controlling	You're not their father, you're their partner. It's not your job to micromanage their every affair as when you do, you become the parent to a rebellious teenager.
Humorous	Laugh More. Stress Less. Love Endlessly.
Intimate	Intimacy is a constant effort over time. Step up your game. Get outside your comfort zone for them. Often times your partner is reluctant to share their true desires, so it's up to

	you to test the waters and embrace their smiles.
Present	Yesterday is gone. Tomorrow's never promised. But today...today is a gift; that's why we call it the Present! Be Present. Truly enjoy your moments.
Appreciative	Constant validation towards your relationships is needed. Don't focus on needing to tell them everything though, as validation is shown much more beautifully in actions.
Reciprocating	Every relationship in life requires reciprocation. Although it doesn't have to be tit-for-tat, the level of attempt to satisfy needs must always be equal.
Attentive	Awareness is everything. Although love may be blind, your partners are not. It's time to pay more attention to the needs they verbalize and even more importantly, the needs they don't.
Flexible in needs	Sacrifice, compromise, and tolerance are some of the main pillars in a healthy relationship. Embrace them.
Eating Healthy	You are what you eat. Put effort into worshiping your body with quality nutrition so that you may transition healthy worship to others.

Committed	Lead the path. Prove your commitment every chance you can, focusing on actions over words.
Drinking Enough Water	Your brain and heart are 73% water. Feeling hurt or imbalanced physically? Drink UP!
Not dependent on drug or substance consumption	Allow you to control you. If you're controlled by substance, you're no longer fully available to others.
Open to spontaneity and change	Death is serious. Everything else should be an effortless flow; just roll with it!

You just broke UP with someone you thought was best for you even though you were neglecting yourself and others in so many key areas.

You can't even imagine how much better your next will be as your focus becomes on building you.

With my x, I exercised less from her stress, ate junk food that she stocked us up with, watched too much TV, and even started day drinking from being content in a dysfunctional stressful relationship. Now, I'm networking with endless powerful connections as I go out more, I'm getting into the best shape of my life, and instead of that excess TV, I'm instead currently writing this badass book just for you ;-) xoxo!

Understand the absolute fact that the only role your x will serve you moving forward is in pushing you to obtain levels of success and ability you never would have otherwise, and once achieved, always ensure to throw in a thank you!

Step 5: <u>You're Sad</u> - <u>So TF What</u>

"If you're sad about a failed relationship,
then you honestly have no idea how lucky you truly are"

Break UPs like this are often an uncomfortable and recurring presence in our lives.

Even though I just told you that it's only a failure if you fail to grow from this, most of you still feel like the entire world is coming to an end. So at this point, I'm going to do my best to put these false beliefs into perspective. <u>21 Short Stories</u>:

- I found the love of my life.
  She didn't.

- He promised he would wait for her forever.
  She kept him to his word.

- It was a lot.
  It just wasn't enough.

- He woke up, rolled over, and reached for her.
  She wasn't there, and never would be again.

- They told me they could save either my wife or my son.
  They were wrong.

- After months of waiting he finally saw his wife.
  He'd never been happier but he knew he'd have to wake up soon.

- He never wanted to leave his wife.
  But it was getting late and the graveyard gates were about to be closed.

- My owner won't wake up.
  My food bowl has been empty for so long.

- I pick up your little collar and leash, and I almost expect you to come running at the sound. I will never get used to the awful silence.

- I rock my baby in my arms and sing softly to her.
  It helps me pretend she is only sleeping.

- I had carried her to the hospital, half conscious and overdosed, but alive. I was the only one who waited with her for her recovery, and every day she would reiterate how much she loathed me for it.

- I became an EMT to save people's lives.
  Twenty minutes of CPR on my dad proved that was a lie.

- The heart monitor chimed its final tune.
  Come the end there was no applause.

- I told her she would be okay.
  That was the first lie I ever told.

- "He's not coming, is he?" I asked, squeezing my mother's hand, the multi-colored party hat on my head slipping down. My mother squeezed back, and without a word walked back inside the house.

- 9 months of excitement came to an end.
  She never cried.

- I kept the ultrasound.
  Someone I never met.

- Mommy promised her the monsters weren't real.
  But mommy didn't know that daddy was the monster.

- Parent backing out of driveway unknowingly runs over and kills his 3yr old daughter.

- Holocaust: families torn from the arms of their loved ones while being maliciously gassed and burnt to ash.

- 9/11- attempting to call loved ones while burning alive in a collapsing building and trying to summarize your final message of love for them on voice mail.

- Childhood cancer: comforting your 6 year-old daughter as you try and make sense for her life as she's looking for meaning as to why she must die.

And you're sad because **you chose to stick in a relationship with someone who treated you like shit** and failed your needs in endless ways!? And you call this YOLO'ing it UP! C'mon! WAKE UP! You're better than that.

If you're telling me you're broken and lost from THIS, then you clearly have no idea how blessed you are to never yet have felt actual factual tragic loss.

Nobody can make you feel anything; know that you are purposely choosing to feel these feelings of emptiness and loss, and if you've taken nothing else, please embrace the second half of this book:

PERSONAL GROWTH OVER EVERYTHING. As you grow and build, so too will everything around you!

Aug. 25, 2020 – 2 month (Favorite x) Anniversary

Step 6: <u>Throttling Up</u>

"You are not your past. Your future will be defined by what you do next."

As discussed in Step 4: Understanding Their Role, you now have a list on all things you're going to begin controlling and building. The time to take action on picking yourself UP is NOW!

Focus on the fact that success is always a process, and you're already dead square in the middle of it, so let's turn it up with these simple actual things you will start doing TODAY and every day after!

- **Show Some Respect To Yourself**
- **Made Service**
- **Big Primpin**
- **Add Value to Others**
- **Assert or Hurt**
- **HYPE-Man**
- **Object vs Target**
- **Be Selfish**
- **Embrace Confrontations**
- **Get Good at NO**
- **Amazing Fruit Cocktail**
- **Super-Computer Connect**
- **Ideas vs Stories**
- **A Series of Small Wins**
- **Ball Tickling**

- **Make Em Respect Your Time**
- **CritiKing**
- **Break Through with Humor**
- **Maximize Discomfort**
- **Master Rejection**

1) Show Some Respect to Yourself First

As your body is your temple, it's time to start worshiping yourself today. I was blessed enough to learn the fundamentals at the young age of 18 where I was able to pay my way through college as a Personal Trainer helping others obtain their fitness goals through posture, working out, and nutrition.

Posture: your foundation for all motion. Posture is also your single greatest communicating factor where body language accounts for over half of all communication towards others.

Included in your book purchase is my video course on showing you exactly how to easily correct bad posture and maximize good posturing in everything you do, but I'll try to lay out the basics below.

Head hanging forward, shoulders rounding forward, and your pelvis tilting forward are the main aspects of bad posture as hunching forward communicates weakness and insecurity.

Simple stretches and tightening of muscles along your backside will quickly fix all where you then can hold your head high and chest out everywhere you go. Go to JeremySigal.com and request your free video course on rapidly correcting posture today.

Working Out: Our bodies require strength to process nutrients, avoid injury, and maximize a healthy long life.

If you're like most, working out for 2hrs/day just is not an option, but if this is an area you're in need of, sign up for my video course on 15mins for Mass where I'll walk you through how to rapidly whip your body into shape in 15min workouts 3x/week...that's it!

You can do cardio in your own time, but muscle is what burns fat, so it's time to get some. The three biggest muscle groups are Legs, Back, and Chest.

Although you may have certain areas you want to build as well, focusing on your three big muscle groups is the single fastest way to obtain results in trimming down and toning UP.

Chest: Flat Press- hands slightly above the nipples, chest out, shoulders back. You can do this with pushups, barbell, dumbbells, cables or a machine.

Back: Pull Downs (UPs)- wide grip, elbows back, chest out, full extension up. Rows: Arms mid torso, full extension, pulling from your mid-back, getting your elbows all the way back.

Legs: <u>Squats</u>/<u>Leg Press</u>- pushing from your heels and squeezing your butt the whole time. Ensure you're getting low enough for a 90 degree bend at the knee, and make sure that your knees are not extending forward over your toes. Squats are about moving your hips back, not pushing your knees forward. <u>Lunges</u>- feet spread out as far as comfortably possible, chest out/shoulders back/leaning back or at least straight, drop straight down until the knee is just above the ground, then press up using your forward foot's heel and glute (butt).

These simple exercises will begin to change everything, and for the complete thorough visual step-by-step instruction, go to:

<u>JeremySigal.com</u> and signup for my **15 mins for Muscle** video course.

2) Made Service

Any guesses as to my most liked Facebook/Instagram post? I'll give you a hint: It wasn't a picture of me with 10 hotties or me in fancy cars. It wasn't a picture of me with the coolest people or holding the largest amount of money. It wasn't a landmark birthday or even my release from prison. Give up yet- you may as well because even I never saw this one coming.

A picture of my bedroom f'ing closet! I received four times more likes with a picture of my closet than any other post before or since. Suck that IG Influencers lol!

Made Service- not "maid," but "made" like Made-Man.

When her hair's done just right and her perfume smells amazing, we're all impressed and attracted to her high level of self-respect. We similarly remember when our friend picked us up in their filthy car with the inside looking like a fast food dumpster, where we all then associated that level of filth with our friend's personal respect level.

When we're trying impress our peers and earn their respect, the single most important impression you can make is one of extremely high self-respect for how you treat your personal space and personal things.

Your personal space defines you.
Your personal space is you.
Made Service

Your home, your car, your clothes, your office, and your friends are all an extension of you, so make sure they represent a high level of respect because they will literally define the respect and status you get from others.

Adapt to your surroundings = <u>Weak</u>
Adapt your surroundings to you = <u>Strong</u>

Made Service- it's more about <u>who you are on the inside determining what you deserve on the outside and from others.</u>

When you're looking to <u>Break UP Not Down</u>, keep your personal area cleaned and organized. Show a high level of respect to yourself first so that you can get a high level of respect from others later.

In prison, inmates associate your personal respect level with the respect you show your things, where guys that are highly respected all maintain an immaculate cell, clean clothes, and a clean body. Even though I'm out of prison now, everyone in my new arena knows how extremely clean and organized I am. Same routine, different arena, and it pays the absolute highest dividends every time.

One of my favorite tricks for staying ready is most recognizable at my Highrise residence. As I entertain groups of guests quite frequently, I never want any awkward or uncomfortable moments to exist. For example, when we're out having fun at night and then return to my place, my unit's AC's are already blasting cool air. My LED soothing indigo lighting is already on, and the upbeat chill music is deep into its rhythm. My toilets are cleaned, my unit is spotless, and there are no negative distractions. The only thing guests notice when they're in my house is how amazing they feel as their every sense is overwhelmed and intimidated at the exact same time.

In the arena of school or employment, although you may not be scrubbing your toilets, you most certainly will be judged & respected by your ability to maintain a clean well-organized working area. Allow this habit to include all your personal areas and belongings as well, and Breaking UP all the way to the top will rapidly become your story.

Made Service = Freedom? Absolutely. One of the most beneficial aspects of **Made Service** is that you eliminate distractions. I have extreme ADHD which means that everything requires my attention at the exact same time. For this reason alone, I maintain clean and organized personal spaces so that I can focus only on moving forward. Another word for extreme focus on everything ahead of you; **Freedom**. Made Service Keeps You In The Moment. **Made Service Keeps You Free**. When growing through your Break UP: **Utilize Made Service**.

3) Big Primpin

While in prison, I was locked in an actual cage for the worst of the worst and I needed to be ready for every single possibility outside my cage door whenever given the chance. Knowing that every possible opportunity existed the moment my cage door opened ensured that I never walked out of my home until I was ready for everything and everyone. My teeth were brushed, my hair was combed, my clothes were clean, and my body smelled goood. Showered and shaved, I was ready. Afterall, I might run into the warden with a problem I needed solved or the legendary female I lusted endlessly over, and the last thing you'd want to do is offend the person you're looking to connect with by having bad breath, matted hair, dirty clothes, or body odor.

Big Primpin

Since you never know when the opportunities you need will present themselves, make sure you stay ready to connect with them when they do. When your mission is to rise, you need to stay ready for the opportunities you need.

Big Primpin- When You Stay Ready, You Ain't Gotta Get Ready.

Make sure and put effort everyday into your details <u>BEFORE</u> you leave your cage. First Made Service. Get your place ready for whatever may happen next. Then:

- Shower
- Shave
- Maintain a clean hair cut
- Brush your teeth (and your gums)
- Clean and match your clothes
- Clean shoes: similar to stained clothes, spotless shining shoes look amazing, so clean them every time you wear em
- Fitted clothes: studies show people make more judgements about your personal trustworthiness and successfulness based off the fit of your clothes than any other Primpin act.
- Apply deodorant/cologne and again,

DO THIS ALL _BEFORE_ YOU LEAVE YOUR SPACE

Now obviously these are the basics, but the point of these details is that you need to have them done **before** you ever walk out of your house, you need to do it every single day, and you need to do it every single time. For example, I live in a Highrise residence, and every time the elevator stops on my floor to pick me up, there is a chance I might be walking into a small room with a powerful business contact I'm looking to connect with or maybe even the girl of my dreams. **Big Primpin**: Stay ready for every opportunity by nailing down your details **before** you leave your cage.

4) Add Value to Those Around

One of my favorite things to tell my sentencing judges and the parole board was this line:

> **"I work hard every day to turn this punishment into an opportunity."**

Is that a gem or what! The most frequent advice I give to people going through a Break-UP is similar, where I tell them to focus on this one thing, **Throttle UP**. What I mean by this is that most people become sad and desperate while going through a Break UP, where they internalize their pain and reach out begging their x to return.

I'm not just saying this just to sound cool, but seriously, What The F are you thinking?! I mean, your x already left you, probably for someone exceling in areas you were slacking on, and now you think they're just gonna come rushing back into your life because you've added "desperate" "weak" and "crybaby" to your lengthy list of faults!? Forget That! C'mon, You're Better Than That.

ThrottleUp - Add Value

You're new in the arena of being single, and the fact remains that people want what other people want. It's time to be desired by those around you and as they validate you, you will in return remember just how special you truly are. **Become Desired. Become Valuable. Become Validated.**

Focus on the things you can control:

a) **Fitness**- start exercising more and looking sexy
b) **Nutrition**- start eating better and feeling sexy.
c) **Financial**- start working harder and building bigger.
d) **Smiles**- cultivate them every place you go.
e) **Socialize**- your every opportunity is outside your cage. Get out, get involved, and get connected to things bigger than yourself.
f) **Big Primpin**- stay ready so you can be ready for the next one.

When you see someone successful that you're looking connect with, never ask them to help you just because. Instead, **get busy focusing on the value you can add to them** and your journey alongside them will become self-fulfilling.

Constant Education has always been my biggest value add. I surround myself with knowledge and with people who know more than me; people who challenge and allow me the ability to constantly absorb more information to be added back into my group at a later date.   Be a **Bank Account of Lendable Knowledge**. Be appreciated for who you are.

5) Assert or Hurt

We've all heard the old rhyme that _nice guys apparently finish last_, but why? I mean, isn't being nice like the easiest way to make everyone like you? So why are we finishing last when we're making everyone around us happy?

Well, the lengthy complex psychological reasoning goes a bit deep, but the underlying theme for why nice guys finish last is mainly because they're passive pussies, plain and simple.

If you're not saying hi,
then she's definitely saying bye.

- <u>Passive</u> =   you have respect for them, but not for yourself.
- <u>Aggressive</u> = you have respect for yourself, but not for them.
- **Assertive** = <u>when you have mutual respect for each person.</u>

Bullies are aggressive and although nobody likes a bully, studies show that being passive is likely to get you even less in life. When you're being passive, what you're actually doing is suffering by habitually failing to act on your own best interests & desires.

The most common regrettable passive situation I hear about is when a someone is pursuing the person of their dreams and is too scared to act on their desires. Being reckless and bold in the pursuit of your crush will literally define their attraction towards you. However, failing to act will similarly solidify a message that you don't care enough about them to let yourself go for it.

For example, by the time a woman is wondering "is he going to kiss me", that magical moment between you has already passed. Being polite is one thing, but failing to act on your own whims because you're too afraid of failure is the absolute definition of being a pussy.

Being nice is easy and that's why most everyone is. **Forget Easy**!

Telling people how you really feel and **what you really want** is called being **courageous.** You know who else is courageous - warriors, and much of the time we speak about warriors, we refer to them as heroes.

My question to you is this: Do you wanna be walked all over because you're a pussy or is your preference to be revered and celebrated as a hero? If your mission is that of the hero role, then this book is for you ☺. When your goal is Breaking UP Not Down as you climb up and conquer everything along the way, then you're gonna need to master this part:

Assert or Hurt

Practicing perfecting the art of planting your feet, speaking your mind, and staying connected to your group. Be Assertive and Stay in Control.

The problem with being passive is that your long-term failure becomes self-fulfilling because in your every future relation,

"Nobody is going to respect you more than you respect yourself."

The same is true for being aggressive with others. The recipients of a bully's aggression recognize instinctively that they don't enjoy being taken advantage of. They feel pressured into submitting and immediately build resentment towards their aggressor. As an aggressor, your failure will become self-fulfilling as others begin to avoid you, and eventually begin to aggressively plot against you.

Master being assertive, even when an aggressor aggressively attacks you. Being assertive means that even when you can destroy a target, you always focus on a win/win outcome where you can put in the minimum effort and achieve the maximum result. Embrace **certain words** and **phrases** that have **the power to change the course** of a relationship.

Being assertive is all about setting boundaries. For this process, use this layout.

I feel _____

when you _____

because _____.

In the future, I need you to _____.

If you don't, I will _____.

No arena will allow Mr. Nice Guy to rise to the top. **It's time to Assert or Be Hurt**. Healthy relationships are acquired when we protect their interests and inspire greatness which is why people can never love a pussy or a bully the way they love Mr(s). Assertive.

Being passive is easy, and when you're angry, being aggressive comes naturally. Learn to make being assertive easy, and aggressive hard, by focusing on sticking to your agenda and taking as many deep breaths along the way. **Deals rarely get worse** when you're willing **to walk away**, and people always appreciate realness in whatever form it's delivered.

Being assertive is easy when you're with your inner circle, but to conquer your new single life arena, you must begin to master being assertive with everyone around and obtain the confidence to hold people accountable. Being assertive not only means holding others accountable, but also requires that you hold yourself accountable.

Remain accountable to your mission and your position, and when others step out of line in relationships, be assertive and hold them accountable as here it truly is **Assert or Hurt.** My favorite trick for being assertive is to approach the situation **Neutrally** and **Non-Threatening**:

a) **Reduce Anxiety**- don't roll into being assertive just after you've caught feelings. Take a moment to separate your emotion from your objective and begin with some seriously deep breaths before/during your dialogue. You'll speak slower and in a more controlled tone when you're calm, or at least as calm as possible.

b) **Celebrate Them First**- roll into your assertive dialogue by telling the other person a couple specific things you love about them and why you enjoy having them as part of your group.

c) **Assert**- after you've built their ego up really high, cutting them in half with your assertive position will still leave them feeling massively appreciated and in control.

d) **Reiterate Your Appreciation**- finish your request with another reminder of why you value them so much and reiterate your vision for them as an important part in the future in your life.

Examples:

A) Baby, I love you and I absolutely love providing for you.

B) The way you make me feel when we're hanging out together is incomparable to any other feeling I've ever felt, but

C) I fell really unappreciated when you fail to clean up after yourself in the kitchen even though you were home all day while I worked tirelessly at the office earning the funds needed to sustain our lifestyle.

D) In the future, I need you to be more considerate with our space so that I can come home to a relaxing clean environment after a long day's work (because),

E) I know that the two of us at our best could never be a stronger relationship.

or

a) Hey Chris- that was really cool of you to take me out the past few nights as I always have an amazing time, (and)

b) I really enjoy our time together as you're my single favorite person in the entire world, (but)

c) I feel really overwhelmed from never having anytime to myself to process my day and my thoughts when you forbid me to go anywhere by myself.

d) In the future, I need you to allow me occasional space so that I may remain strong and balanced for you. If you don't, it's only going to hurt my love for you as I won't have the strength to give you the things you need.

Warm into being assertive, otherwise you just come off as being an emotionally aggressive dick. Another part of excelling at assertiveness is being confident in your **Negotiating Skills.**

Negotiating skills are actually a massively important component of being assertive and getting others to agree with your position. One thing I do really well is that I practice my negotiating skills in damn near every transaction I encounter. I do this not because I need a discount, but because I want to master my negotiating skills for when I do need the deal. Also, because I'm Jewish and I hashtag got you!

When people who aren't my inner circle ask me for something, always try and ask for something in return. Known as a "**mutual concession**," make them move just as they're asking you to move which will ensure that your relationship and positive state of mind remains intact after the transaction.

- **Them**: Hey Jeremy, would you be able to lend me $100 until payday?
- **Me**: I'm really low right now. I got you this time, but would you mind holding off on future requests for a while as I stock back up?

- **<u>Them</u>**: Jeremy, I know you said you wanted to sell your car for $50,000, but would you be able to let it go for $40,000 instead?
- **<u>Me</u>**: I can bring the price down to $45,000 if you can pay in full by today.

Mutual Concessions- make them move with you. Be assertive, make mutual concessions, and be rewarded.

Another negotiating skill I use is the phrase: "**would you be willing to**..." Asking someone if they're "*willing*" personalizes your request more and requires that the respondent base their response off a deeper internal moral picture rather than just asking if they "like" or are "interested" in something. "Would you be **willing** to meet with me over lunch to discuss my proposal?"

Be Assertive and Ask For It

Most people are too passive to ask for things they want from others. Swallow your pride when you have nothing to lose and everything to gain. Similar to going in for that first kiss, even if you're rejected, you still experience a massive gain as the other person knows you are confident and willing; both are a major win.

ASK FOR DISCOUNTS and DEALS.

- "Do you guys offer any discounts?"
- "What's the best price you can do on this?"
- "What's up with a friends and family discount?"
- "What's up with a cash discount?"

I recently picked my Dodge Viper up from the dealership and was sincerely unhappy about the invoice price I was being asked to pay. I knew what a fair price was, but rather than engage at such a high starting price, I used this phrase assertively instead, "This price is way too high and if I have to pay it, I promise you I'll never come back here again." We both knew the price was way to high...Bam 50% off! Another phrase I like when asking for discounts is:

"I'd be a really satisfied customer if..."

Telling a business that you're an unsatisfied customer is one of the most devastating things a business owner can hear. Again, not only are these vendors risking losing your business, but they're also risking losing the business of your friends, family, and the community through a bad review.

Be Assertive. Tell them you're unsatisfied and what it would take to make you a satisfied customer. If they agree, thank them for making you a very satisfied customer once again. If they don't, threaten them with a bad review and be willing to completely avoid them for life. Employ being assertive with everyone you encounter and practice holding everyone accountable as much as you possibly can.

this is one of the single most important skills in this book.

YOU WILL _NEVER_ OBTAIN A HEALTHY RELATIONSHIP IF YOU ARE TOO ILL-EQUIPED TO ASSERT YOURSELF.

6) HYPE-Man

"Invite people to like you with great enthusiasm to meet them"

- Only 7% of communication is the actual words you use.
- 38% of your communication is your tone, so make sure you hit the right note especially when you have everything on the line. If you want your new arena to think you're lame, boring and average, then PLEASE continue acting lame, being boring, and speaking about average.

On your Day One, you need to utilize this chapter and make sure anyone you encounter thoroughly enjoys your interaction and the easiest way to do this is to make your tone exciting.

#ENTHUSIASM

When we're looking to create quality new connections, then it would shock you to learn that most people put such minimal effort into sparking interaction with those around. Remember that your **new connections** are only going to **blossom if they enjoy you.** When you're trying to get people happy & excited to meet you, then the first thing you need to do is be excited and happy to meet them!

Get excited about *Everything* **they say**!
Be excited about them and they'll get **excited about you too.**

Just as in life, we all come into this world by ourselves and it's only by choice that we stay alone. Humans are instinctively social creatures and we're naturally pack orientated for multiple reasons, mainly for survival and success. We've evolved to thrive from the incomparable strengths of a group while remaining safe where we're much more powerful and capable together than alone. Running solo in a world full of powerful groups and challenges can be absolutely detrimental to your safety on a daily basis.

Don't risk danger in being separated from society just because you're failing to inspire excitement and gain strong connections with your peers. **Begin all interactions with EXCITEMENT** and **ENTHUSIAM.** Be excited about what you're talking about and sound super excited about whatever the hell they're talking about too; it's the easiest trick you can use to connect!

Some strategies I use for enthusiasm are:

1) **Ask questions focused on excitement-**
- "Doing anything exciting today" **vs** "how are you."
- "What was the best part of your day" **vs** "how was your day"
- "What are you most excited about right now?"

2) **Avoid dull conversation** about vague, serious, or boring topics such as the weather, geography, and "how's your family" kind of shit. Afterall, most people keep those topics at the bottom of their totem pole of excitement anyway.

3) **Make the conversation about things you <u>like</u>** vs things you don't like. This tends to keep things more positive and upbeat.

Number "3" is massively important in the current online dating scene where many people will detail a long list on what they're not looking for. By the time you've read the 15th thing these single folk detail that they hate in a person, you start to have a really clear picture of exactly why these people are single! **Drop the negative chit chat and gossip**. Instead, forge deep meaningful relationships with those in your arena by using positive enthusiastic dialogue to:

- learn about their deepest desires
- focus the conversation on topics that motivate and inspire them
- learn about their greatest current challenges
- what are they most excited about in their personal life
- what are they most excited about in their professional life
- what are they most excited about for today
- do they need help solving any problems you can bond over
- what current agendas should you be made aware of
- pay them sincere specific compliments
- be inclusive and encourage their opinion with something
- talk about life and all the most beautiful mysteries contained within

Stop restricting the boundaries of conversation and allow your new group members to take the conversation wherever TF they want! The three main fears people share with me about meeting new people are:

a) "I understand I'm surrounded by people I want to meet, but it's hard for me to do it."
b) "I've tried to meet people, but I have nothing to talk about with them."
c) "I'm not interesting, and no one is going to be interested in me."

Now, although these are understandable concerns of many, each of them is unrealistic and reveals that these concerns only exist from an extreme lack of preparation and proper education.

The solution is simple: **HYPE-Man**
Enthusiasm while placing **their validation <u>before</u> yours**

Forget needing to be interesting or having anything exciting to talk about. Make your **entire interaction about them.** Get excited about everything they say and leave them feeling special. Afterwards, I guarantee you that they're going to be actively seeking the opportunity to shower you with excitement. Similar to when you receive a killer compliment and all you want to do is dodge it and throw one right back at them! **HYPE-Man,** #PassTheBall.

<u>ENTHUSIASM</u>: **Tone, Pitch,** and **Intensity** of your voice. Whatever the content of the things we say, it's our tone that communicates what we're feeling when we say them. When another person you don't know is staring at you like you're his dinner, you're probably not going to be consumed with happy feelings and the urge to bring that person into you're circle, but, you absolutely will disarm their strongest defenses with a sincere smile and a positive energy that screams "I think you're awesome and I want to make your life better!"

Understand that when you're new to your arena, **enthusiasm is even better than confidence,** mainly because **confidence is about you,** whereas **enthusiasm is about them**.

74

When your focus in on a subject or person that's important to you, then chances are you'll find yourself overtaken by enthusiasm, and here comes an avalanche of positive energy and inviting tone. You'll be energized, your voice will sound stronger, your hands will start gesturing, you'll find your whole body moving as you warm to your task. You'll lose your self-consciousness and be lost in the interaction itself, in the words and ideas you want to get across.

Enthusiasm is highly infectious. Think of a time when you heard someone talk about a subject you previously had no interest in, but they were so enthusiastic about it that you couldn't help but absorb their excitement as you found yourself intrigued- even fascinated. There's something **contagious about** the body language of **enthusiasm**; when you see someone talking excitedly, smiling, gesturing, full of energy and keen to share what they know, you can't help but respond.

<u>Energetic Mood Matching</u>: Don't come in hot! Adjust your tone, pitch and rhythm to where the other person's mood & energy is at. If they're calm and relaxed, don't bust through the front door waving your arms spitting the voice of intensity. Match their energy to connect and build.

For example, when you're stepping onto a football field for a big game, your energy is that of jumping about while you yell and hit yourself in the face; great for that connection, but about the extreme opposite of walking into a Library. When you're looking to connect, match their mood, copy their energy, and allow that mutual comfort to blossom into deep connections.

When you find yourself interacting today and beyond, curl your tone upwards towards the end of each statement, smile when you speak, and let them know how excited you are to meet them by complimenting a specific strength or two of theirs.

After you meet the people you're trying to meet, make sure your conversation remains balanced. Many people become nervous and unaware when meeting new people where they never shut up and end up strangling the entire conversation.

- **Don't strangle the conversation.**
- **Don't talk about yourself the whole time.**
- **Never focus on negatives.**
- **Never interrupt the person talking.**

Perhaps the worse of these is the interrupting part, as the message you're sending the other person is- *"my every fleeting thought is more important than your most sincere passions in life."* #ForgetYouWithThatMessage. When you're new and you're looking to make Family-Deep Connections, encourage their personal dialogue.

People become comfortable when they feel they can talk to you, so don't sabotage your connections; just listen, smile, nod, and STFU!

As far as talking about yourself, duh! One of the single most used words in conversation is "I." That being said, what do you think the person you're having a conversation with wants to discuss; #THEMSELVES! Their lives, their kids, their jobs. Do yourself a favor and when you're looking to connect, **DON'T TALK ABOUT YOU**. Get them talking about them, get excited about everything they say, and watch your relationship blossom to the max every time.

7) Objects vs Targets

"Targets are something we aim to destroy, whereas Objects are something we respect and avoid"

- Objects are selfless and use their strengths to benefit their peers.
- <u>Targets base their self-worth off others</u> and are full of false pride.
- Objects have the actual value, strength and depth needed by their peers.
- **Targets have zero depth**, one purpose, and are easily destroyed.

Don't be a target.
Never place yourself above your peers.

Striving to be an object, my mission has always been never to hurt anyone for personal gain. In truth, I've never felt good about winning any fight as the loser is left hurt, upset, and seeking vengeance. Your goal should always be to win at the least cost to your competition and your group.

8) Be Selfish

"Be selfish enough to gain well before you're selfless enough to give."

Being selfless is a luxury you must earn.

The luxury of being selfless is a reward earned by fighting for depth as you rise to the top in numerous arenas. However, when you're starting out at the bottom, you're gonna need to resist the temptation to be weak so that you can amass the strength you'll need to conquer, thrive and obtain successful relationships. **Be Selfish.**

Your agenda of Breaking UP, not Down isn't anyone's agenda except yours. To push your mission and stay your course, you'll need to have incredible core strength. **Build Your Value. Be Selfish.** Amass as much value for yourself so that you will become needed, appreciated, and eventually sought after as a life-long partner to those around.

After my Break UP, I started by **showing respect to myself first** where I built my physical strength to improve my value and appearance.

Get Selfish and Get Strong

I became selfish with my health. Where I was eating more snacks and unhealthy foods with my x, I began cooking more, eating out less, and cutting sugar/sodium/empty calories wherever possible.

Similar to studying material for a promotion, you'll never pass the test if you don't embrace a selfish moment or two learning the information.

As most breakups are more one-sided, the person on the losing side becomes desperate and further devalues themselves by begging the other to return.

Don't get desperate and beg your loved one to come back. **Being Selfish** teaches us that we can work hard enough to flip the script and eventually have them be the one begging us to return.

Be Selfish. (then) **Be Selfless.** (then) **Be Fondled.**

Add Value to yourself including physical, financial, social, emotional, spiritual value and more. The less time spent stalking your x is more time you can invest into yourself and as you rise, so too will their level of attraction towards you. Personally, I never worry about going through a Break UP because as I'm constantly becoming better, so too is the woman I'm about to get next. The more value you add to yourself, the more value you can offer your group. **Be Selfish** and **Rise.**

9) Embrace Confrontations

*"Sometimes you just gotta put your back to the wall
and get busy swingin"*

It was Halloween night, 1996, and I was crossing a street as a pedestrian when I was struck by a vehicle at 50 mph. I recovered well enough, but I did get hooked on Oxycontin for over 15 years. Now, although I'm better for the whole experience, one of the best rewards I was given through my addiction was multiple court-ordered drug rehabilitation programs and prison time!

#Winning ☺

Interestingly enough, one of the first skills you learn in a drug rehab is healthy "confrontation skills." Weird, right? Why is this one of the first skills they teach you during a rehabilitation program for drug abuse?

The long of the short answer begins here, where normal people address their issues as they arise, drug users avoid addressing issues by running from their problems with distractions like getting high instead.

The theory goes that people who habitually avoid their problems basically remain the same age mentally as when they became addicted to distractions such as drugs, or like for another x of mine, excessive spending and travel was hers. For this reason, even drug rehab is mainly about maturing people addicted to distractions and teaching them healthy social coping skills instead.

Understand that using drugs is not these people's problem; it's their underlying issues that cause them to use drugs. Drug use also isolates users where they become self-centered and further limit their ability to be part of society in a healthy capacity. The opposite of running is called being assertive, and when looking to master **Assert or Hurt**, the most fundamental skill for success in being assertive is the ability to nail **Embracing Confrontations**.

In our culture, confronting another person is often a very difficult, unpleasant and uncomfortable task which is why it's no wonder that it's impossible for most.

Many in society would rather tiptoe around the "obvious blatant unpleasantness" in the room and stay in the "safe zone" rather than **Be Assertive** and **Embrace Confrontation**. Although engaging in a confrontation is never an easy thing to do, when done correctly, **confrontation skills** will reap you the **single greatest** dividends in your journey to Breaking UP compared to any other skill period.

Nice guys finish dead last because they're passive and never **Embrace Confrontations**. When we avoid disagreements, we remain on the other's path. STOP running from confrontations and start welcoming them instead.

Never allow other people's mistakes to be your own.

Confrontations don't have to be violent or chaotic. The only thing confrontations have to be is momentarily uncomfortable and that's it. Being confrontational isn't about being aggressive; it's all about being assertive and making progress towards a mutual goal.

<u>Benefits</u> & <u>Strategy for Confrontation include</u>:
- Confronting an issue provides clarity
- Confrontation clears the air
- Confrontation always starts with praise
- Give them direction, not ultimatums
- Always finish with praise

Embrace Confrontations. Change their behavior, maintain your direction, and continue to the top!

10) PROGRAM

"staying busy and having direction
are two completely different agendas"

Routines allow us to become efficient with our efforts and time. When you're new to an arena and you have a long journey ahead, making the maximum progress in the shortest amount of time possible is your only option.

Similar to the concept of working hard versus working smart, most people in prison are consumed with staying busy, yet they never get anything done if that makes sense. That's because there's a massive difference between:

Busy vs Direction

Tip: Pound 2 bottles of water in the morning BEFORE anything else. Staying properly hydrated allows all your organs to function at an optimal level, including helping your liver metabolize fat. I drink at least one glass of water every hour, where I look amazing, I feel even better, and I haven't been sick in over 10 yrs. Hydrate UP #LikeALOT

Routine vs Direction

Your day doesn't have to be all planned out, but it must have direction and progress towards your goals. Your **PROGRAM** needs to **bring you closer to your goals each day**. The importance of routine is this: *"Routine builds the bank of account of strength available to borrow later."* Invest in your routine so that you can maintain a steady pace and progress towards your objectives.

Healthy Structure

You're where you're at due to a combination of unhealthy relationships, unhealthy employment, unhealthy goals, unhealthy communication skills, unhealthy hobbies, unhealthy physically, unhealthy habits, and/or more. The point of Healthy Structure is to fill your life with all the healthy positive routines and habits that you need to succeed.

The point of Healthy Structure is to focus on **what we can do every day** to fill our voids and climb to the top with a win.

Healthy employment. Healthy relationships. Healthy hobbies. Healthy Social Skills. Healthy fitness habits, and more. When you're newly single and in need of big change to rise to the top, then you can't afford to be like most people who just stay busy at best. Remember:

"There's no growth in the comfort zone, and there's no comfort in the growth zone."

Become consumed with actions instead of thoughts. Be seen as a doer and watch your arena seek out your value. Let's make some moves. Get a Healthy Structure and **PROGRAM** for Progress.

11) Get Good at NO

*"I'm so good at **NO** that you're likely to appreciate me and my **NO** more than them and their Yes."*

- "Hey man, can I get a job!"
- "Yo Jeremy, you mind if I borrow your car tonight?"
- "Hey bro, can I crash at your place for a few days?"

Ugh, no, No, and NO!

Although you're likely yelling in your head **NO**, remember that it requires vulnerability to reach out and ask for something, and the pain of rejection stings no matter how annoying of a person you are. No one wants to say yes to every request, but when you're climbing to the top, you're gonna have to **Get Good at** not only saying **NO**, but also minimizing their discomfort when you put your foot down.

Fact: rejection stimulates the same part of the brain as physical pain.

Rejection actually hurts.

When you're trying to establish new connections and build healthy relationships, learn to minimize discomfort in your arena by mastering this section: **Get Good at NO**.

"The difference between successful people and very successful people is that very successful people say no to almost everything."

- *Warren Buffet*

1) How do I get good at delivering bad news?
2) How do I say **NO** to people while preserving their admiration for me?

Get Good at NO

Happiness comes from an equal combination of giving and receiving. Being too "nice" and accommodating will always leave you feeling frustrated, angry, devalued and disrespected.

Don't Hurt - Assert

If the transaction leaves you feeling disrespected, then the end result will eventually be a loss of relationship, the consumption of negative energy, and a permanent loss of time. Loss of time is perhaps the worst as the losing party becomes consumed with their bad decision and is left constantly fuming and unable to stop thinking of ways to get even or get over the whole thing. **WHY ARE YOU HURTING YOURSELF?**

The first step in **Getting Good at NO** is building your core strength so you have the confidence to be taken seriously.

The reason we hesitate to say **NO** is because we sense the other person's feelings will be hurt by our rejection, and we're right. Well, if you can't man TF up, then at least appreciate some tricks from my book on how to **Get Good at NO**.

1) Apologize Your NO Without Saying It:

- *"Sorry, I don't really have it like that right now."*
- *"I'm not in a really great position right now either, sorry."*
- *"Man, I wanna help, I really do, but that's gonna put me in a bad spot, I'm sorry."*

2) Don't rush into an important NO:

- *"Yeah ok, lemme process that and let you know a little later. Is that cool?"*

3) Tell Them Why Yes Is Not an Option:

- *"I'm gonna be honest John, that's not something I'm even comfortable considering for a multitude of reasons. I'm sorry it's just not."*
- *"There's no way I'm going to jeopardize our friendship on all the ways that situation goes wrong, I'm sorry, I'm can't."*

4) Pass It Off to The Future:

- *"I can't do that right now, but maybe we can look at it again in a couple weeks or so?"*
- *"Right now wouldn't be an option, but I'd be okay processing that further when Stephanie gets back in town."*

5) Don't Overexplain NO:

- *Have confidence in your stance. Be brief, be firm, and let them tell themselves NO.*
- *Don't over speak your NO out of insecurity. Have the confidence that you are strong and valuable enough to them know that your NO is to be accepted, or forget them, right!*

6) Deliver NO and STFU:

- *#Silence*
- *Let them finalize to themselves that your NO means NO.*
- *Explain your NO however the F you want, and be silent. At this point, "he who speaks first loses."*

7) Put Their YES On Them:

- *Make them put in work for their yes by asking them for more information. Send them on the hunt to figure out their problem further which with that done, you will have more info to base your NO off of.*
- *"I'm not saying it's a bad idea, but I would like to know how you guarantee you'll be able to sell your products for $10. Get me some more information on what the current market is for products like yours and at that point we can consider this further."*

8) Easy NO's or a Hard Yes:

- *When you can't say NO, at least make them work hard for your yes with mutual concessions.*

One of the strategies I mastered in prison was simple: **Make them say no to themselves** by **inferring NO** rather than saying it.

Would If I Could, #CantSoiWont

This simple enough strategy worked like a charm 99% of the time, as their feelings were preserved in that I never denied them; I merely let them tell themselves that I would if I could, but #CantSoiWont!

People are less likely to hold their rejection against you when they're the ones rejecting themselves. There's bound to be occasions where this tactic doesn't work immediately, at which point you can have the confidence to check em as now they're just being annoying. At this point, I recommend **offering a mutual concession**, an **"I will/If you"** kind of statement. For example:

- "Alright baby, I'm willing to go out with you tonight if you promise we can be done by 10:00p as I have an important business meeting planned for tomorrow morning,"

- "I know you want a new car this week, and I'm willing to provide that if you help me with the digital marketing of my new business."

When you fulfill an uncomfortable and big request **without a concession, they're just going to "give a mouse a cookie"** syndrome your ass.

Make Em Work Hard For That YES.

In this strategy, I have them make concessions with me, so that they have to bring something I want as well (except you Grandma xoxo).

For example, one situation I find myself in a lot is struggling to put together the right balance of people at parties and events that I host. The problem is that parties are actually alive with energies and rhythms and the wrong people can throw the entire party off. Rather than telling the wrong people **NO** you can't come, I instead raise their barrier of entry with a mutual concession that they can attend but need to bring something to make the party better, usually a date is best.

Since my fear is that the wrong people will suck the life out of the party, I hold them accountable to supply their own fun by bringing a date, and at that point it's a win/win. Either they'll bring a date and enjoy the party with their own group, or they'll fail the barrier of entry set for them, thus allowing your party to remain on target to thrive as a success.

Night clubs have the same barrier of entry to force people to tell themselves **NO** by requiring a specific dress code and charging a higher amount for entry. "I'll let you into my party if you wear exactly as I say and give me $40."

Great achievers are not only **Good at Saying NO**, but they're also **Great at Delivering Bad News**. When it comes to delivering bad news, I try and get it out as quickly as possible; some fluff or praise at the beginning, then the bad news, maybe a suggestion if possible, then have the confidence to go silent and listen as they process their feelings.

With confrontations or uncomfortable interactions, you're gonna need to master the art of **sitting on your emotions**. Don't immediately respond to your emotions. Take a moment instead to process what you're feeling so you may lead with a **Logical Response vs Emotional Response**.

Don't Rescue Other's Feelings all the time. These people are grown and they have a duty to themselves and their group to man the F UP and handle the things and feelings they need to handle. It's not your job to hold their hand through every uncomfortable feeling or situation. You're not their father and it's not your duty to provide the comfort they need within, not to mention they need to grow and learn to self-soothe, so don't steal that from them. **Allow them to Learn. All them to Grow.**

My good friend Jo just went through a breakup with his girlfriend who after three months of dating was just fed up with her complete lack of **Made Service** at his house. I asked Jo if he ever told her **NO** and explained to her that her behavior in his home was unacceptable, and what do you think he told me? "No, but I shouldn't have to." Yeah, you're right, BUT, being in a healthy relationship means you'll be training their behaviors in the new relationship like you'd train a puppy in a new home. HELP THEM. **Get Good at Telling People NO** so that your relationships can thrive instead of die.

12) Amazing Fruit Cocktail

"when positive is all you see, positive is all you'll have"

The way you see the problem is the problem. For me, being imprisoned was a state of mind, and where most inmates allowed themselves to be imprisoned as the victim, my positive optimistic mindset allowed me to be freer than anyone on the yard, staff included. I honestly always felt free even while in a maximum security prison for many years.

One of the most unattractive qualities you can embrace is negativity, where focusing on the negative only breeds more negative. You know what is sexy? Positivity!

Negativity Is Easy and **Cheap**! You just state the obvious BS that surrounds us all where others are happy to get cheap with their moments and chime in on the easy yuck around us. Well Done Cheapo! C'mon, you're better than that. **Stop being cheap with your moments**.

Drop The Negativity. Where most prisoners would whine about the shit food we were served every day, I would always compliment something fantastic on our tray instead. Sometimes I would notice how soft our pancakes came out or how perfectly flavored our fake meat was. I remember one evening specifically when the whole meal really was junk and my table mates laughed as I praised the fruit cocktail (it really was amazing though ☺).

Positivity is inviting and causes others to willingly seek out and look forward to your interactions. Negativity is the exact opposite where I don't know about you, but I absolutely positively completely avoid negative people who are likely to discuss negative things. Life's too amazing and they're simply too weak & cheap.

Fun Fact: Cheapness is the most anti-seductive quality you can embrace.

Another common problem is where people bring their group down by discussing negative situations that have no upside. When you're feeling like shit and it's a matter of time before you feel better, then discussing with your group how horrible you feel all the time will only bring them down with you. **Drop the victim mentality**. Understand that **victims have no control**. The only inmates that were truly "imprisoned" were those who considered themselves victims (basically 99% of them). Stop placing yourself in the line of fire. Try embracing the following words of wisdom from the Serenity Prayer:

> *"have the serenity to accept the things you cannot change,*
> *the courage to change the things you can,*
> *and the wisdom to know the difference"*

Be Positive and Be Free.

When your mission is Breaking UP, then become consumed with solutions that advance your peer's agenda with positivity, optimism, and vision. Focus on providing smiles rather than frowns.

Where most people Breaking Down complain about every little thing all the time, I became addicted to complimenting the beauty everywhere I went. My entire focus began to shift towards all the things I couldn't see or enjoy with my x, and in that sense, I began to become empowered and free.

With positivity, "**your presence is a present**."
Be Positive and Be Free

13) SuperComputer Connect

"the bigger your webbing, the greater the influence you'll wield"

When computers were first created, they were extremely large and got very little done. On its easiest explanation, a computer "computes" by reading code created by many sequenced switches in on/off or "0/1" positions. The ability to severely shrink the size of the switches/processers and place **a substantially greater amount of connections in the same area** is the reason we're able to have so much **more computing power**. Even more so, a "supercomputer" is basically a massive amount of processers capable of more computing power with the ability to obtain the greatest solutions and results compared to any other.

In your new arena, there will always exist an absolutely massive advantage in having access to a greater number of processers or access to "peoples brains." In your new arena, be like a supercomputer of connections and obtain the results that others can only dream of.

Become Connected & Become Desired.

People want what other people want. When you're competing in an arena, **Connection is Life** and **Disconnection is Death**. When your goal is to obtain healthy relationships, then you'll need all the support you can gain from everyone in your arena along the way. Even more important than just making a quantity of connections is to make sure your connections are of quality as well.

You want Family-Deep Connections for ALL

Family-Deep Connections are relationships built off unconditional trust and support for your positions/direction. When competing in your arena, it's your **Family-Deep Connections** that keep you safe along the way.

Invest In Your Relationships. You can't be selfish and deeply connected at the same time. Allocate quality time for your relationships and make them Family-Deep in order to rise.

There is no foundation without deep connections. When your goal is climbing out on top, understand that your objectives will fail every time unless you invest in an equally deep foundation, so make sure you build as many **Family-Deep Connections** as possible. Choose to thrive with solutions rather than thrive with problems.

Quick Connect Tip: Group yourself together with words. An x of mine would always refer to all her friend's family members as auntie or uncle. I remember this showed an instant closeness and to this day I call my friend's mom "mom," and their dad "dad." Grandma/Grandpa too. Try this on your date's parents and if you survive the weirdness, you'll have already obtained a **Family-Deep Connection**. Group yourselves together with a "we" or an "us" even if you just barely met; instant closeness.

Even though I may only meet some people in my group once or just in passing, there still exists tremendous power in connecting with each of them. Even if you don't like someone or don't want a close association with them, it's always a major asset to maximize their positive regard for you.

Real vs Vague

Even when I meet a person only one time in brief passing, I always ensure to create a deep connection with them by speaking enthusiastically about something real and specific with them instead of commenting on a vague topic like weather or sports. Put a little effort into meeting these people, and in a world full of polite vagueness, expect to earn deep connections when you get specific and real with those around.

SuperComputer Connect for your superpower of obtaining the best solutions and results needed to get you to the top!

14) Ideas vs Stories

*"where stories keep you stuck in the past,
ideas will inspire a new future"*

Stories Keep You Exactly Where You're At

One thing I've learned is that the best guarantee for repeating your failures is to be consumed with them. When your goal is to rise to the top, then the first pattern you need to break is that of cycling back towards the bottom, and the easiest way to do this is to **consume yourself with ideas** of a massive new future rather than romanticizing stories about your small troubled past. **Where your past is definite, your future in Infinite.**

It takes confidence to dream up a new future and bring others along the journey, but great achievers who rise to the top are masters in surrounding themselves with **Ideas vs Stories**.

<u>Breaking UP Not Down</u> means that you'll eventually need to turn your selfish gains into selfless offerings to empower your peers.

Stories fill our time with things we already know and keep us exactly where we're at. Things like watching TV and gossiping are more addictive than heroin which is why everyone is hooked and doesn't stand a chance at quitting.

- I don't watch TV.
- I don't follow sports.
- I don't play video games.

- I don't hang out with the same people doing the same things every day.
- I don't listen or partake in any gossip (for the most part ☺).

I spend as much time as I can socializing with experts where I constantly learn new things and continuously plan my bad ass future.

Venting vs Processing

When things aren't going well and you've become upset at the actions of another, you should **Never Vent**. Venting is a system designed to reignite flames while you continue to upset everyone around during your angry story telling. When you're upset like this, **focus on processing the issue with direction towards a solution**. Once you've figured out the solution, you can now become fixated on how you will resolve the issue and now once again you're consumed with **Ideas vs Stories**. Douse the flames of anger with solutions and direction.

Stories are fun, but unless they inspire and support your ideas for a greater future, then the only purpose they fill is comfort. **Comfort is the killer of growth**, so maximize growth and focus on consuming yourself with **Ideas vs Stories**.

15) A Series of Small Wins

"start with the fights you know you'll win before the ones you think you'll lose."

Winners Effect: a term used in biology to describe how an animal that has won a few fights against weak opponents is much more likely to win later bouts against stronger contenders. For males, as they win more, they release more testosterone becoming more risk adverse and more likely to succeed.

Winning is a process, not an act.

Most people go through their day with the least amount of friction as possible. They prefer not to disrupt others or upset the balance, where they instead spend their free time enjoying tasty snacks, watching meaningless TV, discussing small talk, and all that while every hope at obtaining greatness fades away more each day.

It's extremely difficult to be optimistic and positive about your future when all the dialogue in your life is negative, consumed with stories, and you're surrounded by laziness. This is the reason most people fail to change, and this is why most people rarely do anything great with their lives.

When your mission is to rise, then you're gonna **need constant battle** with a steady **push towards victory**. Don't get stuck on the daily grind at the bottom; take a page out of my book and get into a rhythm of small wins before you begin swinging at the big ones. **A Series of Small Wins.**

When I say small wins, I mean that you need to beat up all the things you're guaranteed to win; things you can control like **Made Service** & **Big Primpin.**

A Series of Small Wins – Winners Effect

Studies shows us that the first thing we should do in the morning is **Made Service** where we make our bed, clean our cage, and organize our day. On to **Big Primpin** where we must shower, shave, do our hair, brush our teeth, cologne up, and dress to impress. With those small victories complete, you move into PROGRAM, where you make a healthy breakfast, enjoy a nice cup of coffee, and clean everything up immediately afterwards. Victory complete.

Cleaned and fed, you'll continue your PROGRAM where you move into physically demanding battles pushing through an intense exercise routine to balance the strength of my body with the strength of my mind. Victory complete.

Next, you move into mental battle next where you focus on pursuing your studies and/or research for any current projects, whether it's working on correspondence with my relationships, ideas for your future business or positions in situations fighting for success. Victory Complete.

Now that your morning has already experienced **A Series of Small Wins**, you're ready to step up to the plate and swing for your homeruns. **Winners Effect**. More likely to win the big ones now too.

16) Ball Tickling

*"capture the movement of their lips as they smile
upwards and ride that current to the top."*

When mastering the ability to connect with every individual is an absolute requirement, then make sure you embrace the most surefire strategies for success. If you had any guesses as to what the one universal communal desire we all seek is, what do you think it would be?

- **Money?** For many, yes, but not even close to all.
- **Fame?** Again, some people crave this, but not all.
- **Power? Love? Likes?** Maybe yes on the likes, but since my grandpa doesn't even know what a "like" is, we'll have to continue searching for that one constant. Give up yet, I'll help:

SIGNIFICANCE and VALIDATION

#NailedIt

Although we may not all want money or fame, one thing we all crave is to be validated as significant in one aspect or another. This is one quality you can always appeal to in another that will always equate into their appreciation, smiles, and happiness towards you.

When you're an outsider looking to get in, your best method of entry is paying it forward by offering significance and validation to everyone around, and you do this by **placing their validation BEFORE your own.** It's a fact that sincere compliments absolutely disarm those with daggers out, and only with their weapons holstered are your peers able to receive your message of love, protection, and guidance. It takes confidence to make yourself vulnerable and put other's validation before your own.

I thrive to the top of Breaking UP because I master **SuperComputer Connect** and forge endless **Family-Deep Connections** using my one main skill; **Ball-Tickling**. My greatest success came from my ability to make people like me through validating them as significant where I'd then begin to act as a human can opener to see our path for connection.

Whether complimenting a new contact on their physique and asking them for workout tips, or complimenting a boss on their power & ability in leading a group, **strong people of power** and **authority always appreciate you fondling their balls.**

This strategy only works when you come off sincere, but the good news is that coming off sincere is usually effortless when you're passionate about your mission. As I actually care about the people in my arena, I make sure to focus on areas of tickling where my compliments will be received as sincere.

People love killer compliments, especially when they're specific to them. When you're giving them a glowing specific compliment, you're showing them how much you know and care about them. You're similarly extending them an olive branch into a friendship with you which is bound to happen as you've made sure the other person enjoyed your interaction and is surely looking forward to the next one.

Fun Fact: we're great at remembering faces because our species developed a larger frontal lobe to help us easily identify details in a person's face because as we all used to look identical in a tree. Therefore we had to know which monkey would rip our face off and which identical looking monkey would let us suckle some teat. Remembering names is nowhere near as evolutionarily fundamental especially when you're calculating 20,000 different notes about a person as you're introduced which is why we're all great with faces and terrible with names. #FixThat

Tip: Tickle away as you remember their name when no else does. I focus on emptying my mind while I repeat their name to myself and then once to them in a sentence. Nothing is more flattering than someone taking the time and effort into remembering your name.

It's a lot harder to be mean to someone when they like you. It's one of the reasons I did so well negotiating settlements for personal injury law firms. I always made sure the insurance claims adjuster liked me, and it was always harder for them to be a dick afterwards.

When I'm with my friends in front of a girl they like or a job they want, I'm always the first to tell that job how talented my boy is or tell the girls how great of a lay he is. Empower your people and rise!

17) Make Em Respect Your Time

"never get into an argument that you know you will win"

When we don't earn it, we don't respect it. When things are free and available, we don't value them. When something you want can be yours anytime you choose, then it's obviously not very special to you.

Be Special. Be Valued. Be Earned.

When your goal is to Break UP, then your new connections need to: respect you, value you, and consider you special. The foundation to achieve this single objective is to make sure your peers respect your presence and respect your time.

People will eventually get comfortable and steer the path for their own gain. When your goal is to rise, then you must **put effort into your new relationships upfront,** otherwise you're likely to be forced to do the max in hopes of correcting their problematic comforts later.

- **Make Em Respect Your Time.**
- **Don't Be Easily Accessible.**
- **Don't treat em like your long-lost friend.**
- **Make Them Earn Your Respect**

How to make them respect your time:

1) **You respect your time**. Don't be too accessible.
2) **Be assertive** with the conversational direction.
3) **Be busy**. Have other appointments or tasks you need to do.

4) **Hold people accountable to a timeframe** by stating your availability, "hey man, I got a couple minutes until I gotta get on the phone, what's up?"

5) **Don't let talkers hold you hostage**. Have a catch phrase handy to exit a conversation such as, "hey, I appreciate your time but I gotta dip; lets hookup on Friday and keep me posted on your issue."

6) **Make an impact** with as few words as possible.

The 6-Minute Rule:

Making a phone call was never easy in prison due to high security and overcrowding. Either way, sometimes a 6-minute phone call every other day was all you could get, and I learned then that a 6-minute call was all you really needed to have a full conversation. One thing I noticed quickly was that the longer 30-minute calls on lower security yards lost their good energy and rhythm towards the middle and/or end of the call.

Even when I was able to enjoy 30-minute phone calls, I never forgot the short call lesson where I eventually bought a watch and set a timer for 6-minutes max time per call. My goal was always to ensure that the other person left our call on a high note and eagerly looked forward to our next interaction, so rather than strangle every last minute outta the call, I would instead jump off during a high note where our energy would remain until we spoke next.

Leave on a High Note.
Make Em Respect Your Time.

I did this especially with the ladies where I would call infrequently with an amazing exciting conversation back and forth, then dip out on the conversation at an absolute high note leaving them there eagerly anticipating our next conversation. Similar to people who match on a dating apps and don't respond quickly, the message they're attempting to send is that they're busy, their time is valuable, and they are to be respected as such.

Don't be too accessible.

Whenever I'm throwing parties, I never let them die or end on their own. I pay TF attention to the energy and I always end the party on a high note so that everyone leaves with great energy and only the best quality memories.

End On a High Note.
Never arrive too early.

When you're showing up for a meeting, don't show up 30 minutes early because "you have time to kill." Time to kill means that you don't have enough going on in your life and that your time is not that important. On the flip side, when you're always punctual with a few minutes to spare, your group will come to understand that your time is to be respected and appreciated as they can always count on you.

Never overexplain yourself.

Have confidence in your words, and unless you stuttered, don't over explain anything to anyone. Don't make your words or thoughts too accessible. *"Never get into an argument that you know you will win."* Once your position is stated, kindly shut the F up!

Trust: Anytime someone I care about is trying to hijack my time lecturing me on an issue where I know I'm right, I'm always quick to assert that our relationship is based on trust and if they don't trust me enough, then I'm gone. If you're continuing to accuse me and stress me out even after I've delivered my answer, I'm out because my time and my health are more important than your false attacks.

It's not easy to argue that point, but at the same time, allowing another person to stress you out and steal your time when you know you're in the right is a "Shame On You" type of incident. Make em respect your time by setting clear boundaries on things you're willing to discuss and things you're unwilling to discuss.

One thing we would always say in drug rehab therapy programs was **"10 words or less**." Basically, make an impact with your words and get to the point fast, especially as most people drone on explaining their feelings rather than the actual problem that needs to be fixed. Lucky for me, I absolutely mastered the art of helping people get to their point quickly while working in law firms as everyone calls all the time for you to solve their every problem under the sun. *"I've got two minutes; tell me what you'd like me to do about it."* Learn to make your impact and get TF out!

Another skill I use to make people respect myself and my time is that I would explain why I trust and respect them first. When I give them a glowing specific compliment about the qualities I respect most about them, we are in that moment in agreeance that those qualities actually exist. I mean, I gave them the opportunity to

#SpeakNowOrForeverHoldYourPeace, right? Then we agree; you are all of the above ☺.

Example: I currently have three cars and no driver's license. My cars are all paid for, so they just sit at home but every once in a while, a good friend will ask to borrow one of them. Now, although it is a major stressor thinking about all the borrowing-gone-wrong situations, I quickly realized that once I decided to lend them the car, then lecturing them about "not f**king my car up" left a very negative connotation associated with my good deed.

I realized that If I trusted them enough to borrow the car, then I didn't wanna ruin the moment by shaming them through a lecture. **Make Em Respect You and Your Time** by praising them on why you trust them instead and how happy it makes you to be in a position to help them.

18) CritiKing

"critique is your single greatest tool for change"

Criticism: the expression of disapproval of someone or something based on perceived faults or mistakes.

The reason we're unable to easily critique others is that most people associate being wrong with being a failure. For most, being wrong is associated with not being good enough, and when people feel rejected by their peers, they typically launch into an all-out counterattack putting forth their best defenses to prove their worth. Not only that, but once criticized, these people tend to as they say, "catch feelings, not flights." Simply put, **criticism is a positive attack on their soul.**

People are extremely sensitive in defending themselves after having spent a lifetime trying to be perfect. This is why it is near impossible to challenge their soul and simultaneously make them appreciate your input to the extent they willingly implement your message for the betterment of the group. Knowing how sensitive people are should tell you that:

- number one, not every fight is worth pursuing, and
- number two, much of the time we critique, we end up causing more harm than good.

However, when your mission is to Break UP, then you must thrive with this chapter: **CritiKing- become the king of critiquing.**

When people feel challenged but unable to fight to the top in a big arena, they usually resort to withdrawing into a smaller one. Although we don't all need to be part of a large group, it is a fact that the smaller your group is, the less challenges you will likely incur, the less well-rounded you will become and the smaller the success you will obtain.

Again, living in a small world with a small mind and a lack of challenge isn't a losing concept, unless your mission is to rise and obtain your greatest relations yet. When you're part of a large arena battling for the top, then being **able to challenge** and **correct**

issues is an absolute requirement for your success. You must become an expert at both issuing and receiving criticism.

Your ability to accept criticism is the result of significant personal strength, confidence and very high self-worth. However, being able to properly issue criticism to others is an entirely different set of skills and in an arena like prison that I was trying to conquer, it was nearly an impossible task.

I would honestly argue that no group is more sensitive and ego driven than prisoners. Again, most convicted criminals spent their entire lives creating a small world where they could reign king, and people who are used to being the king are damn near impossible to critique. Thank you Prison; no better place to master this skill than with a yard full of kings ☺. Three things I quickly learned about critiquing others was:

1) **Don't rush into your critique**- foreplay here will do wonders, and
2) **Don't issue critique in front of others**- bladder shyness is a real problem, and
3) **Two Back-Pats, One Jab**

     Let's break these concepts down a bit further.

1) <u>Don't rush into critique:</u>

- Whatever the other person did to upset you most likely already has you (and maybe them) emotionally charged. The most important aspect in connecting for change is **Do Not <u>Attack</u> Back**.

- Critique isn't about you feeling better delivering a counterattack; it's about obtaining a positive permanent change within the relationship for the betterment of yourselves and your future.

- Take a few deep breaths, walk away for a bit if you can (even a day or so sometimes) and think about the underlying message you're wanting to deliver.

- Format your critique through the lens of what you want your relationship to look like in the future.

- Emotion vs Logic: Address the situation with logic rather than emotion. Logic focuses on the agreement moving forward, whereas Emotion focuses on you validating your ego; in getting even or getting ahead.

2) <u>Don't Critique In front of Others:</u>

- Time your critique to when your recipient is most relaxed and receptive.

- People are naturally egotistical and defensive, all of which is amplified around others.

- Always pull them aside to a safe setting.

- Don't let the crowd control your recipient's response.

- People will take your words more seriously when they see how much effort you put into the setting.

3) **Two Back-Pats One Jab:**

- Loosen UP your recipient prior to battling them so they'll be exposed to your weapon of truth.

- Help your recipient lower their defenses by praising them with how great they are, how much you appreciate their position in your life and how much you look forward to their future success in the relationship.

- Give your recipient two positive messages first; two sincere detailed compliments about what you love about them, what others love about them, and keep them connected to the future vision of the relationship.

- With their ego's strengthened, they can now stand to take a hit.

- Deliver your **CritiKing** Jab with Love.

- Deliver your critique with a soothing tone, zero frustration, and exceptional body language so they stay calm and remain receptive.

- Hold your head high and your eye contact strong during delivery.

- Ensure your message to them is inclusive and is phrased in terms of longevity for the group.

- Substitute the word "but" for "and." Instead of praising them and then cutting it all away with the big "but", praise them and continue their positive message by using the word "and."

Example:

But: "You're one of my favorite people in my life and you're exceptionally enjoyable to be around "**BUT**" I need you to take better care of your health so that you can be the strong partner that we need."

vs

And: "You're one of my favorite people in my life and you're exceptionally enjoyable to be around "**AND**" I need you to take better care of your health so that you can be the strong partner that we need."

Guide vs Attack

Your peers are more likely to accept your critique when they feel your intention is to guide them rather than attack them. **CritiKing** is an especially necessary skill to master when your mission is to conquer hearts because **healthy relationships require holding your partners accountable** towards the relational objectives.

19) Break Through with Humor

"humor diffuses conflict, builds trust and increases the acceptance of new ideas"

How often can you make a genuine smile while being legitimately angry? I'm assuming it's probably pretty difficult, and if it's not, then I'm also assuming that you're mentally unstable like my x or probably wanted by the law for a crime spree or something.

If the opposite of anger is happiness, then mastering the strategies of making people happy is one of the best ways to rise UP and conquer even the most difficult people in your path. Life has shown you that people are more likely to support your agenda when they like you, and one of the easiest ways to make people like you is to make people smile.

Using humor is obviously one of the best ways to make people smile, but the power and abilities of humor extend lightyears beyond just obtaining smiles.

30 Benefits of Using Humor with Your Group:
1) improves productivity
2) reduces stress
3) prevents burnout
4) provides motivation
5) increases size of paycheck
6) boosts overall brainpower
7) improves decision-making
8) increases the acceptance of new ideas
9) triggers new connections
10) enhances one's ability to solve problems
11) gets people to listen
12) improves memory retention
13) boosts persuasion
14) assists in learning
15) increases likability
16) connects us with others
17) fosters rapport
18) reduces status differentials
19) builds trust
20) encourages collaboration

21) enhances perceived leadership skills

22) diffuses conflict

23) creates more opportunities

24) builds credibility

25) improves ratings

26) increases ability to cope

27) strengthens the immune system

28) relaxes muscles

29) burns calories

30) increases happiness

Aside from laughter being proven to help cure cancer, live longer, and break through the defensive walls of your arena, I've found one of the best uses of humor is to connect with others. When you're looking to make deep connections, it's important to focus on how you make people feel. When I go out of my way to connect and interact with another, my purpose is most always that I want them to leave our interaction with three things:

1) a smile,

2) a positive association with our relationship, and

3) an eager desire to meet again

When we meet with people, we want them to enjoy our interaction, and there's no better way than to **Break Through with Humor**, as leaving them with a sincere smile says it all.

Be Light-Hearted and Playful as much as possible.

Death is serious, but life is about happiness. It's easy to be serious and straight forward, but one thing I learned is that we all have within us a strong preference to interact in a light-hearted playful way rather than a constant boring serious demeanor. **Being lighthearted allows us to stay in the moment** and **ride the wave in the excitement of now**. Unfortunately for the masses, people are always quick to jump away from the excitement of now straight into the comforts of the past. Here comes Mr. Serious and guided conversation as exciting as an interrogation:

What do you do?
Where're you from?

Does that line of interrogation sound fun to you? If so, you're reading the wrong freaking book; please pass it along to someone who actually wants to conquer their arena and leave the biggest f'ing wakes behind as they plow through everything in their way.

- **"What do you do?"** - No single question is more judgmental, uncreative, and non-sexy than this. **<u>DON'T USE IT</u>**. When someone has a job they love, then trust me- they're gonna volunteer exactly what they do and they're gonna do this pretty quickly. Most people don't have a job they love, and they don't enjoy that question. Instead of **What Do You Do**, ask leading light-hearted, exciting & creative questions such as:

  - "What keeps you busy?"
  - "How'd you end up here tonight?"
  - "How do you spend your time?"

Not only will people respond to these questions basically telling you "what they do", but more importantly, you'll allow them to steer the conservational path in a direction most comfortable to them and making people like you means making people feel comfortable with you.

- **"Where're you from?"**- C'mon! Are we gonna talk about the f'ing weather next! **DON'T!** I personally hate this question mainly because IT'S THE SAME DAMN QUESTION EVERYONE ASKS ALL THE TIME; it's completely unoriginal and if you just **open your eyes to the moment, you'll see there exists much more relative, clever, connecting** and **exciting things to discuss** which also keep you right where you wanna be; In That Sexy Ass Moment!

Don't ask the same boring routine unsexy questions like everyone else. Use some creativity, individuality, and humor when dealing with your relations, especially when you're new.

Playful vs Serious

Playful conversation flows with its own rhythm, whereas **Serious conversation is directed by questions**. Where serious conversation is guided & restricted, **playful conversation flows easily, is unpredictable**, and even just thinking about one produces a massive smile on my face. According to the ladies, **the single greatest factor in my success with them is my playful communication style,** #ImFunny ☺.

Allow your conversations to flow with playfulness and avoid engaging in unnecessary serious conversation as much as possible.

Light-Hearted and Playful: I'm absolutely surrounded by super connectors and joyful people most of my day, and my favorite conversations with these powerful people are always the ones where we talk for a while without saying anything of substance. Basically, our conversations are about 98% disrespecting each other with name-calling & humiliating weaknesses, and only about 2% substance. Most of our conversation may just be our need to relax our mind from our intense days because all we really wanna do is #smile.

People may not wanna take a stance on an issue important to them, speak about something traumatic from today or worrisome about tomorrow, but everyone has in them the desire for easy pleasant conversation all the time.

One thing I do extremely well is that although I ensure my interactions are mostly light-hearted, **I rarely waste the interaction with vague meaningless information**. Every time I interact with people, I make sure and hit some strong points; something important to them, and then something important to "us". The only thing I do better than picking the right topics is how I deliver them: Stab With Humor. Be Light-Hearted and Playful.

Break Through with the Humor your arena craves and use it to break through every barrier so you end up on the winning side of every battle every time.

117

20) Maximize Discomfort

"there's no comfort in the growth zone"

Success is earned and attempting to earn anything is called a challenge. Risking a loss through a challenge is uncomfortable, but therein lies your blueprint for success: **Embrace Discomfort to Achieve Success.**

Change is hard for most, but when you're growing through a Break UP, **change must become you**. Although relearning everything and trying new things can be extremely uncomfortable, **maximizing your discomfort will vastly accelerate your rise** to the top.

The reason most people fail to rise is that they **maximize comfort** and **minimize growth**. Most people fail to strive for advancement because they're content with exactly what they have and where they're at. Once you've accomplished your dreams and you're in cruise control, then there's nothing wrong with comfort in your success, but comfort is a luxury you're never going to enjoy while trudging through battle along your way to the top. Socrates said it best when he said,

"Discipline is the highest form of intelligence."

Maximize Discomfort

After having my heart broken by x in ways I had never felt before, the last thing I wanted to do was get comfortable. I wanted to **fight Everything Everyway Everyday** until I forced the universe to place the partner of my dreams directly in my path. I knew this path would be massively challenging, and as my mission needed

118

everything I had, then spending time like other lost souls lying in bed all day watching TV meant a guaranteed death to my dream.

"There's no growth in the comfort zone and there's no comfort in the growth zone."

This chapter tells us to **Maximize Discomfort** for the purpose of personal growth, and the reason people never obtain their dreams is that they spend their entire lives chasing comfort.

Maximizing Discomfort means surrounding yourself with people who know more about success than you. Where most people are quick to hate on people doing better than them, I was always quick to **embrace people better than me** so that I could absorb their success for myself.

Maximizing Discomfort means **holding people accountable**. I loved my x in ways I never knew possible, but as I provided so much and asked for so little, I was always quick to assert my boundaries which only always caused her stress. As she may have been more incapable of properly handling stress than any other I have ever known, I knew that every assertion would be a fight, and with her, fights were always aggressive and her outburst had become increasingly physical.

But what other choice did I have. If I was seeking change towards her treatment of us, I needed to embrace the discomfort in hopes of maximizing any chances of change.

When you're full of core strength and confidence, **Maximizing Discomfort** becomes easy and obtaining your success comes naturally. Learn to **Maximize Discomfort** and shoot to the top every time ☺.

21) Master Rejection

"Allow rejection to drive you and success to guide you."

If success were easy, it would be called by a different name like "everyday normalness," but it's not. "Success" is a title we earn over time while taking risks, accepting challenges, and fighting our way to the top. The cliché "life's too short" is annoying, but in this instant it's extremely appropriate because **success absolutely takes time**. Success in Growing Through a Break UP is often a lengthy process where you simply cannot afford to get side-tracked or discouraged along your rise.

Master Rejection - Master Success
Recognize that: <u>The Way You See The Problem Is The Problem</u>
Never Let Another's Rejection Define You.

Any time I approach a woman in public and proceed to hit on her, most women will instinctively reject you because they're uncomfortable with the public situation. Most women don't even have the confidence to talk on the phone when they first meet, text only, so what the F do you think is likely the reason that they're running from you in public? **They're Uncomfortable with Themselves.**

Master Rejection and KEEP MOVING FORWARD

When someone rejects your position, consider that their rejection may have nothing to do with you. Even if you're beyond perfect or even horribly inept, their rejection towards you could just as likely be they're in a relationship, they're shy, or for a million other **reasons that have nothing to do with you.**

Rejection Is A Gift
Rejection Is Your Blueprint For Success
"Victory Favors The Bold." #BoldMoves

Learn to let go from the feeling of rejection as quickly as it hits you because focusing on rejection is a surefire way to maximize its label upon you. Anytime I feel rejected, I either ignore it completely, or I **Process vs Vent** and make sure I focus on the solution for success rather the pain of the problem.

While the entire city of Las Vegas was emptying out of their first professional team game ever- Vegas Golden Knights Game One on 10/10/2017- I was walking back inside against a crowd of 20,000 and was blessed enough to lock eyes with the most beautiful woman I had ever seen, where I absolutely squared my shoulders and blocked everything in her way so I would be her only thing in that moment. I ended up in a relationship with this woman for the next two years and owe most of the best moments in my entire life to that single moment; that single bold move. **Master Rejection, Master Success.** #ShoutOut @StephanieSibley #AlwaysAndForeverBaby #xoxo #☹

My ability to **Master Rejection** allowed me to pull off one of my favorite bold moves I've ever executed towards a woman, where I'll never forget meeting my x-girlfriend Gentille. She was with a few girlfriends in a booth at a bar when I went straight up to them and was lucky enough to hold the conversation for the ten minutes that I did. Gentille was almost as playful and witty as I, so our moment was exhilarating; so good in fact that I was feeling the need to go in for our first kiss and needed to **Pull Her Aside**. The only problem was that she refused to step away from her friends and I was forced to pull out a bold move.

I got up from their table, grabbed the armrest to the barstool Gentille was sitting in and began dragging her and her stool through the crowded bar all the way to the balcony where I stole our first kiss. #ShoutOut @Gentille.Chhun #SmileForMe

Bold Moves + Master Rejection + Embrace Success

I was on my first date with Graziela, where I ended up meeting her for the first time with her girlfriends at a bar. As it was me plus three women, I held back to be polite for as long as I could.

GO IN FOR THAT FIRST KISS GUYS
(Build enough comfort to go in for that first kiss within 10 minutes)

After about 20minutes of proximity and caressing her shoulder, I turned to her girlfriends, asked if they wanted to watch our first kiss, and then confidently grabbed Graziela by her sexy face where we all enjoyed our first embrace. #ShoutOut @GodsBabyPrincess <3. Now I understand that this is likely a crime in some countries, but that's the entire f'ing point of this chapter:

Follow Your F'ing HEART
Never Let Rejection Control Your Agenda
Victory ALWAYS Favors The Bold

I was flying to Miami for work and I happened to have a beautiful girl sitting next to me on the flight and I was not about to pass up the opportunity to connect on the maximum level we (probably more I) desired. I'm not Mr. F'ing Nice Guy and neither should you be.

So TF what if we're surrounded by everyone in a close area and blasted in bright afternoon sunlight during the flight; #ImGoinForIt. She was going through a breakup(down) and flying home from Las Vegas, and after having an enjoyable conversation, I told her that I would help her practice being single by treating our flight like a date. #YoureWelcome

Sure, it felt a little weird putting my arm around her and holding her hand, but who cares. What are you afraid of? Rejection LMFAO! I eventually went in for the kiss where she aggressively fought me off stronger than an Air Marshall, but the point here is the same: **Master Rejection** and **SUCCEED**.

One thing I've always noticed is that even when a woman fights you off from the first kiss on a (*consensual) date, she ends up respecting you more for it and even gets excited afterwards. In these cases, **I may be batting a thousand for success on my second attempt**.

This was the case for my plane date, where the second kiss attempt went over like an absolute charm! Kami and I sincerely enjoyed each other's time and even remain friends until this day, so please tell me again about rejection defining you?! #ShoutOut @KamiP #ThankYouForOurMoment #wassup ☺.

Success after Rejection IS ALL anyone will remember about you. Although I can guarantee you I've scared off more women than you've probably ever talked too, what I can also guarantee you is that these women will never forget the rush of excitement they enjoyed during my bold pursuit. Rejection itself will never define you; it's what you do afterwards that no one forgets. Your ability to master rejection will become the sexiest thing about you.

Victory Favors The Bold - Just Go For It

The worst decision you can make is indecision. Where most people are consumed with what they're "GONNA" do, to achieve your best yet, you'll need to become obsessed with taking action and DOING things every day that progress you towards success.

Rob Brough (My BFF):

"Be a DOER and Always Avoid the "Gonners."

Become blind to failure by seeing only success.

Allow rejection to drive you and success to guide you.

The difference between ordinary and extraordinary is that little extra. Accept the fact that although each of these actions are relatively simple and doing any one of these actions may appear miniscule, the fact remains that I absolutely kill the f'ing game of life ONLY because I **embrace these actions EVERYDAY**. It really is that simple because as you build each, you obtain depth, and once you have depth, nothing can ever knock you down.

- **Show Some Respect To Yourself**
- **Made Service**
- **Big Primpin**
- **Add Value to Others**
- **Assert or Hurt**
- **HYPE-Man**
- **Object vs Targe**
- **Be Selfish**
- **Embrace Confrontations**
- **Get Good at NO**
- **Amazing Fruit Cocktail**
- **Super-Computer Connect**
- **Ideas vs Stories**
- **A Series of Small Wins**
- **Ball Tickling**
- **Make Em Respect Your Time**
- **CritiKing**
- **Break Through with Humor**
- **Maximize Discomfort**
- **Master Rejection**

You're not available when you're weak. Recognize the fact that as you gain your strengths, you will then become present where in those moments, the world will bend to you.

Although nothing is promised in life, I can show you success story after success story of people like me who have obtained the absolute most just by being present and available in the right moments. Take for example how I own multiple law groups; only a high school diploma and five felonies, so how did I do it.

In 2009, I went to prison for a year for growing marijuana, and as my home was raided, I literally came out of prison with nothing. What I did have was many of the qualities listed above in Throttling UP, where after getting a front desk job in a law firm, we found that I was a natural fit for managing the office and building their business.

I went from broke and homeless to making my first million just because I was present and available for my opportunity.

The same is true for dating and every other opportunity; build your value, amass your strength, put yourself out there, and capture your moments.

Success is never something we see coming; Success is something we do every single day and only looking back do we realize how intelligent we were to put in all those little efforts to place us available and capable within all the right moments which always equals SUCCESS. Your time to Throttle UP is now!

Post BreakUP Support Crew

Step 7: <u>Finding Yourself</u> and <u>Your Last</u>

"You've waited long enough for you- your time is now"

Think about how many loveless unhappy marriages you know of where partners are trapped and so badly in need of growth?

I look to you in growing through this Break UP and I state with more passion than anything I've ever said, where I tell you that you have no idea how lucky you are to embrace this growth with your best ahead; enjoying the growth that others need so desperately and will never have.

Breaking UP is supposed to be hard, but as you've read above, your best is absolutely yet to come.

Step 1: This is a Break UP and a Break Through.

Step 2: You're Soothing Down and Winding UP.

Step 3: You've admitted your role in the unhealthy relationship.

Step 4: You've come to understand their role IS your future success.

Step 5: You're sad, but you know that your best is yet to come.

Step 6: Your actions in Throttling UP will get you ready for success.

Step 7: Now is the time to Find Yourself and then, Find Your Last.

For my recent Break UP, I physically pushed the relationship to a breaking point because I had no choice. I was too weak to walk away as I love people too deeply, so I kept pushing until she changed or left. With her, I truly felt like I was 5mins from a fatal heart attack almost every single day as she was physically incapable of providing peace or even basic reciprocation. After popping 400mg of ibuprofen nearly every single day just to relax the muscles around my heart from her endless outbursts, pushing her away was my only choice.

So why am I ready to move on where others are not? The reason is because I spent over 15 years working on myself and being selfish in gaining value so that I could finally become selfless with all my gifts.

- I'm in shape, I do it in minimal time, and I thoroughly enjoy aiding others in their fitness journey.
- I've become financially stable and I'm efficient enough with my time to enjoy effortless quality moments with my people.
- I'm an amazing communicator where I am extremely assertive in setting boundaries and extremely receptive & accommodating to the needs of others.
- I'm effortlessly positive and choose to smile and laugh over anything else further cultivating quality moments and relations.
- I always embrace discomfort towards growth.
- I have no fear of rejection and eagerly embrace challenges.
- I'm incredible at motivating and empowering those around me towards greatness.

- I'm 100% secure with my strengths and I'm never insecure of mine or another's flaws. I've worked hard for years mitigating my every weakness and maximizing my every strength.
- I promote peace and positivity.
- I pick and choose my battles to eliminate endless fighting.
- I'm obsessed with Ideas vs Stories to enable growth & success.
- I'm drug free and present in order to give everything my best always.
- Although I don't immediately enjoy receiving critique, I always listen and consider their position if for no other reason than to allow them to be heard.
- I maintain a clean home and often welcome others to enjoy my gains.
- I cook my meals, eat as healthy as possible, and constantly provide these quality nutrients to everyone around.
- I'm great at giving people the skills to be confident and more assertive in their every interaction in life.

<u>Simply put</u>, <u>I am the best me that I can be</u>. For these reasons, I am capable and ready to move forward to my best being ahead, and as you're able to repeat the above in full and in truth, so too will you.

We allowed an unhealthy relationship to consume and define us, and this WILL NOT be part of your future.

Your new mission is not finding another. It's finding yourself. Know that finding your last is the end result of becoming the best you that you can be and as you make this your only focus, I promise that everything you're looking for will quickly find you!

This change and success WILL NOT happen in a day, but in a near tomorrow, you can be assured that your story most certainly will be, as long as you **BEGIN TAKING ACTION** building your value today and every day after.

Only when you're able to offer yourself everything above and love yourself fully is it time to begin scouting for your next, and soon enough, your last.

Focus on being defined by these two single qualities:

- **Authenticity**
- **Boldness**

Authenticity means being honest, open, and fully available. If an asteroid were minutes from striking down the world, most everyone would call their parents as they know, love, and trust them most fully and deeply. When trust is everything, it's time to offer everyone your true open authentic self which is the single greatest way to form rapid deep connections. Let down your walls and let in your loves.

Boldness means you exude unwavering strength in your positions. You have the undying desire and confidence to stand behind your positions and those of your group. FEAR DOES NOT CONTROLL YOU!

As you dive deep on self, you will become aware of your weaknesses and you can use this book and my other materials to convert your every specific weakness into incredible strength by contacting me at:

JeremySigal.com

As you embrace **Authenticity** and **Boldness**, you will then possess the only thing you need to rise to the absolute top as you use this experience to grow and succeed at levels never imagined before.

You're starting to become the person for you that you've never yet been able to be for another.

You need to stop "seeking" a relationship. Instead, begin "attracting" a relationship by first embodying the qualities within that you seek from another.

Although at one point we were the problem, we are now transitioning in full to being the solution. So I say to you, **congratulations** on your **awakening** and **your best** absolutely being always **ahead**!

P.S. I won my flawed x back 2 more times AFTER this book. Then, I won me a better girl!

Get so good you get them BACK or WIN A BETTER ONE!!!

Substituting Loss for Gains 2020

Conclusion: Pleasure vs Joy

This conclusion is a gift to you from the wisest person I know, my Best Friend Mitch.

December 31, 2019 at 7:30p: I spent my final moments of the decade enjoying a phone call with the beautiful insight and wisdom from my best friend Mitch. Mitch had been listening to me process my confusion in being able to easily explain why many "financially" successful people are so unhappy. As grateful as I was for his wisdom, what Mitch unknowingly also ended up giving me was the conclusion to this book via a gracious lecture explaining the difference between Pleasure and Joy.

Simply put, Pleasure is about consumption, whereas **Joy is about creation**. The entire message of this book is learning to create and disperse happiness to others rather than stealing the beauty around for the selfish consumption within. Don't consume; CREATE!

My book is about helping you obtain comfort; comfort in life, comfort in death, and comfort in everything in-between. When we obtain comfort, what we're really obtaining is happiness, and that was the point of Mitch's NYE 2020 wisdom; do you obtain your happiness from pleasure or from joy? Again, I'm paraphrasing, but here goes the wisdom of Mitch:

Pleasure is something you gain from the outside world. Although pleasure makes us happy, the fatal flaw of pleasure is that it's fleeting. Pleasure requires that you take something from the outside world to make you happy. Not only are you focused on pleasure-filled fleeting-happiness, but you're also affecting the world in a selfish manner as a taker. A selfish manner of extrinsic motivation.

This book is about obtaining happiness through affecting the world, but in a manner of giving rather than from taking.

In comes Joy.

Joy is happiness as well, but the difference is that Joy is something you create from the inside with your core strength. Where Pleasure is something you take from the outside and enjoy it within, Joy is something you take from the inside and disperse it to the outside world for everyone to enjoy. Joy is happiness you give to others.

With the self-created happiness of Joy, it doesn't matter which way the wind blows because you're the center and you are always spreading joy. Everybody loves Joy, but only few can produce it because most people are weak and become stuck with the cheapness of pleasure. This is why those who spread joy rise to the top every time, because they're uncontrollably happy people who give it all to the outside world. Joyous people are givers.

Not only do Joyous people have the ability to create their own happiness, but they also have the superpower of being able to create joy and happiness for the countless others around. Even when everything around them is fleeting, their ability to influence the world surrounding us all becomes possible. People who bring joy genuinely love this world and have no need to hurt others, whereas people consumed with pleasure have only one need; that of selfishly stealing the gifts of the world to distract them from their own unhappiness.

If you're weak and wanna affect this world by taking, then we now understand your endless failures and unhappiness. However, if your mission is the willingness to build your core strength and unleash your gains through the endless selfless acts of bettering everyone around, then I look forward to basking in your rivers of happiness #together. In conclusion of my conclusion, my only question to you is this:

As you gain, how are you going to affect this world?

Thank you very much for your time and consideration in reading my book! I look forward to you implementing my strategies for your continued success and happiness every day. Here's to you!!!

Death Doesn't Matter If You Live Everyday
Be Honest. Be Bold. Be Free
You are not your past.

You're Always what you do next!

What's Next:

1) PLEASE **Leave a Review** on Amazon (only if you liked my book or are at least willing to say as much). #HelpMeHelpYou

2) Signup for my new video courses which visually walk you through step-by-step turning your every weakness into massive strengths.

JeremySigal.com

3) Contact me (Jeremy Sigal) with any questions, comments or concerns.

   - Facebook: Jeremy Sigal
   - Instagram: LegalQs
   - Email: me@JeremySigal.com

4) Follow and Like **ALL** of my posts and stay updated on my latest ventures of adding value to your life every way possible.

5) Let's do something GREAT #Together!!!

Notes

Designer: Jeremy Sigal
Author: Jeremy Sigal
Content: Jeremy Sigal
Editor: Jeremy Sigal
Publisher: Jeremy Sigal

Disclaimer: Although every single story actually happened and is true & accurate in description, some names have been changed to protect the privacy of these individuals.

Do Not EVER Start A Fight, BUT
I pray you find the Strength to Finish Every Single One In Your Way!

Now go forth and report to me AFTER your Victory!

I Love You ☺

Printed in Great Britain
by Amazon

28353011R00079